Lies

BESTSELLING AUTHOR
A.L. WOODS

ISBN-13: 979-8780276746

Also by A.L. Woods

REFLECTIONS
TRILOGY

MIRRORS

SHATTERED

AWAKE

Standalones

RAIN

VERITAS

Playlist

"Lie" by Sasha Alex Sloan
"Hurts" by LANY
"Under Your Scars" by Godsmack
"Simple Man" by Shinedown
"Black" by Pearl Jam
"Watch Over You" by Alter Bridge
"She's so High" by Tal Bachman
"Don't Speak" by No Doubt
"Back At One" by Brian McKnight
"This Woman's Work" by Kate Bush
"You've Haunted Me All My Life" by Death Cab for Cutie
"Clair de Lune, L. 32" by Claude Debussy
"Paradise By the Dashboard Light" Meatloaf
"Love Runs Out" by Martin Garrix, feat. G-Eazy & Sasha Alex Sloan
"Come On Eileen" by Dexys Midnight Runners
"Reaching" Cellophane Roses
"Ya'aburnee" by Halsey
"Take My Place" by Lily Allen
"Enter Sandman" by Piano Tribute Players
"Apples" by Lily Allen

"Rich Girl" by Daryl Hall & John Oates
"Nothing Compares 2 U" by Chris Cornell
"Sabbra Cadabra" by Metallica
"All I Want Is You" by U2
"Stutter" by Narrowhaven
"Dream Come True" by Frozen Ghost
"Wasted Years" by Iron Maiden
"World Around Me" by Escape the Fate

Scan this code to access the playlist on Spotify

Foreword

Lies is a standalone novel within the Reflections universe and acts as both a prequel to the Reflections Trilogy and a sequel to Veritas. There will be some references to events from the trilogy and Veritas, some of which are glossed over, others examined more in-depth because of their impact on Penelope and Dougie. If you intend to read those books and would rather not be spoiled, I would suggest coming back to this one.

We read to escape, but often, we read content in a fictional setting that is reminiscent of reality. For that reason, content warnings are important to me.

Lies deals with themes that have the potential to be distressing to some readers and a full content warning can be found at the back of the book.

I would implore you that if any of the listed themes have the potential to be distressing to you, please don't read this.

Chapter One

Dougie

Three years ago...

WHO IN THE *LEGALLY BLONDE* HELL WAS THAT?

Lewd whistles erupted across the hectic construction yard. "You're a long way from Hollywood, sweetheart!" one guy on the crew crooned.

I couldn't make out who had said it, but I wanted to hit him all the same.

Prick.

Laughter filled the site over the whine of drills and whirr of a nail gun popping against the clapboard siding of the house we were restoring back to its former glory.

If it had *ever* been glorious.

Shit had looked straight out of a nineties horror movie when we'd erected the construction fences. Not gonna lie.

"*A cu dela é muito pequena,*" Luis said to the right of me, his eyes distending.

I didn't have a goddamn clue what he said—he barely spoke a word of English, communicating almost only in Portuguese.

He was related to Sean, my best friend and the miserable asshole who owned the house and employed the rest of us.

"You're right. Her ass is small... and flat," Tony wheezed out with the translation, choking on the fumes of his cigarette dangling from his ugly mouth as the cancerous haze masked his features momentarily. When it cleared, I caught him leering at the out-of-place blonde like she was a Kobe steak, all but snapping his jaws at her.

I pegged him with an unimpressed glare.

The clown was married with three daughters under six. Could he at least pretend he had some table manners? Y'know, a napkin to mop up the drool practically dribbling outta the corner of his mouth?

"Why is she wearing heels?" Joey asked, squinting at the blonde as he lifted his hard hat, revealing his sweat-streaked forehead as the obtrusive sun nailed him right in his eyes as he stared.

Even I couldn't take my eyes off the inevitable beautiful train wreck waiting to happen, but I wasn't like these idiots... not really. I was watching out of concern. "She's gonna fall over in those things," I mumbled.

How high were her heels? At least four inches, red-bottomed, expensive-looking spikes that could have doubled for a weapon.

The blonde frowned at our gawking, her rounded eyebrows pinching together. She leveled her chin, appearing dignified, then tiptoed around the uneven gravel, trying to find her equilibrium, all while clutching the strap of a massive brown leather purse over her shoulder that resembled a bowling bag with busy print scattered in a layered cream-colored L and V print.

Why was she wearing heels—never mind open-toe ones—on an active construction site?

Call it a sixth sense, but the urge to rush to her came seconds before her balance teetered, the stilettos and the treacherous terrain threatening to tip her right over. She was going to break an ankle at this rate, maybe smash her pretty face, crack her dainty little wrists when she tried to break her fall.

Her arms jutted outright, windmilling as her mouth popped open and her brows met in the middle helplessly.

Yep, it was happening.

She was gonna eat shit, and these perverted idiots were gonna let it happen.

No one moved, trapping their breaths behind snide smiles.

For fuck's sake.

I dropped the hammer to the ground with a "thud," abandoning the panel of clapboard I'd been adhering that flapped in the breeze pitifully. The guys hooted at her expense all while I gritted my teeth and made a run for it like my life depended on it.

Shit.

Her feet slipped clean right out of her heels—I caught the flash of her bright, fuchsia pink toenails as she went airborne, a helpless cry leaving her mouth over the cacophony of construction and jests. Her hands jutted outward to catch herself, bracing for the brute force of impact.

Nah, she wasn't gonna hurt herself. Not on my watch, anyway.

I didn't consider myself a knight in shining armor, but I was a sweaty asshole in a hard hat with quick reflexes thanks to a short-lived high school football career that went nowhere after I tore my ACL during a scrimmage.

I coulda gone places had that not happened, but in this moment, I was grateful it did.

I might not have been here to catch her otherwise.

A puff of air expelled from her lungs as I caught her easily, her svelte body pressing against mine as she stabilized herself. She glanced up at me through the shroud of her made-up lashes, a mixture of gratitude and curiosity filling her eyes as she held my gaze, embarrassment staining her cheeks red.

My stomach dropped. Holy shit. Was she wearing colored contacts or something, or were those natural? Were they blue or were they green? I swallowed tightly, getting a good look at them, staring longer than what was probably socially acceptable for people like her who reeked of Chanel No. 5., manners and WASP inbreeding.

But that didn't stop my insides from twisting with a misplaced yearning. Nor the prickle of my skin, or the buzzing setting off in my mind that I couldn't clear.

Blue. Her eyes were definitely blue with a distinct ring of chartreuse green and gold streaks closer to her pupil. Atlantic Ocean blue, the shade reminiscent of the best summer of your life spent in the Cape. You remembered eyes like those years later, long after you'd forgotten her face or name. They saw right through you, and made you wanna be better, too.

The ruddy blush deepened in her cheeks, her hands finding my pecs as she straightened, and that swan-like throat of hers worked appreciatively.

"Hi." That single-worded greeting was too posh. Her accent wasn't from around these parts, definitely out of state.

She sent me a demure smile, but her eyes, fringed with her long lashes, were all heated flirtation, and the way her hands remained fastened on my chest left me suspecting she knew exactly what she was doing.

She wasn't shy about shit for someone who screamed manners and old money.

"Hi, yourself." I liked her type—no bullshit, cutting straight to the chase. I could do the guy from the wrong side of the tracks routine with her if that was her vice of choice. I was always someone's vice of choice, someone to sink into and forget about the world around them.

My mouth twisted with a wolfish smile. "You lost, Goldilocks?"

She sobered, clearly not caring for my joke.

I cringed inwardly. *So close, Patterson.*

Goldilocks hmphed, ripping her hands free from my chest. She folded her toned arms across her chest, her profile tensing.

She looked around me, her mouth rocking. "I'm looking for Sean Tavares."

I cocked a brow at her, giving her a once-over carefully. Sean didn't do blondes. He'd done that only once in high school with a broad named Colleen, who ended up driving her car through a bank and—well, long story.

Either way, he swore up and down he was over blondes.

Then he'd dated Francesca—headful of dark, curly hair on that one. Pretty, but psycho. Seriously. She belonged on an episode of *America's Most Wanted* because that girl was an absolute con artist and almost tied him down with a kid that wasn't his. Definitely a doozy of a situation.

Actually, come to think of it, Sean had a thing for the ones that were borderline clinical—blond or brunette. He didn't discriminate against the ones who were one breakdown away from a psychiatric ward.

Either way, Francesca had been the last time I'd heard of him seeing anyone seriously enough that they'd come looking for him at work.

I rubbed my scruffy jaw, giving Goldilocks another once-over despite her pouting. I had to hand it to him. If he experienced a change of heart on blondes, it was worth the conversion. The smooth-haired flaxen woman was gorgeous, but if she *was* fucking my best friend and the bastard hadn't told me yet... well, I was about to cockblock the fuck outta him because she'd picked the wrong asshole from Fall River.

"You don't look like his type," I observed.

I decided I didn't like it when she frowned. The lines deepened in her forehead as she looked me up and down with disdain. Her jaw rocked, her temper flaring off her in thick waves. "I'm here for the *job*, you prick."

My brows jumped. Well, well. Where the hell had the WASPs been hiding this one? She had a mouth on her.

I grinned. "What job?" Goldilocks didn't look like she knew how to handle a hammer, but she'd probably do just fine under my jack-hammering hips.

I shook my head, clearing the thought. *I'm no better than Tony.*

I was spending too much time with these morons that I was forgetting my upbringing and Eileen, my ma, would box my ears if she ever knew where my lewd thoughts were right now. I knew the rules.

You took a girl to dinner first, got to know her, and then maybe if you were lucky...

She huffed impatiently, opening her purse as she dug through the contents and pulled out her phone—one of those new iPhones or whatever—the kind people who didn't worry about money always flaunted.

I liked the way the sun strobed across her hair. She was a natural blond. The late spring rays caught on her hair, appearing closer to spun gold. You couldn't box dye that shit.

"Here," she said, closing the short distance between us, her phone outstretched. Her hair smelled good, like peaches and ginger, with a trace of vanilla. She tapped the screen with the tip of her manicured finger, and I noticed her nails were painted the same color as her toes. It almost distracted me from the constriction in my lungs as she zoomed in on a name.

That name.

The last one I'd wanted to see or think about.

"Maria Tavares set up the meeting."

I staggered back. That fucking name made me see red, but it paled compared to the ache pervading through me. I kneaded my chest involuntarily, reliving that night all over again for the briefest moment.

Maria was Sean's older sister and had been the epic source of my fifteen-year hard-on for the longest time.

The oldest Tavares sister was, for a lack of better words, gorgeous, wicked smart, and a coldhearted man-eater. Last year, she let me warm her bed for six months after I signed a nondisclosure agreement, promising to be discreet because she was trying to make partner at her stuffy firm, and as the only woman, she couldn't afford any kind of scandal. Period.

But I wasn't trying to be a scandal. I was trying to be her boyfriend, to finally love her and be loved back.

When I asked for more? She crushed me under her red-bottom shoes that looked a lot like the ones Goldilocks was wearing and reiterated the terms.

We were just fucking, so I left. If not for the sake of my dignity, then to spare myself anymore agony because the fantasy of Maria that lived in my head rent free was slowly killing me.

And sure, I might have walked out on Maria, but it was because she was steadfast on her decision that I was just a convenient cock for her to ride.

And now she'd sent this one in to torture me. I'd learned my lesson and I wouldn't make it twice, especially with someone cut from the same cloth as Maria.

My jaw ticked, annoyance flanking me as my shoulder blades snapped together. "Follow me," I said gruffly, turning on the heel of my work boots, heading for the house.

Goldilocks struggled to keep up, but this time, I didn't make any exceptions for her. If she knew Maria, she could handle her own, and my short-lived eye fucking session was over. I darted around a group of guys carrying in another slab of drywall. The crunch of Goldilocks's spiked heels cutting into the uneven ground was distinct over the hammering, and her desperate, winded puffs leaving her as she struggled to keep up.

She wouldn't dare complain.

Stepping up the porch steps, I jerked the front door open, leaving it wide for her to follow. The scent of cut wood, drywall and wall mudding hit my sinuses as I stepped into the living room. My best friend had his back turned to me, the muscles in his back twisting under his shirt, his hard hat ditched by his water cooler. Sean was as stubborn as a mule. As soon as he started sweating, the hard hat came off, no matter what the Department of Labor's OSHA stipulated.

I cleared my throat, but he didn't pay me any mind. The asshole got tunnel vision when he was working.

Sighing, I called his name. "Sean?"

"What?" he growled at me, a nail clenched between his teeth as he lined up another piece of drywall, his big hands caked in dust.

I glanced at the blonde, realizing I hadn't grabbed her name. "What's your name, sweetheart?" I didn't know why my instinct was to keep throwing terms of endearment at her, but I couldn't seem to stop myself.

Yep, I was as bad as Tony.

No wonder Maria hadn't wanted to date me. I was kinda pathetic.

Goldilocks bristled, her cheeks heating once more. Straightening, she tucked her short hair behind her ears, kicking her chin out. "Penelope."

Penelope.

Yeah, I'd remember that name just like her eyes.

A pretty name for a pretty girl, even if it screamed blue-blooded pedigreed former debutante. Hell, her bone structure alone had that done for her.

I glanced back at my best friend as he took the nail out of his mouth, lined it up and then pounded it into place with two solid "thwacks", his forearm flexing.

"Penelope's here for the interview."

"Penelope?" he repeated, looking at me over his shoulder, his expression a combination of confused and unimpressed as he lowered his arm, testing his grip on the handle of the hammer.

If she thought I was a prick, she was in for a real treat.

Sean was grumpy.

All. The. Fucking. Time.

Or at least he had been for the last decade. Personally, I thought he just needed to get laid regularly, but he'd turned into Mother fuckin' Theresa since we took this project on.

Sean used to get it in before.

Sometimes.

But even then, he'd been kinda prickly, which left me with the impression it wasn't all that satisfying and closer to a mutual exchange of bodily fluids.

I was fairly certain he was going on three months of his new act of celibacy. "Who the fuck is Penelope?" he asked, bewildered.

Penelope tapped her foot behind me, clearing her throat. "*I'm fucking Penelope.*"

I barked out a laugh, glancing at her. Maria's minion or not, she had spunk. I'd give her that.

Sean was anything but amused. His lips twisted into a scowl. He was about four weeks overdue for a shave, and extra short on patience. His clothes seemed permanently stained in joint compound, sweat sullying the front of his chest.

Today was a bad day.

Then again, every day for the past decade had seemed to be a bad day for him. It didn't help that this restoration was turning into a giant money pit, and we all knew it. Problem after problem seemed to be unearthing. The odds of him recuperating his expenses during a recession weren't looking good.

"You're the interior designer, right?" Katrina's dulcet voice hit my ears as she rounded the corner. She was the youngest of the Tavares siblings, ten years younger than Sean, making her twenty to his thirty. "The one Maria heard about from work?"

I paused, watching Penelope's body language. She didn't react to Maria's name at all. Maybe she didn't personally know of Maria after all, which meant maybe I wasn't down for the count after all.

Penelope gave Trina the once-over—it was hard not to when Trina's hair was currently the color of a traffic cone and she looked as out of place here as Penelope did. Trina wore about eight pounds of makeup on her face—five pounds around her eyes alone—a silver hoop in her septum that enraged her ma and paraded around with one earbud in her ear, the other draped around her neck, blaring some kind of screamo shit that was going to destroy her eardrums one of these days.

Penelope smiled warmly at her, nodding her head. "That's me."

Sean ignored her, homing in on Katrina. "What did I tell you about those headphones in your ears?" he growled.

She smiled sweetly at her brother, batting her spiderlike lashes. "The same thing you tell everyone about hard hats," she piped back, sounding every bit as sarcastic as she intended. "That it's a 'hazard'." Her gaze fluttered from her brother's discarded hard hat to him, her dimples deepening.

I whistled low. She was dead. Sean was an active live wire with a short fuse these days, and with his family, that fuse was even shorter.

He scowled at her, then dropped the hammer to the unfinished floors, fiddling with his tool belt as he kept her in his line of vision. Trina was small, sprightly, and could outrun her brother easily. He was two hundred hulking pounds of muscle and well over six feet tall, but there was no contending with Trina's petite, agile, and nimble frame.

On cue, she squeaked, taking off at a dead bolt across the house.

"No running in the house!" He adjusted the tool belt, weaving it back into place. He shook his head, gritting his teeth, his jaw tensing under the pressure. "I'm gonna fucking kill her."

Yeah, working with family didn't seem all that appealing. Trina was a lost soul who, frankly, didn't want to be here at our giant sausage fest —not that I could blame her. Their ma tossed her out this year after she'd had an abortion. Naturally, as older brothers do—both by blood and by loyalty—we'd taken care of the asshole who'd skipped out on her. We hadn't heard a peep about Charlie in Fall River since. Trina lived with Sean now, and he had tried to keep her onsite, working odd jobs to give her something to do even if she bitched and complained about it. He didn't get a break from family.

Ever.

Which I suspected also contributed to his celibacy pact.

If I knew anything about Maria's true intentions, she recommended Penelope for her siblings' sake. She was selfish, sure, but nothing meant more to her than her siblings. Except maybe her job.

In her mind, Maria probably figured Sean would get a woman's influence around here to help move the property quicker, and it would entice Trina to work here full-time rather than mourn that asshole who knocked her up.

My stomach rolled. *Ugh.*

I still didn't want to think about Trina having sex. Anytime I thought about her being pregnant, I got flashbacks of her uneven pigtails and rabbit teeth while she wildly peddled her rusting, hand-me-down bicycle on wobbling training wheels up and down their driveway. She would ride as fast as she could with concentration pinching her tiny features, never daring to go past the wooden split-railed fence around the property lest she get an earful from her parents.

Why couldn't she just stay a kid forever? She was never dating again, not if Sean or I had anything to do or say about it.

I would hand it to Maria, though. She knew what her siblings needed without them realizing. It was too bad that kind of emotional adeptness didn't translate into her romantic affairs.

Yeah, I was still a bit bitter.

"Is this natural oak?" Penelope asked, pulling me out of my reverie. "I love the herringbone pattern." She breezed by me, dropping onto her haunches to touch the floor with her hands.

She had delicate hands, slender fingers with perfectly polished fingernails. Too dainty for a construction site, better suited for...

Nope. Think of your ma in her nightgown. I wasn't like one of those barn animals outside... was I?

Her hands curved, testing the floor, and I could think of all the other things that gorgeous crescent of her cupped extremities could do.

At least she was seeing the floors after we'd buffed out the spray-painted pentagram on them. I only wanted her to see beautiful things.

I ripped my gaze away, concentrating on Sean instead for a focal point. I couldn't get hard over my best friend even if he was the last human alive. Not 'cause he wasn't good looking for a guy, or whatever, he was just a miserable son of a bitch. Imagine trying to cuddle up to that burly beast postcoital? Hard pass. You'd get more warmth out of a boulder.

"Yep," Sean clipped, staring at her as she examined the flooring.

"We should refinish and stain them," Penelope announced, rising to her feet. She planted her hands on her hips, tapping her foot with thought, eyes surveying the room. "And paint these walls gentleman's gray."

"*We?*" Sean questioned, unimpressed.

I liked her gumption and usage of pronouns.

"Yeah," she said absently, wandering over to the windows. She gave us an indulgent head tilt. God, her neck was pretty. "The midday lighting would look whimsical against a dark wall, don't you think." It was a statement, not a question.

"Sure, whatever," he said, waving her off. "I don't care about that shit."

"Well, you should," she argued, failing to mask her aggravation. "We're trying to lure the hipsters out of Boston into suburbia." She extended her hands out in front of her, like she was trying to mime a picture frame, her expression relaxing as she transported herself else-where, getting into her element. "This house needs something to make it stand out. We have to build the space, set the mood, and tell a story that'll resonate with them days after they leave here."

"*Hipsters*. Right." He rolled his eyes, lifting the corner of his shirt to wipe the sweat off his forehead before it dripped into his eyes. I studied her to see if she checked him out because on top of working construction, Sean had to show us all up by working out six days a week and eating clean.

Penelope didn't pop a glance, her eyes traversing the room.

It relieved me. I was shorter than Sean by a couple of inches, brawnier and more confident than him, too. I didn't want to have to fight him for her.

What the hell was I saying?

Clearing my throat, I allowed the extended silence to envelop me as I studied Sean. Instinctually, I knew we were both thinking the same thing—hipsters weren't leaving Boston for *Eaton*, of all fucking places.

"What's your rate?" he asked, indulging her as he rubbed his boot against a scuff on the floor, scowling at the mark. Idiot. He'd been the one to do that when he dropped the hammer. Like I said, tunnel vision.

Penelope propped the tip of her shoe on the floor, studying the smooth ceilings as her lips parted just a little, letting out a whimsical sigh. "A hundred and fifty an hour."

He released his wrinkled shirt, his hands balling into fists. "Are you out of your goddamn mind?" he growled, baring his teeth.

Oh God, here we go.

Sean looked feral. Money always stressed him out. That was what happened when you got ripped away from your dream to support your family by doing something you kind of hated for financial stability. It made you bitter.

I stepped in front of her, throwing him a silent warning. The luxury of being best friends with this tall, uncultured motherfucker, since well before either of our balls dropped, meant I could communicate with him almost exclusively in looks.

Calm down, asshole.

I'd help him pay for it if I had to, even though my bank account was drier than the Sahara. I could apply for another line of credit,

credit card, work a street corner, or sell my truck. Anything to keep this one around.

She was fun and sprightly. We could afford to have some fun around here.

Penelope examined her fingernails, her nose wrinkling. "My rate is reasonable."

"Sure, maybe in New York."

"I'm from Connecticut," she corrected, raising her chin. That explained her accent. Her cadence was even, each vowel enunciated clearly, as though she'd attended a fancy boarding school.

Shit, she probably had.

"I don't care where you're from." His jaw tightened. "You're too expensive."

She nursed her lip, then tried a different angle. "There are no upfront fees. I can get a fifteen percent discount through most materials distributors, so you'll see that the savings I bring you are worth my price." She had the aptitude of a saleswoman... or maybe a politician.

I'd vote for her. She'd sold me.

Sean blinked at her, no doubt considering the option. Fifteen percent wasn't anything to scoff at, especially with a project this size. The addition had been his brilliant idea to bring the square footage up, but that had been before the house of horrors started revealing all its issues. By then, it was too late to renege.

He glanced around the room, looking for answers. "How many hours do you need in a space like this?"

"That depends. How involved do you want to be?"

His face reddened, arousing my wince. He hated a question being answered with another question. "*That depends. How* much is it going to cost *me*?"

"Okay, how about this?" she suggested, clasping her hands together as her face lit up. "We can do a flat-fee structure. That way, things like phone calls or color swatches don't eat into the budget. And," she grinned, her eyes gleaming, "I'll always be around here."

My insides fluttered.

I loved her smile. Her lips were thin and disappeared a little when she beamed, but her teeth were squared, even and white, and you could tell that every grin came from a genuine place.

I'd do unspeakable things to make her smile.

"Christ," Sean groused, drawing me from my thoughts as he drove the heels of his palms into his eyes. "What's *that* going to run me?"

She chewed her lip, looking heavenward. "For the entire house? Twenty-five thousand?"

He laughed sarcastically, but his face... yeah, he was pissed. "You must think I wipe my ass with hundred-dollar bills, don't you?"

"It's a four-thousand-square-foot house with five bedrooms and three and a half baths," I interrupted, earning his murderous glare. Sean's anger alone was a vacuum that sucked all the oxygen out of the room.

Yep, I was next on the chopping block.

He was going to take my head off clean, but my stupid mouth kept going a mile a minute. "At a hundred and fifty an hour, that's what?" I looked at her for support, my brows jumping to my hairline. "Two hundred hours?"

Penelope's mouth popped open, her eyes widening with surprise that I was supporting her. "Yeah, exactly."

I had ulterior motives.

"Tell you what," I said, studying her like it was just the two of us in here. I was already a dead man, may as well make it worth it. "Can you stretch those hours over a couple of months? We're running behind here."

We should have already been knee-deep in the design stage.

Sean made a noise of displeasure, but I was too enthralled with Penelope and the way her skin flushed like she was overheating. I hoped it was because she was experiencing the same fluttery bullshit I was. Apparently, I was in the eighth grade again and really interested in finding out whether her lip gloss tasted like bubblegum or cherry.

Her tongue poked out to brush against her bottom lip—taut and bright pink, probably capable of doing all kinds of things.

Do not get hard at work. Do not get hard at work.

My cock twitched.

"Yeah, I can do that," she replied, sounding out of breath.

"Fine," Sean bit out, accepting he'd lost the war and pulling us both out of our alternate universe. "Come back on Monday with your contract." His gaze dropped to her shoes. "And find better footwear. You're a liability. I don't want you rolling an ankle."

She brightened, giving him a thumbs-up. "I'll see you on Monday, then." Her grateful blue eyes moved to me, another smile playing with her lips. "It was nice meeting you...?"

I held out a hand to her. "Dougie."

"Dougie." She repeated my name, her hand slipping into mine. My fingers closed around hers, my thumb brushing against her knuckles. I wasn't into romantic movies, but goddamn, was I a newfound believer in them.

That feeling circulating between us was instantaneous—like lightning had struck me, a blast of energy rocking right through me at a single touch. My heart skipped an actual fucking beat. This feeling was better than the Sox winning the World Series or the Patriots winning the Super Bowl.

Shit, it might have been better than sex.

But maybe I'd change my mind if the sex was with her...

Her stunning eyes widened for a moment. It made me wonder if she felt it, too.

She must have. The way her lips parted, a controlled breath escaping her slowly as though she were remembering how her lungs functioned.

Sean cleared his throat, interrupting the moment. Only then did I regretfully let her go. I'd still feel her hand in mine for hours later.

Penelope touched her lips with the tips of the fingers I'd been holding, then inched back, creating a reluctant distance between us. "See you on Monday, Dougie."

Dougie. How could I get a recording of her saying my name on a loop? I watched her walk away, my eyes tracking her through the living room window as she headed toward her silver Range Rover. This time, when one of the guys catcalled her, she held up a middle finger.

"Up yours!" she hollered, dropping the WASP act. "Not even in your fucking dreams!"

I chuckled. That shut them up. She was gonna be a breath of fresh air around here. I liked that on the surface, she gave off rich girl airs, but when she opened her mouth? She was a bit of a Masshole-in-training.

"Hey, jackass," Sean called.

Heaving a sigh, I let Penelope leave my line of vision, regarding him. *Figures.*

When he didn't immediately speak, I kicked my chin at him. "What?"

Sean crooked a thick finger at me, his glare thinning.

I rolled my eyes and wandered over to him, resigning myself to my fate. He slung a sweaty arm around my shoulders, pulling me in tight against his hot chest—nasty—then drove his knuckles against my hard hat, the pressure making my head ache.

"I'm only doing this because Maria thinks her influence will be good for Katrina and will help me offload this money pit faster." His voice dropped low enough for only me to hear. This time, the mention of Maria's name didn't bother me. I was too alive with thoughts of Penelope's presence on the site a few hours a week. "I don't need any more headaches. So do me a favor and don't fuck the new girl, Douglas."

No problem, 'cause I wasn't going to just *fuck* the new girl.

I was going to marry her.

Chapter Two

Dougie

Present

WE WEREN'T ALWAYS THIS WAY.

My wife and me, that was.

Nah. We used to like each other. A whole lot, in fact.

I'd be so bold to say we used to love each other, too.

Now… I stared up at the exterior of our house, my wipers working across the windshield in uneven streaks, revealing our beginning. It had been a home once. A place where we whispered our dreams and fantasies to one another in the darkness of night, where we held each other close and swayed in the kitchen to music with our breaths mingling and our foreheads pressed together, losing ourselves in the steady thrumming of our hearts beating in unison.

We couldn't get closer to one another unless we shared skin and bones.

The colonial had been the place that started it all—our unlikely love story—and our unexpected destruction.

Maybe the house was cursed, despite its reconstruction, the refinished floors and the gentleman's gray paint on the walls. None of the pretty details would mask that the life force that had once existed in this house was as good as dead.

Just like we were.

Penelope and I were always destined for chaos because in every poor guy/rich girl plotline, the asshole from Fall River never got to keep the former debutante from Connecticut.

I mean, shit, if you had told me when Penelope stumbled into my arms I'd marry her someday, I would have laughed.

Sure, I'd deluded myself with the fantasy the same way kids believed they could be superheroes—but I didn't think it would ever come true.

Never mind any of the things that came after.

The soft pitter-patter of nocturnal raindrops cleared momentarily on a tidy streak, only for the splatter of droplets to return. The sound was hypnotic, a balm on my racing mind as I noticed all the things I hadn't gotten to lately in my intentional absence.

Our driveway was littered with a thick blanket of glittering, wet leaves from the proud copse of maples lining our driveway. Raking hadn't made it high on my list of priorities. That was largely impart to the fact that I was never home. I kind of hated being here now—and frankly, I was fairly confident, she hated me being here, too.

But let's go back to the beginning. That's how all these stories went.

Once upon a time, a construction foreman met a pretty interior designer who was wildly out of his league, and she gave him a chance. A chance he never probably deserved, but one he thanked his goddamn lucky stars for.

Wasn't that how all happily ever afters went?

That chance included sneaking off into the basement of the very jobsite they'd met on just to sample her mouth before his boss and best friend hollered bloody murder at them from the top of the basement steps. Or driving to the outskirts of town to fuck in the woods when lunch rolled around, only to come back after and send each other lewd texts every opportunity they weren't desperately pawing at each other.

Fucking led to dates—her idea despite her initial ambivalence toward dating. Dates I'd never thought I'd get the chance to take someone like Penelope on. Dates graduated into sleepovers, her place first—and eventually, when I got over my embarrassment—mine. She hadn't cared that my window air conditioning unit wasn't functional, or that the place was empty. She'd snuggle up against me in bed, even with beads of sweat clinging to her hairline, mewling with content-ment in her sleep as though she were sleeping on one of those pillow-top mattresses seated on a four-poster bed frame.

Penelope hadn't cared that I couldn't rub two pennies together because I didn't have 'em. She just liked me, for me.

"You're kind and nice to me," she'd told me once, tracing the pad of her slender finger over the bridge of my crooked nose, a small smile playing on her lips before she lifted her eyes to mine. *"I like nice guys."*

For the first time, I believed nice guys finished first.

She was everything I'd ever hoped for, and more.

And I fucked it up, because as it turned out, I wasn't much of a nice guy after all. I was an asshole who never deserved her to begin with.

Just like her parents had warned her.

With that thought bouncing errantly in my mind, I reached for the keys in the ignition, turning the engine off. The colonial was dark, not even the porch light was on.

Pen used to leave them on for me. I'd be able to see our house as soon as I pulled onto our street. Every exterior pot light lit up, the porch a beacon in the darkness, beckoning me down our meandering driveway back home to her. It was a little sign she cared.

If I was a betting man, I'd put it all on black with a surety my wife would like nothing more than for me to trip over my own two feet and crack my fucking head open. Maybe bleed out on the porch steps.

Not that she needed the insurance money, but she wanted to hurt me, even at the risk of her precious fucking porch.

She wanted to get back at me for the way I hurt her.

And I had hurt her—immeasurably so, in a way I'd spend the rest of my life paying for. I heard it in the hitch of her breathing as the emotions lodged in her lungs. I caught it in the knitting of her tight shoulders and the way her haunted gaze dropped to her wedding band and engagement ring any time I was around.

Pure unadulterated agony, she relived repeatedly.

One mistake. That was all it took to set our happily ever after aflame.

Reluctantly, I opened the car door. The brisk October cold swallowed me while the growing, incessant raindrops fell from the sky, splattering across my exposed skin and perfuming the air in petrichor. Leaves crunched under my heavy footfalls as I lumbered toward the porch, nerves already coiling my insides.

That porch made Penelope want to buy this house. It captivated her because where she was from—the land of white-tie aristocrats and old money entitlement—no one sat out on their porches in Greenwich, Connecticut. Porches served a decorative purpose only. Somewhere to put planters made by landscapers who remembered how much you hated geraniums and a place for a meticulously decorated porch bench to live unused and unfulfilled because no one would ever be caught dead sitting out there.

It was all about illusions and pretenses.

But here in Massachusetts, in a homely bedroom community like Eaton that never ended up appealing to Boston's hipsters, people sat out on porches. They knew each other's names. They raked their leaves themselves in a timely fashion, hung holiday lights come December, and always separated their trash from their recyclables.

Back then, before we'd made this house ours, I'd hear her shoes belting across the wooden planks, announcing her presence, and my heartbeat would kick up a notch. I knew I wanted to hear that sound for the rest of my life the day I met her.

When I'd gotten her pregnant a few months after we'd met, she proposed we buy this place together—and despite my initial misgivings, tight finances, and general nerves, it was a no-brainer to me because finally, I'd gotten everything I'd ever wanted in life.

I got the girl.

I got the house.

I got the kid.

We had everything.

Penelope might have been Greenwich born and raised, but back then, she was a far cry from her upbringing. She liked I came home a dirty, sweaty mess, and didn't mind my hard hat, callused hands or my high school diploma. She hadn't cared that I lacked accolades, that I was the first Douglas Seamus Patterson in my family. That I had a paltry 401 (k), too much credit card debt, and could only name one Ivy League school in the country.

She loved staying up late for me, so we could sit out on this porch in the summer when my shifts ran later to take advantage of every ray of sunlight before a miserable, cold winter descended upon us. I could still feel her sticky, lean legs draped across my lap. In my memory, I could hear the shrill chink of her reusable metal straw against her glass when her lips wrapped around the straw, sucking on iced tea perched on her pregnant belly while her pretty blue eyes meandered across the stretch of green space that made up our yard.

Then her reverent gaze would settle on mine, and she'd smile. Pen had the best smile—small, albeit sexy.

But that smile was for me, and me alone.

I hadn't seen it in a long time, just like we didn't use this porch swing anymore. Hell, I couldn't remember the last time I'd witnessed a smile on her face at all.

Debris covered the porch swing, wet leaves sticking to the wood, the chain creaking miserably in the biting October night breeze. It was as weather-beaten as we were.

We hardly did anything together, 'cause I fucked it up.

I fucked it up, and I couldn't fix it.

I put my key into the door lock, twisting until I heard the click of the lock releasing, then pushed down on the latch. The interior was a lot like the exterior—swathed in darkness and uninviting, despite how beautiful it was. It was just another lie to mask the truth. The inside, perfumed by her favorite sweet-scented Bath and Body Works wall-flower, black cherry merlot, tangled with traces of whatever she'd thrown together for dinner.

Based on the distinct notes of garlic, oregano and tomato in the air, likely pasta.

Penelope wasn't much of a cook. She'd grown up with a live-in cook and two housekeepers, one who had raised her. She'd never had to learn, but when we'd met, she always tried.

Locking the front door, I set my keys into a decorative catchall bowl on the credenza carefully. It was after ten. Our son, Christopher, normally went down around seven thirty p.m., and Pen…

To be honest, I wasn't really sure what her schedule was anymore.

My body ached—and not just from a long day—as I wandered through our living room, heading in the kitchen's direction.

I missed her. God, I fucking missed her.

Swallowing the painful lump in my throat, I flipped the light switch on. The hum of the dishwasher running greeted me. Unlike our porch, there was nothing remiss in our kitchen. It was showroom worthy. Three years ago, Pen had loved every minute of designing the color palate for this room with Katrina. Black quartz with creamy veins made up the countertops, standing proud against the macadamia nut cabinetry. The farmhouse sink, devoid of dishes, not even the drying mat had anything on it. The stainless-steel appliances didn't so much sport a single, wayward fingerprint smudge. Hell, you wouldn't think a toddler lived here if it weren't for the highchair tucked in the corner.

She kept everything in its place to hide the blemishes that lived beneath the surface. It was how she remained in control.

It was what made her stay.

Sliding off my worn-in denim jacket, I slung it over the rear of a high-back bar stool tucked against the kitchen island. I disturbed the pristine appearance, but my jacket and I would be gone before she got down here in the morning.

I always made sure of it.

Ambulating to the fridge, I pulled the door open. There was no evidence of whatever she'd made herself and Christopher tonight. There never was. I was the shadow in the house. The stain who returned home when it was late, and slipped into bed without so much as making a noise to stir her awake because I was afraid that someday, she'd go sleep somewhere else.

And then I'd have lost her for good.

I pulled out a plastic container with cold cuts, not bothering with the rest of the sandwich condiments. It wasn't unlike me to shovel food into my mouth out of necessity, not out of interest. Everything was a necessity now—sleep, food, bathing, work. I hadn't experienced pleasure of any kind in almost a year.

It was lonely.

Closing the fridge, I tossed the cold cuts to the counter and surveyed the kitchen. Inwardly, I wanted to smash the room to pieces because it was a fucking lie disguising the truth.

Perfect and put together while the rest of our life was in fucking shambles. I was falling apart, slowly, maddeningly. Everyday tested the frays on the rope keeping me together, tugging a little harder, wearing me down just a little more.

My vacant stare fixed on the cold cuts. I wasn't hungry after all. Not enough to stuff dry turkey slices in my mouth for a third time this week and convince myself that I had it together, that I could do this. I tossed the container back in the fridge and killed the lights on my way out of the kitchen.

Double-checking the lock on the door, I made my ascent up the stairs just as the rain outside hailed down harder, creating a deafening white noise engulfing the house in its barrage. My legs throbbed with exhaustion as I took the steps one at a time, clinging to the railing until I got to the top. Taking a right, I kept my footsteps nimble as I edged toward Christopher's room. With my hand on the knob, I held my breath and turned the knob with care. The tinkling of soft music permeated gently from the nightlight projecting a cerulean starry night scene on his walls as I jutted my head in the small clearing of the door.

At two years old, he was looking more like his ma than he was me every day. But I hoped one day, when he was a man, he'd look like me. I just prayed he was better. That he learned to appreciate what he had when he had it, even when it got hard.

The soft nest of his golden curls spread on his pillow. I suspected he'd have Pen's aristocratic bone structure, currently masked under plump, dimpled cheeks, but his lidded eyes were all mine—forest green with a curtain of dark lashes.

A smarting of pain worked through my chest when I thought of this morning. I always got him up and ready for the day. That was my time with him while Pen stayed in bed a little while longer or got herself together.

Most days, he was fine. He liked it when I woke him up. My palm flushed against his back, sweeping back and forth. I'd sit on the edge of his bed between the safety rails and his footboard, waiting for him to stir. He'd crawl into my lap with sleep still in his eyes, thumb finding his mouth—no matter how much I tried to discourage him—his head finding my pec. I'd soak in that moment, reveling every second until he was ready to get dressed and go get something to eat.

But today, today, he was a toddler with big emotions. Today, I couldn't seem to do anything right without him crying uncontrollably. I couldn't reason with him or console him enough, and that only got worse when Pen flew into the room ten minutes into his tantrum, menace polluting her tired features.

She'd decided whatever upset him was my fault. She scooped him up from off the floor, his small limbs twining around her. Each breathless hiccup made me sicker by the minute as his red, tear-stricken face buried into the crook of her neck and his agonized *"Mama"* left his mouth.

"Just go," she told me, rocking him while her fingers brushed his curls away. *"You've done enough."*

I knew she wasn't just talking about Chris anymore.

So, I did. I went to work and thought about all the ways my family would be better off if I wasn't there ruining their dynamic. A dynamic I had been a part of until I wasn't. I was the interloper now, the outlier who didn't belong in a family I helped create.

A family I loved.

Sure, rationally, I recognized two-year-olds cried sometimes. He was at the height of his emotional development, and not every tantrum made sense—I knew that as much as the next dad. But it was the way she looked at me like I should have known better, like I continued to disappoint her every day. *That* fucking killed.

But I guess, I deserved it. I'd turned out to be the inferior scumbag her parents warned her about, so could I blame her?

I closed his bedroom door, the anxious knot already forming beneath my belly button as I moved in the darkness toward our bedroom.

Pen's bedroom with the king-sized bed we used to sleep in the middle of, wrapped up in each other. The bedroom I got a couple of hours of fraught sleep in, keeping myself as close to the edge of the bed as possible. My hand extended to the door, but the constant and even purr of…

What was that?

My heart hammered, my ears homing in as awareness slammed into me, and the soft familiar moan I'd heard hundreds of times slipped from her, penetrating my memory.

Was she?

Hot rage pooled in my stomach. My molars connected, adrenaline punching into overdrive as I twisted the knob and shoved the door open roughly. The thump of it pulsated against the door stopper, melding with the steady drone of a vibrator.

Just as I expected, Pen startled, lurching upright, the buzzing somehow growing increasingly louder as she remained transfixed in horror. The heady scent of her arousal hit my nose, a flash of memories I had no business recalling, rushing at me. I wanted to bite my fist to keep from punching something because I'd never been more fucking frustrated in my life.

"Seriously?" I demanded, heaving a tight breath.

I didn't even know she owned a vibrator anymore.

Then again, I guessed I didn't know the woman I married all that well.

I wasn't the only one with a secret. My wife had some, too.

The only difference was mine remained exposed on a lens under a microscope, while hers were still under lock and key.

Pen's shoulder-length flaxen hair stuck in all directions. Her wild blue eyes flared with worry. She fumbled under the bedsheets, the buzzing ceasing as she retracted the hand nestled between her legs, her erratic inhalations filling the heavy silence, chest heaving.

She must not have heard my controlled movements downstairs over the torrential downpour. Or she had, and just thought she had more time.

I shook my head. *Unbelievable.*

So, my wife wasn't uninterested in sex.

She was uninterested in *me*. That thought… it tore up the remnants of my self-worth. But I deserved this. It was my fault, after all. My actions brought us here.

Why would she want me after what I'd done?

Penelope didn't rush to speak. She never did.

She was still trying to collect herself as I strode toward the adjacent bathroom, hitting the light switch. Pen had picked a white-and-blue color palate in here. The white bulbs in the decorative-caged geometric-metal chandelier emitted soft shadows against the white porcelain tiles.

She'd wanted a clean and expensive look in all the bathrooms long before she knew she wanted to buy this house, and she'd gotten it. I made sure of it behind the scenes, because whatever Penelope wanted, Penelope got. Period.

I peeled my dirty, long-sleeved Henley off my body, tossing it into a hamper behind me. My skin smelled like sawdust, remnants of my deodorant from this morning still lingering over the distinct scent of sweat from a long-ass day.

My hands, though. They ached. My knuckles split at some point today, and my fingers and palms throbbed.

I'd stayed at work until the rain came in, arranging bricks for the chimney we were repairing. It had been meditative work; work I would have done forever if it meant not coming home to feel the frosty chill that contended with Mother Nature's.

I met my own eyes in the bathroom mirror, hatred filling them. Not toward Pen, I could never hate her… but at myself.

Self-depreciation and degrading myself were becoming a second language I was fluent in. My callused hands found the white marble counter, my body leaning at the waist as I tried to slow my racing heart and soften the current of anger pumping in my veins. I didn't care if she was getting herself off. That wasn't it... it was...

Her soft footfalls hit my ears, her shadow filling the threshold of the bathroom door. I didn't want to look at her, but like a moth to a flame, I turned my head, finding her weary blue eyes.

Penelope folded her arms over her chest, her thin lips pressing into an even thinner line. The blush the same shade of pink as her tank top and sleep shorts stained her cheeks, 'cause I'd caught her. There was no way she was talking her way out of this.

Her stare was flinty, moving from me to the tips of her polished toes. "I just needed something for myself," she explained.

Yeah, I got it. I jerked off to thoughts of her a couple of days a week just like I had in the old days, sometimes more—because it was the closest I was getting to touching my wife. If it wasn't because we'd had a son out of wedlock, I would have contested whether we had ever consummated our marriage.

We hadn't, in case you were wondering.

I hadn't had sex with my wife in what would be a year come January, and to put that into perspective, we'd only been married for seven months. Initially, I had chalked it up to wedding stress—for the wedding we hadn't really wanted. At least, not like that.

Of course, I'd *wanted* to marry her. I'd always wanted to marry her. Ever since I saw her climb out of her Range Rover, wearing those ridiculously expensive shoes outside of this house three years ago when it had been a construction site.

Men knew when they'd found the one. Don't let anyone tell you otherwise. They knew when they met the person who could bring them to their fucking knees with a single look, and I'd known with the confidence of my last name that I wanted her to be mine. That I wanted to put her in a house just like this and have as many fucking babies as we could before she was beating me off her with a stick. Penelope was addictive—a constant hit of dopamine I wanted in an IV. I was gonna grow old with her and go on cruises that catered to the elderly. I was gonna die with her because I loved her more than life itself.

And then we'd started planning our wedding. Something small and intimate that warped and twisted seemingly overnight into a massive, gaudy-as-fuck affair for her parents' society club—and everything changed.

She changed.

And in a way, so had I.

"Yep," I replied, offering her a curt head nod. "I get it."

She exhaled. It wasn't of relief. No, it was an agonized wheeze like the breath found itself trapped in her lungs like a steel band and no amount of oxygen would help ease her pain.

"But." God, was I about to prostrate myself? "I'm right here, Pen." If she'd just let me hold her. I didn't even need to have sex with her, just to twine my fingers with hers, trace her jawline with the tip of my busted nose, or touch the short strands of her hair.

Anything.

My throat worked, a thousand tiny blades scoring me. "Whenever you want me, I'm right here."

Her expression fell, her eyes squeezing shut. She shook her head in one quick, short stroke that killed me. "I can't."

Can't.

Yeah, I was familiar with that word—but I was also tired of hearing it with no further explanation as to *why*.

I'd own my fuckup for the rest of my life, but it didn't excuse her from never explaining to me how we got here to begin with. "And I can't do this for much longer." Why wasn't I entitled to answers?

Her eyes opened, her pupils all but dilating. "Over *sex*?"

Was she kidding? I missed my wife. Desperately. Not just burying my face between her thighs and lapping up her release when she came on my face.

I missed talking to her. The way her face lit up, recounting something goofy Christopher had done that day.

Her laughter.

How she cranked Iron Maiden at an offensive level while doing chores and proudly paired band tees with high fashion.

This wasn't just about sex anymore. This was… this was slowly going insane from the isolation and the absence of love.

"Over everything, Penelope." I pushed off the counter, scrubbing a hand over my features, the muscles in my abdomen tightening as I braced myself for her backlash. "I desperately need you to talk to me."

She combed her fingers through her hair, tucking the strands behind her ears the way I always used to do for her. "There's nothing to say."

"There's plenty to fucking say," I groused, extending a hand to her. "You're in bed, pleasuring yourself. And I'm desperate for you to just let me in, anyway possible."

Let me just hold you for a minute. Thirty seconds, tops. Remember what it feels like to be in my arms again. Acknowledge that we're still husband and wife and we said 'til death do we part—

"Then let's get divorced," she uttered matter-of-factly, dropping her loose arms to her side. Her features grew cold, and I knew she meant it with every fiber of her being. She always brought that word up any time I pushed too hard. That's what made me back down every single time, because even if I was alone, I was afraid to lose her and Christopher.

But it didn't change that I was tired, too. Tired of feeling sick. Tired of groveling with no end in sight.

I staggered back, appraising her through narrowed eyes. "That is *not* what I'm saying."

"You said you can't do this for much longer, didn't you?"

"That's *not* what I meant," I reiterated.

I was dying without her. Didn't she see that? The D word. The word I swore would never be a part of my vocabulary because I was not getting divorced. Ever.

I loved my wife.

I loved my wife so much I almost fucked it all up to shit. *Almost.*

"Then what did you mean?" she demanded, her hands balling against her exposed thighs.

"I need you to fucking talk to me!"

"Lower your voice," she hissed, ire flashing in her blue eyes. "Do you understand the shitstorm you left me with this morning? I couldn't get him to calm down."

I scoffed. "Don't pin that all on me."

"You don't know the first thing about being a dad, Dougie." I recoiled, and the veil of anger adorning her face vanished as she clapped a hand over her mouth, her eyes distending. She couldn't believe she'd said that any more than I could.

But that's who we were now. We said things we didn't mean in moments of duress, and we were always under duress.

Pen drove the heels of her palms into her eyes, rolling her lips together. "You're just not here *enough*." Her shoulders sagged when she dropped her arms to her side. "That's all."

That wasn't all she was saying, but it was part of it. Sure, my absence probably played a part to the way things were right now—but that was because she'd made it perfectly fucking clear that she didn't want me around, either.

I schooled my expression, nodding my head. "I need you to talk to me," I repeated. Desperation enveloped every single word, my remorseful stare pleading with her. Anything. I'd give anything for her to let me crawl inside of that head of hers and understand how we got here.

I knew my role. I knew what I'd done had pushed us off the fucking cliff, but I didn't understand how we'd found the cliff to begin with.

We'd had everything, and then we had nothing.

And that was all she was giving me now, too.

Nothing. She gave me nothing.

Every. Single. Time.

Pen turned around, padding back to bed. That emptiness I should have grown accustomed to by now choked me, consuming any remaining tendril of hope I had.

I should give her what she wanted—a divorce, her freedom.

But I couldn't. 'Cause even though I was the interloper, it had been lies that brought us here—hers and mine.

The only chance we had in hell of surviving this was the truth.

Chapter Three

Penelope

Three years ago…

"WHAT'S SO FUNNY?" I ASKED TRINA WITHOUT LOOKING AT HER. THE PADS of my fingers brushed against a sample of textured wallpaper I was considering for the powder room. Stabbing the salad nestled on my lap with a cheap plastic fork with my other hand, I lifted the sample up, tilting my head appreciatively. Wallpaper got a bad rap, but I always thought that if you used it appropriately, it could add dimension to any space.

There definitely wasn't wallpaper in my childhood home—which was what partially made it so interesting to me. Anything "out of the norm" in the eyes of my parents and their society friends had always fascinated me, including design choices, musical preferences, and taste in men. Or as they'd call it, "a suitable husband."

No thanks.

Trina made another ornery sound, her laugh gurgling in the back of her throat. "I've known Dougie my *whole* life, and I've never seen him this way before." And there came the onset of the kaleidoscope of butterflies fluttering in my stomach.

She flittered her honey-brown eyes at me, her lips pursing to suffocate the childish smile. I liked Trina. At only twenty, she was a far cry from her uppity older brother, who could seriously afford to lighten up —he didn't even eat lunch outside with the rest of us. His lunch came in the form of a very green, nasty looking protein shake that he drank without so much as flinching.

Every. Single. Day.

The sound of the mixing ball hitting the plastic and stirring the contents of his shake was the Pavlovian signal that it was time to break for lunch. I'd catch sight of his long legs extended in front of him when he sat on the floor, his expression hard. He was a grumpy asshole and willingly opted to isolate himself from everyone except for his sister and Dougie.

He didn't like me. At all. He hired me, sure, but he never missed a moment to remind me he was only doing it to keep Katrina happy and get this house off his plate as soon as possible.

Message received—loud and clear.

I was the expensive nuisance here to save the day, and he was desperate for any opportunity to remind me I wasn't pulling my weight.

I'd show him. He'd get top fucking dollar for this place with my help, even in a recession.

I was that sure of myself.

Where Sean was in a permanent state of annoyance, Trina evoked a sort of laissez-faire attitude to just about everything. Over the past month and a half, she'd been happy to help me with whatever I was working on and didn't mind being a conversational conduit between Sean and me when it came to making decisions.

I wasn't scared of Sean, but he just messed with my positive sunshine vibes. He was a gray rain cloud who needed to get laid or smoke a joint and take a load off. Trina could handle him better.

Still... even though her brother was a dick to me on a near daily basis, it made me want to try harder with him for some reason. He might not have liked me, but I was only fifty percent confident it had to do with what I was charging him—even if it was fair.

He called me "an unnecessary distraction on the job site."

It kind of sucked when your client hated you. But that wasn't the feeling everyone had toward me on the site, which I suspected was exactly what he meant by suggesting I was a distraction.

I thought some of the crew might like me around here, especially now that I'd gotten comfortable slinging barbs back at them. You needed a thick skin to survive on an active construction site. Someone was always yelling at someone, for one thing or another.

Trina sipped the remnants of her soda noisily, the dregs slurping through the straw sandwiched between her teeth, her central incisors slightly larger than the rest, making her appear rabbit-like. She released the straw, rolling her plump pout with mischief. "All he does is stare at you."

I didn't need to ask the who she was referring to, because the staring over the past couple of weeks had been mutual. The only difference was one of us had trained at the best schools money could buy and remained well versed in the art of remaining furtive.

It was no secret that the true crux of Sean's argument that I was an unnecessary distraction on the job site was because Dougie wasn't covert about anything.

It was why I liked him.

He wore his emotions on his face and said exactly what he meant, just as he meant it.

Lifting my Clubmaster Classic Ray-Bans to the top of my head, I found the magnetic set of green eyes across the yard with ease. Dougie was sitting on his lunch cooler away from everyone else, legs parted, elbows perched on his knees. His tired orange-and-yellow work vest was folded and resting at his feet. There was a half-eaten sandwich in his powerful hands, and I wasn't sure he was really enjoying it at all with the way his exhausted jaw worked.

I had plans for those hands. He just didn't know it yet.

Dougie always brought his lunch, and every day, he ate it the same way. He offered me an inscrutable smile, the warmth of lust licking up the inside of my thighs, creating an ache desperate for relief. That smile was dangerous. He may not have been furtive, but that smile was impossible to read.

It could mean all kinds of things.

I ripped my eyes away, trying to keep the blush off my face, but I could feel the curl of heat crawling up my neck, before finally settling on my cheeks.

Dougie was cute. Different, but cute.

Not in a bad way. When you grew up with parents who'd meticulously planned your every move in life right down to which legacy Ivy League asshole you married, with his coifed haircut, the armoire full of Ralph Lauren polo shirts hung on velvet hangers, and an unrepentant affinity for unsatisfying missionary sex—you welcomed different.

I'd always felt a little different, too. On a superficial level, sure, I was exactly what I seemed like on paper. Fair-featured former debutante with parents who'd carefully begun curating her life resume since the moment of conception.

They'd known my name would be Penelope Louise at the verification of my gender—in homage to my grandmothers. They picked the best therapists, so I'd know how to manage the inevitable stresses of life—which really just meant ensuring there would be no scandal. No deranged, pregnant, pill-head daughter for my parents to hide away from their society friends lest I embarrass them. Before I'd even taken my first breath, they'd confirmed I'd attend boarding school at Hotchkiss, and then began making hefty donations to Yale to ensure I went there next—just like Daddy, legacy student or not. I'd have Mother's good cheekbones and flaxen hair, play piano at an almost grade eight level, maintain an unrepentant need for perfection, and with any luck, a low dose Ambien prescription to help me sleep someday when the facade inevitably crippled me.

As the daughter of Evelyn and Walter Cullimore, I'd grow up to make them proud, continue the artificial legacy and play my performative role dutifully.

They decided everything for me.

And I despised it.

I didn't want to be reduced to the role of a submissive wife to some asshole named Harold Huntington III, even if he photographed nicely and his father played golf with mine. The idea of going to Yale and studying law when I'd never get to practice because I'd find myself preoccupied with breeding like a purebred Arabian mare made my skin crawl. I wanted to get the hell out of Connecticut, far away from the weight of my parents' expectations of me, from their high society, club etiquette, missionary sex, and contrived way of being.

It was a big fucking lie, anyway.

I'd applied to Boston University's English literature program behind their backs—and no, Mother still hadn't forgiven me—and welcomed a life free of debutante balls, prudish dinner parties, and high tea where one of Mother's friends would inevitably suggest I date her son even though he was a misogynistic prick with a Napoleon complex, and a fast car he didn't know how to drive because it was a stick shift.

I wanted a man who knew how to handle what he was packing.

Falling into interior design after graduation had been a happy mistake, one that had changed the course of my entire life. Design provided me with a creative outlet I'd always been seeking, free of judgment, and expression was encouraged. I was good at what I did. I knew I was.

Even if my parents didn't see it. Daddy and Mother had given me every opportunity to be exactly like them, but all I'd ever wanted was to be me.

I didn't want to eat salmon because it was low fat and high in omega-3s. I wanted to eat a greasy slice of pizza with questionable meat on it from a hole-in-the-wall that was one health infraction away from being shuttered.

I wanted to wear short skirts that barely covered my ass and go to dingy bars with live music where no one knew me. Find a hot guy I'd never see again and let him take me against a gross bathroom wall just because he could, and I wanted it. Then go freeze my ass off outside and recount the experience while my best friend, Raquel, smoked a cigarette because only one of us had ditched the habit and it wasn't her.

I wanted to listen to music, the kind that my parents hated. Debussy was fine—I could play "Clair de Lune" with my eyes closed—but have you ever listened to Iron Maiden's "Hallowed Be Thy Name" with noise canceling headphones with a lit joint pinched between your fingers and the smoke melting all the tension in your body after a long day? I had, and it made me cry every single time. Debussy had never done that to me. Debussy never made me feel like I was alive. Debussy never made me see color swatches differently or given me the confidence to experiment with an unconventional piece of furniture in a sterile room.

I just wanted to live. Really live.

Trina straightened with an excited lurch, ripping me from my thoughts. "He's coming over here."

What? I glanced upward. Sure enough, Dougie had wrapped his sandwich back up and shoved it into the cooler. He kept his posture relaxed, gait unhurried, as he headed in our direction. His eyes flittered to Trina and the house, communicating in silence. I could almost hear him and his hard accent. *"Beat it, kid."*

She let out a little squeak, clambering to her feet. With a short wave over her shoulder, Trina called out, "See you in a bit."

Shit. Why was I so nervous suddenly? I had been approached before, dozens of times. But never by someone who looked at me like he recognized there was a societal disparity between us and didn't care. Dougie couldn't have been taller than five foot ten, with a broad set of quarterback shoulders, and dark brown hair cut into a taper fade crew cut. He had about four days' worth of stubble across his jaw, chin and upper lip and the most incredible hypnotic green eyes I'd ever seen—as verdant as the deepest part of the woods this house backed out to. He moved with a kind of swagger that wasn't contrived, head cocked to the right, a panty-melting smile testing the corners of his mouth.

I flattened a hand against my stomach, willing my coiling insides to settle as he stopped in front of me. My stare dragged from his strong hands, tracing the course of his defined veins running up the length of his exposed forearms, until I found his eyes.

Dougie observed me, like he saw me. The real me.

My heart was in my throat. I couldn't exhale the way I wanted to, not without giving up my cover that I was overly aware of him, that I loved the way he looked at me.

"Hey." He squinted under the relentless summer sun, holding a hand like a visor over his eyes. "How's your day going?" Dougie had the best accent. It was unquestionably New England, his rhotic hard. My ears always perked up when I heard it around the site. My pulse would quicken and a silent plea to get a glimpse of him would whirr through my brain.

I tucked my legs under the foldable camping chair he'd set up for Trina and me when we'd gotten back from Wendy's with our lunch.

I noticed Dougie doing things like that over the last couple of weeks. Not just the camping chairs, but when I said something, it was suddenly taken care of.

I really need a coffee. He would send Trina on a Dunkin's run with a crisp twenty in her hand and a smirk plastered on her face.

My tire is flat from the gravel. Dougie would have the spare put on before I left for the end of the day.

He was thoughtful and kind. I liked kind. I'd never done kind before, but I wanted to know how kind translated in other areas.

I mirrored his pose, shielding my eyes from the sun with my hand, tipping my head back to stare at him. "It's going okay, yours?"

Sean had told me off an hour ago about the countertops I was thinking about for the kitchen. He reminded me this wasn't the set of an HGTV show and we didn't have a money tree. I'd walked away wounded with my tongue sandwiched between my teeth, but a few minutes later, I'd heard Dougie's voice curtailing his ire… *"Don't be a dick. She's just doing her job, alright? We'll figure out the money."*

"Good, good." He nodded enthusiastically. I almost missed the tight constriction in his thick throat as he swallowed. "You need anything?"

I smiled, chewing on the inside of my cheek to prevent it from blooming into a full grin. A little mystery never hurt anyone. "Not that I can think of."

"Okay." He dropped his hand. "If that changes, just let me know."

"How was your sandwich?" I wasn't one for small talk, but I wanted to prolong our conversation a little while longer.

Dougie laughed, shaking his head. "Awful." He glanced at my half-eaten salad, kicking his chin. "And your salad?"

"I should have gotten a burger." At that, he laughed.

Playing with the fork, I speared more lettuce and popped it into my mouth, taking my time to drag it out. My salad was fine, but he didn't give a shit about it anymore than I cared about his sandwich. Who was interested in food when you were in the presence of someone who made you hungry in other ways?

The gesture garnered the exact reaction I'd wanted. He shifted his weight from one foot to the other, his stance widening as his gaze heated. Dougie cleared his throat, the timbre in his voice dropping. "So, I'm thinking you probably know why I'm really over here," he hedged.

I rested the fork against the edge of the plastic container, swallowing my bite. "I bet it has nothing to do with my salad or how my day is going, right?" I teased.

He held up his hands as though he was guilty as charged. "Let's go out."

My teeth found the corner of my mouth. "Go out?"

"Yeah," he tested, suddenly unsure if he'd misread the signals. "On a date." After all that preamble, he cut straight to the chase.

Dougie had a face you didn't want to lie to, so I was honest. "I don't date."

I liked the freedom and flexibility of being single. I was in no hurry to be tied down by something else. My parents' expectations had already burdened me. I needed to remain autonomous.

I regretted the words immediately, the boyish expression ghosted from his expression. His jaw flexed, brows punching inward with thought. "Uh, yeah, okay." He straightened, harrumphing. "No problem, sorry." Dougie gave me his profile for a moment, then nodded.

"Also, you might want to consider wearing some sunscreen out here or get a hat." He tapped his nose, taking a step back. "The tip of your nose is turning red."

I touched my nose, feeling the budding promise of a sunburn there. He was right. Lowering my hand, I watched as he turned to leave. "That's it?" I asked, waylaying him.

He glanced at me over his shoulder, his expression pinching. "I've got sunscreen in my truck if you want me to get it for you." Now I knew why he always smelled faintly like sunscreen over his deodorant and the spice of sawdust.

"That's not what I meant."

He paused, then cocked a brow. The muscles in his arms flexed as he hooked his hands on the back of his neck. "What do you mean?"

A month and a half of us dancing around each other, and he was already out? "I tell you I don't date and you're out of the game?"

He shrugged, slipping his hands into the pockets of his tired jeans. "I don't play games, Pen." His tone was sober, his eyes absent of mirth.

Pen. I liked how he called me Pen. How he said my name with an easy familiarity even when it was clear he wasn't thrilled by what I'd told him. The only other person who called me Pen was Raquel.

But he was the first man I'd ever heard "I don't play games" from.

"How about fun?" I rolled my lips together, my skin tingling as his molten stare studied my mouth and his teeth involuntarily found his bottom lip, dragging against it. "Do you like having fun?"

He softened, grasping my insinuation. A faraway look touched his eyes, transporting him somewhere else, and I wasn't sure if I liked it or hated it. Most men brightened at the suggestion of a no-strings-attached situation, but I was grasping Dougie wasn't most men.

"Fun, huh?" he repeated lowly.

My head tipped back, the back of the fabric chair cradling my neck. "I bore easily," I confessed, touching my chest. "I won't waste your time, but I'm down for having fun."

Seriously, my blow jobs were renowned back in college. I was proud of myself.

It seemed like he was considering it for a moment, the tip of his work boot resting against the gravel driveway. His mouth rocked from side to side, then he nodded. "Yeah, I can have fun."

Good, that settled things. I expelled a controlled sigh of relief. Untucking the lid from the container, I fastened it shut, and then plopped my salad remains into the greasy bag Trina's burger had been in. I adjusted the links of my dainty wristwatch to snag a look at the face.

My heart kicked in my chest, the words flowing out of me. "Wanna show me what you can do in twenty minutes?" I was brazened. I always had been. In college, I'd operated on Marlboros, Maiden and muscular men. I'd given up the cigarettes by graduation, but my penchant for Maiden and muscular men remained steadfast. I didn't know what his music preference was, but he certainly fit the bill on the muscular part. The sleeves of his T-shirt struggled to contain his biceps, but I knew I wanted to dig my fingers into them when I rode him.

Dougie tested the inside of his cheek with his tongue, then laughed through his nose. "Meet me at the end of the street."

"The end of the street?"

He nodded, jerking his head a little toward the crew. "Don't let any of these idiots see you getting into my truck. They're distracted by food right now, so we've got some time."

My mouth pressed into a tight line, dread pooling in my stomach. Why? Was he embarrassed by me?

"It's not because of you, Penelope," he assured, as though detecting my errant shift in mood. "Guys like me don't get women like you. That's not the way the world works. I'm just too cocky to let a good thing pass me by without shooting my shot, but if they see that..." He gestured at them with the jut of his thumb, their booming laughter swallowing the sorrowed crooning of a Portuguese Fado song permeating the yard. "It'll invite them to do the same with you and I don't want that."

I didn't know why the unembellished observation bothered me. Of course guys like him could get women like me. Why couldn't the world work that way? Who cared if those guys saw?

Not me.

He offered me an amiable smile. "I'm gonna grab my keys. Start walking."

I liked his hand on my thigh. Strangely, it felt like it had always belonged there.

Dougie's massive palm naturally settled there as soon as we pulled away from the end of the street, the pads of his fingers tracing the seam of my jeans. There was nothing lewd in the gesture, and he didn't inch his hand upward like any other guy would have.

But I wished he would. Every brush of his fingers created a dull ache between my legs and a gnawing hunger in my gut, desperate for friction and pressure.

The tires bounced on the wooden planks of the covered bridge with the pretty cupola as we edged into the town's outskirts. Dense thickets hugged the road when we cleared the bridge.

"Where are we going?"

"Privacy," he murmured.

He could have brought me back to his place... if he wanted to. "Do you live in Eaton?"

Dougie tested his grip on my thigh, the pulse under my belly button throbbing, sweat breaking out against my spine. It snatched my next breath from my lungs. "No. Fall River." Right, I guess the journey would have eaten into our time limit.

The truck slowed, his hand leaving my thigh so he could hit the indicator—ever the law-abiding citizen, even when no one was around to witness his adherence to the rules of the road. He pulled the truck onto a hidden dirt path wide enough for only his truck. The tires crunched twigs and overgrown shrubbery as he drove us further and further into the depths of the woods.

When he decided we were far enough, he cut the engine.

"You took me all the way to the edge of town... into the woods?"

Horror movies started this way, didn't they?

Dougie frowned, his hand reaching for the keys in the ignition.

Uncertainty quirked his brows as he searched my face. "Yeah… is that bad?"

I shook my head. No, it wasn't bad. Unconventional, sure, but not bad. Glancing up at the gangling tree limbs, I felt a sense of calm and safety in the way they formed a canopy over us, reminiscent of an umbrella. It was intimate out here, shut away from the rest of the world, in our own reality where the spotlight on our differences didn't exist and I could be as vocal as I wanted. It kind of turned me on.

Unbuckling my seat belt, I allowed it to retract back into place. Twisting in my seat, I tucked one leg under me, sizing him up. "You going to put your seat back or what?"

Dougie chortled, unbuckling his seatbelt and then lolling his head to the right. He studied me carefully, his eyes tracing over my features, and I felt as though he was taking snapshots in his memory. "You're pretty bossy, aren't you?"

"You don't know the half of it."

"Oh, yeah?" he husked, reaching to his left, his seat shifting back. The seat reclined a little. Dougie parted his legs, patting his lap. "Come and show me."

Finally. Crawling over the middle console, I extended one leg over his waist, bringing myself into a straddle on his lap. His muscular arms banded around my waist, pulling me closer and just as I suspected, it was better than I imagined in my head. Like the fitting of last two puzzle pieces coming together in a five-hundred-piece kit. A restrained groan left him, his eyes hooding as he stared at me. I felt the twitch of his stirring cock against the crotch of my jeans, the denim creating just the right amount of friction when I rolled my hips. I matched his groan with a breathy, satisfied sigh that got his attention.

Dougie let one of his arms around my waist free, his hand extending to touch a lock of my hair. He tested it in his fingers, relishing in it for a moment before the brush of his callused fingers tucked the strands behind my ears. The gesture made goosebumps break out across my skin. "You feel good."

"I'm gonna feel better in a minute."

"Yeah, I know you are," he agreed, focusing on my mouth. "Can I kiss you, Penelope?"

I smiled, my forehead puckering with disbelief. "Are you always a gentleman?"

He shook his head, his mouth crooking to the right. "Just with you... so?" His pointer finger found my upper lip, following the outline of my cupid's bow as he waited for his answer.

My acquiescence came in a way that aroused a curse from him. Leaning forward, I enveloped the thick digit with my mouth, cheeks hollowing as I sucked the length back, my hand clutching his.

"Pen, fuck." The low, wretched sound of his voice made my pussy throb, a hot flush of warmth spreading through me.

I worked him until the semi in his pants was fully erect, hard and ready for me. He pulled his finger out of my mouth. It was difficult to read his expression—intimate, and yet... pensive.

Dougie shifted forward, skimming the tip of his nose with mine, his hot breath falling over my face. "I'm gonna kiss you now, Pen. And if you want," he leaned closer, his mouth inches from mine, my skin scorching hot and desperate for more of him, "you can kiss me back, too."

The tentative feathering of his lips met mine, his stubble tickling my face as time seemed to slow. My insides flipped and my heart hammered wildly as I sank into the kiss, wanting more, despite the conservative approach he was taking. He slipped one hand into my hair, cradling the back of my head as he deepened the kiss.

I'd been kissed before, sure, but not like this.

This I'd never forget.

The tip of his curious, taut tongue licked the pleat of my lips with permission, and just when I thought the kiss would remain restrained, he released his inhibition and devoured me. His tongue massaged mine, causing me to squirm in his lap. The rapturous fervent kisses left me panting, my hands fumbling with his shirt. I wanted him naked. *I* wanted to be naked.

But as my hands reached for his jeans, he snagged them, clutching them tightly.

I broke the kiss, my chest rising and falling as I tried to collect my breathing. "What's wrong?"

That wasn't a bad kiss. I knew for a fact it wasn't.

All he did was smile, like he was in on a joke I wasn't privy to. He drew me back to him, placing my arms around his shoulders. His lips were back on mine again, taking what was his—just not all of it.

Why?

My blood thrummed through my veins, my mind flustered and intoxicated by my arousal as I tried to process why he wasn't taking advantage of the fact that I was ready for a lunchtime-dicking appointment. That was the whole reason I'd suggested "fun."

Not that this wasn't fun. He was a great kisser, and I liked that his rigid cock pulsated against me. Every hungered sound he made set off another flurry of goosebumps and made my pussy swell some more.

But he wasn't… "Do something," I demanded.

Take my top off, lose my bra in your truck, motorboat me. Anything.

"I *am* doing something," he murmured, brushing the tip of his nose against mine. "I'm kissing a really beautiful woman."

I stilled, the statement mainlining inside of my mind. It spurred something inside of me, something that made me want to cry for some inexplicable reason because I wasn't used to gentle.

"You can touch me, you know?" I whispered. "Anywhere." Did I really need to spell it out for him? Put his hand on the small swell of my breast? Shove his hand in my pants so he knew I was wet and desperate? Hell, I might not even balk if his finger brushed against my asshole, even though that wasn't really my thing.

But all he did was nod. Dougie slid both hands through my hair to tip the back of my head forward. "I know." The words fell across my lips, just as his descended upon mine. "And I will."

"When?" Could I pencil it into my calendar? Try to line up my next waxing appointment in preparation? Maybe ensure I do some yoga that day, so my body was extra pliable.

He broke out into a laugh, his head falling back against his headrest as he surveyed me through hooded eyes that I swore I'd see in my dreams tonight when my hand inevitably found its way between my legs tonight. "When I'm done exploring your mouth, Pen."

I glanced at my wristwatch. Disappointment had me pushing air through my vibrating lips. "Lunch is over soon."

Dougie hooked his fingers through my belt loops, dragging me against him. The moan escaped me involuntarily, the thick ridge of his cock creating just enough friction against my clit that my body came to life with each guided motion of my hips like he was driving himself into me.

Every hair on the back of my neck raised to half-mast, my skin breaking out into a horripilation under my clothes.

"Yeah," he groaned hoarsely. "That's what it's gonna sound like, huh?"

My fingers speared into his hair, my nails dragging against his scalp as I pressed my forehead to his. "Are you going to fuck me or not, Douglas?"

He smirked at the usage of his given name. "Eventually." His commanding grip tightened against my ass, urging me to roll. My pelvis came down on his cock again, another desperate sigh leaving me as I rocked against him. "But not today."

My neck bowed, my hair falling over my shoulders, the column of my exposed neck proffering to him. "I'm too old to dry hump." I'd done seedier things with strangers, the kind that would have gotten me disowned.

This was juvenile, and yet...

He leaned forward, the coarse stubble of his beard brushing against my skin. Dougie's mouth traced my jaw, his mouth finding my ear. "But you're going to anyway, aren't you?" His voice was liquid sex, all gravelly and possessive. It made my nipples turn into tight points, chafing against the lace of my bra.

All I wanted was for him to ravish me, to unbutton my jeans and slam me on his cock, over and over again, instead...

"Show me how good you'd give it," he commanded, nipping at my earlobe. "Give me something to stroke off to later."

"Dougie..." My hips bucked hard against him. All the argument fled my body, the carnal part of my instincts coming online and taking over. I quickened my rocking, crushing down on him until the gnawing need pervaded through my pussy and twisted with agony under my belly button.

"You'd want me to fuck you hard?" he grunted, rolling my body alongside his. "I'm going to ruin that tight pussy of yours, Penny. Just wait and see."

"Oh God." My body tingled with pleasure; the panel of my thong soaked as I chased the outline of his cock. It was big, big with the promise of ruining me, just like he'd said.

I wanted it. Bad.

My mind slipped into fantasy, where our clothes didn't exist, and the tight constraints of his truck weren't an issue. Sweat licked up my spine as my skin grew heated, my body bearing down in an uncoordinated figure eight against his cock, chasing my release.

"Fuck, fuck, fuck," I cried out, my fingernails sinking into his muscular biceps that tensed under my grip. My skin tightened as pleasure licked up my thighs and detonated in my pussy as my orgasm broke free.

"Yeah, that's a good fucking girl," he murmured, brushing his lips against my cheek. "You took it so good, didn't you?"

I fell forward, trembling as the aftershock of the orgasm racked through me.

What the hell was *that*? Was it even legal for him to make me come that hard without having actually fucked me?

His lips skimmed mine, my skin tingling under his touch. "Lunch is over," he murmured, patting my thigh.

I nodded breathlessly, then shifted back in my seat. Sure, I was satiated, but also terribly fucking confused.

This was far from finished. No, this was closer to my salad, an appetizer at best. I wanted the entrée. Hell, dessert, too.

"What are you doing after work?" I asked. I wasn't sure what I intended to do with the information, but I wanted to know if I could invite myself over to his place.

Dougie corrected himself in his seat, his hands adjusting the weight of his stiff erection constricted in his jeans. "Watching the Sox play at Sean's."

"Oh." He winced, the repercussions of his attempt at gentlemanly altruism no doubt coming back with a vengeance. I swallowed the pooling saliva in my mouth, my gaze shifting from where his hands were fastened against his crotch to his pinched profile. "I can take care of that for you." No, I wasn't being benevolent. I had selfish motives. I just wanted to see if he was as big as I thought he was. Extending a hand, he caught it before I ever met my mark, waylaying me. *Again.*

What was with this guy?

Dougie's thumb pressed against the center of my palm gently. "I'm okay, really." He placed my hand back on my lap.

The truck vibrated back to life, my mouth ajar as I appraised him. "That's it?"

"What do you mean?" he asked, reversing the truck out from the clearing.

"You don't want *anything* from me?"

"I got what I wanted," he replied, putting the ignition into drive when we edged onto the road. He leaned back in his seat.

"Blue balls?" I demanded incredulously. Was that some weird kink? He asked for something to stroke off to later, so maybe…

Dougie chuckled, then shook his head. "Nah, I could do without that." His thick fingers drummed along the steering wheel to the beat of Tal Bachman's "She's So High", crooning softly from the radio. "I got to kiss you. That's all I wanted."

"To kiss me?" It was cute, but *ugh.* "How old are you?"

"I turned thirty in January, you?"

A nineteen-seventy-eight baby—the release year of Meat Loaf's uncut "Paradise by the Dashboard Light" on a 45 RPM and Van Halen's debut album—which made him two years older than me. Clearing the thought away with the shake of my head, I blew out a frustrated breath. "I'll be twenty-eight in October, but I didn't actually want to know how old you were. I just meant—"

He cleared his throat, interrupting me. "That you wanted me to fuck you without remorse and then spend the rest of the afternoon pretending you don't exist?"

"Wh-what?" I stammered, my eyes flashing. Not exactly, but…

"That's what you're used to, right? That's why you bore easily?" he surmised, his mouth rocking with consideration. "Be the asshole first so you don't get hurt?"

I harrumphed, turning my head. I didn't ask to be scrutinized right now, even if he was right. "It's just easier."

"For who?" I didn't have a brilliant answer for that, it was just the way I operated. It felt easier. The thing with the spoiled-rich-girl routine was that while no one would ever take pity on you because of your privilege, it didn't change they wanted you like you were a guaranteed meal ticket—even the other trust fund babies who ran in your inner circle. If they burned through their inheritance, they had the contingency of yours. What was better than being rich already? Reproducing with someone else who was wealthier than you.

It made me feel like shit, so I always kept my cards close to my chest. I got what I wanted from people, and then I moved on. But Dougie didn't seem to give a shit about that.

At all.

"Look, Penelope. I'll be honest. I want to date you, properly." He heaved a pained sigh through his nose. "But I'm good to have fun with you if that's what you want. It's just..." His throat weaved with a noticeable swallow. "It's been a while since I've been with someone. Give me a bit of time to get my head back in the game."

The confession drew my attention back to him. He was honest, sure, but what did he mean it had been a while? Was that why he wasn't rushing to get into my pants?

I studied his profile. The right side of his face was even, the afternoon sun highlighting his skin. You could hardly tell there was a twist in his nose—he'd sustained a break at some point. Maybe an injury from his childhood that had healed badly.

His lips rested together; his concentration fixed on the road. But even though he kept his features neutral, there was something there, something I could pick out despite it being unarticulated. "Did you get hurt?" I asked softly.

He brought the truck to a perfect, gentle halt at a stop sign. "Didn't we all at some point?"

We were quiet the rest of the drive back to the house, but I couldn't help but marinate on what he'd said. He'd gotten hurt, and while he was right that we all experienced heartbreak at one point or another, his had clearly scarred him irreparably. Dougie pulled the truck over to where he'd picked me up, idling as he glanced at me expectantly.

I didn't look at him as I told him, "You can take me to the house directly, please."

In my peripheral, Dougie waffled for a moment more, his mouth opening as though he was going to ask me if I was sure. There would be no ramifications for him, but for me—no, I was adamant. I didn't care. Those assholes could shove it up their asses. After a beat of a second more, the truck was back in drive, gravel under the tires sputtering as we pulled into the unpaved driveway.

As he predicted, everyone stared. But I didn't care.

I wanted them to see me with him. I wanted them to know he could get me.

That he had me.

But I wanted him to know it, too.

Even if I had to date him to make that clear.

Chapter Four

Penelope

Present

I HATED OUR WEDDING PHOTOS, SEATED IN A PRETTY PICTURE FRAME, taunting me from its home on the dresser.

They immortalized the lies.

Someone once told me I'd never look or feel more beautiful in my life than I would the day I put the mermaid-style wedding dress on and walked down the aisle surrounded by hundreds of people I didn't recognize. They assured me my heart would swell with so much joy, my legs would threaten to give out on me as I clung to Daddy's arm and he gave me away to the man who made me a mother, the man who'd always treated me better than anyone.

But I didn't feel like a princess on our wedding day. I felt trapped, as though the walls were closing in on me and every bead of sweat clung to the champagne lace of the dress. It was too hard to breathe in that gown, surrounded by unfamiliar faces and a life I'd been so certain I'd escaped from. It had been a negotiation to get my feet to move, to keep my spine ramrod straight, my chin leveled, and my neck elongated, just as I'd been trained.

Overnight, I'd become what I hated, and I'd wanted the day to end as quickly as it had begun, to return to our lives before my parents got involved. Before they hired Moira, the wedding planner. I needed the day to end like I needed my next breath—for my parents and their expectations to go back to Connecticut.

For the wedding stresses to be over and tell Dougie the truth, to apologize for my behavior leading up to our day.

I'd been unfair to him, cruel.

Cold.

A stranger.

That entire day, I desired nothing more than for my husband to look at me like the first time he'd met me. I needed to see it in his eyes, that none of this glitz mattered to him anymore than it did to me. That when our nuptials were exchanged, when these people went back to their inconsequential lives, it was just about us. That after the wedding that had gotten out of control both in size and cost—we could go back to being just him and me.

But Dougie didn't look at me—not the way I needed him to.

He looked at her.

He looked at her like he should have looked at me, and it was my fault.

I pushed him straight into her arms. Leading up to our wedding, I'd been pushing him away for months, weeks, days.

Everyone filled my head with the promise of unbridled happiness and the fairy tale ending akin to a fucking Disney movie, and all I'd gotten was heartbreak. And the chasm where my sadness lived only deepened when, days later, I found myself confronted by a horror of another kind.

I was defective.

Perfect Penelope Louise Cullimore, who had retained her familial last name out of spite—my parents had wanted Dougie to take my family last name and he rightly refused—wasn't so perfect after all.

The evidence had lived all over our bathroom floor.

My feet dangled over the edge of my bed—our bed—as my stare fixed on the sturdy and thick maples lining the leaf-littered driveway as gray morning light filtered in. Droplets from last night's storm still clung to the glass of the sash windows. A small gust of wind loosened leaves, the tawny auburn and bright red dancing as they made their descent.

I loved the fall. Had loved the fall. Now it was just another reminder that a year ago, things had been different. We'd been happy. We'd played in those leaves and laughed. We had spent mornings like these in love and wrapped up in each other.

I wanted to scream until my lungs threatened to give out, for it all to just fucking stop.

But then I heard it—the urgent footfalls of tiny feet in hot pursuit belonging to the glue keeping us together.

I dug deep inside of myself for a smile, because if anyone deserved my best, it was our son. The doorknob turned in an uncoordinated manner, Christopher's head poking through the opening.

He grinned at me, displaying his tiny baby teeth. I felt the sharp edges of my anger soften, the smarting in my chest abating only for a moment. "Mama." His curls were a golden mess. My fingers twitched against my legs to fix them. He pushed the door open wider, waddling over to me sans pants.

"Where are your pants, honey?" I asked, earning his giggle while he flexed the toes of his sock-clad feet against the floor.

"I was working on that," Dougie said gruffly, holding up a pair of sable-colored corduroy pants. My cheeks heated seeing him, recalling the compromising position he'd found me in last night.

It wasn't... it wasn't that I didn't want my husband, despite everything.

I just... I didn't know how to be with him that way anymore. I was no longer the woman vying for his attention on a construction site. No longer forward enough that I'd clamber into his truck one summer evening and demand he fuck me properly and then take me out.

I was his wife. His wife who'd stopped having sex with him several months ago and no longer knew how to be intimate with him out of fear that he'd see my deficiencies, too.

And then what would be left? Right now, we had an illusion I could maintain, even if it was a lie.

But I was throwing the vibrator away.

He bristled under my attention, his jaw flexing. He wasn't mad about what he'd seen—it hurt him—which was worse. Could I blame him? After everything I'd done, every attempt at affection he made thwarted, every evasion of his innocuous gestures of intimacy. If I were him, I'd be hurt, too.

But he'd hurt me, too.

Short of accidentally touching me in bed or our hands brushing when we were handing Chris off to the other, we hadn't intentionally touched each other in a long time.

I disguised my need to wither on the spot with a frown, staring at Christopher's striped blue-and-red shirt. "Those don't match his shirt," I clipped, deflecting my thoughts.

Resentment.

Resentment was safer than vulnerability, the same way projection and conflation of issues were.

I may have hurt him in my dismissal, but Dougie's actions ensured we'd never be the same again.

He glanced at the pants, his brows bending inward, then looked back at me. "I thought it looked okay."

My ribs tightened, the unadulterated anger returning as it heated my veins. "I said it doesn't match," I repeated with a snarl.

His eyes flashed, his nostrils flaring. The promise of an argument percolated in the charged air, my heart hammering in anticipation. But as quickly as the force had stirred, it vanished.

He wasn't interested in doing this with me today.

"Fine." Dougie ripped himself from the doorway, storming back to Chris's room.

All I wanted to do was tell him it didn't matter. It didn't matter that Chris didn't match because I'd be changing his shirt and pants by noon after he ate something he'd inevitably end up wearing. I wanted to tell him that I was sorry that Dougie had gotten stuck with the girl who had promised him fun and love and everything he deserved, but instead, brought him nothing but misery.

I was desperate to tell him it didn't matter what happened. No, that was another lie, wasn't it? My throat tightened, the lump forming there painfully, and I swallowed it back. I had to swallow it because in a marriage, you either communicated or you endured.

I chose the latter, emulating my parents' motto, because if I communicated, it made it easier for him to leave. And as angry as I was, I couldn't handle being left—no matter what I said to him in moments of blind anger when I demanded a divorce. I didn't want one, and I was partially to blame for our downfall.

I slid off the mattress, my ass hitting the floor. Opening my arms, Chris charged at me with a cheeky smile. He wrapped his soft arms around my neck, rubbing his nose into my cheek. He still smelled like his baby shampoo from last night and something sweet on his breath, like he'd just finished eating oatmeal.

"Mornin'," he squealed in my embrace, his excitement seeping into my bones as he bounced against me. I wanted his enthusiasm. I wanted to be the best mom for him. "Mornin', Mama."

He and Dougie deserved so much better than me.

My bottom lip trembled, the tears stinging my eyes. I couldn't. I was selfish, but I could lie. I'd become too comfortable being deceptive.

"Morning, my precious boy." I kissed his cheek, blinking the tears back. He was my purpose. His existence was the only thing keeping our fragile family glued together.

Dougie's jaw remained razor sharp when he rounded the bed, gray pants in his hand. He tossed them on the bed, planting his hands on his waist.

I heard his sharp intake of breath struggle through his deviated septum as he lowered himself into a squat. "Chris, Daddy's gotta go to work. Can you give me a hug, buddy?"

Work. I missed when he and I used to work side by side. After we'd finished the house we ended up buying, we worked on one more together until I gave birth. We thought it would be better if I stayed home, but I missed the stolen kisses, the intentional, heated brushing of his fingers against mine when he passed while I was putting together color mood boards. Or how he'd brush my hair over one shoulder and plant a kiss on my neck and not care that the crew would erupt into hollers because we didn't give a shit about what anyone else thought.

We were in love, and we wanted everyone to know it.

Now we weren't, and we hid it.

We closed ourselves off from everyone else, because if they saw that our brief marriage was already falling apart—what hope would there be for happily ever afters anymore?

We lied—to ourselves and to the rest of the outside world.

"No," Chris whined, his arms tightening around my neck.

I smoothed a soothing hand over his back, the rumbling onset of a tantrum vibrating him. "Chris, tell Daddy 'bye'," I murmured.

"No!" He stomped his foot, letting me go. He pouted at Dougie, his small brows crushing together, his face flushing red. "No, no, no!"

The reaction incited Dougie's frustrated head shake. "Wonderful."

"He thinks," I swallowed hard, willing the words to come because I understood our son's feelings, too, "if he throws a fit, you'll stay." I watched as Chris's eyes swam with glossy tears turning the shade of his eyes emerald, his chin trembling.

Dougie looked upward, exhaling. "He's the only one who wants me to stay these days."

The comment met its mark. My chest smarted, knocking the breath out of my lungs. *That's not true,* I thought.

My chin tipped downward. "I guess."

"I gotta go," Dougie repeated, righting himself. "Love you, little man."

"No," Chris repeated, crossing his arms over his chest, stomping to the corner between the wall and my nightstand to bury his face in it. "Daddy bad."

Dougie's posture stiffened, but I heard it under his breath as Chris wailed. "Yeah, he is." He glanced at me, offering me a curt head nod. "See ya."

I still love you.

Have a good day. I'll miss you.

Don't be late.

All the things I should have said, but all that came out was, "Bye."

Chapter Five

Dougie

Three years ago…

"Trouble in paradise with Blond Satan?" Sean asked, removing his tool belt, placing it next to his hard hat that had spent more time on the floor than on his head today. Most of the site had cleared for the day. What remained of the lingering crew hung around outside, engaged in a boisterous conversation, resonating through the whole yard.

"Don't call her that," I complained with a scowl. I didn't know what the fuck his issue was with Penelope, but he made no attempt at masking his disdain. He was a grade A dick to her on the regular.

Sean smirked. "If the shoe fits." He shrugged his shoulders.

"You need to get laid," I seethed.

His brows jumped as he untucked a pencil from behind his ear and sent it to the floor alongside his tool belt. "I think you're doing enough of that for the both of us despite my warning."

"I'm not fucking her." And I wasn't, despite how it looked when we returned to the job site every afternoon with our clothes mussed and her skin flushed.

I'd done a pretty bang-up job of avoiding having sex with Penelope. She was fine to grind on my cock throughout her lunch break if she wanted to, though.

I had my reasons.

"Right," Sean replied sarcastically, kneading the knot in his shoulders. The tension brewing between us over this was coming to a head.

He was a goddamn dog without a bone about her. She couldn't even breathe right, which was making me suspicious. The only time you had that much of a hard-on for someone was if you... God, I didn't even want to say it, but...

"What's your deal?" The hair on my arms rose with alarm as my query formed, my molars connecting. "Are you into her or something?"

We rarely liked the same type of women. Sean liked the broken ones—him and his stupid fucking hero complex. Or they just made him feel less bad about himself because it meant there were other people in the world a little more fucked-up than he was.

He scoffed with disgust. "Absolutely *not*. Princess isn't my type." Yeah, I didn't think so, but I needed to be sure. "She's irritating and costing me a small fucking fortune," he continued. Sean probed the inside of his cheek with his tongue, his attention shifting to the kitchen with a jut of his chin. "She's talking about Caesarstone in the kitchen."

"So?"

His forehead puckered. "*So?*" he echoed with a growl, his upper lip curling back. "Do you know what that's going to run me?"

Yeah, I had an inkling, but it felt like there was something he wasn't saying, so I went the antagonistic ambivalent route. "She gets that discount."

"Dougie." He barked my name as though the force should incite sense into me. Sean scrubbed both palms over his face, groaning.

"*What?*" Just fucking spit it out.

He pinched the bridge of his nose. "Forget it."

"What's wrong?"

For a moment, I thought he was going to wave me off again, go storm off and seethe in a corner somewhere, but he surprised me. He dropped his hand, pitching it on his waist. "Shit's tight, man," he muttered, surveying the room with a shake of his head. "Really fucking tight."

Worry sank like a brick in my stomach. For him to confess that to me, it wasn't good. Sean didn't make a habit of airing his shit. "How tight?"

He blew out a breath. "If this place isn't done and sold by the fall, I'm going to need to get another line of credit, and I'm already maxed on the one I have." He glanced at me, his lips flat. "Rewiring unexpectedly set us back sixteen thousand. We completely blew through our contingency fund, never mind the foundation issues we ran into." He shook his head. "We'll be lucky to break even in this fucking economy."

That was why he looked like he hadn't been sleeping, why he'd let his hair grow out, curling a little over his ears and why his beard was out of sorts. Yeah, the recession wasn't doing anyone any favors, especially real estate. Fuck. That was bad, and completely out of character for him.

Sean had always run a tight ship, but there had been anomalies in this project from the beginning. Things we thought we could have salvaged only to realize they were too far gone for a sound but practical patch solution.

There were eight of us on the crew, and next to Penelope, I was the biggest number. He overpaid me, for reasons, and we both knew it. Which meant I understood what I needed to do now.

I opened my mouth to speak, but he held up a hand. "If you're going to tell me not to worry about it, I don't want to hear it," he intoned. "You mean well, but that shit pisses me off."

"I wasn't," I assured, holding both hands up to pacify him. "I was gonna suggest you lay me off for a bit." I could find another job. Probably.

His nostrils flared, his upper lip curling back. He glared at me as though that was the dumbest thing I'd ever said. "Go home, asshole."

"I'm just saying—"

"Your suggestions fucking suck," he stressed, shaking his head. "Go home before you say anything else as profoundly idiotic." He turned his back to me, plodding away.

I'd had an inkling he wouldn't go for it, but it was worth the shot. I'd never suggest he let any of the guys go. They had families to worry about, and any of them could do what I did with a bit of patience.

Even if Sean was short on that in abundance. I stared heavenward, wondering if the late João Tavares was taking in the shitstorm his lies had left behind for his son. Sean wasn't supposed to be in construction or restoring homes. He was supposed to be in a kitchen, wearing one of those fancy chef coats. Tavares Construction was his father's business, but his dad passed away ten years ago from cancer. When they went to book the funeral, they realized there was nothing in the accounts. The Tavareses were half a million dollars in debt, had a second mortgage on their home to fund Maria's Harvard tuition, and Sean had no choice but to drop out of the culinary program he was in just to get them out of red and back into black. He had two kid sisters to help his ma feed.

It was a shitload of pressure for a then twenty-year-old kid, and how I'd wound up working for him. I'd never let him go at it alone. He was my best friend, practically my brother.

We were in this shitstorm together, and eventually, he paid it all back, helped Maria pay for Harvard, and kept food on his ma's table and clothes on his younger sisters' backs.

I couldn't imagine Trina handling it, and she was twenty now.

Don't get me wrong. His dad was a good man who made bad choices, and those choices had a ripple effect that changed my best friend's life forever.

Ten years later, and money still made him anxious, debt even more so.

I just hoped that someday he'd get the chance to reclaim his dream, that he'd let go of his fear of something happening to his family again.

Striding to the front door, I snagged my lunch-box-sized cooler by the stairwell and then braced myself for the wave of insufferable humidity to slam into me. The air was as thick outside as it was inside the house. The heatwave hadn't broken in days, which made my shit-hole apartment an unbearable oven.

I was gonna be able to afford air conditioning someday.

The sun snuck through the limbs of the maples lining the driveway as I headed to my truck, gravel crunching under my work boots. I spotted Penelope's Range Rover at the end of the driveway, but she was nowhere to be found.

Weird. Glancing around the yard for signs of her, my search yielded zero results. Had I missed her inside? I considered going back, but then remembered we'd kind of gotten into it over lunch.

Kind of. If you could call it that.

I hesitated, stopping. I needed to apologize, but she needed to understand my why, too.

Fiddling with my car keys, I hit the unlock button, the headlights flashing on the F150. I'd ditch the cooler and then go find her. Opening the driver's side door, I tossed my cooler in the back, alongside my vest, and just as I was righting myself in my seat, the passenger door flung opened.

Penelope didn't meet my eyes as she settled in the seat, her chin leveled, attention directed toward the house as she futzed with her seatbelt. Every so often, she gave me a glimpse of her upbringing. It came out when she got annoyed. Her posture grew perfect, her chin held high, and her concentration pointed.

Little Miss Prim and Proper was a disguise for the deviant under it all.

Penelope was noiseless. She didn't even huff out an exhale when she settled against the seat, her hands clasped tightly in her lap against her jeans, appearing dignified.

I rolled my lips under my teeth to suppress a laugh. "What are you doing, Pen?"

A small, unimpressed tick appeared in her jaw. With her hair tucked behind her ear, I studied the small studs lining her lobe. Three to be exact. There were two gold hoops hugging her cartilage, and a bejeweled, star-shaped piercing in her tragus. For someone so otherwise girly, it came across as another act of rebellion; a subtle "fuck you" to her parents.

The ones she scrunched up her nose for every time they called, and she let it go to voicemail.

"I've figured it out," she began, offering me a diplomatic head nod. "You're not going to fuck me until I date you, right?"

I narrowed my eyes, then reached for my seatbelt, clicking it into place. My fingers lingered on the strap, playing with the polyester. "What makes you say that?"

She tossed me an aggravated glare over her shoulder, as though to ask, *Really?*

The chuckle I'd been trying to hold in broke free. I guess we were continuing our lunch time discussion after all.

"It's not funny," she groused, shoving a hand into her golden hair, tugging at the strands by the roots. "It's frustrating as hell, actually."

Of course it was. I was frustrated, too. "That wasn't my intention, however..." I parked my elbow on the windowsill, rubbing my dry lips with two fingers. "That's an excellent strategy. I should consider that."

Her startling Atlantic-blue eyes bolted to me, the gold speckles melting into the green and blue. She was done pretending to be level-headed. "Dougie," she hedged, clenching her jaw. I could detect her annoyance undulating her body. "If it's not that, then what is it?"

I cocked my head. She was unreal. "You really want me to fuck you in my truck, Pen?" She jolted at the word choice, my fiery stare journeying over her body. Right on cue, she thrust out her chest in offering, preening under my attention.

Unlike Sean, who was an ass man, I was a tits guy. And Pen's could make a dead man salivate. The tight, no-more-than-a-handful perky swells looked great in the gray-ribbed tank top, the channel between her breasts all but begging to give my cock a new home.

God, she was determined as hell. I flicked my eyes upward, zeroing in on hers. "Really?" I stressed.

"Really," she insisted eagerly. "I really want you to fuck me in your truck." Penelope chewed on the corner of her lip for a beat of a second. "And *then* you can take me out."

Huh? I pegged her with a bemused smile. "What do you mean?"

She bowed her head, appearing demure. "On a date."

What had changed? More importantly… "Can't I take you on a date first, *then* fuck you?"

She shook her head, pushing her resolved shoulders back. "No. I need to know if breaking all of my rules for you is worth it first."

I huffed out another laugh. She really was something else. The way she prioritized her order of operations was a mystery, and I could keep arguing with her, or… I could give in. To be honest, in that moment, I really wanted to fucking give in. I was pretty sure my right forearm was officially visibly stronger than my left one ever since she waltzed into the yard.

"Douglas Patterson." Her usage of my full name made warmth flood to my balls. "If you don't take me back to our spot right now and fuck *me* properly, I'm going to fuck *you* here. Do you understand me?" she growled, jerking her thumb at the house. "And whoever is still kicking around is going to see. Is that what you want?"

My expression fell, the scowl slipping into place. I didn't want anyone to see her like that. "No." Although the visual of her fucking me was kind of nice.

"Then turn the truck on and take me. Now." She held her chin high, exposing her neck as she made her demand, but even under all her confident statements, I saw the nervous flash in her eyes as though she worried, I'd rebuff her again.

I was at an impasse. As hot as Penelope was, I didn't really want to hit it and risk her quitting it if she decided she didn't like me after all.

She was dangling the carrot in front of my nose with the potential date afterward, but I was tired of being the dependable fuck for someone, only for them to toss me aside when I wanted more.

I wanted more, long term, with Penelope.

Her eyebrows furrowed, her gaze falling to my car keys in the ignition. "Stop overthinking, Dougie." She skimmed her fingers over her lips, lips I had every intention of kissing until they bruised. "We can talk about the date after."

I turned the truck on.

Penelope flung off her seatbelt before I even got the truck into "park" when I stopped the truck under the hardy umbrella of trees in the middle of our clearing. In my peripheral, a flash of gray flew by as she pulled her tank top off. A groan slipped out of me as I caught sight of her breasts swathed in soft pink lace.

I'd known they were going to be perfect under her shirt, but not that perfect.

Before I could wonder if she was the type to match her bra and panties, she was already popping the button on her jeans open. She lifted the small curve of her ass, pulling the denim down in a hurried shimmy over her toned legs.

She matched. That flimsy little piece of lace was all that was keeping me from seeing what shade of pink her pussy was. My body heated at the thought.

"Get undressed," she demanded breathlessly, kicking off her shoes. Her jeans puddled at her feet as she kicked them off alongside her lace-less solid black ankle boots.

"Pen," I whispered, despite my cock stirring at the first flash of her shirt being pulled off. "Just slow down."

"No," she blurted. "I've slowed down long enough, c'mon." The complaint lived in the statement's force. Her chest rose and fell rapidly as she squirmed in her seat. She fixed her mussed hair, glancing down at her body. "I'm starting to take this personally," she echoed from lunch.

I resisted the urge to sigh, shifting uncomfortably in my seat. "And I already told you not to." She'd gotten sullen about this earlier and sulked the entire ride back to the house.

I could say I didn't understand. I always got her off even if it was juvenile in her eyes. I'd give myself blue balls all summer long until she understood I wouldn't treat her like an easy piece of ass.

But still... with her half-naked in my truck, the notes of her perfume tangling with the sweet potency of her arousal filling the truck's cabin, and her exposed needy pulse vibrating in the column of her pretty throat... I might be too far gone.

My mouth grew drier by the second, my heart thumping painfully as my gaze kept slipping from her eyes to her gorgeous, lithe frame. The valley of her breasts rolled into her taut torso and her narrow waist, and that dipped into the sweet spot I really wanted to bury my face against.

I shifted, more heat flooding to my cock that was no longer in the semi-hard territory, even if the pangs of unworthiness seeped into my skin.

A body like that belonged in a bed with two-thousand-thread-count sheets, in a room that was temperature controlled with blackout curtains to keep the sun out come the morning.

Not in my dirty truck. But I didn't have any of that.

I had a broken air conditioner unit that hadn't worked in two summers, and a mattress with springs that dug into my spine when I made the mistake of sleeping too close to the middle. My sheets were cheap, and my pillows were ten years old. I had blinds that were broken and older than me. My building smelled like stale cooking oil, and decay from the garbage my neighbors left by their doors rather than taking it to the dumpster behind our building. And my place was fucking ugly. The exterior of the triple decker was the color of shit brown with overgrown weeds wrapping the perimeter, and my neighbor above me was a real crotchety witch who enjoyed vacuuming at five a.m.

I didn't belong in Penelope's world any more than she belonged in mine. The rich-girl-and-poor-boy trope were the oldest story in the book. Yet, she was here, with a desperation glowing feverishly in her eyes and a visible tightness in her limbs as she second-guessed herself when I didn't immediately plaster her body with mine.

"Am I..." she anxiously began, touching the ends of her golden hair. She squeezed her eyes closed for a moment, exhaling an extended breath as she wrapped her arms shyly around herself. I didn't want her to hide, not from me. Ever. "Am I not enough?"

My brows snapped together, frustration creating a pit in my stomach. Not enough? Was that what my self-doubt and attempt at exercising control made her think?

"Put your seat back, Pen." She opened her eyes, confusion flooding as I released my seatbelt from its confines. "Go on," I insisted, finding the hem of my shirt. Her mouth popped open when I pulled my shirt over my head, bunching the fabric and tossing it to the dash. "What are you gawking at?"

I glanced down at myself, understanding flanking me. I might not be Sean, but I had a body that had done a lot of shit in unsavory conditions—carried bags of concrete by myself under the cold barrage of raindrops in the fall, swung blocks of brick when refacing a house in the dead heat of summer. Muscle memory had me engaging my core rather than straining my back every day, bending with my knees and never my back. I used my body, day in and day out.

And it showed.

A lump shifted in her throat as she swallowed tightly, her gaze unusually shy. "Are you going to feel emasculated if I say you're beautiful?" she asked, sounding sheepish as her cheeks grew ruddy. "'Cause you are. You remind me of one of Michelangelo's statues."

I smiled, laughing through my nose. Yeah, that was probably where the similarities between Michelangelo's statues and I started and stopped.

But I'd show her that myself. That was one part of me I *was* proud of.

"The seat, Pen," I murmured, my heavy fingers aching to touch her. She could think whatever she wanted of me. It would all pale compared to what I thought of her.

Pen fumbled with the lever, the seat jerking back. She let out an electric combination of a surprised yelp and an impatient moan when I climbed over the console, my right knee tapping the inside of hers to part her legs. They butterflied immediately, her breath falling over my face with her exhale as I lowered my body against hers.

"I'm still sweaty as fuck," I warned her.

She smiled, offering me a short headshake. "It doesn't matter. I like you sweaty." Her nerves lived in her hands as she placed them tentatively on my biceps, her fingers testing my skin.

Resting all my weight on one forearm, I touched the underside of her chin, drawing her stare to mine. "Promise me you'll never, and I mean never, forget how special you are." That was one thing that did matter to me. One thing I hoped she'd always remember.

Her eyes softened just as she began to say my name. "Doug—"

My mouth slammed against hers, that spark igniting between us as her needy cry crawled up her throat and into my waiting open mouth. It pissed me off, thinking that she'd internalized my desire to take my time with her as being a fault of her own, some kind of hidden shortcoming.

She wasn't defective, not by a long shot.

There was nothing wrong with Penelope—she was perfect. But that's what made her too good for the likes of me. One day, she'd wake up and realize slumming it with the poor boy was a novelty that had worn off.

And I'd get hurt again.

But I could appreciate the time we had together until she got it out of her system. I could savor the frenzy in her kiss when her tongue dove into my mouth, gliding expertly across my own. If I listened to the rules of our agreement, I could protect myself from getting hurt. I slid my hands into her hair, reveling in the way the soft strands felt closer to silk in my roving fingers. Pen bowed her back into me, the laced cups of her bra brushing against my chest.

I needed to feel them in my palms, without the fabric shield.

Sliding one hand behind her, I edged closer to the clasp just as she broke the kiss. Pen shifted to help me with her bra, her arms curving behind her. "The clasp on this bra is a pain in the ass, I—"

I pinched it free easily, the straps falling over her shoulders. She arched a suggestive brow at me. "You have too much experience with that, huh?"

Yeah, I'd admit—I'd had my fun. Had fucked around enough for Sean and me to last a lifetime. I'd been a cocky son of a bitch in the past, who'd never thought twice about who he got it in with.

Which was why when the full package presented itself to you, you didn't lose your load on the first day just because she gave you "come fuck me" eyes and had a pretty smile.

You prolonged it, hoping eventually she might see your worth, too. Even if that was naïve.

All I offered her was a smirk. My fingers hooked around the straps, pulling them down at an agonizingly slow pace. Her skin pimpled under the attention, her head leaning to one side as her lips parted. Pen's chest heaved as I tossed her bra to the backseat, studying her carefully.

Her tits were better than I expected—more than a palmful, but not too much that they'd spill out of my grasp. Her rosy, pink nipples complemented the swells of her creamy skin. The beads tightened into hard points with anticipation alone. I lowered my mouth, my eyes falling shut to savor the sensation while my cock throbbed.

Her hands found my shoulders, my name leaving her lips on a desperate pant, the blunt edges of her nails sinking into my skin just as my mouth closed around one of the tight beads.

Pen was responsive as hell under the attention, just like I'd known she'd be. She trembled under me, my mouth oscillating from breast to breast—sucking, nipping, and soothing, to arouse all kinds of sounds out of her—taking my time with my exploration. Her skin was hot against mine, the sun bearing down on us from the sunroof.

But for once, neither of us seemed to mind that it was hot in here. Her grip on my shoulders tightened as I dragged my tongue down her sternum, dropping my weight between the tight space of the dash and the floor. My fingers hooked around the lace of her thong, my stomach dipping and my chest hollowing as she lifted her ass off the seat to help me.

As soon as the paltry piece of lace cleared her ankles, her legs parted once more. Jesus fuckin' Christ…

I glanced up at her, watching as her hands slid across her breasts, rolling one of her nipples tightly between her fingers, her eyes hooding as she watched me watch her.

My balls ached painfully, the crotch of my jeans too snug. If I'd thought her tits were great, it was nothing compared to her pussy. She was hairless, save for a tidy strip of hair above her clit, the same shade of gold as her hair—definitely a natural blond—the lips swollen with need, her entrance glossy, beckoning me forward.

I wanted a taste. My hands hooked under her thighs, dragging her closer to me. She gasped as her spine slid down the seat, her feet finding the dash when I settled her legs over my shoulders. Anticipation had her squirming, my enthusiastic cock pulsating under the gesture. Her mouth fell open when she squeezed her breasts once more, her nipples clenched between the webbing of her fingers.

She was so fucking hot, and I needed her. I needed her more than she'd ever need me. My head tipped forward, the tip of my busted nose brushing against her clit as my unyielding tongue laved at her opening. She practically levitated off the seat, her arms extending as her right hand grasped at the armrest of the door, and her left hand found my hair and tugged.

Her partially lidded eyes found mine, her quickened breaths ghosting my face as I stared up at her. "Your pussy tastes good, Penny," I husked, fortifying my point with a swipe of my tongue across her seam.

"Dougie," she whined, her grip in my hair growing more intense. I could have sworn the remark had more arousal pooling out of her.

I had suspected the first time I'd let her dry hump me in my truck that Penelope got off on being spoken to during sex, but now, tasting her arousal firsthand on my tongue, I had it confirmed.

I dipped my tongue inside of her entrance, my cock throbbing as she jerked against me, her hips rolling forward. God, she could fuck my face into oblivion for all I cared, cut off my air circulation and put me into an early grave. I wouldn't be mad about it. It would be a hell of a way to go.

Pen's frantic breathing turned into heavy pants as my tongue fucked her, my thumb settling over her clit, massaging her tenderly.

"Oh, God!" she cried, as I feasted, sucking on the engorged lips of her pussy hungrily, my lips smacking together. Her legs flexed around me, her muscles constricting.

I was kind of glad we were in the middle of the woods. No one could hear her. Those eager cries were just for me. I shifted my thumb away from her clit, my mouth closing around the sensitive bundle of nerves.

"Ah!" Pen trembled under my assault, but it paled compared to the way her hips lurched when I tested her entrance with the thick tip of my middle finger.

I was going to hurt her if I didn't prep her. I knew I would. The channel of her pussy was so tight, her walls flexing around my finger as I sunk in until I was knuckle deep. She gushed around my finger, her pelvis grinding against my mouth while the hand that had been bracing herself on the console closed around her breast once more.

Her head tipped back, her stomach tightening as she tugged on her nipples. My body tingled with the observation as I tasted her. My index finger tested the opening, my extended middle finger rolling to relax her enough to accommodate my second finger. We were still a long way from home. I wouldn't attempt to penetrate her with my cock until my ring finger was seated inside of her, too.

She moaned when I dipped my index finger inside, her pussy contracting around my fingers. I buried them forward, my fingers hooked in search of...

"Fuck, fuck," she moaned, her whimper brandishing my memory. *Bingo*. I grinned against her, nipping at her clit as she ground against me, uncoordinated, desperate, and mine.

So fucking mine.

Her body didn't reject my ring finger, but her eyes blazed when she realized. Her arousal practically saturated my hand, my mouth still massaging, nipping and stroking her cunt as I pumped into her. "I want to come on your cock, Dougie," she exhaled. "Please."

I lifted my head, studying her eyes. Her palms came to my bearded cheeks, cradling my face. "Please," she repeated, drawing me closer. "Give it to me."

"Pen." She robbed the argument from me by caressing her lips against mine, her arms twining around my neck, not caring that she could taste herself on my mouth. She pressed herself against me, the heat of her wetness rubbing against the denim ridge of my cock.

I didn't lift my head as my arm shifted for the middle console, lifting the lid. I blindly dug around in search of the strip of condoms I'd shoved in there as a precaution in the event I'd lost my self-control to her, kissing her back until she grabbed hold of my hand.

"I'm on the pill," she said.

That made me break the kiss. I studied her eyes, a sharp exhale leaving me despite my cock jumping at the invitation. "That's not a hundred percent, Penny."

The temptation twisted my insides, my cock engorging to the point of pain as the fantasy played out in my head.

I wasn't an asshole who fucked a woman he wasn't dating without a condom. I'd never been that asshole, and yet, she gave me that unyielding needy look—the one that turned me into that reckless asshole who was going to do exactly as she asked.

This felt dangerous. The hair on my arms rose in confirmation as I regarded her through tapered eyes, even though my cock kicked with willingness. One of my heads needed to be responsible, and I knew which one wasn't.

The sight of her bright pink tongue dipping out of her mouth to brush against her bottom lip nearly killed me, the corner of her mouth lifting with mischief. "Neither is a condom. You've made me wait for this for weeks." Pen drew my hand away from the console, settling it against her slick pussy.

I groaned, my fingers brushing against her out of reflex. "Penelope, you're gonna kill me. I don't wanna—" *taint*. The word I wanted to use was taint. "I don't wanna risk the chance of getting you pregnant."

"If you get me pregnant, you'll just have to marry me," she teased with a moan, rolling her hips against my fingers still pressed against her entrance.

My nostrils flared at the suggestion. She had no fucking idea how fast I'd do just that, with or without a baby.

Which was a crazy thought. I'd only known her six weeks.

She was playing with me, though. I could play right back. I just needed to get out of my head. "What ever would your parents think?" I growled, nipping at her. I wanted to vacuum her skin into my mouth and leave a trail of marks on her flesh, claiming her as mine, but I resisted. "I fucked their precious little girl, defiled her." Dragging my nose along her sharp jaw, I fit my mouth against the shell of her ear. "Put a baby in her."

"Of course you put a baby in her," she moaned, the sound so fucking musical it made both my heads swell. "Fucked her so good, you filled her right up with your cum until it leaked out of her."

I tensed. My pleasure receptors were about to go fucking nuclear with the filth spewing from her mouth alone.

Jesus, she was crass. It made my cock pulsate.

"Too much?" she asked, her blush deepening. "I can dial it back."

My teeth found my bottom lip, my head shaking. "Keep running your mouth," I assured hotly. "Let me hear what else you want me to do with you."

She slid a hand between us, cupping me expertly on the outside of my jeans. "I want you to fuck me like if you don't, you'll go insane."

"I'm already going insane, Penny," I replied. "I stroke off to you twice a day."

Her eyes flared. "You do?"

"Sometimes more," I murmured as I undid the button of my jeans, while she pulled my fly down. Shifting the denim off my waist, I shoved my pants and boxer briefs over my ass, my cock springing free.

"What do you think about when you do—" She cut herself off, her gasp slicing through the air, whirring in my head. "Oh. My. God." She studied my cock for what felt like an eternity. Pen lifted her anxious eyes to mine, the nerves melting into hunger as she gave me a lewd smirk. "You really are going to ruin my pussy, aren't you?"

I swallowed hard, watching as her palm glided across her entrance, gathering her arousal and then swiping it across my cock.

"Fuck," I bit out as her slick hand closed around my cock, pumping slowly.

She slid her freehand between her legs, her hips bucking as she circled her clit, and then dipped two fingers inside of herself. Her fingers were too slender. It wouldn't help. She arched her back, flicking her heated, lust-filled gaze at me. "Put it in."

I hesitated only for a moment, but then I lowered myself against her, resting all my weight on my forearms. The head of my cock crowned her entrance as she gathered her arousal on my tip with her hand, her eyes nearly bugging out of her skull when she felt the girth.

"We'll stop if it hurts," I assured her, hooking her legs around my waist.

She nodded her head, wiggling her cunt against my cock, anticipation pummeling through us both. "Do it," she insisted on a breathy exhale.

I found her lips, kissing her as I pushed my hips forward. She stretched around me as I entered her with a pensive precision, only getting a quarter of the way through when I felt her stiffen under me.

Her fingers scored my back, a small whimper leaving her. *Shit.*

I stopped, retracting my hips.

Pen opened her eyes. "Don't stop."

"I'm hurting you."

"Don't. Stop." Her hands slid down my spine. Finding the muscles in my ass, she urged me onward. "Don't stop, Dougie."

We needed to change positions. "Put your legs over my elbows," I murmured. "It'll hurt less." I adjusted my weight, redistributing all the pressure on my knees so I wouldn't crush her, while also correcting the angle so there was less pressure on her cervix.

I was admittedly used to this part. Everyone thought they could handle it until it was time to penetrate, then it felt like they were being impaled with a two-by-four even if they hadn't been a virgin for years. Most of the time, it was flattering, but I never wanted to hurt anyone. Especially her.

Pen did as she was told, and sure enough, I slipped further inside of her, her body relaxing when she realized the pain didn't accompany it. We groaned in symphony when I filled her to the hilt, seated snuggly inside of her. She flexed around me, a happy sigh leaving her mouth as her body molded into mine.

Penelope skimmed her lips against my own, rocking her hips under me to encourage me to move. My body tingled as I moved, pumping in and out of her slowly until her increasingly louder mewls turned those slow and controlled thrusts into urgent strokes. I couldn't get close enough, deep enough. Some part of me just wanted to meld into her and keep her forever.

It was a pipe dream.

My pelvis drove against her clit relentlessly, goaded on by her frantic cries. Her breasts brushed against my chest as the piston of my hips quickened into a desperate rut—long, relentless strokes. The harmonious wet squelch of her pussy filled the rocking truck, her lids dropping shut as her mouth popped open.

She was close. I could hear it in the way her breathing shifted, each intake sharp like it wouldn't balloon her lungs. Sweat glistened against her flushed skin, the strands of her hair slick against her face.

"You take it so good, Penny," I husked. "Tightest. Fucking. Pussy. Ever." I punctuated the statement with my hips, crushing my pelvis against her clit, and that was it.

She detonated, a steady stream of sharp cries leaving her, her body quivering under me as the euphoria of her orgasm blasted through her. I slowed my strokes, wanting to watch the way all the tension fled her body.

But she surprised me. She opened her eyes, heat burning deeper as she chased away the aftershock of her orgasm—refortified in her purpose. Pen's legs circled my waist, tightening until they bound me against her. "Fuck me until you fill me with every drop," she said hotly.

Ah, fuck. My body hummed with the tantalizing demand, the primal part of my brain rushing into overdrive. She wanted me to fill her? Fine, I'd fill her until she still felt me leaking from her hours from now.

Or at least, I would in my mind. I was pulling out.

"You want just that, don't you?" I growled, pressing my forehead against hers, my hips taking off into urgent thrusts once more. My heart thundered in my chest, her fingers gripping my ass as I drove myself into her harder.

Pen nodded her head. "I want to still feel you when I'm at home in my bed alone." She bucked under me, meeting my thrusts this time. "I'm going to fantasize it's your fingers dipping inside of me," she murmured. "Fucking me so good."

My body buzzed at the visual. Penelope was dangerous. I lunged at her mouth, tugging at her bottom lip with my teeth before she opened her mouth for me. "C'mon, Dougie," she cried into my mouth, sweat glistening on her face. "Give it to me."

My body shuddered, the heat rushing through my balls, shooting through my cock. I pushed the bind of her legs wrapped around me, but she held on like a vise, jerking me closer.

Shit, shit, shit.

Didn't she realize I'd said all of that in the heat of the moment? I'd meant to pull out at a minimum.

Pen just clung on, her neck curving back as she milked my cock, the walls of her pussy contracting around me. The ceaseless and most intense orgasm I'd ever experienced just kept going and going, spilling inside of her, nearly robbing me of my vision.

I sagged against her, the shudders racking through me, while what remained of my pleasure spiraled in my stomach until it died.

Damn it.

I pressed my forehead against her cheek, the aftershocks zipping through me as my heart rate slowed.

What a brat. She'd done that on purpose. "Don't do that again," I warned her, brushing my nose against hers. "It's not safe."

"You're paranoid," she complained, massaging her lips against mine. She offered me a flirty smile, framing my face with her hands. "You liked it, didn't you? Live a little."

I scowled down at her. Of course I fucking liked it, but it didn't change that it was irresponsible. "Penelope," I warned.

"Douglas," she rebutted, offering me another one of her sexy little smiles. "You're never fucking me with a condom. Ever."

My lips vibrated in my exhale, my eyes tapering. "You're stubborn."

"You're learning." She ran her fingers along my bicep. "Besides, it's not like I do that with everyone."

That made me feel a little better. "Spoiled brat."

She blinked up at me, trying for petulant, but the smile broke out, consuming her pretty face. "I always get what I want," she sing-songed.

I opened the middle console once more, pulling out a stack full of napkins I'd ditched there this morning from my Dunkin's run. I shoved them under her pussy as I retracted my hips slowly. My seed spilled out of her in a rush once the plug of my dick was removed. I bunched the cheap napkins, collecting as much as I could until she was mostly dry.

She shifted upward on the seat, mewling contently. She was trouble. Pure fucking trouble.

And addictive as hell. "Take me back to your place," she suggested.

I paused. Embarrassment swam in my veins as I considered both the empty state of my apartment and the condition of the building. "How about I take you to dinner?" I countered casually instead.

"Okay," she agreed, stretching her arms above her head. "And then you can take me back to your place."

"I don't think that's a good idea." I opened one of the unsoiled napkins, using it to wrap the bunch I'd used to clean her up. Then I grabbed another to wipe my cock, bunching it to join the others.

It almost distracted me from the burden of her stare. "Why?"

Why? I wanted to laugh. But as I found her stare, she just looked at me expectantly, as though I owed her a good explanation. "My AC unit is busted, and it's easily a hundred degrees in my place."

She blinked, and then her forehead puckered as though it was a nonissue. "So?"

"So, you won't be comfortable."

She glanced at me, to her naked frame, and then up at the setting sun. "Well, it's hot in here and I feel pretty comfortable now."

"That's different."

"Why?" she pressed. Pen pushed her weight up onto her elbows, cocking her head to the left. Sweat glistened on her face, giving her a pretty afterglow. "I can handle the heat, so why don't you want to take me back to your place?"

"Because."

"That's not an answer."

No wonder she and Sean didn't get along. They were both stubborn as fuck and had an uncanny way of pushing all my buttons. "Just drop it, for fuck's sake," I snarled.

Her expression fell, her mood sobering as she realized we weren't playing around anymore, and this wasn't something she got to kick up a fuss about.

I probed the inside of my cheek, shame heating my skin. "I'm sorry. I just don't like anyone at my apartment."

No one ever came over. Ever. Not my ma, not Sean, not any woman.

There was nothing to see there.

Penelope was quiet, gnawing on her bottom lip. She surprised me when she extended a hand to touch the underside of my bearded chin, settling her stare on mine. If it upset her that I'd lost my cool, she didn't show it. There was an easiness alive in her eyes, an unspoken understanding filtering between us. "I just want to spend more time with you," she began, her tone soft and unhurried. "That's all."

It was more kindness than I deserved at that moment. I snagged her hand, brushing my lips tenderly across each of her knuckles. "I'm sorry I snapped."

"I'm sorry I pushed you to show me where you live." Her lips lifted a little. "But if you're up to it, you can come to the city on the week-end," she tried instead. "Stay at my place."

"Oh, yeah?" I teased, running the pad of my thumb along her ring finger absently. "You got AC?"

She laughed, nodding her head. "Yeah, I've got AC." I was sure whatever air conditioning unit she had pushed air imported from the French Alps.

"Where do you live?" Pen scrunched up her nose as the blush painted her cheeks, running her free hand through her tangled hair as she mumbled out a response.

I'd heard her just fine. "What did you say?" I craned my head, making a show of cupping my hand around my ear to amplify her voice.

Pen resigned herself, repeating her response a little louder this time. "Beacon Hill."

There it was again—the contrast in our worlds. She lived in one of the most affluent neighborhoods in the state, with its cobblestone roads, picturesque Federal-style row houses and gaslit lanterns, and I couldn't afford to replace my air conditioner unit or pay my credit card bill in full.

We were different. We'd always be different. But only one of us was making our financial differences an issue—and it wasn't her.

She studied me for a long time. "Dougie?" I met her eyes, my shoulders slumping. "Don't ruin this, okay? We're just having fun." My expression collapsed, the statement robbing me of my next breath.

That's right. She was slumming it with me, having fun. At the end of the day, it didn't matter where I lived. One day, I wouldn't see her on the jobsite anymore. I wouldn't concern myself over her flat tires, or her need for a coffee, or a chair for her to sit on. My truck wouldn't still smell like her perfume long after she left. My heart wouldn't race at the sight of her, because she wouldn't be part of our crew anymore.

She'd be gone.

I needed to not repeat the same mistakes twice with another woman. I nodded my head, despite the smarting of pain ricocheting through my chest. "Yeah." I knew where this was going. I'd heard the same speech from someone else once.

I understood the rules. We were having fun. That was all. Under no circumstances was I to fall in love with her or try to change the terms of our arrangement.

So it didn't matter if I fucked Penelope in my truck on our lunch break or on the floor of what I assumed would be original hardwood in her million-dollar apartment.

We were just having fun.

Fun.

"And I enjoy spending time with you," she added. "With and without our clothes on."

I reached for my shirt on the dash, nodding absently at her. "Yeah."

"So, will you come over to my place this weekend?"

I made a show of hesitating. "I don't know. I'll have to check my schedule."

"Got another hot date?" she teased, but I didn't miss the underlying hint of jealousy in the query.

"Does it matter?" I asked, pulling my jeans back into place. "We're just having fun."

Penelope hesitated, her eyes tracking me as I crawled over the dash, settling back into my seat. "I guess not, but..." She cleared her throat, searching for her bra. "I'd appreciate transparency. Just 'cause..."

"'Cause you want me to fuck you bare, right?" I stared at her. Her brows dipped, her mouth forming into a thin line. "I won't fuck anyone else, Penelope. Don't worry."

She looked like she wanted to say more, but she didn't. She nodded her head absently, picking her bra up and feeding the straps over her arms.

"I won't either." She cleared her throat, hooking the clasps back into place. Penelope elongated her neck, trying to tack her shield back in place, but I already saw the gaping chink in her armor, her hurt filtering through. "You can take me to dinner now."

Chapter Six

Dougie

Present

I was the first one at the site.

I was *always* the first one at the site.

Then again, everyone else had a reason to make every minute at home count—a few more minutes with their kids who wanted them around, and a warm, whispered promise in the ear of their wives about all the things they'd do to them later, followed by a lingering kiss or two.

Not me, though. My house was a purgatory—neither heaven nor hell.

Honestly, these days, I'd show up much earlier if it wasn't because the sun rose a lot later. The current project was tucked deep in the woods on the outskirts of Eaton, too far away to capitalize on street-lights, reliant only on daylight.

Eaton was a bucolic bedroom community in butt-fuck-nowhere Massachusetts, and that was coming from someone who grew up in Fall River, a city with under a hundred thousand inhabitants.

It was forgettable. It wasn't a destination spot. It didn't pull tourists in like Salem, fascinated by the witchcraft trials. It didn't have the historical charm and old-world lore of Boston. Hell, it didn't even really offer much for leaf peepers.

It was just there, and for the last couple of years, it had been home.

To myself, my wife, and our best friends.

The ones we didn't talk to anymore.

I appraised the Victorian from my spot in the truck while Pearl Jam's "Black" crooned quietly from my radio. My body ached with the reminder from the late night I'd had yesterday as I spotted the bricks I'd neatly stacked by the chimney until well after the sunset. Chimneys were a notable feature on colonial-style Victorians, and this one's had crumbled to shit over the years of neglect.

Then again, it had sat abandoned for over a decade.

And Katrina, much like her brother Sean, had a penchant for the damaged ones.

I wasn't just referring to their restoration projects.

Although, I supposed Sean's once-hardened wife was redeemed now, wasn't she?

She'd become the person my wife should have been.

The sound of slow tires crunching along the driveway that the earth had reclaimed drew my attention to my side mirror. It was the thrum-ming bass and heavy drumming of a song cutting through the quietude of morning that tipped me off on who it was.

There was only one person who blasted that shit she called music at seven thirty in the morning. The tawny headlights of Katrina's older cherry-red Jeep Liberty flashed across the dense trees and shrubbery fringing the quarter acre of property the Victorian sat on.

She was early. I wasn't expecting anyone else here for at least another half hour. Katrina met my eyes briefly in the window as she passed me, pulling her SUV in front of my truck. Her music quieted before she cut the engine. Flinging open her door, her tightly laced and scuffed-up tan work boots searched the ground before she slid out with a triumphant humph.

Katrina was the youngest of Sean's three sisters, and the most petite. When she was a little kid, I used to tease her she was small enough to stuff in my pocket and no one would ever be the wiser. Her dark blue jeans clung to her legs, the knees intentionally torn. Her faux fleece-lined corduroy chore coat was three sizes too big for her and I was certain had belonged to Sean at some point. Trina was notorious for lifting clothes from her siblings' closets without their permission—even now, when she no longer lived with them.

She'd dyed her hair bright blue recently. The messy locks—I doubted she'd managed a foray with a hairbrush this morning—pulled into a sloppy bun on the crown of her head, loose strands framing her made-up heart-shaped face.

She leaned back into the car, her left leg lifting from the ground as she reached for something. Trina straightened, two large Dunkin's coffee cups in her hand. We took it the same way, regular—cream and sugar.

Her breath left her mouth in hot vapors, consumed quickly by the unusually harsh October air when she locked eyes with me and lifted the cups to her face as she donned a brittle smile.

I didn't like it when she looked at me like that. She reminded me of her brother when she gave me that bullshit, fragile smile. He'd always done that right before he was going to drop shit on my lap I didn't really want to hear.

I wasn't in the mood. I was still reeling over my argument with Penelope over Chris's fucking clothes, never mind the visual I'd conjured up in my mind of her getting herself off.

Short of me driving off, though, I wasn't getting out of this. I turned the truck off, bracing myself for the inevitable.

Trina clipped her door shut with her hip just as I opened my door.

"You're early," I said, trying for casual, as though it was no big deal that I was here well before I had to be, and it clearly wasn't a coincidence she was here, too.

Trina might have been the boss now, but she was also perpetually late and a little irresponsible. She was a night owl, and I'd heard rumors back home that she'd been spending her evenings exploring abandoned places nearby—which was kinda sketchy and, y'know, illegal.

Then again, if any of the Tavares' siblings were going to have a penchant for trouble, it was her. Age had turned her into a total fucking adrenaline junky, but I'd leave it to her family to lecture her. It was none of my business.

Not anymore.

"Yeah," she replied, matching my tone as she took long strides toward me. "We've got a lot to do today." She handed the cup to me, bringing her own to her lips and taking an exaggerated sip. Her eyes narrowed on the pile of bricks by the chimney, the wing of her thick liner folding with her squint. "You unloaded?"

I shrugged like it was no big deal, taking a drink from my cup. I'd had the time. At least now the cleared trailer could go back to the stone yard.

"When?" she pressed, drumming her fingers against the cup. Her fingernails were a chipped mess. She'd peeled her black polish back, and I'd bet if I looked at the floor of her driver's seat, the layers of nail polish would pepper the car.

Last time her nails looked that bad, she'd confided in me about her pregnancy. Her family still didn't know she'd told me first. It was just another secret I had with someone else.

Which was why I knew whatever she was going to say to me was going to be really fucking bad.

I finally replied, "Yesterday."

Trina hummed, attempting indifference. "The stone yard only dropped off the shipment at ten to five," she commented, her manicured brow lifting knowingly. "When did you move them?"

"Yesterday," I repeated with a little more force. Did it fucking matter when?

"I see." Christ, she sounded like her older siblings when she got disdainful. Her head tipped forward as she studied the tip of her shoes, her teeth clenching as though she was contemplating something. "Can I talk to you?"

"We're talking now, aren't we?" I observed, keeping my tone dry.

Trina flinched, as though she hadn't expected the force of my snark. We'd always had a playful relationship. She always treated me like another older brother, and I had no siblings. Sean's sisters may as well have been my own.

Well, except one.

I stared at the barren treetops, clearing my throat, changing my answer. "Yep."

A few years ago, Sean had stepped back from his family's construction business and Trina took over. To be honest, despite being perpetually late, she was much better at it than he was. She had a natural acumen for construction, and these old buildings seemed to commune with her in some weird way. Things came to her second nature in a way they hadn't for Sean. She woulda made her father proud.

Katrina jerked her head toward the dense woods, edging toward a small manmade clearing. The crew enjoyed walking through there and causing shit—climbing trees, wrestling in piles of leaves like a bunch of barn animals despite the risk of getting bit by a tick, attempting to catch fish with their bare hands at the nearby stream. I never took part, but sometimes, I missed the casualness of just shooting the shit with them, being content with life.

I kept to myself now.

The crisp fall air enveloped us as we entered the clearing, the light dimmer among the hardy sentinel trees densely packed together, looking down at us in judgment. My jaw smarted with pain as tension set in the longer we walked. I suspected I knew what this was about. It was the same conversation every couple of weeks.

"Where are we going?" I questioned, ducking under a low-hanging branch.

"For a walk."

My hackles shot way up. "I don't have time for this, Trina."

"No?" she mused, glancing at me over her shoulder, her lips pursing. "You've got a lot of work to get through 'cause you gotta rush home to your wife and son, right? Make it home for dinner at six?"

I tapered my eyes at the back of her head, realization dawning on me. Right. She hadn't been asking me about the bricks and the when for no reason.

She'd seen the security feed. I'd fucked up.

A couple of years ago, one of our projects had gone up into flames —intentionally set by a couple of assholes who'd gone after Sean in retaliation over his involvement with his then girlfriend.

Ever since, we had a camera feed installed on every project. Trina monitored it like parents did with baby monitors—like a hawk.

Resigning myself, I shoved the hand not holding the cup into my pocket in search of warmth, following her lead. The autumn leaves crunched under our footfalls, the silence a welcomed reprieve from the sound of the bumbling stream in the woods. In a few more weeks, it would freeze over and then all we'd hear is the overwhelm of our own thoughts out here.

I hated it.

"You shouldn't be staying here all evening, Dougie."

There wasn't much else for me to get home to. "We're ahead of schedule. That's good."

"Yeah," she considered with a half-shrug, giving me her eyes briefly over her shoulder. She looked a lot like her ma, or at least, she would if her hair wasn't blue, and she took that septum piercing out and wiped off her makeup. Trina changed her hair like a chameleon. No one ever knew what they were going to get. It was almost like she was hiding from herself sometimes. "But..."

Here we go. I blew out a breath. "But what?"

She stopped, huffing out a sharp exhale, keeping her back to me. "But there's something you're not telling any of us."

Us. Her family.

My best friend.

My lips buzzed, my posture stiffening as I watched her resume walking through the woods. "There's nothing to tell."

It was none of their fucking business.

Trina adopted a hard tone, her footsteps faltering as she pivoted to face me dead-on. "You wanna continue to act like you and Penelope are fine, and I respect your need for privacy, but I also don't think it's fair that you froze Sean," she inhaled sharply, "*and* Raquel out."

Had I mentioned my best friend married my wife's best friend or how fucking annoying that was when you were avoiding them both now?

Katrina didn't need to speak for them. Her brother had plenty to say. I still had the voicemails buried in my phone, and I was sure Penelope's inbox looked the same. "Katrina, don't concern yourself with issues that aren't yours."

Her eyes ignited with fury. "She almost died," Trina hissed at me. "Raquel could have died. She needed you both." I gritted my teeth, my jaw flexing as that night came rushing back at me at full speed. "And you just…" she waved her hand in the air, "*disappeared.*"

The night Pen found me where I shouldn't have been.

The night that put the final nail in the coffin of my marriage.

The only one I wished I could do over.

Katrina tried to embolden herself, planting her hands on her hips. She blew a lock of her hair out of her eyes from the corner of her mouth, then fixed me with a stubborn stare. "Look, Dougie, we love you guys. I know you would never do this to us for no reason. You're family—"

"We're *not* family," I growled back.

Family didn't fuck family, literally or figuratively. Ever.

She recoiled, her honey-brown eyes flaring before she arched a suspicious brow at me.

The wince ricocheted through me inwardly. I shouldn't have said that.

Regardless of my history with the oldest of the Tavares's daughters before I'd met Penelope, what I'd done after my wedding, or my wife's inexplicable resentment and eventual shame, directed at her best friend —Katrina, of all people, didn't deserve that.

Honestly? None of them did.

The Tavareses had always welcomed me as one of their own, and I'd frozen them out at my wife's request without remorse because allowing them in meant I had to acknowledge that my marriage was dead and there was no one to blame but myself. I'd followed Penelope's lead on this one. She shut down, and I mirrored that. It was easier.

But it was also fucking lonely.

I looked away, watching as freed leaves helicoptered in the air, landing at our feet. In another couple of weeks, snow would claim them and the soft, buoyant earth beneath my boots would harden—another season ending and starting. The onset of the holiday season—I didn't even know what that looked like for us this year—and then the end of the year.

I doubted we were hosting our annual New Year's Eve party.

I sensed Trina was waiting for me to say something, anything, but there was nothing.

After another moment, she cleared her throat noisily, clucking her tongue against the roof of her mouth. "Okay, I can't keep doing this," she announced, taking another quick sip from her coffee, and then, with the casualness of announcing the weather, she threw my world off kilter. "You're fired."

What the fuck had she just said? I scoffed, incredulity punching through my veins. "You *can't* fire me."

"Actually, I *can*," she retorted, crossing one of her arms over her chest. "Who's going to stop me?"

Who was going to stop her? Sean? He wouldn't say shit to her, because I hadn't said shit to him in months. My wife had fucked over his, and in turn, I'd fucked him over.

This brat had just backed me into a corner like a comeuppance. Trina always had the upper hand on everyone.

"Don't be an asshole about this, Katrina." I fucking needed this job. I needed an outlet, a purpose. I needed a place where I felt valued, where the constant reminder of my indiscretion didn't live in Penelope's eyes, and the claustrophobia of our house didn't exist. I could breathe a little out here. At home, the walls were closing in on me, one torturous second after another.

But Katrina wasn't afraid of me. She wasn't afraid of anyone. The barb seemed to embolden her, because the tiny little shit stepped into my space with a finger jutted in my direction like a weapon.

"Then you don't bitch out on *our* family," she snarled back. Trina wasn't dropping it. She wouldn't let me ex-communicate myself or erase my existence from their brood. "Either tell me what they did to you, or man the fuck up and get over it."

My ego wouldn't let me. It was a relentless son of a bitch. I sniffled, the bitter air making my nose run. Fine. That's how she wanted it to be? Done. "They're going to deliver the replacement sash windows in the next week or two. Make sure that Luis doesn't install them. He's got butter fingers."

Her self-righteousness vanished as the realization settled over her. I wouldn't fight her. She huffed out a dry laugh, her expression tightening.

"Joey's installation is a little more even." Not as good as mine, but decent enough. "And if you need an extra set of hands," I paused, the impending low blow bubbling in my gut, "You could call Adam."

The remark did exactly what I had wanted it to. She saw red. "You fucking piece of shit," Trina spat, seething. She jerked away from me as though I'd slapped her. Her hand clenched around her coffee and if I didn't know better, I could have sworn she considered chucking it at me.

Yeah, I deserved that.

I didn't need to bring up her ex, nor remind her she'd gone snooping through his past when she shouldn't have a couple of years ago, or what kind of domino effect that had set off for Sean and Raquel.

Her single action had nearly estranged her brother from her family permanently. But the Tavareses weren't the only ones who could stick their noses where they didn't belong or jab their dirty fingers into festering wounds that just wouldn't heal.

I could play that way, too. I reached into my pocket, pulling out the house key, then tossed it at her open palm.

"This is for your own good!" she yelled brokenly at my back as I walked away, the sky carrying her tear-stricken voice. "You're going to thank me some day."

"Shove it up your ass, Katrina." I flipped her off.

"Daddy!" Christopher burst from the living room as I shut the front door, the October air zipping through the foyer. The distinct sound of a knife working against a cutting board in the kitchen ceased. He raced to me; his arms extended as he enveloped my leg.

And just like that, I was absolved of my sins from this morning.

I only wished it was that easy with his ma, too.

The innocence in the gesture made my eyes sting like hell. His ma used to greet me with excitement, too. When he was a newborn, when we'd been happy. I could still recall with perfect clarity the way she'd lean over the banister from the landing, that soft smile on her face.

"Welcome home. I missed you today."

I hadn't heard that in months.

Shit, the last time I'd heard my wife tell me she loved me was our wedding night and I was almost one hundred percent confident that had been out of obligation. I winced, my chest tightening.

I wondered if she loved me at all anymore, but part of me didn't want to know, either.

The tugging on my pant leg brought my attention downward. "Hey, buddy." I ruffled his flaxen hair. He looked up at me in awe, offering me a toothy grin.

If you asked me where I thought we'd be a year ago, it wasn't in this place. Truthfully, I thought by now, Pen and I would have been discussing expanding our brood—or at least actively trying.

We'd had a lot of practice in that department, before she'd shut down on me, and before I... I guess it didn't matter now.

Instead, I walked on eggshells, always bracing myself for the shoe to drop or the utterance of the D word in her perfect boarding-school lilt.

Penelope cleared her throat, her arms crossed over her chest. She had tucked her soft brown cashmere slouchy turtleneck in the middle of her dark jeans, her hair framing her face.

Her brows bent in the middle, her mouth a severe slash as she studied me wearily. "Why are you home?"

Not, *why are you home so early?*

Nope. Why are you home, interrupting our dynamic, the one I wasn't a part of?

How dare I.

"We gonna play," Chris interrupted, bouncing with excitement as he reached for my hand, trying to tug me. "Play trucks."

I swallowed tightly, escaping his ma's intense gaze. "Yeah," I agreed, nodding at him. "Just let me get out of my jacket and we'll play, okay?" He beamed at me, the disparity between his ma and him practically impaling me. How the fuck was I gonna get us out of this mess? "Go wait for me by your toy box."

He nodded, then raced back to the living room.

"Dougie?" Penelope pressed, my name a demand.

Sliding out of my coat, I hung it on the hallway tree. I didn't look at her. Her oppressive stare was uncomfortable enough as it was. I bent over, undoing the laces on my boots, tossing them on the mat.

When I straightened, she was still staring at me. It was like she was observing an intruder in her house but was too shell-shocked to react. She wasn't covert about her annoyance that I was home before nine a.m. on an ordinary Tuesday. And that almost made me remorseful that I hadn't tried to strong-arm Katrina into amending her decision.

I couldn't work for her, but I could still be on the site, right? I could just... watch or something.

No, that was stupid.

I just didn't want to be here when it was clear I wasn't wanted. What the fuck were we doing anymore? Most of the time, Pen appeared to resent that I was here. She did everything in her power to make me feel like I was the interloper. If we weren't arguing over bull-shit, then we were ignoring each other or exchanging the bare minimum we needed to in order to co-parent.

Scratching the back of my neck, I spit it out, "I got fired."

"What?" she blurted, the undiluted shock painting her expression as her arms dropped to her sides. She couldn't believe it any more than I could, but it was true.

I nodded, passing her. Our living room was fancier than anything I'd ever had growing up, closer to a showroom despite the toys sprawled all over the place—they'd be cleaned up by the time he went to bed. The gray-colored sectional she'd swapped our couch out for last year sat in the middle of the room, centered with the fireplace on the left. Throw pillows in pewter and a hazy blue with tassels were positioned perfectly on either ends, the stylish coffee table positioned on a braided cream area rug in front of it. She'd recreated a gallery wall with varying mirrors over the fireplace in a similar style to when we'd been staging this house for sale—before she'd suggested we buy it.

"Why?" she called at my back.

I stopped, glancing over my shoulder.

Really? She wanted me to spell it out for her?

Gee, I don't know, Pen. Maybe we were assholes for shutting our best friends out for no goddamn reason and expecting that it wouldn't have a ripple effect in my working life when I worked for my best friend's family. What do ya think?

Her expression softened, understanding touching her eyes. "Oh." She dropped her chin, staring at her feet. "Katrina can't force us to talk to them."

No, she couldn't. But it didn't change the fact I missed my grumpy best friend and his South Boston wife who I'd developed a soft spot for even though she'd hated me at first.

It didn't excuse me from feeling like shit that we'd missed out on so much in the last couple of months. "Can I ask you something?"

She lifted her uneasy eyes, her brows pulling inward. "What?"

"What did Raquel do to you that made you so mad at her that we don't speak to them anymore?" I swallowed, watching Penelope stiffen and suck back a labored breath as though she hadn't expected the question. "Especially after what nearly happened to her." It never made any sense to me. She was pissed at me, so what did Raquel and Sean have to do with it? "I never understood why you demanded we stop speaking to them over something *I* did."

'Cause whether I wanted to admit it or not, Katrina was right. Raquel could have died that night.

If she hadn't gotten to the phone.

If she'd broken her neck during her fall.

She could have died and left Sean widowed and potentially child-less. What then? It would have fucking destroyed him in a way that paled to his father's death.

Would we still be doing this? Punishing them for my indiscretion?

Pen's face crumpled, her lips pinching tightly to control the trembling, but just like everything else, she gave me nothing to work with.

"You said something to me a few months ago, do you remember?" I charged on. She stared at me blankly, but her posture grew rigid as she braced herself for impact. "'Why does she get to be pregnant with twins? She didn't even want kids,'" I recited, watching as she inhaled sharply. "Why did you say that about her?"

It didn't make sense.

She dropped her eyes, shaking her head. "Don't."

If Pen had wanted more kids, we could have discussed it. I could have explained to her the very basic principles of procreation.

It started with sex.

Which we weren't having.

The one-eighty shift in Pen's personality back then had disturbed the fuck out of me. No one loved Raquel more than Penelope. No one. Sure, Sean married her and worshipped the ground his wife walked upon but Pen always looked at Raquel like she could do no fucking wrong even when she did. I used to tease them that if shit ever hit the fan, it would be those two who vanished in the night together, all Thelma and Louise.

Sean hadn't found the suggestion funny—sore spot—but those two always turned into cackling hyenas over the idea. They loved each other, and short of a detailed play-by-play of every minute of their day, they were always engaged with one another.

Until they weren't. Until after the wedding, when Pen pulled away at the height of Raquel's third trimester, avoided phone calls, didn't return texts or emails. When she made us park our cars in the garage and pretend like we weren't home so we could ignore the knocks at the door with the curtains drawn and blinds closed over the main floor windows.

It was like marrying me had destroyed Pen in some way.

Now my wife stared at me like I was the bad guy, as though I'd been the one who ignored the phone calls and messages. This hadn't been my idea. I wished she would tell Raquel what I did if that's what she rightly felt embarrassed about.

I'd rather deal with it head-on than this bullshit.

She had nothing to be embarrassed over—I was the one who fucked up and I'd deal with Raquel's rage.

Instead, I changed the subject. "Most crews are winding down for the season." I probed the inside of my cheek with my tongue. "But I'm gonna call around for some snow removal gigs." I could rely on Mother Nature to keep me busy and out of her hair for the winter.

Maybe we'd get lucky with a couple of winter Nor'Easters.

"Okay." I wasn't used to her voice growing that soft, but it was the guilt speaking. I didn't blame her, but we were both complicit in our circumstances. She wrung her hands together and shifted her weight from foot to foot. "If we need it, I'll ask—"

Hell. Fucking. No. "You'll do no such thing," I interrupted with an edge in my voice, rage roiling in my stomach. I'd sooner sell a kidney on the black market before I asked her parents for fuck all.

My family, my responsibility.

That had been our agreement when we bought this house. I had a paltry initial investment in it, but I wasn't comfortable with her buying it in full even though she could. Then it would be her house, not ours. Pen was a trust fund baby, on an irrevocable payout plan. She'd gotten an initial payout on her eighteenth birthday, another at twenty-five, thirty, and she'd get what remained when she turned thirty-five in four years' time.

Then there was the eventual inheritance when her parents passed on. She was an only child.

It was part of what made her parents thrust a last-minute prenuptial agreement at me. I'd never cared about Penelope's money, ever. If anything, it made me kind of uncomfortable and that had nothing to do with feeling financially emasculated by her ability to manage everything on her own, and everything to do with knowing that people looked at her and me like we were different.

But for some reason, she'd still wanted me. Still wanted our life together.

So, I put in what I could on the house, and she put in the rest and reinvested her money for Christopher and her own stock portfolio. I covered most of our living expenses outside of whatever additional things she wanted. Those she bought herself.

She wasn't about to insult me now and go to *them*. As if I needed another fucking reminder I'd turned out to be the abysmal failure they'd warned her about.

"Do you understand me?" I asked her after the prolonged silence.

Pen's skin grew ashen, her head weaving with a nod as shame touched her eyes. "Okay."

Which brought us to the next issue. "I'm going to be around here more, so I need to know something." She lifted her weary eyes to mine, waiting. "Do you want me to move out?" I asked, keeping my tone neutral.

She'd asked for a divorce yesterday. She always did when I backed her into a corner. So, I shouldn't have felt relief that she didn't immediately blurt out a "yes."

But her refusal to speak didn't make me feel any better, either. "It's a simple yes or no, Penelope. Nod or shake your head."

"No." She folded her arms across her chest once more, brushing her fingers along her biceps as though she were self-soothing.

"Fine."

"But I think it would be better for us to sleep in separate rooms."

Ouch. The cords in my neck tightened painfully, sweat licking up my spine. "Alright."

"You're not sleeping well," she replied.

That's because I was trying to avoid disturbing her, attempting to prevent this very thing from happening—being dismissed from my bed, the last link I had to her. "How considerate of you to notice," I gritted, turning away. This conversation was more than over.

"Dougie." She had the gall to sound like she was doing this out of concern for me.

"Save it, Pen."

"I'm not trying to hurt you."

That was the first time in months she'd bothered to consider that I wasn't the only one who had fucked up, that maybe she wasn't the only one hurt anymore. That maybe, just maybe, I was a victim in all of this, too.

But it incensed me all the same, especially when she tried to hide behind selflessness.

I spun around, widening my arms. "Too fucking late," I snarled. She flinched, but I wasn't finished. No, if we were both going to take off the punching gloves, she may as well hear it. "You can get yourself off in peace now. Congratulations."

Venom sprouted in her eyes, her shoulders hitting her ears. "You're an asshole."

I was, wasn't I? But I hadn't always been. Before, I'd only been an asshole sometimes. Now? Now it was a daily thing. "This marriage made me this way."

Her bottom lip trembled with the realization that the statement was true. Before her, I'd been the nice guy. I would have climbed Mount Everest just to get a smile out of her. I would have laid down and taken a world of hurt for her because she'd been worth it. Penelope brought out the best and worst in me. She'd turned me into someone I didn't know anymore. And I'd allowed it.

But love did that to people, didn't it? With the snap of your fingers, it could turn you into someone unrecognizable.

"Fuck you!" she shouted at my back, dropping the pretense that we were trying to ensure Chris didn't pick up the word. Honestly? Who the fuck cared? It wasn't like he had anyone to repeat it to.

He was a prisoner in this house, too.

His parents were completely and utterly fucked.

But her telling me, "fuck you,"—well, that was a fantasy. "I wish you fucking would, sweetheart." I laughed, storming away. "Then maybe we'd both get some sleep."

Chapter Seven

Penelope

Three years ago…

"I'VE BEEN THINKING," I STARTED, SHIFTING MY WEIGHT FROM FOOT TO foot, closer to a sway.

The pencil Dougie held in his hand stopped moving against the piece of wood, his eyes lifting to mine. "Uh-oh," he sang, followed by a gruff laugh. He set the pencil down on the worktable, turning around while shoving his safety glasses up. I swallowed tightly, staring up at him through my lashes. He was sweaty around his hairline thanks to the summer heat and the overexertion of his muscles, the veins in his forearms tight with protrusion.

We'd already gone on lunch, and I was pretty sure Sean might berate us if he found us in the basement alone again, but...

Dougie offered me a smirk, his eyes scanning the yard for everyone else's whereabouts as though he were thinking the same. Satisfied by what he saw, he settled his hands on my waist and pulled me in, his lips melding with mine, making my head buzz.

My arms twined around his neck instinctually, my height raising on the tips of my toes to bring me the few extra inches I needed to get closer to him. Dougie's kisses were always hungry, like he was seconds away from devouring me. He groaned low, breaking the kiss with a pant of regret.

"What were you thinking?" he probed, placing a kiss against the tip of my nose and stepping away from me just as the front door opened and two of the guys on the crew walked out. They headed toward a trailer that contained the kitchen cabinets they were unpacking.

I'd picked a macadamia white color in there. Something that would play with the veining in the countertops that Trina and I strong-armed Sean into relenting on.

He'd get his money back on his investment, even if it hurt initially.

I chewed on my bottom lip, wishing like hell I wasn't so nervous about my ask. "I was thinking, maybe... instead of my place this week-end, we could go to yours?"

We'd been doing that for the last couple of weeks. Dougie knew what my world looked like, what laundry detergent I used, how the rain sounded against my apartment windows, and what coffee table books I had. I wanted to explore his world, too.

His face fell. "No." His tone said the answer was final and brooked no argument.

Except, he forgot I was born ready to debate. "Why not?"

"You don't belong in a place like that." He gave me his back, picking up his pencil from the table. He adjusted the glasses back on his face, then resumed what he'd been doing.

What did he mean I didn't belong in a place like that? A place like what?

I wasn't satisfied, and if that explanation was supposed to mollify me, it only made the curiosity worse.

Just as I opened my mouth to debate, his voice cut through with an edge to it. "Please don't be a pain in the ass about this."

"Why can't I see where you live?" I pressed, dropping my voice.

His grip on the pencil tightened, his jaw constricting. "Pen." He exhaled with control. "I don't bring women back to my place."

Well, that was fine, except for one tiny detail. I squared my shoulders, kicking out my chin. "But I'm not just a woman, I'm—" I paused.

He looked at me dubiously, his left brow rising just an inch, waiting for me to finish the sentence. I was what, exactly?

Hadn't I said I just wanted to have fun? Hadn't I established the very rules he was diligently following?

It bothered me. For some reason, it hurt that he rebuffed me. That he didn't push me to be his girlfriend. That he didn't dare to step even a toe out of the lines I'd defined. Wasn't I good enough for him to want to beg me for commitment instead of this arrangement? Dougie didn't kick up a fuss about anything. He was good-natured, levelheaded, and didn't make my life hard.

But over this, he wasn't bending.

When he said he didn't play games, I didn't think that meant he didn't break the rules even a little.

"We can grab burgers from that place in town that you like before we head to the city, okay?" No, it wasn't okay. His lips moved, murmuring something else under his breath that sounded a lot like a math equation, his pencil making a small mark on a piece of wood.

"I don't want burgers," I whispered, as good as they were from Four Corners.

He offered me a half-shrug, not looking at me. "Okay, we'll grab whatever you want then." He'd eat sand if I asked him to, which was why I didn't understand why he wouldn't even give in a little on this.

"Dougie." I said his name urgently, my heart kicking in its cage when he tensed. His green eyes found mine, worry flashing in them. "Please." I brought my hands to my chest, clasping them firmly there. "I just want to see where you live."

"Why?" He rocked his jaw from side to side. "It's nothing like where you live."

Well, that was kind of the point. It was nothing like where I was from, and that made me curious. He knew that my condo in Beacon Hill was a thousand square feet with ten-foot ceilings, delicate crown molding, and had an antique wood-burning fireplace I'd never used. He'd stood in my galley kitchen in muted awe, eyeballing the Wolf appliances and the white cabinets, and quartz cream-colored counter-tops with his arms pressed tight at his sides like he was afraid to touch anything. But I didn't have a clue what life looked like for him. Where did he sleep when he wasn't in my bed? What color was his shower curtain? Was he naturally tidy? Did he leave his dirty socks on the floor?

We spent most of our time at my place. He took me to nice places he looked up beforehand. I'd treated him this week, though. Or, Daddy had, unknowingly. I'd gotten tickets to a Sox game from him that had been intended for one of his clients who bailed, so he gave them to me. They were situated directly behind the dugout.

Dougie had been nervous. Of course, he'd been to a Sox game before. But he'd pointed out where he and Sean usually sat, way at the top in the nosebleeds, closest to the blistering sun. He'd never been close enough to make out every strand of hair that made up Josh Beckett's goatee.

I was convinced he sweated more that day than he ever had at work. But once the first crack of the baseball bat against the ball sounded, he'd grown animated.

Happy. He was handsome when he was at ease, when he wasn't thinking about protecting me from what he thought was a broken, diseased part of him.

Desperation had me vying to be in his world. I wanted to see his things, and to feel his sheets against my skin. I wanted to wash my hair with his shampoo even if would dry out the ends, or to eat a meal off his dishes and drink coffee in his mugs.

Why wouldn't he let me in? "That's the point," I informed him. "I'd like to experience something that's yours."

He sniffled, rolling his lips together. "No one's seen where I live."

How was that possible? "Not even Sean?"

"*Especially* Sean." Worry entered his tone, chilling me to my bones. Dougie looked back at his work, the pencil slipping from his fingers once more. He straightened at the waist, looking down at me over the bend in his nose I loved running my pointer finger over. "There's something you should know about me, Pen, for transparency's sake."

Oh, God. What? What was it? Secret love child? Undercover cop? Ed Gein wannabe?

My chest squeezed, my pulse thrumming deafeningly in my ears as my mind raced to conclusions. "What is it?"

He gave me an apprehensive smile, embarrassment touching the fine lines near his eyes. "I'm, uh, broke."

Huh? I tilted my head at him, confusion flooding me. "What do you mean?"

"I mean, I'm not like... penniless, I've got a little saved. I'm just... yeah, I guess money is just real tight. I gotta stretch it out." He cleared his throat. "So, I don't own a lot and my place is kinda empty." I blinked at him, trying to conjure the visual. When I didn't say anything, he constructed the setting for me. "I have a broken recliner I salvaged from the curb a few years ago, and my TV sits on a couple of milk cartons. My mattress is on the floor, and sometimes, I can't pay my rent on time because a couple of years ago," he kicked his chin at his truck in the distance, "I thought it would be wise to blow my wad and buy that gas guzzler. I'm still on the hook for two more years before it's paid off."

I had a wild imagination, but this? This I couldn't visualize.

Dougie studied me, waiting for my reaction. I didn't know what to say, truthfully. It made me embarrassed in some small way that I'd practically flouted everything I had that he didn't.

God, I was stupid. A stupid, spoiled little rich girl. Everything I'd never wanted to be.

I'd always scoffed at my parents' wealth. Money had never been of any consequence to me because I'd always had it. I hadn't had to worry about where my next meal was coming from.

I'd been overindulgent, born with a silver spoon in my mouth.

Entitled.

Privileged.

I'd bought and renovated my condo in Beacon Hill from top to bottom once I was out of college with the first pay out from my trust fund. Daddy and Mother bought the Range Rover for my graduation present.

Nothing I owned was actually mine. It was just inherited wealth. A trust fund. I was a trust fund baby who'd never wanted for anything because I'd always had it within reach.

I'd never gone to bed hungry or lived in a place barren of things.

I never thought twice about swiping my credit card, or worried about defaulting on a payment.

I never even noticed furniture at the curb, because I'd never had to.

My privilege bothered me suddenly—a lot—because inadvertently, I'd been rubbing it in his face. God, what he must have thought of me.

My hands fell to my sides, my gaze finding the house, knowing Sean was mindlessly installing the fixtures in the main bathroom while likely bitching someone out for something. If Dougie was struggling, that implied he was being underpaid, right? Why wasn't Sean paying his best friend enough?

Dougie's eyes followed my lead, as though reading my mind. "It's not his fault."

It seemed like the simplest explanation. Sean had kicked up a fuss about what he had to pay me. I could imagine what that meant for Dougie. "But if he paid you more—"

I hated how ridiculous I sounded, ignorant almost.

"He pays me more than he should already, Pen. Trust me on that." Dougie folded his arms over his broad chest, blowing out a breath. "He's not as cheap as he comes across, not when it comes to people he cares about." He flexed his hands, huffing sharply as though he were resigning himself to something. "My ma has bradycardia." As my brows bent inward with confusion at the medical term, he continued, "It means her heart beats too slow. She was getting bad fainting spells." He dug the tip of his work boot into the ground, kicking a rock away. "She fainted at work a few years back and knocked herself out."

I let out a little gasp, fighting to remain rooted where I was to not crowd him. It made me think of the last interaction I'd had with

Mother that had ended up in an argument when she'd asked whether I'd gotten the middle-class lifestyle out of my system.

After hearing Dougie's story, I didn't think the way I was living could be considered middle class by any stretch of the imagination.

He looked skyward, his throat bobbing. "She knew she'd need a pacemaker eventually, but she kept it from me. Didn't want me to worry." He let out a clipped laugh, followed by a quick shake of his head. "Anyway, when it came down to it, her choice was she got the pacemaker, or..." he didn't finish the sentence, but I knew.

Get the pacemaker or risk dying.

"Shit isn't cheap, unfortunately, and she couldn't keep her job at the warehouse. It was too high-risk."

"Your mother worked at a warehouse?" I didn't know why the visual was hard for me to place. Not that there was anything wrong with working at a warehouse. My mother had never worked.

Before she'd become Mrs. Walter Cullimore, she was the daughter of Mr. and Mrs. Samuel Spencer of Hartford, Connecticut—a homemaker and a newspaper publisher.

She was the cliché kept woman, as were her mother and grandmother before her.

What was Dougie's mother like? Did he look like her? Where was his dad?

He nodded his head. "She worked the night shift at a shipping warehouse back home." He scrubbed his callused palms against his jeans, as though bracing himself for the next part. "My dad left when I was a kid, so it's always just been her and I." Dougie stared at me, his posture stiff and uncomfortable. "So, I make sure I keep the lights on in her place." He laughed. "She fuckin' hates it, proud as hell that one. But she's my ma, y'know? You gotta take care of your family. She's got no one else but me."

I shook my hands out at my sides, processing the information. Dougie wasn't broke, not by a long shot. He was rich in kindness and love. He was self-sacrificing. How could he ever believe that I wouldn't think he was good enough?

I couldn't stand it any longer. I rushed to him, crashing against his sweat-slick chest with my chin tucked into my neck, my arms binding around his waist. "You're a good man." A really good man. Better than anyone else I'd ever met.

Anytime someone in my parents' society club did something for someone they knew, it was for the press and the clout—not because they gave a fuck about anyone but themselves. But Dougie, he did it out of love.

A couple of howls broke out from the yard. I was aware it was only a matter of time before they aroused Sean's notice and he came out to yell at us, but I couldn't help myself.

"Pen." Dougie moved to break the link of my arms, growing uncomfortable at the attention, but froze when he felt the heat of my tears spilling against his chest, mingling with his sweat. "Are you crying?"

How could I not? I was such an idiot. I'd let him take me to these restaurants, and pay for our outings, and it could have been me all along. He could have bought groceries for three months, and I was just… pathetically clinging to him like a life raft, sobbing. I should have never let him take me out.

"Shh, c'mon now," he soothed, pressings his lips against the crown of my head while his arms looped around my shoulders, holding me tight. "Why are you crying?"

I looked up at him, my heart aching at the softness living in his green gaze. How could he ever think he wasn't good enough for me? If anything, I wasn't good enough for him.

"You're a—" I hiccuped, blinking back more tears. "Re-really good person."

Dougie smiled, thumbing the tears away. "Well, you don't have to cry about it," he teased with a wink, but I caught the faint blush on his cheeks. "Sometimes, I'm an asshole, too."

Never. He'd never been an asshole to me, even when he got upset when I pushed him about going over to his place. "But you don't belong in my apartment, Penny. You belong at home."

I wanted in his world, even if I had to force my way into it and create a spot where I never had to leave. "Please let me spend the weekend at your place," I begged.

He opened his mouth to argue again, but he hesitated. He looked away, his muscular arms slipping to bind around my waist. Dougie blew an exasperated raspberry. "I'll make you a deal," he began, his expression compressing. "You can see my place, and then we'll go back to yours."

Okay, this was a start. I placed my hands on his chest, his strong heartbeat pounding in the solid cage. "Okay, and then..." I trailed off.

"Then I'll make you dinner."

His body hardened in my grasp, as taut and tight as a rope. "I can buy you dinner, Pen." There was an edge in his tone, like he didn't trust my intentions came from a genuine place.

"No," I insisted. Eating out was so expensive and gluttonous. "Honestly, I want to try eating at home more and—"

"Pen," he warned, his eyes tapering. "The whole reason I *don't* tell people about my situation is because I don't want pity."

I knew that. Maybe I hadn't experienced that firsthand, but I'd seen that fight for survival in my best friend, Raquel. She didn't like hand-outs or sympathy, either. She held her own, and didn't want anyone feeling sorry for her, no matter what kind of bullshit hand of cards life had dealt her.

I wondered if they'd get along. God, what was I thinking? Raquel met none of my—none of my what? Fuck buddies? Dougie wasn't just a fuck buddy. He was something more. I cared about him. I wanted to spend all my free time with him, and grow as a person with him.

I liked him. I really liked him. That was why I wanted inclusion in every facet that made him who he was. "No, really." I cupped his cheek, savoring the overgrown stubble peppering his face. "I can make pasta."

"Pasta?" he repeated, smirking. His beard tickled my hand when he spoke. "You can cook pasta?"

Well, no, but I was going to learn on the fly. How hard could it be? Put pasta in a pot, add sauce, and... wait, did you cook the pasta before the sauce? Okay, maybe I didn't know what I was doing, but I'd figure it out. I broke out into a laugh, arousing his own.

We'd disregard the fact that I hadn't eaten processed carbs in years.

He tapped my nose, a small sigh leaving him as he brushed his knuckles over my cheek. "You're too much."

The sash window on the side of the house overlooking the window jerked open, Sean's distorted features appearing in the screen. I could feel the brute force of his anger from outside. It made the summer heatwave feel frosty in comparison. "I swear on the fucking Pats upcoming season, you two are on my last goddamn nerve!" Trina's wild shrieks of laughter behind him carried out through the window. "Cut it the fuck out and get back to work!"

Dougie chuckled. "C'mere," he murmured, tilting my head up. "Let's give him something to get really pissed about."

"Dougie!" Sean shouted. The yard broke out into another chorus of laughter.

I couldn't help but join them, the giggle freeing itself. I knew exactly what would solve all of Sean's issues. "He needs to get laid," I suggested as Dougie's mouth inched closer to mine.

"You have no idea, Penny."

Dougie pulled the truck into a spot in front of an exhausted-looking triple decker. Thick, prickly, overgrown weeds wrapped around the uncared for perimeter. The concrete walkway to the small porch cracked in some places, crabgrass growing in the slivers.

He was nervous. "This is it."

I said nothing. My hands reached for the eject button on the seatbelt, my attention trained on the building. I could sense the weight of Dougie's stare as he studied me carefully, looking for some sign of my hesitation, waiting for me to flee.

All I did was smile.

Fall River wasn't like Greenwich. It ran along the Taunton River, and though it classified as a city, its population was only twenty thousand more than the town I'd grown up in. Greenwich gave off the impression of a place found in a Hallmark movie, but parts of Fall River could fool you into believing you'd flown over the Atlantic Ocean and found yourself in one of Portugal's archipelagos with the way Portuguese flags flew proudly and the number of restaurants we

passed. Dougie told me that had to do with almost half the city identi-
fying as Portuguese. Their influence was potent here. I liked it.

"Just watch your step," Dougie said, as I opened my car door and
stepped out into the oppressive late summer heat, away from the cool
confines of his truck. The concrete was uneven under my shoes as I
edged closer to the front porch. "I'm on the second floor, so we gotta
enter from the back." He extended his hand out for mine, palms slick
with sweat when his fingers enveloped my own.

His verdant eyes flashed with worry, his jaw tensing as he led me
around the back to a fire exit, moving at a pace closer to walking to his
own funeral. He let me go up first, the metal creaking under our
weight as I gripped the rickety railing. The stairs were a bit unsettling.
They felt loose against the vinyl clapboard siding wrapped around the
structure. I was grateful we only had to go up the one flight of stairs,
and not all the way to the top.

I heard his keys sliding along the ring as he searched for his house
key over the heavy sound of his breathing whistling through his nose
when we cleared the stairs. "Dougie?" He lifted his head, the key sandwiched between his fingers. "It's okay."

The lump in his throat shifted with his swallow. He edged by me,
shoving his key in the lock and twisted the knob. Opening the door, he
stood out of my way so I could enter first.

He wasn't kidding. There was next to nothing in here, and it was
hotter in here than it was outside. Almost unbearably so. My eyes
flitted to the window air conditioning unit he had described to me, and
sure enough, no air pushed from its vents. A thin blanket of dust
coated the top of the box from being unused.

The recliner he'd mentioned sat in the middle of the room, the
pleather torn on the arms and worn in the middle. I wasn't sure how
much of that was him or the previous owner. His television was the
nicest thing in here, and that made me want to laugh. It seemed like
such a guy thing.

The under pad of the dark brown carpets was thin, and something
told me if we took a box cutter to the edges, we'd find gorgeous hardwood under it. Old buildings like these almost always had hardwood

underneath. His walls were a dingy cream color, and the blinds over his windows broken in places.

"See?" he tested. "Nothing to see in here." It was an invitation for me to leave but I didn't take it.

I moved to take off my shoes, but he stopped me. "Leave 'em on." He shut the door behind him, then he placed his hands in his pockets. Dougie's posture was pin straight, his discomfort palpable.

"What color is your shower curtain?" I asked, toeing toward his kitchen. He had yellowed Formica countertops on top of honey cabinetry, basic circular cabinet hardware in a brass color, no doubt upcycled every decade when they finally got around to making renovations. The peeling linoleum floors with a textured effect aroused a wince—God, if there was hardwood under here, the glue from the laminate would destroy the planks. It was tidy in here, though. There was a tiny coffee maker and a single slice toaster, nary a crumb to be found on the counter.

"My shower curtain?" he questioned, watching as I examined the burst of colorful fridge magnets. He had a lot of fridge magnets for someone who kept nothing pinned to his fridge. "Clear."

"Clear?"

"Clear. Kind of hard to find a color that matches pink."

I tilted my head at him, my eyes gleaming. "Is your tub pink?"

He jerked his head to the left. "Go check it out."

I smiled, my insides giddy. At least he wasn't trying to rush me out of here like I'd previously worried. It was almost like he was trying to give me free rein to allow me the opportunity to decide when I was ready to leave.

The carpet from the living room transitioned into laminate wood. There were three doors in his narrow and short hallway. On the right-hand side, more linoleum, this time with a checkered tile pattern in the bathroom. The skinny door at the end of the hallway no doubt a linen closet, and I suspected the last door on the right was his bedroom.

I'd go there next.

He wasn't kidding. His tub was pink, flushed against taupe tiles. "Wow," I exhaled.

"Told you," Dougie said sheepishly.

I glanced at him over my shoulder. "Pink was quintessential in the seventies." The pedestal sink under a medicine cabinet doubled as a mirror was clean, his toothbrush in a cup next to a tube of toothpaste squeezed within an inch of its life. The faintest traces of bleach lingered in the air, like he'd cleaned recently. "It's clean." There wasn't even the slightest hint of mold in the grout.

Dougie laughed. "I have no excuse to be dirty."

"True," I replied. "But sometimes, open spaces are an invitation for messes." I turned around to face him. He leaned against the bathroom doorway, a visible flush in his countenance that I could've chalked up to being due to the heat in his apartment, but I knew the actual source. "I like it here."

He guffawed, then rolled his eyes. "You're sweating bullets, and you like it in here?"

I touched my sticky hairline, then shrugged. "Sure, it smells like you."

"Like me?" Over the bleach, I could pick out his scent easily, and it made me weak-kneed and happy.

I nodded, approaching him. "You always smell like the earth." The space between his brows folded with interest as I settled my hands against the covered hard muscles of his abdomen. "Like fresh cut wood and crushed pepper," I added.

He nodded his head, his lips puckering like he was trying to keep from laughing. "That was strangely specific."

I placed my chin against his chest, tilting my head back to regard him while my fingers found his belt loops. "I've had a lot of time to think about it." His gaze heated, but he blinked it away. "Tour's almost over, huh?" He could show his bedroom to me, if he wanted. He'd said he'd never had a woman here, which suggested that maybe no one else had ever slept in his bed. I wanted to be the first.

"And then we're getting out of here, yes." He touched the ends of my hair, his fingers threading through the strands to cradle the back of my head in his firm grip, his thumb rubbing over my steady pulse in the tendon of my throat. "Thanks for not laughing at me."

I tensed. "Why would I ever laugh at you?"

"I've lived here eight years, and this is all I have to show for it."

"It's honest, Dougie," I murmured. "You're an honest man, and that, by extension, makes you a good one." I felt his gaze on my lips, my skin tingling with anticipation.

God, I was so nervous suddenly. Even though I grasped his belt loops, I felt clumsy. "Can I say something?"

"You're asking for permission?" he teased. "You always blurt the first thing you're thinking."

"Not when I'm nervous." No, when I was nervous, I defaulted into old habits. I stiffened and turned into a carbon copy of my mother with her good posture, and my shoulders squared with my chin even like a quintessential WASP. I over thought my every single move and wanted to ensure no one knew I was worried. Almost like it was a well-rehearsed facade.

People couldn't hurt you when you gave off the impression that nothing could penetrate the ironclad surface of perfection.

He dropped his hand from my hair, creating a sliver of space between us. "I like you," I blurted out.

Dougie's expression clouded, his stare dropping to the floor. He huffed as he pushed off the bathroom threshold, shoving his hands in his pocket with a sniff. "Yeah, I knew this was a bad idea."

Huh? I frowned.

He tilted his head back to stare at the bathroom ceiling before he finally looked at me. "Okay, you like me, *but?*"

"There was no but." At his prolonged silence, I dry washed my hands, then shook out my fingers. "That was it. I like you, and I wanted you to know that."

Dougie studied me, struggling to contain the shock from his face, the muscles in his jaw jumping. I mean, of course he knew I liked him enough to let him fuck me repeatedly, but it was different saying the words out loud with moxie and my stare trained on his, so he knew I was dead serious.

I liked him. I liked him a lot, and I wanted him to read between the lines and just...

Ask me to be his and only his.

But he didn't. He looked at me as if I'd sprouted two more heads and spoke to him *dans en Français.* This went over differently in my head. In my mind, he plastered me against the wall and showed me how much he liked me back, not appear as though he'd calcified into place like a Jurassic Park fossil.

"Oh."

Oh? His eyes were rife with something I couldn't place. Uncertainty, doubt and then... God, was that boredom? He cleared his throat, backing out of the bathroom and away from me. "You can check out my room while I pack my bag and then we can get going."

Unbelievable. That was a green light to tell me how he felt about me. The opportunity to tell me the feelings were reciprocated and that he liked me, too.

Instead, I felt like a warm, dependable hole he shoved his cock into. The girl with the fucking air conditioner and the Red Sox tickets. It hurt. Why did it hurt so much?

My teeth gritted. What an asshole. I thought him questioning me meant he liked me back, but I was wrong. The shock hadn't come from a place of relief, it was an inconvenience.

I didn't want to see his room anymore. I just wanted to go home. Breezing by him, I rushed in the front door's direction.

"Pen?" Dougie called, confusion wrapping around my name.

I didn't dare look back at him, not trusting myself not to cry. "I'm gonna go wait in the truck."

"Don't you want to see my room?" I didn't look back at him.

"No." I jerked the door open just as the tears broke free—damn it. I kept them out of my voice. "You were right. It's too hot in here."

I didn't have it in me to tell him not to bother coming over.

Chapter Eight

Penelope

Present

IN HINDSIGHT, I THINK I'D ALWAYS LIKED HIM MORE THAN HE LIKED ME.

I'd always been the forward one; not just with him, with every guy. Sure, I liked the chase, but I enjoyed the pursuit more. I saw something I wanted, and I went after it.

I never pussyfooted around how I felt about him. I made it known from the beginning that I wanted him when I stumbled into his arms the first time we met. And sure, he may have asked me out initially, but he'd always been so strict about staying within the parameters once he learned how I felt about dating. He could play within the rules of that, but when it came to our marriage...

The rules ceased to exist when they were no longer convenient.

Dougie had been playing with Christopher for almost two hours—Chris's excited shrieks ringing out through the room followed by Dougie's gravelly laughter. It continued that way until I'd interrupted, muttering about Christopher's nap. I killed the mood instantaneously.

We hadn't uttered a single word to each other since.

How the hell were we going to navigate this? I had a husband at home full-time now. A husband who was now raking the front yard like each fallen, wet leaf had personally wronged him, the sharp, tinny scraping filling the air as he mumbled things under his breath, the words leaving him in hot vapors. He'd stop raking every so often, panting heavily as his eyes dragged around the yard. It would take him days to get that sorted, maybe weeks. The trees weren't completely barren yet, and there were almost a dozen maple trees in our backyard alone. But he just kept on raking, the muscles in his back flexing as he worked.

He was going to be around me every waking moment of the day and I didn't know how the hell to function anymore. He couldn't stay outside forever. Eventually, he'd get the yard sorted. There were only so many make-work projects I could find around the house before our paths inevitably crossed. I needed to talk to Katrina, get this figured out. Our marriage was none of her family's business. They were taking this too far.

If we didn't want to talk to them, it was our choice.

So why did thinking that alone make my chest hurt? My mind wandered to the countless voicemails on my phone, the ones that expired every thirty days only for a new one to take its place. The text messages I never replied to, the apology flowers—ones I'd never been deserving of—that had wilted in a vase on the kitchen table months ago. Dougie and I weren't the only casualties in the demise of our marriage, nor was our son. Our best friends suffered, too.

The kitchen phone ringing made me jolt in place, my shoulder blades pinching together as I padded over to the wall, lifting the receiver with unease when my eyes examined the unfamiliar number on the caller ID.

No one ever really called the house anymore. "Hello?"

A silvery-toned woman spoke on the other end. "Hi, this is Doctor Correia's office calling. Is Penelope there, please?"

I swallowed tightly, my insides heaving as the acid crawled up my throat. I'd been waiting for this. Relief should have been coating my insides, not dread. Confirming Dougie wasn't approaching the house with a quick glance, I spoke, "This is Penelope."

The sound of her typing on the other end filtered through. "We're just calling to confirm your two o'clock tomorrow."

I exhaled, but my heart frantically stuttered. I nodded, forgetting she couldn't see me. "Y-y-yes, I-I-I'll be there." Finally, I'd have all my answers tomorrow. Tomorrow, I'd confidently know what was wrong with me. Then I could act accordingly.

My eyes fell to the baby monitor on the counter near the phone. Christopher slept soundly, the infrared LED screen illuminating his tiny features in the darkness of his bedroom. Observing him always strengthened me.

"Great. If you could just bring any medications you're taking with you."

My head felt heavy. I cleared the thickness from my throat. "Okay, thank you."

"See you tomorrow." Placing the phone back on the receiver, my frame trembled as the chill raced through me. I'd been waiting for this appointment for months, ever since...

The flashback charged at me, my teeth clenching tightly together to keep the sob contained. There'd been so much blood—more blood than I knew what to do with. It had looked like the scene of a horror movie, droplets staining our pristine, snow-white bathroom floors and soaking my panties.

Out of reflex, my hand searched the air for the lip of the bathroom counter, even though I was in the kitchen. I'd clung to that counter for dear life that night, and even now, phantom cramps squeezed in my abdomen, reminiscent of contractions.

I'd sat hunched over the toilet with sweat clinging to every fine hair on my body, nausea racking through my insides, my head swimming.

I could hear Dougie's faint footsteps on the other side of the door, approaching.

Please don't come in. Please don't see me like this.

But he couldn't read my mind. He couldn't hear my silent plea. All he knew was that we were late for the airport. We were supposed to be going on our honeymoon.

The honeymoon that was going to help us get back on track for a marriage that just started on the wrong foot.

In my memory, the tentative knock came first, but I couldn't free the words from my mouth fast enough to stop him, the pain consuming me. The door opened, the hinges creaking.

The tips of my fingers brushed against the kitchen wall, recalling the way his face grew pallid and his green eyes widened, transfixed in horror that night.

"Pen?" Dougie didn't know where to look, his expression growing ashen, eyes distending. He swung his gaze from the droplets on the floor, my saturated, crimson-stained panties bunched at my ankles, collecting the remaining blood that had traveled down my legs before I'd made it to the toilet, and then finally, I felt the weight of his worried stare fall on me.

I recalled lifting my forehead from where I'd pressed them against the tops of my knees, anger pummeling my insides. *"Get. Out!"* I screamed at him.

I'd never screamed at him. But now I had, and he ripped himself out of the bathroom door threshold, slamming the door behind him. In his absence, I had the audacity to cry for the loss of his presence and this tiny life I'd kept a secret from him. After every cruel thought I'd had about the inconvenience leading up to this moment, I had the gall to feel like my body had betrayed me in the ultimate way.

But it was me who had betrayed the tiny life and my marriage.

It was all my fault.

Dougie had assumed the most obvious thing had occurred, and I let him. I played into it, murmuring an apology a few hours later about my period and bad cramps.

We never made it to the airport, and it felt like our marriage had bypassed the honeymoon stage entirely. If he truly knew, it would have made everything that much worse.

This wasn't supposed to happen to us.

"What was that about?" I jumped at the brassy baritone of Dougie's voice penetrating the dark place my thoughts had wandered off to. My hands flushed against my stomach as I spun around, my eyebrows gathering in the middle.

I'd only taken my eyes off him for a moment. I hadn't even heard him come in, almost as though he was slinking around on purpose to catch me off guard as soon as my back was turned. He must have seen me on the phone from the garden doors. We kept them uncovered because I'd always liked how the sun filled the kitchen.

He was panting as he shrugged out of his jacket, his cheeks rosy from the October chill. Dougie slung his jacket over the back of the high-back stool near the kitchen island, his head sloping expectedly. He wanted an answer.

One I wasn't entirely prepared to give him. I fidgeted on the spot, picking at a piece of pilling on my turtleneck. "I have an appointment in the city."

He studied me while rolling up the sleeves of his plaid button-down shirt, his veins flexing in his forearms as he worked. "For what?"

It was a normal question. It was to be expected a spouse would want to know what the other was doing, but it pissed me off all the same. This was exactly why I didn't want him at home, snooping around, keeping his eyes on me all day while searching for anomalies.

I kept my tone even in my response, desperate to keep him uninterested. "It's just a doctor appointment. I've already arranged for Chris to stay with your mom while I'm gone."

It had thrilled Eileen by the prospect of spending a few hours with her grandson. She was a kind woman, but she saw right through people too easily.

She knew something wasn't right between her son and me. Where she would have normally stuck her nose in our business, meddled and tried to orchestrate a solution, she was hands-off, telling me only, *"It'll work itself out, Penelope. Marriage is hard work."*

She would know. Her husband left her when Dougie was young while she had no family to lean on. Yet, she was still so optimistic. It made me wonder how the hardship hadn't left her jaded. How could she remain so positive?

Dougie sniffled, his nose still running from the cold. His jaw contracted, green eyes tipping to the floor as he processed my response. "Really?" he pressed.

His mistrust unnerved me, making my shoulder blades punch together. He scratched at his jaw absently, his eyes working around the tidy kitchen until they settled on the unmarked calendar on the fridge. I had never put the appointment down there.

I hadn't wanted him to ask too many questions, and I hadn't expected him to be home to disassemble my answers, either. I'd gotten away with it this far, going to various specialists, the hospital, our family doctor, undetected, right under his nose. None of them were marked on the calendar. I put down what he needed to know, reminders pertaining to Chris, bill payment due dates, car service appointments.

But not the doctors' appointments. Never the doctors' appointments.

He licked his bottom lip, his gaze hardening. He didn't believe me. "A doctor appointment, huh?" Dougie echoed.

I folded my arms over my chest, slanting my head to the right. "That's what I said."

He scoffed, clearing his throat as he braced himself against the back of the bar stool. "If you're going to see a divorce lawyer, I'd like to have an actual conversation first."

The accusation infuriated me. My pulse elevated, my blood pressure whirring in my ears. Despite what I'd said to him, divorce was the furthest thing from my mind. It was something I said in the heat of the moment. I knew it hurt him, but it got him to back off.

Unlike his apartment so many years ago when I'd confessed my feelings and he said nothing back, Dougie always wanted to talk about our marriage, always had something to say. But nothing he could say would fix this.

There was nothing to discuss.

I moved for the kitchen threshold, his taut voice waylaid me. "Penelope, I'm really fucking trying here. You need to meet me halfway."

Demands.

He always seemed to make demands of me now, too.

Asking me for things he didn't deserve.

The tightness in my chest made my next breath scant. "I do not need to do *anything*!" I spat, stabbing the air between us. "You made that choice for us when I found you with her."

He had the gall to look at me like that again—wounded. Like I was the one who kept picking at the indiscretion until it bled, as though I was the reason the wound just wouldn't heal.

"You misunderstood what you saw," he said, gravel entering his tone.

I hadn't misunderstood shit. I knew what I'd witnessed. The betrayal burned in my stomach like poison, flashes sprouting in my vision as I recalled that day.

Him with her. I didn't need to see her half-naked or smell her perfume on his skin to fill in the blanks.

The image of her in his passenger seat, blotting her red-rimmed eyes, lived in my memory rent free.

It was everything I needed to know.

She'd become his home, and I'd become his hell.

I wouldn't let him gaslight me into believing otherwise. "Don't insult my intelligence."

Dougie held up his hands, his features growing pained. "I'm *not*. If I did what you were accusing me of, I'd tell you by now," he insisted with no fight in his voice, his tight breath wheezing from his nose. "You know me better than that."

Funny. I thought I did. I thought I knew everything about my husband—the good man—but it turned out I didn't.

The version of my husband I knew before we said "I do" would have never found himself caught dead with her. They'd always avoided each other, and he'd reassured me years ago that there was nothing left there. So how did they end up in his truck together if not for something illicit?

Dougie just stared, watching me with open palms held up at his sides like he was showing me his hand, trying to prove he had nothing to hide. But the turmoil-driven acid coursed through my veins all the same. Why was it, every time I thought of that day, hatred polluted me and all I wanted to do was hurt him back?

This wasn't a marriage. This was a mess. Our mess. The fight fled my body, the familiar sorrow taking its place. I felt so defeated, so... empty. "I'm not going to see a divorce lawyer."

He forced a laugh, crossing his arms over the breadth of his chest. "I don't believe you."

"And I don't believe you didn't fuck her, so I guess we're even," I hissed.

His stance widened as his arms dropped once more, his fingers curled at his sides. "Penelope, I swear on my ma's life, I *didn't*." He'd sworn it up and down for months, weeks, days.

Any opportunity he had to say it, he took it.

But I didn't want to hear it.

I tensed, ripping my stare from his. Dougie loved his mother. He loved his mother more than I loved my mother. He'd taken care of her. He still took care of her.

Even if some small part of me questioned the merit of my accusation, why was I struggling to believe him? Why couldn't I entertain the idea of forgiving him?

He had been with her. He had left our house after an argument and sought her out.

And like a series of unfortunate events, I found him by mistake, parked a few car lengths away from my car in the hospital parking lot. Raquel had gone into labor early. She'd had an accident.

I thought I'd jinxed her.

I needed him. I needed him to assure me it wasn't my fault, and he didn't answer the phone because he was with her.

The familiar sensation of all-consuming adrenaline slammed into me while the tears pooled in my eyes as the memory played on the back of my lids like a vignette. I'd watched numbly as the source of his unrequited love left his truck with tear-stained cheeks and her makeup smeared on her face like they'd gotten into a lover's quarrel. She'd lumbered numbly toward the hospital doors in stilettos—always with the fucking stilettos, constantly with her head held high and the airs of self-entitlement.

To her family.

To my best friend.

That woman.

The one I'd always been covertly insecure about, and for good fucking reason. Even the day I'd run into her at our unknowingly shared therapist's office, she'd made my skin crawl. It'd felt like another reminder that nothing was mine and mine alone. My husband, my therapist, my best friend—her goddamn sister-in-law—we seemed to share it all.

She was the bane of my insecurities.

That woman was the one Dougie had looked at with repentance in his eyes on our wedding day, his hand firmly wrapped around her bicep as they exchanged a moment in silence.

How did he expect me to believe nothing had happened between them when he should have never been in the city, when all the signs pointed to his case of buyer's remorse?

But fine, if he wanted to do this, we could do this—my way. "If you want me to believe you, tell me why you were in the city that night." My pulse quickened as the question extended in the air between us.

He had no reason to be in Boston, not even to pick her up if she was too emotional and distraught to drive. She had a boyfriend for that.

Dougie's chest visibly caved. I'd only asked this question once, the night I'd caught him with her. Since then, we'd never gotten this far in this argument. I'd never allowed it, because I didn't want to think about it. I wanted nothing to complement the visual that lived in my head rent free.

"Can we sit down?" he asked, trying for gentle. He bit the inside of his cheek, his eyes growing naively hopeful. My mind screamed at me to be rational, to finally hear him out and stop torturing myself, or us. But my heart, my emotions, that was what did all my thinking for me these days.

"No." Sitting down left me vulnerable. It would give him the opportunity to look at me, *really* look at me and crawl back into the place in my heart that had always been his.

A place he'd abandoned.

Dougie licked his lips, his Adam's apple bobbing with his thick swallows.

Nothing. He gave me nothing, and the self-made vision rushed into its place—her red-lacquered talons trailing over his tight skin, her plush red mouth on his, her body taking what he gave her—what had always been for me.

Tears pricked the back of my eyes when he didn't rush with another explanation, my lips growing flat. "That's what I thought." I turned to flee the kitchen, but he charged after me.

"I didn't fuck her," he gritted, stopping me.

I just wanted to scream. "But you were going to, right?" I demanded, spinning around, no longer caring to keep my consternation in check for Christopher's sake upstairs. "You were going to fuck her, and then you got caught by her *boyfriend*."

When I'd rushed to the truck, long after she left, Dougie had gotten out, sporting a bruise that could have only come from the blow of someone who'd felt the sting of betrayal, too.

Dougie flinched, my observation meeting its mark, and my insides soared with self-righteousness. I'd pegged the situation correctly. I knew that was exactly what he intended all along. Maybe he hadn't done it, but intent mattered.

Intent still made him guilty.

His posture sagged as he backed away. He opened his mouth to say something, but immediately closed it.

I was right.

He scrubbed a hand over his face, his fingers lingering on his unclipped beard. "I'll admit I thought I wanted to," he breathed. "But I didn't."

But he didn't.

That was supposed to comfort me. The tears slipped free at his confession, my pulse pounding in my ears as the betrayal racked through me.

He'd wanted to.

He hadn't, but he'd wanted to.

Why the fuck did that feel so much worse? My husband had *wanted* to cheat on me.

Sure, he hadn't, but he went to her with an affair on his mind. After what I was going through already in silence, after what I'd lost, he had wanted to have sex with someone else.

Not just someone else—but with *her*. Knowing full well how she made me feel.

What remained of the unhealed scabs ripped free from the wound, the pain feeding the anger that was always within arm's reach inside of me. "I hate you," I cried, my chest heaving. "I *hate* you." The brute force of my statement stunned me, my insides shredding as the urge to scream clawed painfully at my lungs once more.

It was just another lie, wasn't it? I didn't hate him. No matter how desperate I was, I couldn't hate him, but I wanted to. I couldn't reconcile the thought that he'd left the house that night after an argument with me in search of her.

All I wanted now was for him to sweep me into his arms and beg. But he remained rooted in place while the weight of his admission sunk in my gut like a brick and my heavy head spun. He didn't scramble to take back what he said, to try to overexplain it. He said nothing; the statement existing between us now like a corporeal, tangible thing.

An entity in our marriage.

Dougie's chin lowered to his chest with shame. "It wasn't because I wanted her," he croaked.

That was worse.

I averted my gaze, my head shaking. "So, anyone would have done the job, huh? She was just convenient?" My body trembled, my rattling knees threatening to give out on me. Of course she was convenient. She and I were alike in more ways than I wanted to admit. We'd always gotten what we wanted. "How could you do that to me?"

I almost wished it hadn't been her. Maybe then I'd be able to visualize getting over it. I wouldn't spend every waking moment measuring myself up against her. She'd been at our wedding, for God's sake. He'd assured me repeatedly that they'd never been serious.

Her brother didn't even know.

Everyone lied to each other, but somehow, Dougie seemed to be at the helm of all the deceit.

"How could *you* do this to *me*?" he charged back quietly, lifting his eyes. "How could you freeze me out and—"

He was going to turn this around on me? "And what?" I demanded.

I wrapped my arms around myself, bracing for impact.

His chin jutted to the right, as though he was processing what he was thinking before he said it. "The wedding wasn't us."

"Not this again, Dougie." I shook my head, my rage overpowering me. "Always about the fucking wedding." So what? It got a little out of hand. It was one day in our lives.

"That wedding changed *us*, Pen. It changed *you*."

"It didn't." But I knew it had. I knew he was right. I just didn't want to hear it. Acknowledging that I was complicit in this mess in more ways than I wanted to admit was too difficult. I didn't want to carry the burden of the responsibility because then it would mean that I had to concede that there had been things I was lying about, too. I didn't want to be part of the problem—I wanted to be the victim who needed to remain angry at him.

If I wasn't, the self-loathing would consume me.

"You didn't want me," he said brokenly, shaking his head. "You didn't want me, and you rebuffed me for months."

That wasn't true. That wasn't... "And you went to find it some-where else, huh?" I accused, the tears dripping from my chin. I let out a bitter laugh, smiling tightly. "At least I give it to myself. I don't go looking for it elsewhere."

He stared at me, watching the tears gliding over my cheeks. I saw his fingers twitch. Another lifetime ago, he would have wiped my tears away. Now, he was the source of them.

Resignation, blending with humiliation, skated over his features as a low, bitter sigh left him. "I felt like..." he shook his head.

"Like what?"

His shoulders hunched. "Like I could have been any guy on our wedding. That it didn't make a difference you were marrying me, after everything."

Oh, give me a break. "So, you went to go fuck your ex?"

The presence of his rage slammed into me. "Penelope, I *didn't* fuck Ma—"

"Don't you dare say her name in this house!" I screamed at him. It was bad enough that I still remembered every place she'd ever sat and stood in this house from the first time I met her.

I didn't want to hear her name. I didn't want to think about her under my husband, pressed up against him, touching him.

Our paths crossed because of her, because of her decisions. She hadn't wanted him. She'd never wanted him the way I did. She was an entitled new-money snob, prepared to ruin a marriage and a young family.

She didn't want him, but I did.

I'd always wanted him.

I'd always loved him.

My husband was never second best. He was always number one.

My first pick. My ultimate choice.

But I'd never been his.

"I'm sorry," he whispered, closing his eyes. "I'm so sorry, Penny."

Penny. I couldn't remember the last time he'd called me that. "I wish I knew how we ended up here."

I wished I knew, too.

Christopher stirred on the monitor, his whine hitting my ears as I backed out of the kitchen. If we were making wishes out loud now, I had one, too.

I slipped the wedding and engagement rings from my finger, chucking it in his direction. The ping of the gold bands struck the ground, bouncing at him, his sharp intake hitting my ears, but I didn't watch to see the hurt filter in his face.

"I wish I'd never married you."

Chapter Nine

Penelope

Three years ago…

"Why do you sit like that?" Raquel's harsh South Boston accent summoned my attention. I knitted my hands tightly in front of me, my palms growing increasingly clammy as I stared at the plate of French fries she was mowing through.

She was hungry. She always was, but I supposed that was to be expected when she lived off coffee, cigarettes and instant noodles.

"Why do I sit like what?" I asked, offering her a forced smile. I was grateful for the din of the shithole bar we always went to, O'Malley's. It masked the sonorous pounding of my heart.

She licked the ketchup from the corner of her mouth, swallowing her mouthful. "Like you're a contestant for a Miss America pageant and your special talent is sitting with a stick wedged up your ass."

What? I glanced down at my posture. Sure enough, she was right. I was sitting like I'd been raised—legs crossed at the ankles like a proper lady, the arches of my nude Louboutin pumps elevated, shoulders even with poise, spine straight.

I never sat like this anymore. Only when I was nervous. It helped foster the illusion that I had my shit together and wasn't on the verge of going home to pop a lorazepam for the first time.

I dropped my posture into a slouch, something she was more familiar with from me. Tugging on the neckline of my black, rolled-up Metallica T-shirt, I tried to buy myself breathing room, then tucked my hair behind my ear.

Raquel just stared. "Alright, weirdo." She brought her drink to her mouth, her eyes roaming around the bar. O'Malley's was a hole-in-the-wall in Boston's North End. Raquel liked it, even though the rats outside were the size of fucking raccoons. The bar's owner, Ronan, was a friend of her late father's. I think it fostered the illusion in her mind that there was a place safe for her in this city—one where her monsters weren't allowed.

Ronan made sure of it.

Taking a fortifying breath to slow my racing heart, I knew it was now or never. I had to tell her.

"I met a guy," I announced, trying for casual as I brushed my fingers against the condensation built on my glass.

Raquel didn't even so much as make a face. She reached for another French fry off the plate seated between us on the table, dunking it enthusiastically into a dollop of ketchup and then popping it into her mouth.

I stared at her expectantly, waiting for her to say something.

Instead, I earned an eye roll. "Cool."

That was it, no further questions. The conversation, in her eyes, was over.

Raquel didn't date. She didn't even really fuck. Not really. Save for that worthless fucking mistake she crawled into bed with once a year —the one who shall remain nameless... *anyway.*

"He's hung like a horse," I added, trying to garner her interest with a joke.

It worked as I'd intended. Her brows shot north as she reached for her glass again, tipping the remains of her whiskey down her gullet without so much as a wince. She studied me over the rim of her glass, her forehead puckering when she pulled her stare away to glance at Ronan with her glass raised. The grizzled man acknowledged her with a head nod.

Finally, she replied, "TMI, Pen."

"Well, you didn't really care about the fact that I met someone." I leaned back in my seat, my ankles instinctually hooking once more. I attempted to drop them, letting them dangle on the bar stool.

"Yeah, because you're *always* meeting someone," she replied with a tight laugh. "That's what you do."

That was what I did. Just like I'd told Dougie, I bored easily. I swapped people in and out, changed up my roster when it felt convenient. But I wasn't inclined to do that this time. I found myself determined to slow down time.

I wanted to tell her it was different, because it... it felt like it was.

Things had changed between Dougie and me lately. Ever since I'd confessed to liking him, despite him not saying it back, it felt there'd been a shift in the gravitational pull, bringing him closer to me. He'd become more brazen with his affection, plodding right up to me in the morning and pinning me against my SUV to kiss me. Any moment I wasn't working or with Raquel, I was with him.

I liked him—more than I'd let on that day in his apartment, more than I'd ever liked anyone before. But it scared me to say those exact words to Raquel because admitting it not only changed the weight of what I felt between Dougie and me, but it risked the dynamic I had with her. I was all she had.

Raquel was important to me. We were closer to sisters than we were best friends. We did practically everything together. Ever since I waltzed into our shared room at Boston University a decade ago, I knew we were going to be best friends.

Even while she stared at me horrified, as if I were a rejected Spice Girls member with my soft pink cardigan tucked into a pleated skirt and shiny kitten-heeled Mary Jane's and curls in my hair. It was a stark contrast to her light denim-blue high-waisted jeans, black spaghetti-strap top with a red, white and black oversized plaid shirt on top, beat-up combat boots, and her then mess of long dark hair tucked under a beanie.

Where Raquel looked like she belonged in the front row of a 90s grunge band show—exactly where I wanted to be in about two hours' time once I ditched the combined 320-lbs of Connecticutian expectations standing behind me with disdain on their faces—I looked like I belonged on the set of the movie *Clueless*.

"*Fucking wonderful. A WASP,*" she complained, not even attempting to modulate her voice. Mother gasped, and Daddy cleared his throat noisily. They weren't accustomed to people saying exactly what they thought. That was frowned upon in Greenwich.

But I loved it. I loved it almost as much as her nasally accent and hard inflection.

I hadn't helped the situation by behaving borderline saccharine, making a show of being excited. My heart thumped, watching her, watching me while remaining transfixed.

I had a role to play still, and I needed her to go along with it for a few minutes more—to get pissed at me, to reassure my parents that there was no universe in which we liked each other.

Her mouth hung open and her hands balled into tight fists at her sides like all it would take to set her off was to put up a Backstreet Boys poster on her side of the room.

"*It's not too late to get you into Yale,*" Mother had whispered.

"*One phone call, Pearl,*" Daddy added, watching Raquel curiously.

Fuck Yale. I was staying at BU. "*I'll be fine,*" I assured them, kissing both of their cheeks politely. "*It'll be good for me to see how the middle-class function.*" That comment had Raquel clenching her molars.

Perfect. I'd make it up to her in a moment. My parents just needed to leave. Satisfied by what they saw, they departed after I promised to make sure I called them.

Mother and Daddy weren't even out of the building before I spun around and sent the Mary Jane's flying with two deft kicks of my feet and popped the buttons on the cardigan open, to show off the Iron Maiden T-shirt underneath. I'd pulled Mother's vintage sterling silver Tiffany & Co flask from my bag, filled with Daddy's whiskey, waving it in Raquel's line of vision. All she did was raise an eyebrow at me.

She didn't trust me, but that was okay. She would. I hoped she liked having fun. I loved having fun, but it had been impossible to get a read on her.

Even though she seemed a little lighter over my hidden attire, there was something about her that still gave me the impression she'd been raised to always be on guard. I wondered why.

She remained silent, staring at me.

I extended the flask to her like an olive branch, a sly and knowing smile tugging on my lips.

She hadn't known it yet, but I knew she was going to be my best friend.

"I'm Penelope. I like Maiden, Marlboros, and muscular men. Not necessarily in that order, but I would take all three at the same time. What's your name?"

Just when I thought she was going to snub me, she accepted the flask with the slightest flash of a smile.

We'd been inseparable ever since.

There were people in life you met that you got gut instincts over. Their existence jolted some dormant part inside of you that set your synapses nuclear. Something that told you there was something within them that set them apart from everyone else.

The same way that instinct had helped me determine that she and I were going to be best friends was also how I knew Dougie was... well, different.

I wished I had another adjective for different.

Which was probably why I was fumbling around for words, feeling closer to a fish out of water, floundering on sand. I had a degree in English literature. Words should have come to me naturally, but I could feel the beads of sweat taking shape on my spine, my insides twisting. "I know, I just…" I broached.

She watched me, her cinnamon stare darkening. She didn't want to hear this. She'd freak. I knew she would.

Raquel and I had a pact. A pact that included abandoning New England for a life filled with adventure, traveling around the world, exploring new cultures, and eventually, planting roots somewhere else. Over the years, I'd showed her real estate listings periodically in California when she came back to my place after a night out. California seemed appealing—tepid weather year-round, the weight of our respective legacies thousands of miles away.

I'd gotten overexcited by the prospect. I'd show her listings for big, sprawling houses with beach views, an office for her to write in, and a gourmet kitchen, even though neither of us cooked, vaulted ceilings and massive swimming pools, a short walk to the beach.

But lately… without her noticing, the listings I'd showed her had changed. Sure, superficially, they looked the same. Six-bedroom homes —more bedrooms than we'd ever need—a huge family room to comfortably host all the parties we'd never have, Mediterranean-styled structures, but… there was one recent addition.

A nursery. Seemingly overnight, I'd been thinking about kids, about starting a family and settling down, my way. With someone I might really love. The idea had come on out of nowhere, but now that it was there, I couldn't seem to get it out.

I was hoping she'd get the hint that maybe my wants had changed, too, but it had gone completely over her head. And now, I felt scared to tell her, because I knew it would change the dynamic between us. She needed me. She needed me just as badly as I needed her. Raquel kept me grounded. Sure, I made the choice to leave my parents' lifestyle behind, but it was Raquel who unknowingly ensured I stuck to it. She was my anchor as often as I was her flotation device.

But what did that look like when I wanted to open my sails and explore uncharted waters?

"You just…?" Raquel pressed for an answer at my extended silence, sounding every bit as unimpressed as she appeared.

I wrinkled my nose, my face splitting into a smile I didn't feel.

"You're right. We're just having fun, it's nothing serious." The lie tasted like the ash from her cigarette she'd stabbed against a brick wall before walking in here. There was just one minor problem. "But would you be up to meeting him?"

"Meeting him? The not-serious guy you're fucking who's hung like a horse?" she questioned, exasperated. She appraised me carefully, chewing on the inside of her cheek. "If you let me order nachos, I'll think about it. I'm still hungry."

The nachos here, much like the fries, sucked. "Food freeloader." It was a joke. We both knew it. I'd buy her the whole goddamn menu if she wanted. She was withering away. I didn't think I'd ever seen her wrists so frail under the cuffs of her denim shirt.

It scared me almost as much as being honest with her about my feelings for Dougie.

Raquel was a columnist at a small-town paper in Eaton. She was an amazing writer, but that paper was sucking the creative energy right out of her. In college, her stories had been gritty, passionate. Now, they were formulaic.

I'd bought her an antique mahogany wood secretary desk for her twenty-fifth birthday nearly three years ago, with delicate gold curlicue. Something to remind her I believed in her, that I knew she could do what she really wanted to do. Raquel should have been an author by now, but she was too afraid to try again after all the rejections she'd received that she kept hidden in the secretary drawer.

We didn't talk about it, but the eternal optimist in me still hoped that someday, she'd try to go after her dreams again.

Raquel stuck her tongue out at me. "You say food freeloader, I say poor girl power move." Poor. I felt like I heard that word a lot lately, like a cognitive bias. Raquel, like Dougie, stretched every dollar she earned. She'd grown up in a rough pocket of South Boston and had seen shit I didn't want to think about, but she got out.

At least, mostly. There were other parts I wished she'd leave behind for good, but the past had a funny way of catching up with her—some of which she invited back in, out of a false sense of safety.

I still tried to remind her she deserved better. Naturally, I'd offered to ask Daddy for a favor to get her a job at the *Boston Globe*. He was friends with the paper's publisher, John W. Henry, but she'd declined. Mother hardly tolerated Raquel, but Daddy pitied her. She got a job at The *Eaton Advocate* instead, which meant any lunch I wasn't riding Dougie, I was with her. Hardly anyone in that town read the paper, but it was a job.

Raquel didn't like handouts. She'd sooner starve herself. But she knew the rule when we went out—I was buying.

She drummed her fingers against the worn edge of the table we were sitting at. "When do you want me to meet him?" she asked, resigned.

It was the cue my phone needed to buzz to life, Dougie's text flashing across the screen.

Just parked. Coming in.

Her eyes shifted from the phone to me. She wasn't even trying to be stealthy. I heard the indifferent sound crawl in her throat.

Was now too soon?

I hadn't said it, but the way she slouched in her seat told me she understood all the same. Raquel studied me with disbelief on her heart-shaped features. She was pretty in one of those Disney-princesses totally-unaware-of-it ways. Her hair was dark brown and short, running a little past her shoulders and bluntly cut at the ends like she'd done it herself. Knowing her, she probably had. She had full brows that were feathery and somewhat untidy, and a smattering of freckles over the bridge of her nose. Her nose was pert and cute on her face, the tip crinkling as though she'd tasted something sour while she waited for me to confirm what she already knew.

I stared at her hopefully. She rolled her eyes, waving me off with concession. "Fine."

Reaching for my phone, I thumbed out a response to Dougie, letting him know where we were sitting in the bar. O'Malley's wasn't huge, but it was easy to get lost in the crowd once the place got busy. A few minutes later, the tiny, fair hairs on my arms rose, detecting his presence.

Raquel shifted uncomfortably in her seat. I smelled him first, the fresh cracked pepper in his aftershave, the subtle woody earthiness enveloping me. Glancing over my shoulder, I watched as he shifted past a group of ornery girls behind us who were hollering a drunken and off-key rendition of Neil Diamond's "Sweet Caroline."

Tourists. Definitely tourists. It was the same shit every time we were here. I'd felt like them once, but Raquel had cut that off quick.

I swallowed the nervous lump in my throat as Dougie's strong, familiar hand cupped my shoulder. He squeezed it awkwardly, like he was unsure of the etiquette, his eyes slipping from me to Raquel.

God, if looks could kill, she would have decapitated him.

Dougie seemed unsure of what to do. We weren't dating. We were sleeping together. While he'd agreed to meet me here, he seemed equally perplexed, too. I liked him. It seemed only natural to introduce him to the other most important person in my life. The one who looked like she was one drink away from throwing an absolute fucking fit.

"Hi," he finally said, extending an open palm to her. "I'm Dougie."

Raquel studied his fingers like each digit was a live bomb waiting to detonate. When she didn't move to accept it, I nudged her with my foot under the table. Basic manners had always escaped her.

She straightened with a sigh, her expression vacant. Finally, she reached out, but rather than accepting his hand, she plucked a French fry from the plate, popping it into her mouth.

What a fucking dick move. She ignored me when I glared at her, her jaw working as she chewed.

"This sweet cherub is Raquel," I said for her.

Dougie dropped his hand, then snorted out a laugh, arousing her attention. "You think that's funny, huh?" she intoned, her distinct accent thickening, ire palpable.

His brows jumped to his hairline, his smile deepening. "Wicked accent. Southie?"

She scoffed, then studied her fingernails. "The Dot." Dorchester.

"But you grew up in Southie," I volunteered. The scary part of Southie, anyway, not the new, gentrified waterfront parts where the condos for young professionals and families were going up.

Raquel's jaw flexed, indicating I'd said too much. "So?" she spat, lifting her eyes. "That's not where I live *now*." She was prickly about where she'd grown up... for reasons. That didn't excuse her from being a brat now. What crawled up her ass today that she couldn't be pleasant for ten minutes?

Before I could try to pacify her, she slid out of her seat. "Where are you going?" I called.

Raquel always ran away when she got irritated.

"The bathroom." I had half a mind to chase after her. I didn't trust her not to climb the pedestal sink and weasel her way out of the tiny window above it. Lord knew she was scrawny enough to fit.

This first-time meeting went differently in my head. I watched her move through the crowd, disappearing through an opening that led into a hallway with the stairs to the bathroom downstairs.

The stool next to me dragged across the dinged hardwood. Dougie settled next to me, his calloused fingers reaching over to tuck my hair behind my ear. "She's a bit of a harpy, huh?"

I tossed him a look, withering in my seat. "I'm kidding," he assured. "Sorry, bad joke."

Even if he was kidding, the comparison was sadly appropriate. "Not always," I offered. "She's just..." I searched for a word, struggling to find the right one. "Protective."

He gently rolled the ends of my hair between his fingers. "I can tell."

"She's had a hard life, okay?" Raquel didn't deserve it at this moment, but I rushed to her defense. I always did. "Her dad and sister died months apart, and her mother is awful, and—"

"Pen, it's alright." He softened, touching my chin. "If she's important to you, she's important to me."

I liked him and hearing him say that about my best friend may as well have been akin to him professing his undying love for me. Raquel was an acquired taste, like Vegemite or something—salty and bitter. But she was important to me, and even if she was harsh, I wanted him to like her, and for her to like him, too.

It was in moments like these where the booming voices around us melted into white noise, and my insides floated in the warmth of his gaze where I thought maybe I was falling in love with him.

The guy who wouldn't even say he liked me back out loud.

The guy who was making me think about starting a family. Ugh.

"She kind of reminds me of Sean," he observed, drumming his fingers against his chin.

"Sean?" My brows snapped together as I tried to see the comparison. They were both grumpy, but...

Dougie nodded. "Both got dealt a bad hand of cards. Their anger and grief mirror one another. They just use it differently." I softened. He was right. I didn't know as much about Sean, but Trina had made me aware he hadn't gone into the family business because he wanted to. It had been done out of necessity.

It was sad, but honorable. He was an asshole with a heart, and Raquel was snarky, but she meant well. Dougie was right. They were alike. I wondered if Raquel and Sean would ever get along... who was I kidding?

Dougie fitted his palm around my cheek, then tilted my head forward so his lips could massage against mine. The nervous knots living in my stomach uncoiled, my heart thumping to life as he deepened the kiss with a groan. I turned in my seat, fitting my hands on his thick thighs and sliding upward.

Dougie broke the kiss after another moment or so, pressing his lips to the tip of my nose. He leaned back in his seat, shifting around, appearing uncomfortable.

"Are you okay?"

He cleared his throat, locking eyes with me and then guided my gaze downward to his crotch.

I laughed, my cheeks heating at the sight of the slight tenting in his pants. "Are you hard right now?"

"I think you underestimate what you do to me, Penny," he said hotly, cocking a thick eyebrow at me. "You're dangerous."

Too dangerous to ask me to be your girlfriend?

Shaking my head, I offered him a smile. I could keep hoping he'd ask... eventually. "I'm going to go check on her," I said. Sliding off the bar stool, I started to walk away when a current of worry zipped through me, making me stop and glance back at him. "Don't mention to her I told you anything about her life. She's extremely private."

"Okay, I won't," he replied, smiling at me. "I'm gonna sit here and think about my ma in her nightgown."

I laughed.

He hunched forward, his elbows finding the table, trying to protect his modesty as his hands clasped together, his expression a combination of pensive and playful. "I'm pretty sure it's illegal to be this hard in public over a kiss, Pen. Or in general."

Well, that was an invitation for me to check for myself. Returning to him, I placed my palm back on his thigh, loving the way he sucked back a breath. His body stiffened as my hand slid upward, fingers outstretched, until I brushed the hardened length contained by the denim, cupping him. His cock kicked in my palm, a suffocated, melodic groan hitting my ears and making my pussy pulse in tandem.

"You have no scruples," he husked, his eyes locked with mine. "Especially in public."

"None," I concurred, giving him a gentle squeeze. "Not with you."

"What am I gonna do with you, huh?" he asked, blanketing my hand with his, gripping.

Make me your girlfriend. I shrugged, retracting my hand. "Guess we'll find out."

I retraced Raquel's steps, darting around people until I found the wood-paneled hallway she'd disappeared through. I took the basement stairs, the scent of mildew and mold hitting my sinuses when I cleared the last step. I shoved the door indicating the women's washroom with both hands.

Raquel was washing her hands at the sink when I burst through the door, the hinges squeaking loudly behind me, colliding with the door stopper. She didn't even startle. I stared at the open stalls, and once I was satisfied it was just us, I glared at her. "So, you *did* actually have to pee."

She frowned at me in the bathroom mirror. "Uh, yeah?"

"What is your deal?"

Her confusion deepened. "Well, I did just have to make two squares of toilet paper stretch—"

"That's not what I meant, Kell," I interrupted, crossing my arms over my chest. "What's your deal with Dougie?"

"My deal with *Dougie*?" She spat out his name like it was a curse, killing the water from the faucet. She shook her hands out, water flinging everywhere.

God, she could be so fucking inconsiderate sometimes. I ripped a paper towel free from the dispenser and handed it to her.

She tore it from my hands with a scoff. "I could have gotten it myself."

I rolled my eyes. "Yes, I know that you're independent and you don't need anyone."

She bared her teeth at me, stepping forward. "What the fuck is your problem?"

"*My* problem?" I demanded, closing the distance between us. "What's *yours*?"

"You just flung him on me, Penelope!" she shouted back, throwing her hands up in the air. "I don't care *who* you do in your free time. You're going to replace him in a couple of weeks, anyway."

I opened my mouth to argue. No, no, I wasn't. I wanted to keep this one.

Why couldn't she see that? Why did I have to spell it out for her in digestible, bite-sized pieces so she wouldn't have an epic meltdown? She was my best friend. Why couldn't she read between the fucking lines?

Who was I kidding? I couldn't even get Dougie to read between the lines.

I stared at the grimy tiled floors. Dirt, bodily fluids, and who knew whatever else caked in the grout. "Kell—"

"What?"

I looked up at her, her unyielding brown eyes hard and her mouth a flat line. "You're my best friend, and he's my—" I stopped myself. He was my what?

She staggered back, her spine hitting the pedestal sink. "You're *what*?" Agitation with the slightest hint of fear laced her query.

I dragged my teeth over my bottom lip, examining her. She looked betrayed. I hadn't said a thing, and I could already feel the shift of change percolating between us. I didn't like it. "He's someone I'm spending a lot of time with," I supplied instead, hating myself just a little for the lie.

Even if it was for her sake.

Raquel sagged with relief, as though what I'd said was any better than just announcing he was my boyfriend. "It's important for me you two get along. We've been seeing each other for a few months now, so."

"So what?"

"So, can you please try to be nice?" I pleaded. "For me?"

"Until you're off that job and you move on to someone new?" The remark stung, anger heating my insides, but I didn't argue this time. At my silence, she gave me her profile, her jaw constricting as she fixed her gaze on the wall. "Fine."

I stepped toward her, opening my arms for her. Raquel pushed off the sink with a sigh, wrapping her arms around me. She smelled like vanilla, citrus and cigarettes—familiar and safe.

But not the scent that made me feel like I was home. "He really is a nice guy," I murmured into her hair.

"A nice guy?" She patted my back sympathetically. "I'm sure he is really nice while you're on your back."

I broke the hug to flick her ear, earning her hoarse laugh. "I prefer being on top."

"Pen," she whined, slinking to the bathroom door. "You're the queen of oversharing."

"You started it," I sang, following her out of the bathroom.

Dougie's head lifted when he saw us approaching him. He tacked a smile on his face—one I was sure he didn't feel as Raquel homed in on him. She flopped onto her bar stool, her stare never leaving his.

This meeting wasn't perfect, but it was a start.

Now, I just had to figure out how to get Dougie to ask me to be his girlfriend, and how to get Raquel to accept that maybe my dream for my future had changed.

I wanted to have my cake and eat it, too.

I just hoped she'd support me and hand me a fork.

Chapter Ten

Penelope

Present

"Hɪ," ᴛʜᴇ ᴠᴏɪᴄᴇᴍᴀɪʟ ʙᴇɢᴀɴ, Rᴀǫᴜᴇʟ'ꜱ ᴠᴏɪᴄᴇ ꜰɪʟᴛᴇʀɪɴɢ ᴛʜʀᴏᴜɢʜ ᴏᴠᴇʀ the patter of rain against the sunroof of my SUV, laced with defeat. *"It's me… again."*

She exhaled, falling silent for a moment. I could easily envision her shoving a hand through her hair, chewing on the inside of her cheek. *"The twins are teething."* Had that much time really passed? Teething already? I swallowed the lump of emotion in my throat, listening to her background noise. The ding of a spoon spinning in what I assumed was a coffee mug resounded from her end. *"I remember when Chris started teething. How he got that low-grade fever, and you gave him children's Tylenol and that lukewarm bath..."* she trailed off.

I had done that. She'd gone to get the children's Tylenol for me because I'd been too worried to leave Chris's side and Dougie had been working.

"I didn't want to call Sean's ma. She makes me feel incompetent most of the time, but I remembered you did that, and I tried it... it helped." Her tentative sigh made my insides hurt. *"I burned a pot yesterday trying to make quinoa... God, the smell. Sean laughed it off, but I think he was a bit miffed I ruined the pot. I'm gonna try again tonight, though..."* she hesitated. *"Uh, I miss you, Pen. I wish I knew what I did that made you this upset."* I heard the heartbreak in the statement. *"Was it because I wore Keds at your wedding?"* She tried for levity, but even that couldn't stimulate a smile.

Nothing really made me smile anymore. It wasn't her. It had never been her.

"Sometimes I think back to when I knew when you were pissed at me. You'd call me on Saturdays for happy hour at O'Malley's without fail." Her voice broke, but she cleared her throat, and continued, *"Remember that shithole?"*

How could I ever forget? *"They had the best fries. I think the secret was their oil. Or Ronan salted everything with cocaine, I don't know."* God, Ronan. I hadn't thought of that grizzled Einstein doppelgänger of a barkeep in forever.

She was wrong about the fries. They were awful—greasy and over-salted to the point my tongue stung. They were bad, but she wasn't.

"I kind of miss it sometimes," she whispered. *"Don't get me wrong, I love my life, and I'm grateful, but I just... I'm nostalgic, I guess."*

Yeah, I knew what she meant. I missed those times, too. The simplicity of it. Going through life believing I owed nothing to anyone, only to myself. Living each moment fully. Finding fun in everything. I wasn't having fun anymore. I couldn't remember the last time I'd lived in the moment, and my anger and guilt gave me tunnel vision.

I bit my bottom lip, catching my reflection in my rearview mirror.

My eyes glistened with unshed tears, the familiar ache swallowing my insides. I was so sick of crying.

Would she still miss me if she knew every horrible thing I'd said about her in the last few months? No, definitely not. Her Southie accent would thicken, and her features would twist before she told me to get fucked and rot.

I was sure of it. I was thinking the universe had punished me proactively, knowing full well the kind of person I truly was underneath the polished surface.

I deserved what I got, what happened to me.

A faint cry echoed in the call's background. *"I have to go,"* she said absently, as though I were on the phone with her. *"Bye, Pen. I love you. Call you tomorrow to let you know how the quinoa saga goes. I'm gonna get it right this time."*

She loved me, and I didn't deserve it. Raquel would call me tomorrow, and the day after that. She was surprisingly tenacious when it counted. She'd fill my phone up with voicemails and texts, photos with her kids' milestones—the kids I'd envied her over. Or photos of a *Pinterest* recipe she attempted to impress her chef husband with and completely bombed.

My best friend, if I could call her that anymore, never wanted to be a mother, and without even trying, she got two.

Two beautiful babies who had Sean's nearly black hair. Their son had his eyes already, but their daughter… her eyes were still blue, nearly erring on the shade of green, just like Raquel's late sister. It seemed fitting, given that was the baby's namesake.

Two babies she'd nearly died delivering.

Shame had kept me away from her. Shame that I'd ever envied her, that I'd ever spoken ill of her. I'd allowed myself to be jealous of her when I'd always had everything, and she'd had nothing until this moment.

I was a horrible person, and the reminder made me feel sick. "You wouldn't love me if you knew, Kell," I whispered, even though she couldn't hear me. "You'd hate me, too."

Hanging up the phone, I stared at the medical office I parked in front of, knowing the answers I desperately needed lived inside of that building. I reached absently for my wedding and engagement ring, needing to twist them both nervously.

But the only thing I found was the subtle indentation where they'd once lived.

Why had I thrown them at him?

That's who I was now. The banshee. The angry wife who threw the word divorce around in fits of anger, and banished her husband from their matrimonial bed, who told him she hated him and whipped her rings at him with all the rage consuming her.

And then, despite our argument yesterday, I had the gall to sit in the SUV he'd refilled the tank for me this morning and cry for him. Cry because I'd sold him a lie.

I wasn't supposed to be this fucked up.

Grabbing my purse from the passenger's seat, I flipped the sun visor down to stare at my reflection in the mirror. Hooking my index fingers, I wiped the tears that had gathered on my bottom lashes away, sniffling.

I hated the person looking back at me. Hated who she had become.

I dug out the compact from my purse, pressing the cushion into the powder and blotting my red nose. Conceding that this was as good as it was going to get, I closed the compact with defeat, pulled my keys from the ignition, and opened my car door. Slinging my purse over my shoulder, I held my arm above my head to protect myself from the thick bullets of rain that fell from the sky relentlessly, my heeled ankle boots clicking urgently across the asphalt parking lot.

The effortless automatic doors glided open, the artificial heat enveloping me as I brushed the rain from my hair and walked over to the elevators, pressing the up button. I stepped back, watching the marker as it descended from the fourth floor, down to the ground floor.

The doors from the cab opened, and I sucked back a pained breath.

I would never get used to seeing expecting mothers.

I'd been them once.

The woman couldn't have been any older than me, her smile kind as her eyes found mine. Her round belly exited the elevator before she did, her jacket too small to close around her middle as she waddled past me.

That could have been me again.

The elevator doors pinged, the doors rolling shut, pulling me out of the abyss of my mind. I lurched forward, clapping the edge of the closing doors to stop them. The bell chimed once more; the doors sliding open. Stepping inside of the cab, I hit the button for the fourth floor, the same floor the woman had just come from.

My heart hammered in my ears as the doors and the cab began its ascent. I'd been to dozens of doctors' appointments over the past few months, in desperate need of an explanation for what had gone wrong.

I was young. I had a clean bill of health.

It shouldn't have happened.

Stepping out of the cab when I got to the fourth floor, the laminate hardwood absorbed my footfalls as I hastened toward the doctor's office.

I knew what awaited me on the other side, and I knew I couldn't cry.

Taking a fortifying breath that didn't quite reach my lungs, I turned the knob. I ignored the weight of curious eyes on me, or the way their eyes trailed over my frame.

Remember who you are, Penelope.

I elongated my neck, my spine straightening while I kept my gaze trained on the receptionist's desk, stopping when I arrived at my destination.

Digging into my purse for my wallet, I fished out my insurance card. I slid it across the counter tentatively. "Hello, I'm Penelope Cullimore. I'm here for my two o'clock with Doctor Correia."

The receptionist's knowing gaze flashed from the monitor to me, but I caught it.

Pity. I was the one who'd called on a near-weekly basis, trying to get an appointment.

Do not cry.

She accepted the card, then fiddled with her computer mouse, her fingers moving across the keyboard as she logged the details from my insurance card. "Are you still at five-eighteen Riverside Avenue?"

"Yes, but..." I paused, slouching my shoulders. "Could you email me the invoice?"

She looked baffled, her eyebrows climbing to her hairline as she contemplated my request. Every place had different policies, and before, I'd been able to intercept the mail. But with Dougie at home now, I didn't trust that he wouldn't get to the mail before I did.

After another moment, she nodded. "Sure, not a problem." I gave her my email address and confirmed the copay would be added to the invoice. We had one shared credit card, but our other cards were in our own names, so he'd never know I'd been here.

"Please take a seat. The nurse will come and get you shortly."

I nodded, turned around and found a seat in the room's corner, far away from everyone else. Settling into the chair, I reasoned with myself to keep breathing, to fight through the burst of nausea twisting my insides as anticipatory anxiety made my heart beat in my ears.

My body jolted every time a nurse appeared, calling another name, until the room emptied.

And then, finally, "Penelope?"

Ripping my stare from the floor, I found the soft brown eyes of a nurse in bright pink scrubs. I nodded, rising to my feet. I followed her on trembling legs down a narrow hallway, the soft and steady modulated tones filling the silence.

The nurse opened the door at the end of the hallway, holding out a hand. "Doctor Correia will be with you in a moment."

When the door closed, I sunk into a chair against the wall, my body melding with the worn-in grooves. How many other women had sat here before me? How many of them had their dreams shattered or had their hope renewed?

After a few minutes, there was a gentle knock on the door before the knob turned. Doctor Elizabeth Correia couldn't have been over forty. Her curly black hair spilled loosely over her shoulders, a fitted black dress clinging to her soft curves, deepening her warm olive complexion. She was an OB-GYN and the best in the state. I'd been trying to get in to see her for months.

"Hi, Penelope," she greeted, offering me a smile as she entered the room, a file clutched in her hand. "How are you?"

I attempted to return her smile. "I'm fine," I lied. "And you?"

"I'm good." She shut the door behind her, her kitten heels clipping the laminate wood floors as she moved for the seat. Settling herself in a desk chair, she held up the file. "So, I've taken the time to review your files sent over by Doctor Hammond."

Doctor Hammond was my OB-GYN back in Fall River. I wasn't satisfied with his feedback, or the obstetrician I'd seen when I was expecting Christopher, and wanted a third opinion.

There was something Doctor Correia already wasn't saying. I felt it swelling in the air. I shifted nervously under her study.

Finally, she reached for a pad of paper on a clipboard and a pen. "What brings you to me today?"

I mean, wasn't that obvious? Did I have to say the words aloud? I pressed my thumb against my racing pulse in my wrist, my head sloping forward. "I can't seem to get pregnant," I explained with a polite laugh.

When I lifted my eyes, I found Doctor Correia nodding her head empathetically, her pen scratching against the pad of paper propped against her thigh on a clipboard. "When was the last time you ovulated?"

I crossed my legs at the ankles. "I'm ovulating now."

She brightened. "That's good." The pen worked again. "And your periods are consistent?"

"Every twenty-one days."

She gestured her understanding once more, then extended a hand to the open file on her desk. She flipped through the sheets, her finger tracing against a printout. "There's definitely no remaining hCG traces in your blood work." She rocked her mouth from side to side with thought. There wouldn't be. I'd had that miscarriage months ago. "Your ultrasound from two months ago looked clean, and your urine sample also tested fine." She pursed her lips, drumming her blunt fingernails against the pad of paper, thinking. "When was the last time you were sexually active?"

Silence.

My hands clenched against my thighs, my heart stuttering. I mean, of course, that part was a criterion if I… I mean, I wasn't stupid. I was more than aware of what it took to get pregnant. I was just… afraid to even try again.

Hell, I couldn't even be honest with Dougie about it at all. I clenched my teeth together, the backs of my eyes stinging.

I felt her eyes on me. They felt invasive. "Penelope?"

"January." I was speculating, anyway.

No, it was then. That was the night we'd made the baby I'd lost.

I shivered, recalling the January chill that had been present that night. The traveling air circulating the room when our last guest departed from our annual New Year's party. The last guest wasn't even out of the driveway yet when Dougie had hiked my dress up around my waist and puddled my panties at my ankles.

"I've thought about this all night," he'd murmured. After unsheathing his cock, he'd wrapped my legs around his waist and fucked me against the front door hard enough that I bruised. I loved every minute of it.

He was impulsive when he was drunk, and I liked it. Dougie didn't think so much about treating me like I was a fragile piece of porcelain, something to nurture and dote on. He let the primal side of his brain take over and drive.

Strong, potent, mine. The cold wood of the door bit into my skin with each of his punitive thrusts, his hot breath falling across my face as he whispered sweet nothings to me.

Unbeknownst to either of us, things were on the trajectory of change after that night.

In the worst way possible.

We got more intense with one another, borderline hostile, while the wedding we hadn't wanted grew out of control. I felt myself forgetting who I was and the life I'd left behind for the one that I'd chosen.

But now, sometimes, when I was lonely, when I caught a whiff of his bodywash in the air hours after he'd left for work or heard the bass of his voice somewhere in the house—I could still feel him there inside of me, loving me, as familiar as the unescapable hollow ache in my chest.

"Not in a while," I admitted, shame burning my cheeks. "I'm... I'm a little nervous to try again."

I dragged my unwilling eyes to Doctor Correia's. Doctors were supposed to remain impartial, but I caught the slightest tic in her upper lip, her gaze falling to my hand. Even without the rings on, it was obvious that something had once lived there with the way the finger dipped near the knuckle.

Getting pregnant, wanting to get pregnant, when my marriage was in shambles, was the last thing I should have been thinking about right now.

But it was the only thing I could concentrate on to try to make amends for what I'd done.

"I see." She tossed the pad to her desk, exhaling. "Your feelings are valid, Penelope." Crossing one lean leg over the other, her pantyhose chafed when she shifted, her lips curling ever so slightly with an indulgent and polite smile.

But I heard what went unsaid. My feelings were valid, but they didn't warrant taking an appointment from someone who actually needed it. We weren't even trying to have a baby, what was I doing here?

"I know I don't need to explain how conception works to you, so I'll spare you." Her attempt at a joke almost made me smile. Almost. "So, let's start here. If you were to try to conceive again, what would your realistic timeline look like?"

"As soon as possible."

She faltered for a moment, the urgency in my voice throwing her. Her tone grew sterile. "A *realistic* timeline." Yeah, I'd heard her the first time.

I wrung my hands together, tilting my head downward. "I…" God, why couldn't I get the words out? Why was this so fucking hard?

My chin trembled, my emotions betraying me as the tears pricked. I hated this part. I hated I was a leaky faucet, always prepared to cry. They splattered against my knuckles, and it took everything in me to not burst out another curse.

"Penelope." She cooed my name, and I hated it. I didn't want her pity. I'd gotten what I'd deserved after everything. "I know this is extremely difficult, but I want to stress that this is common. And not your fault."

Not my fault.

It wasn't my fault.

But it was my fault, too. It was me who hadn't wanted to be pregnant. I was so annoyed that I was, that I'd resented the inconvenience, the timing. I was mad at Dougie, as though the responsibility fell on his shoulders alone. It had been me who wanted to rely solely on the pill. It had been me who practically forbade him from using condoms. I was too trusting and had learned nothing from our first surprise.

The universe had punished me for my lack of gratitude. My body failed me in the ultimate way, and I drove my husband away, too.

How did I fix it? How did I become the person I once was? Wasn't that why I wanted to get pregnant again? To try to correct my fuckup?

I snatched my bottom lip between my teeth, willing the damn thing to stop quaking. "Conceiving after a miscarriage induces a lot of anxiety in couples," Dr. Correia said, keeping her tone gentle. "And for some, a loss can cause depression."

Was that what I was? Depressed? Did a single word encompass everything I felt? I took a laborious breath, extending a hand blindly toward the tissue box I'd spotted when I'd entered her office.

Induces a lot of anxiety in couples.

Couples. A union. A duo. A collective unit.

What happened when your husband didn't know?

I couldn't tell him.

"It sounds like, and feel free to correct me," she tested, "that there is a lot of lingering worry surrounding intimacy."

"My husband doesn't know," I confessed, running the tissue under my eyes. "He doesn't know that I..."

Why hadn't I just told him? Why was I so ashamed for him to see me that way? He'd found me in the most vulnerable state I'd ever been in with him.

Losing our child, witnessing firsthand how imperfect I was, it killed me.

And I, in turn, killed him. If we'd already been on rocky grounds before that night, I may as well have given him a GPS that drove us straight off a fucking cliff.

I shoved him into her waiting arms, didn't I?

What had I expected?

"Oh." This time, Doctor Correia didn't mask her judgment. There it was, the red herring.

You didn't tell your husband you were expecting, or that you lost a baby? And now you were wasting time and taking an appointment from someone who needed it, to have the science of procreation explained to you?

What was wrong with me?

Plenty of things. I hadn't wanted the baby, had done everything to mask it. It was a later problem for us. Something to deal with after the wedding. Something that I believed would act as a vehicle to return us to the people we were when I was good and goddamn ready for us to deal with it because we'd always wanted a big family.

I hadn't even told Raquel.

Doctor Correia tried a different angle. "Have you considered speaking with someone?"

I nodded absently.

I had a therapist, Henry, with an office not too far from here in Back Bay, who used to keep fake African violets on his windowsill.

Or I should say I had a therapist.

I'd started seeing him when I moved to the city. He'd been nice, but boring and predictable because he didn't challenge me. It was another fucked-up marriage, in a way. It had grown stale, and it felt as though he'd kept me stuck.

But maybe that was my fault, too. I'd gotten comfortable telling Henry what he wanted me to say, and I stopped going to the appointments entirely after I miscarried, because I couldn't be honest with him the way I needed to be.

Never mind my terror over the possibility of running into *her* there when I learned we unknowingly shared a therapist.

All of it just further justified my need to shut down, and simultaneously warped me into this person I didn't recognize, someone who scared me.

I got bitter, resentful.

Hateful.

And now I was just too embarrassed to admit that I was struggling.

So maybe she was right. Maybe I was depressed.

Doctor Correia cleared her throat, arousing my attention. "And have you discussed with them the intention to tell your husband—"

"No, he can't know." Widening my eyes in horror, I straightened in my seat, panting out a breath.

"Penelope." She folded her hands together neatly.

I decided I didn't like it when she said my name. The repetition of it seemed to follow up with something I didn't want to hear.

"You've had one successful pregnancy already. Neither Doctor Hammond, Doctor Chong before him, nor I, can see anything wrong with your blood work, and your test results are perfect. You don't need me right now." Her face softened. But I did need her. I needed someone. "There are reasonable grounds that demonstrate you *can* get pregnant," she continued. "But I think perhaps we need to shift your order of operation here and focus on mending any residual issues surrounding intimacy first before we set our sights on you conceiving again. You should speak to a professional about this."

Fuck her. "That's none of your business." Her head snapped back at my outburst, the air growing frigid. I dropped the prim-and-proper act. "My marriage with my husband is none of your business."

"I never said anything about your marriage," she agreed flatly, then tucked her hair behind her ears, clearing her throat.

Shame stung my skin. No, she hadn't said anything about my marriage, but I had.

"However, procreation starts with intimacy," she continued, her features softening.

I scoffed at the obvious statement. No shit. I knew I had to have sex with my husband, the one I'd dismissed from our bed and banished to the guest bedroom.

So why did the repressed urge to scream exist all the same?

"I'm truly very sorry. Sometimes, we just don't know why miscarriages happen. They're common in fifteen percent of healthy individuals under thirty-five."

I knew miscarriages happened, but they were stories you heard about—not something you ever expected for yourself.

"Having a healthy pregnancy in the future starts with maintaining healthy bonds and taking care of our mental health, too."

I wasn't even listening anymore. She made it all sound so fucking simple. Maintain healthy bonds, have sex with your husband, acknowledge that shit happened.

But shit hadn't just happened. I'd happened.

My stomach lurched, my head spinning.

Just fuck your husband, Pen. No big deal. You've done it plenty of times.

Did I even know how to be intimate with him anymore? Could I let him touch me without seeing contrived images of him with her?

"Let's come up with a plan," she said, interrupting my thoughts. "We'll call it a conception strategy."

I looked at her, feeling hollowed out and numb. My head moved automatically with a nod. Doctor Correia spoke, laying out the things I —we, Dougie and me—could do before we'd consider medical intervention.

But I knew she was indulging me.

It was simple, really.

If I wanted to get pregnant again, I had to have sex. There was no test, no scan, no procedure that was going to be more effective than that.

I had to have sex with my husband and not see images of him with her.

And I was going to.

Tonight.

Chapter Eleven

Dougie

Three years ago...

"Do you wanna go back to my place or yours?" I asked casually, watching as she skipped down the canned goods and jarred sauces aisle, her heels skidding to a halt in front of the tomato sauces.

Her gaze moved from the canned sauces to me. Penelope inclined her head to the right, her lips lifting into a smile. "Are you inviting me over?"

It wasn't the first time I'd done it, but her face always lit up when I did, because it was the one place where she was the only person I'd allowed in. Once the temperature evened out and the nights became a little more bearable, I'd started inviting her over. I knew it was important to her to be in my space, and truthfully, even though my space felt inadequate for someone like her, I enjoyed seeing her futz around my place in one of my T-shirts or waking up in my bed.

"I mean, if you want," I added, watching as she shifted closer to me, something unintelligible flashing in her eyes. "We don't have to. You have all of your stuff at your place, and—" She silenced me with her index finger pressed against my lips.

"I would love to," Penelope replied, moving her finger out of the way so she could feather her lips against mine. I sagged with relief, twining my arm around her waist.

God, she made this easy, yet hard at the same time. All I really wanted was to ask her to be mine. Did she like me enough to change her rules?

"Now, do you want pesto or Alfredo?" she questioned against my mouth. "I'm not feeling tomato sauce tonight."

I huffed out a laugh as she withdrew, shooting me a wink. We were slogging our way through every single premade sauce in the state. It was the only thing she could cook, and I didn't have the heart to tell her she tended to overcook the pasta.

She was cute in the kitchen, and I'd eat whatever she made. This was our routine. We'd go to the store after work a few nights a week. I'd watch her hem and haw over which sauce to get, which pasta noodle to try, her heels clicking across the floors. She'd search the space behind her blindly, seeking my hand. And when she found it, she'd pull me to her, then press herself against my side, her head finding my shoulder.

I liked it. I liked her clinging to me, touching me, wanting me.

But I was afraid that I was becoming too used to this, too comfortable.

"Pesto," I suggested.

"Pesto," she parroted, nodding her head. "I had the most incredible pesto in Genoa." I lifted a brow. Genoa? She filled in the blank. "It's in Italy."

I nodded my head. I'd take her word for it. Furthest I'd been out of the state was Cranston, Rhode Island, for one of those haunted house attractions.

She made a little noise, an unexpected blush hitting her cheeks. "What?" I asked.

"Nothing." Pen shook her head.

She wasn't getting off that easily. I tickled her sides, her giggle hitting my ears as I pulled her against me. "Tell me," I demanded in a growl against the shell of her ear.

"I was just thinking that I'd like to go there with you. Italy, I mean." She nursed her bottom lip, leaning her head back against my chest to regard me. "It's a beautiful country, and romantic, and…" she trailed off, the lump moving in her swan-like neck.

"And they've got pasta," I teased. I'd like to go to Italy with her, too. No idea when the hell I'd ever be able to afford it, but it was a nice thought. I smiled at her rather than bursting her bubble, pressing a kiss to her forehead and releasing her. "What brand of pesto do you want to try?"

She was quiet behind me. "It doesn't matter, does it?"

"Not really," I agreed, reaching for a simple jar with a blue label on it that sounded Italian-ish.

"Not the stupid pesto, Dougie," she huffed out. "You and me."

Huh? I straightened and turned around. She balled her hands into tight fists at her sides, her flinty stare riveted to mine. "What do you mean?"

"I like you," she announced. "I've introduced you to my best friend. I'm talking about wanting to travel with you, and I have no idea how *you* feel about *me*. At all."

I sagged. Oh. I slipped my hands into my pockets, creating a little distance between us.

She was pissed, and I mean, rightfully so. I hadn't been upfront with her. Of course, I liked her. I liked her a fuck ton. I was just trying to follow her rules.

"I like you, too," I replied, watching as she stiffened. "Is that what you needed to hear?"

She jerked her head away, crossing her arms over her chest. "Not if you don't mean it."

I stepped back into her space. "Penelope." I touched the underside of her chin, guiding her eyes to mine. "How could I not like you?"

Her brows furrowed with frustration, her gaze growing petulant. "I've never had to work so hard with a guy before."

"I don't want you to work hard. I'm just letting you drive."

"Why can't you drive?" she asked.

"Because you set the ground rules."

Her forehead puckered with her frustration. "You told me you don't play games."

"This isn't a game to me, Penny," I murmured, brushing my knuckles over the arches of her cheek. She had the softest skin, especially under my cracked and calloused hands. Didn't she see I didn't want to just have fun with her anymore? "I'm giving you exactly what you asked for. Playing a game with you would be me making myself scarce and unavailable, calling you only when I wanted to fuck you. I'm not that guy. I'm just following your lead."

"Well, what if I changed my mind?" she asked.

Jesus. I dropped my hand to my side, trying to get an assessment of what she was implying. Changed her mind in the sense of the novelty had worn off with me? No, that couldn't be it.

But she couldn't be asking me…

Pen reached for my hand, clutching it in both of hers. "I just mean, what if… what if…?" she lifted her eyes shyly, the fluorescent lighting from the harsh artificial bulbs above us creating a glow in her Atlantic-blue eyes. What if what? "Do you want kids?"

I barked out a laugh, my face splitting into a shit-eating grin. "What the fuck, Pen?" That had not been what I thought she was going to say. Why was she asking me that?

"Be serious!" she demanded, stomping her foot playfully, her ire slipping to an uncontrollable smile.

"I *am* being serious," I replied, cocking an eyebrow at her. "We're in a grocery store debating Alfredo over pesto sauce, and now you want to know if I want kids?"

"Well, do you?"

"Do *you*?"

"You can't answer a question with a question."

"I think I just did."

"You're an asshole, Dougie," she groused.

I winked, reminding her, "Only sometimes."

She rolled her eyes, giving me her back as she plucked the jar I'd looked at from the shelf.

Not gonna lie, I was kind of antagonizing her on purpose. Pen was hot when she got pissed, and it set every nerve ending in my body on fire. Her frame stiffened when I wrapped my arms around her waist again, my chin resting against her shoulder, as my nose traced her ear. Her scent was strongest right under her earlobe, the sweetness of peach and the potent spice of ginger layered with Chanel No. 5. She released a soft sigh, leaning into me unwillingly.

"Yes, I want kids," I murmured, for whatever the answer was worth. "I want a house in the 'burbs. I want a lawn I bitch and complain about having to maintain every week because the grass grows too fast, and the weeds are a real bitch." My hands pressed against her thighs, her ass backing against my stirring cock. Even in a grocery store, she made me insatiable. My gaze heated, observing her profile as her lips parted. Thank God this place was dead for a Wednesday at seven in the evening. "And a wife I can't keep my hands off of." She sucked back a breath, giving me her rapt attention as I laid out my fantasy. "I want vacations in Italy, and family trips to Disney. A dog who gives a Dyson vacuum a wicked hard-on." I let her go just as I heard the squeaky wheels of a shopping cart enter the aisle we were in—well, the store was mostly empty. I watched Pen wobble on her heels as she righted her clothes. "And I want chickens."

Her head snapped back, confusion flooding her face when she whipped around on her heel. "What?"

"Backyard chickens."

"Chickens?" she repeated, planting her hands on her waist.

I shrugged. "Fresh eggs, a six a.m. alarm clock, you know the whole cock-a-doodle-do bullshit."

"Only roosters caw at sunrise," she informed me, trying hard not to smile.

"Same shit." I laughed. "Why are you asking me this?"

"I don't know," Pen confessed. "Just curious, I guess."

"What about you?"

She touched my bicep, her teeth snatching up her bottom lip once more. Pen stared down at the pesto sauce in her hand, her thumb running over the matte label. "I don't think I want pesto. Can we have just plain tomato sauce?"

So, she was dodging me now?

"Whatever you want." She placed the jar back in its place, moving back down the aisle. She stopped in front of the jarred tomato sauces, her eyes scrutinizing the organic low-sodium options—never would have thought there were so many options.

Pen's eyes bounced between the variety, her jaw flexing a little, and I just stared.

She had won the genetic lottery—ball-achingly banging body she adorned with skinny jeans and T-shirts for bands she actually listened to and expensive footwear. Her style was grungy and girly at the same time. I loved her high cheekbones and made-up eyes that made her ocean blues stand out.

And her heart of pure fucking gold.

We'd done this shopping experience two dozen times. Two dozen times we'd flitted around Whole Foods, mulling over pasta and sauce options. I'd watched her just like this, thought about her in ways I shouldn't.

Ways that guaranteed I'd get hurt.

Because I wasn't the guy that Penelope got forever with. I was a footnote. A pit stop. A guy she remembered on her daughter's wedding day when a waiter who looked a whole lot like me handed her a champagne flute and the tips of her fingers brushed his. She'd remember my calluses tracing every dip of her body and inch of her skin, committing her to memory.

'Cause assholes from Fall River didn't get to marry girls like her. That was just the reality, as certain as paying taxes and death.

But I wished I could. I wished I could plop her into my fantasy, and we could live out that life. It made my chest hurt, and I fought the urge to knead the ache away as she propped the tip of her boot against the floors and hummed in thought.

I'd have to let her go someday.

Her hand extended behind her again, her recently manicured

fingers flitting incessantly in search of mine. I rushed to accept it with the eager tenacity of a kid because Pen made me giddy.

She grinned at me over her shoulder, flashing her pretty and even white teeth. When Pen smiled, she meant it. She smiled like she did everything else, with her whole heart in it.

So maybe it didn't matter that I could never give her everything she deserved. Maybe I could still be enough. We were as organic and natural as the food in this store. Maybe the way her fingers scissored with mine and the way she made my heart thump was enough to make me ask someday.

Someday, but not now.

Not now.

Not—"Do you wanna be my girlfriend?"

My breath snagged in my lungs until it stung. What the fuck had I just asked?

Pen dropped my hand. The extremity felt like a thousand pounds when it hit my thigh.

Yep, I'd fucked this up. I'd misinterpreted what she'd said, or the conversation on backyard chickens had completely thrown her. I didn't really *need* backyard chickens, but it was legal, and it seemed interesting and…

Had I asked her to be my girlfriend in a fucking Whole Foods of all places? I groaned inwardly. I'd misjudged the mood. Maybe she'd been asking if I wanted kids, so she knew not to continue to waste my time. She could like me, and we could still not be on the same page. I always knew that we were racing against the tiny granules of sand in an hourglass. We had an expiration date. We were almost wrapped up with the project at the house. We were weeks away from the first day of fall, and before I knew it, the house would be sold, and Pen and I would part ways.

I hated it. I hated I was gonna lose her and not just because of our socioeconomic backgrounds or the admission of my stupid fantasy. I'd gone and done something stupid again and fallen for another woman who told me ever so fucking clearly while she was eating a salad that she only wanted me for my cock, nothing more nothing less.

I'd take, "Who's a fucking idiot for eight-hundred, Alex Trebek."

Pen stepped closer to me, her arms twining around my neck. My heart threatened to rip free from its cage.

Wait, what?

Her soft lips caressed against mine, then she whispered the best thing I'd ever heard. "Holy shit, I thought you'd *never* ask."

Huh? A buzzing entered my ears as I processed what she'd said. That wasn't a no. That... I let out a throaty laugh, my insides warming. "Is that a yes?"

She mirrored my smile, dropped her eyelids and slanted her lips over mine. "No fucking duh, Dougie."

Chapter Twelve

Dougie

Present

THE COMMERCIAL FOR AUTHENTIC ITALIAN TOMATO SAUCE PLAYED ON THE muted television. A tired happy family, buzzing around hot, individual servings of carefully portioned pasta. The television's emitted blue light filled the dark room, the flashing depiction of ingredients, spouting words like "freshest" and "sustainable." They skipped out on rhyming off what I knew was probably half a dozen preservatives and a shit ton of sodium because no one liked to think about the shit that could kill you slowly.

The family offered a nice touch that felt closer to a hard kick to the balls. And in case you cared, I didn't think the sauce was authentic, but it was nice marketing.

Then again, I'd also never been to Italy, so what the fuck did I know about authenticity?

Not a lot.

We were supposed to go to Italy on our honeymoon. Eat authentic pesto, just like she'd told me about that day. Our luggage was still packed in the closet. Our passports and flight tickets tucked in a safe in the office alongside our itinerary, untouched.

But Penelope had gotten sick. Really fucking sick.

I absently reached for my beer bottle on the coffee table, bringing it to my lips. It had gone warm. I'd opened it over two hours ago, after I'd heard her go to bed. I'd slipped out of the guest room and came down here in search of a distraction.

She hadn't said a word to me since yesterday, and I had no idea how her "doctor appointment" went. At a minimum, she could have left Chris with me, but she was determined to drive me crazy by isolating me, and getting my ma involved to help with the ruse.

My eyes dropped to her rings I'd placed next to the coaster on the coffee table. I wasn't sure why I felt the need to carry them around like some act of contrition. Maybe I believed that if I did it enough, I'd finally accept that my marriage was over, that she was attempting to deceive me with divorce lawyer appointments under the disguise of a doctor appointment.

My eyes burned.

It was my fault. I'd done this.

I didn't get to cry about shit, but I wished she'd just be honest with me. It would be nice if we could stop lying to one another, if not for our sake, then for Chris's. I saw the writing on the wall. I knew where we were headed, and I didn't... I didn't want us to be one of those divorced couples who put their kid in the middle. I didn't want him to grow up with that kind of representation of what a relationship looked like.

He needed to know that I loved his ma. I'd always love his ma, even if she fucking hated my guts. I'd teach him some day—when he was old enough to understand what not to do in a marriage—what keeping your vows really meant.

He could decide for himself whether he thought his old man knew what the hell he was talking about or not.

I took in a shuddering breath to calm myself, then tipped the dregs of the bottle down my gullet. I wasn't tired. This time last week, I would have just been coming home from work, bone-tired, mentally and physically exhausted, ready to just collapse into bed.

But there wasn't enough to overexert me the way I needed. Now, I just had my thoughts, and they wouldn't stop.

They. Wouldn't. Fucking. Stop.

My head dropped against the back of the couch. I needed to talk to my ma. I'd been avoiding this conversation, because I knew that once she found out what I'd done to bring us to this point, she'd kill me. And if she didn't kill me, the crushing weight of her disappointment would instead.

And then that would cause further complications between her and Connie, Sean's ma. Those two were an unlikely duo who did practically everything together now. For a long time, Connie couldn't stand my ma, but when her husband died—everything changed.

Not just for her, but for her kids.

For me.

I picked at the label on the beer bottle. It used to piss me off when Sean would peel them off, leaving soggy little piles on the table, but now that my thumb was digging at the soiled adhesive, I realized it was kind of meditative.

Soft footsteps moving along the stairwell drew my attention. Pen's shadowed silhouette danced on the wall until I caught sight of her bare legs first, a tight breath leaving my nose. The silk baby-blue nightgown hit her just above the knees, clinging to the dip in her waist.

Nah, it wasn't baby blue. What had she called it… *azure*? I remembered when she brought it home, dumped the contents of her shopping bag on the kitchen table to show me, and then frantically ripped off the price tag before I could see it.

Not that I would have cared how Pen spent her money, but she was always determined to foster the illusion that she wasn't materialistic. She just enjoyed nice things.

Like three-hundred-and fifteen-dollar nightdresses from La Perla. I gave her credit for trying, but her aim was shit. She'd totally overshot the garbage can, and I found the tag a few hours later.

She hadn't worn the nightgown in months, but it was nice to see her in it again even if it wasn't for me. Her hair was damp against the thin straps, the scent of her peach and ginger shampoo hitting me as she cleared the last step. Pen folded her arms over her chest to mask the way her nipples had pebbled under the cool draft on the main floor as she approached the edge of the couch, the muscle in her jaw tight as she stared at the television. I should turn up the heat. She was cold.

I was watching a recap of… honestly, I didn't know. ESPN was on, but I wasn't paying attention. Which made me question what was she doing up?

She remained motionless, silent. Her body language explaining what she wasn't saying—my presence was an inconvenience. "Sorry, did you want it?" I asked, finally sitting up and gesturing to the remote. "I, uh, recorded *New Girl* for you."

Because short of walking on glass barefoot just to make you happy again—and honestly, maybe I would, given the circumstances—I'd do anything for you.

Pen loved sitcoms, good or bad, and I'd always made sure they were recorded for her.

"Oh," she replied, still unwilling to look my way, her concentration pinned to the television. "Thanks, I'll watch it tomorrow."

When she said nothing else and didn't move to sit down, I reached for the television remote, the screen growing dark at the push of a button. My insides twisted as I stood up, guilt shredding me.

How could I have ever done that to her? After everything, why had I allowed myself the moment of weakness.

I kept my eyes cast downward, shifting by her. "'Night."

I could list off all the ways I'd fucked us up from the prison of the guest room. Then I could fall asleep to the fantasy life I'd painted for Pen and myself a long time ago.

Sometimes, I wondered if she really regretted saying yes like she said she did. If she regretted agreeing to being mine. She'd ended up exactly where she would have had she married one of the polo-wearing pricks her parents had wanted her to end up with.

Just keep going, asshole. Stairs, shower, bed, then get up and do it all over again.

Pen's warm, delicate hand attempted to envelop my wrist, making my body tense.

Dropping my eyes to where she held me, my heart nearly ripped through my chest. Slowly, I lifted my gaze to hers.

Her throat bobbed with a swallow, her eyes determined. "You don't have to leave."

She was touching me, and just like that, every hair on my body stood upright, goosebumps breaking out across my skin, every nerve ending ablaze.

When the fuck had she touched me last? Intentionally, and not because cameras were going off, and we found ourselves surrounded by hundreds of people we hardly knew at our wedding.

I exhaled sharply, the gesture burdening me with more thoughts than I could process. Every receptor in my body went nuclear as hope swirled more rapidly.

She touched me. Penelope touched *me*.

"Come sit down." In the darkened room with the soft glow of moonlight pouring in through our living room window, I caught the nervous shift in her throat once more. She tugged on my hand, my legs following her willingly, because even if she would never forgive me for what I'd contemplated doing, I really would do anything she asked me to.

I followed her easily as she rounded the sectional, then settled in her respective spot on the left side, while I took the middle cushion. My aching hands fell in my lap, desperate to brush her damp hair out of her face as her chin sloped downward. The thick silence filled our lungs, enough to choke us both. She brought her knees under her, shifting a little to face me.

Then she did something unexpected.

She fitted my heavy hand around her breast, and I froze.

Her chest heaved, her obvious trepidation falling over her as my mind struggled to process what was happening. I just kept my hand trained there, feeling the hardened point of her nipple under the expensive silk. I wanted desperately for her to just look at me.

When I did nothing, the arches on her face etched with uneasiness.

I drew my hand back.

Pen lifted her chin. Her eyes held my gaze as she pulled the straps of her nightgown over her arms in a way that seemed too well-rehearsed. I didn't want to look. I wanted to revel that this was the longest she'd looked at me in months, but...

My head buzzed, and my throat thickened. Pen reached for my hand once more, placing it against her exposed breast. Soft, she was so fucking soft, and I was fucked. My cock kicked in my sweats, heat licking its way down my abdomen and settling in my aching balls.

"What are you doing, Penelope?"

"Trying to get you to touch me," she whispered, placing her hand over mine and squeezing, the tight pearl of her nipple brushing my palm. Yeah, she'd made that part perfectly clear—but why?

"I'm confused." How could something so normal feel so foreign? This was my wife. My wife, my life partner, the mother of my son, yet she felt like a stranger. She'd thrown her rings at me yesterday.

She told me she hated me.

What the hell was she doing now? Seducing me?

Had this been the advice of her lawyer because it was going to be too expensive? I couldn't even remember the details of our prenuptial agreement. I'd hastily signed it after...

After someone else's recommended amendments.

I wish I'd never gone to her office. I should have just signed the first draft of the prenup and accepted being a penniless idiot with nothing tangible to his name, because Pen's love alone had been priceless.

She shifted on the couch, draping herself in my lap. I sucked back a breath as she leaned forward, her breasts brushing against my face as her hands settled in my hair.

God, she felt good. Too good.

Her warm breath fell across me, making the hairs on my arms rise. The roll of her hips across the rigid tenting in my pants felt uncoordinated, the groan leaving me unwillingly as my body came back online after a long hibernation. "Penelope, stop."

"No," she exhaled, bearing down on me.

Who was I fucking kidding? My hands slid to her waist, rolling the silk nightgown around my fists, and I tugged upward to watch. Nothing. She had nothing underneath. The visual of her grinding against me sent more blood to my engorged cock.

I didn't know why this was happening now, this way, but I could...

"Penny." My head fell back, my hands pawing at the subtle curve of her ass, driving her harder against me. The heat from her core extracted every thought from my head, every argument I had, every answer I desired.

I could get my answers later. My wife wanted me. After everything, she still wanted me. Releasing her ass to cup her face, I tensed when I leaned forward, trying to navigate her closer but she evaded my lips capture. Arching her back instead, she pushed her chest outward and if I hadn't known better, I would have suspected she was nervous.

The feeling was mutual. I hadn't felt this buzzy and hyperaware since I was a teenager—but we weren't teenagers—we weren't even strangers. We were married, and married people kissed.

When she straightened, relaxing a little, I tried again. She dodged me once more. My heart sunk, awareness dawning on me, shredding my insides. No, that evasion tactic hadn't been a byproduct of not knowing how to kiss me or being scared to.

That had been intentional, hadn't it? She didn't *want* to kiss me.

I stilled her gyrating hips, dread constricting around my heart until pain burned in my chest.

Pen choked out a suffocated breath, and I had my confirmation practically illuminated by a spotlight and a banner that reminded me how much of a desperate idiot I was.

She was forcing herself.

For some fucked-up reason, she felt she needed to do this.

My body burned with anger from the tips of my toes to my ears, sweat breaking out along my spine. I needed out of here. "Get off of me."

Pen tensed in my lap, her expression falling. A flash of defiance streaked across her face, reminiscent of when I'd first met her—before I'd ruined us. Her chin leveled for a moment until she tipped her head downward and brushed her tentative lips against mine.

As if the soft, trembling pleat of her mouth was going to fix it now.

No, this felt wrong. This was all wrong.

I pushed against her hips, but she banded her arms around my neck, pressing her mouth harder against mine like this was the remedy we both needed. In another life, it would have been.

A long time ago, a kiss from her ended every argument, brought us both back to reality like an electronic hard reset. It would have been enough to make me roll her underneath me, slide into her and fuck her right into our couch until we both remembered we were crazy about each other. But this was the first time I'd kissed my wife since our wedding day in March.

The first time I'd seen her breasts since January.

Felt the heat of her body pressed against mine.

I deflated. I couldn't do this.

And she knew it, too. "Do you want to fuck me or not?" she hissed.

Of course, I did, but not like this. Not when it felt like an intensive effort, as if she'd spent the better part of the day scripting out each play.

I wanted her passion and her love, not a rehearsed lie.

I shook my head. "No."

Her bottom lip quivered before her jaw set and her eyes flashed with fury. "I bet if I was her, you would."

Unfuckingbelievable.

I pushed at her hips to get her the hell off me. "You're still not getting it." She would never get it, so what was the point anymore?

"Fuck you," she seethed. "How dare you make this about me."

I clenched my jaw, scowling at her. "I didn't *fuck* Maria."

There, I said it. I said her name and neither of us could escape it now.

Pen let go of me, clapping her palms against her ears as her chest heaved. "Do not say her name!"

"I didn't fuck Maria," I repeated a little louder with conviction, pulling her against me, my heart beating wildly in tandem with hers as my arms wrapped around her and she squirmed. "I didn't fuck Maria. I wanted you. I wanted you to fuck me, and to want me and to stop treating me like I was a fucking option."

I didn't fuck Maria Tavares this year. But that didn't make me guilt-free because thinking about it, going to her apartment with the intent to, was still an admission of guilt. A few months after our wedding this year, I let the fact that Maria was happy, when Pen and I should have been after months of ceaseless arguing, cloud my judgment and I made an unforgivable mistake.

With the snap of my fingers, I nearly fucked up Maria's relationship, and I destroyed mine. I betrayed my wife. I let the fact that I was lonely act as a vehicle to be a self-serving prick.

I *had* fucked Maria. A long time ago, in another life.

For most of my youth, I had wanted Maria.

For six months, I had loved Maria.

But not the way I loved or wanted Pen. Maria was an enigma. Penelope was an open book, a burst of sunshine after a monsoon, sweetness on your palate after eating something bitter.

Or she had been.

Pen shoved against me to break my hold. "I never treated you like an option," she argued.

I wanted to laugh. Pen really believed that. She had a special talent for believing anything she said.

It almost made her unwilling to see beyond the bedazzlement of her bullshit that she had treated me like an option. The first best thing. A convenience.

I didn't think it really mattered who slid that ring on her finger the day of our wedding. I got the impression she was marrying me because we'd come that far and her parents needed something to brag about to their society friends, even if I was the last fucking person on earth, they wanted their daughter to marry.

It was the principle now. I'd knocked her up. Her father had made it perfectly clear to me when we'd told them she was expecting three Thanksgivings ago that I was to propose to her immediately and not embarrass them.

That had always been the plan. That had always been the goal.

Marry the girl with the too-pretty eyes, and the easy smile and the stellar taste in music. Spend the rest of my life worshipping her, making love to her, and putting a bunch of babies in her to fill up every fucking room in this house.

But what happened when she didn't want that, too? That wasn't stipulated in the prenuptial agreement they'd thrown in my lap four days before we said, "I do."

Shit, her parents had every fucking lawyer on the Northeast Coast in their back pocket. It had been Pen who suggested Maria look at it— Maria, the corporate lawyer. She didn't even practice family law, for fuck's sake.

Pen shoved me back in her path. She was always shoving me in someone else's path this year. I was a nuisance. Everything I did annoyed her.

Trying to press a kiss against the spot under her ear the way she used to like pissed her off. Brushing her hair behind her ear had her clapping my hand away. Reaching for her in bed—just to fucking hold her for a moment—had her getting out of bed completely, muttering about needing to check on something and only returning when she thought I was asleep.

So yeah, I made a fucking mistake going to Maria's apartment a few months ago after having an argument with my wife, where she said things in a fit of rage. I'd left this house in anger, stopped at a bar, gave myself too much time to think and made a mistake.

A massive fucking error in judgment because I was an emotional fucking wreck desperate for someone to put their arms around me and tell me it was going to be okay.

That I wasn't going to lose everything when I'd just gotten it.

But this farce, this little fucking charade Penelope wanted to perpetuate that she was the only one who'd lost something, that she was the only one who suffered, that I was solely responsible for what happened to us? I was fucking over it.

I would own my part of being the villain, but she needed to own her role, too.

My crime was that I wanted to be wanted—to have someone's

hands on me, to feel the warmth of another person. Her crime had been that she didn't care.

She didn't fucking care about me.

I hoisted her off my lap, dropping her onto the couch. "Keep blowing smoke up your own ass, Pen."

"I hate you," she choked out, her glare searing my skin. "I can't stand you."

"Makes fucking two of us, sweetheart." I stood up, stepping away from her. "But you know something?" I asked with a bitter laugh. "I may not like myself. I might even hate myself a little, too. But I'd rather go the rest of my life repenting for my sins than trying to live a goddamn lie with you anymore."

I wanted to keep her, but not at the expense of either of our sanity.

We'd done enough damage.

If she wanted out, I'd let her free, because I couldn't do this. I thought I could.

The room sobered, but it did nothing to mollify my aching insides. I needed out of this room, and if she didn't let me go, out of this house.

"Dougie, wait," Pen pleaded on a sob, scrambling to her feet. She shoved her hands into her hair, the tears uncoordinated rivers on her cheeks. "I don't hate you. I didn't mean it."

She'd said it. She needed to own it. "Liar."

"You don't get it!" she yelled at me.

"Because you won't fucking let me in!" I roared back, punching the air. "You have *never* let me in."

"I can't," she wailed, whipping her head from side to side. "I can't."

"Then there's nothing here to discuss." I drove the heels of my palms into my eyes, my body feeling weak and heavy. "I never fucked Maria." She winced. "I thought about it and seeing her happy in the way we should have been, it fucked me up and I own it. I hurt you, and I can't take it back. I wish I could. But you," I snarled. "You don't want me, so it's about time you admitted it."

"That's not true," she sobbed, struggling to get the straps of her nightgown back over her arms and her breasts covered.

"Then say you want me," I demanded. "Tell me right now you want me and you want this. That you want to work at us."

She kicked her chin at me, grinding her molars together. "I want you and I want this." God, someone get my wife on Broadway, stat.

I almost believed her for a second.

Almost.

"You're so fucking full of it." I laughed with no mirth, my body prickly and hot. She'd deluded herself. "You can't kiss me, Pen. You can't touch me. Looking at me is hard. Just say it—We. Are. Through."

"Don't!" She charged around the couch, stopping halfway to me, her breaths pumping out of her hard. "You don't get to say that."

"Oh, yeah?" I challenged, rushing to where she stood. "How was your fucking doctor appointment?"

She staggered back, her eyes wild. Her lips pinched together, as though she were suppressing the tremble. "Don't go there."

"What did they prescribe you? Fifty percent of the house, no child support because let's face it," I looked her up and down, "you don't need it. What else? Full custody?"

"Stop it, Dougie." I ignored the warning in her tone.

All I could concentrate on was the all-consuming fury thrashing my insides, drowning my thoughts in acid. My body was buzzing—every anxiety, every worry coming to a head. My legs broke out in a crazed pace, back and forth. "I can't wait to deal with your parents' fucking arsenal of lawyers. Yippee!" I cheered sarcastically, throwing my arms up in the air.

Penelope heaved a series of pants, her stare narrowing. "Dougie. Just. Stop." She clutched at herself, her features pinching.

But I couldn't stop. I wouldn't stop, because I'd always stopped. For her sake, I never said what I wanted to. I allowed us to get to this point. I was always too afraid she'd say she wanted out and mean it, but I'd already confronted the worst plausible scenario, and I was realizing it really didn't fucking matter. We were going to destroy each other at this rate.

"You've got your place in Beacon Hill, so you'll be alright," I continued smugly. "And hey, you're an expert in getting married now for the sake of it, so it doesn't matter who the next asshole is. I broke you in, right?"

If you told me three years ago, when Penelope stumbled into my arms, that we would have ever ended up here—I would have laughed.

Penelope was a fantasy. Penelope was the dream come true. You didn't fuck that up to shit.

Penelope was sweet and fierce. She was funny and sexy.

And my dream come true just slapped me hard enough that I bit the inside of my cheek. Pain detonated in my face, but it was the only thing that took the edge off my anger like a candle snuffer on a lit wick.

I deserved that.

I dropped my eyes to the floor, letting the smarting rip what remained of my contempt away. We were doing exactly what I hadn't wanted to do.

Penelope gasped, her chest caving on her as she flexed the fingers on her open palm, her jaw hanging open. "I'm sor—"

I shook my head. I didn't even want her apology. My limbs tingled as the anger broke, the fever of my rage fading away like a distant memory, sweat cooling my spine.

"I don't want to live a lie anymore."

"Dougie."

"File, Penelope," I said weakly, trying to keep my voice from breaking. My heart was in my throat, but I knew it had to be said. "File and I'll sign."

I was her cage. This house her prison.

And this life, her hell.

But I wouldn't be anymore.

Chapter Thirteen

Penelope

Three years ago…

ACID CRAWLED UP MY THROAT, MY HANDS BRACED ON THE BLEACHED toilet as I heaved, my insides wrenching. My hair clung to the beads of sweat peppering my face, Dougie's T-shirt sticking to my perspiring skin.

From the other side of his bathroom door, I heard his footsteps along the floor. The soft rap of his knuckles against the particleboard of the door hits my ears. "Penny?" he asked gently. "Can I come in?"

I did a body check—what were the odds I was going to throw up again?

High. Very high.

Fisting my hair, I dipped my head into the bowl once more, retching. Jesus fucking Christ, pasta sauce did not feel good coming back up.

I think I was finished with tomato sauce, permanently. I'd need to figure out how to cook something else. Get a cookbook or sign up for a cooking class or something.

Flushing the toilet, I rolled off my haunches and slid to the bathtub, relishing in the cool metal against my sticky body. "Yeah, you can come in."

The hinges on the door creaked as he opened the door slowly, jutting his head in. He was dressed for work, his green-and-blue fleece-lined flannel open on top of a gray T-shirt with Tavares Construction screen printed on the front.

Worry pulled his brows together as he gave me a once-over. "I'm sorry you're feeling sick," he murmured, the door opening all the way. He held out a glass of water to me.

My stomach rolled at the prospect of drinking anything right now. I shook my head. "I don't want it."

"You gotta drink something." He lowered himself to a squat in front of me. Reaching into his back pocket, he held up a sleeve of Dramamine. "Take two of these and sleep it off."

"I can't," I groaned. "The furniture is getting dropped off today."

We were in the staging phase at the house. Sean was listing at the end of the week, and hopefully, he'd be able to sell it quickly.

His check for me bounced when I deposited it yesterday. I didn't care all that much, and Dougie assured me Sean was good for the money. Not that I was going to suffer without it, but it was the principle. I was just keeping that tidbit in my back pocket for when I needed it to put Mr. Cranky Pants in his place.

"Drink," Dougie insisted.

Sighing, I accepted the glass from him. I tipped it just enough to wet my lips, ignoring the way his eyes thinned at my attempt at deceiving him.

"Penelope. Drink."

"I can't."

"Then you can't go to work," he said simply, climbing to his feet. He took the glass from me, placed it on the sink, then held out both hands for me. I let him pull me to my feet, my stomach immediately lurching.

"Nope, nope." I dropped back to the floor, heaving the contents of my stomach into the bowl.

Fuck, this sucked worse than the time I pre-gamed with vodka and then switched to whiskey at Maiden's *A Matter of Life and Death* tour in 2006. Twenty-five-year anniversary of *The Number of the Beast*, and I spent it in the bathroom of Agganis Arena, puking my guts out while Raquel chided me for mixing.

I didn't have her iron stomach. *"Stick to one liquor next time,"* she'd told me.

Dougie scooped my hair off the back of my neck with one hand, holding it out of my face. He rubbed the middle of my back with the other.

"Okay," I heaved. "I'll stay here."

"Trina can handle it today," he assured. "You've gone over the plan with her a dozen times."

He was right. Trina was smart, smarter than anyone gave her credit for. She could handle it, and anything I didn't like, I could adjust tomorrow. I nodded. "Help me to bed?" I asked, flushing the toilet again.

Dougie steadied me, and when it was clear I was stable, he scooped me into his arms. "I can walk," I protested weakly, even though I tucked my head under his chin.

"I know, but I'd rather carry you."

I loved the feeling of his arms bound around me, holding me close. "Show off." He smelled good. Clean, safe. Him.

His chuckle vibrated in his chest as he carried me out of the bathroom and into his bedroom. He'd bought a bed frame recently, informing me he couldn't have his girlfriend sleeping on a mattress on the floor.

It had mattered little to me, but I appreciated the gesture. Although he'd rolled his eyes at me when I'd shown up at his place with new pillows, a duvet and nicer bed sheets from Restoration Hardware.

It was a neutral print, gray and masculine like him. He deserved nice things.

It was still a no-go on a dresser or nightstands. Maybe I'd get him a new mattress for Christmas.

He eased me back onto the bed, pulling the duvet and sheets up to my chin. The mattress sagged when he sat down on the edge. Dougie studied me for a long time, tracing my face with the tip of his finger, a pained sigh leaving him.

"What?"

"Nothing. You're just so beautiful."

I shot him with a look of disbelief, huffing out a laugh. "I just finished yacking last night's pasta into the toilet, and I'm sweating in places I shouldn't." Seriously, my ass cheeks were stuck together.

He chortled, shaking his head. "You're still beautiful."

"I stink."

Dougie sniffed the air, scrunching up his nose. "A little," he agreed.

"Oh, thanks," I replied, feigning insult. I knew he was exaggerating.

"Hey, what do we have if we can't be honest with each other?" he asked, leaning forward to press his lips against my clammy forehead. "You stink, but I'd still bone you."

"I'm flattered, but pretty sure that would give me motion sickness."

He kissed the tip of my nose. "You're probably right."

Pulling away, he stood up. "I'll get out of there early. I'm gonna get your water and the Dramamine. Please try to drink and take them."

It was almost three o'clock in the afternoon when my phone buzzed on his floor. Groaning, I blinked the sleep out of my eyes, relieved nausea didn't immediately consume me. Extending a hand out to the floor, I scooped my phone up from the floor, bringing it into my line of vision.

Mother.

I wasn't in the mood. Putting the phone back down, I hesitated.

Dougie never did that to his mother. He always answered. He was always pleasant and kind.

I could try to emulate that.

"Hello?" I said groggily.

"Penelope?" Mother's plummy voice hit my ears. "Are you asleep?"

"I just woke up," I replied, sitting up. I was grateful the room didn't immediately spin out on me. It seemed like the worse of the nausea was over.

"For goodness' sake," she chided. "What are you doing out there? It's nearly five."

I rolled my eyes. "It's three, Mother. And I'm ill."

Her response was brittle. "With *what*?" I knew what she was really concerned about. I hadn't gotten up and exercised. People in my parents' social circles viewed bodily inertia as the worst of the seven deadly sins.

"I just caught a bug." *I'll be fine, thanks for your concern.*

Mother cleared her throat. "Yes, let's be certain that's all it is."

"What's that supposed to mean?" I challenged, blinking the sleep from my eyes.

She was likely pursing her lips. "That you're not indulging in fast food, drink and..." she dropped her voice to a whisper, as though the phone line had been tapped, "drugs."

"Mother."

"Hedonism is frowned upon, Penelope Louise." Right, the crux of her fear. "Ensure it's just a bug." I'd already detected the accusation in her voice, what she was really saying that she wouldn't deign to utter aloud.

I better not embarrass them with a scandal.

I could hear her playing with the string of pearls around her neck, the delicate smooth beads brushing together. That was her nervous tick. Play with the expensive string of pearls like they were a grounding mechanism. "I'm calling to confirm your attendance for Thanksgiving."

"That's still weeks away." I yawned, looking around Dougie's barren room. He had little at his place, but somehow, it felt homier than my apartment. Maybe that was because he was in it.

"Yes, well, the Rochesters and Huntingtons will be joining us this year."

My body tightened, venom finding my tongue. "Fuck the Huntingtons." They were self-righteous assholes and their only child, Harold, was a pompous little dick who believed he was a god. Our mothers had been desperate to marry us off to one another since birth, but I'd rather join a fucking convent.

When I fantasized about getting married now, it certainly wasn't to that prick.

"Penelope Louise," she trilled. "Honestly, we send you to Massachusetts and you've completely abdicated on the values of your upbringing."

"Because my upbringing was bullshit," I spat back.

"You are an ill-mannered, impudent, ungrateful—"

"Evelyn." Daddy's voice broke through the background. My insides thawed a little. Mother and I didn't get along very well, but Daddy had always tried to be reasonable.

"You spoiled her, Walter. Her insolence is your doing."

No, let's forget I'd left home ten years ago and had practically led a double life when I was right under their noses. But sure, blame him.

Who would Evelyn Cullimore be without her finger pointing?

"Hi, Daddy," I called sweetly, knowing he could hear me now. She must have had me on speakerphone. How very two-thousand-and-eight of her to take the phone call that way instead of the vintage gold Victorian rotary telephone in the sitting room. She was becoming a modern woman, after all.

Mother made an ornery sound, inhaling sharply.

"Hello, Pearl." My parents couldn't have any other children after me, so, he called me Pearl. In his eyes, "I was the most rare and exquisite thing he'd ever seen."

I liked telling myself it was because he secretly enjoyed listening to Pearl Jam when he wasn't within earshot of Mother, though I'd never be able to confirm that theory.

I knew it drove her crazy that he catered a little to my wants. He'd been the one who relented when I confessed I'd applied to BU behind their backs and accepted my admission. Mother had a panic attack and sobbed hysterically that I'd reneged on Yale and tarnished their reputation on purpose. I'd gotten in on legacy status alone because Daddy had graduated from Yale—never mind their exorbitant charitable donations.

But Daddy didn't want me to look back at my life with regret.

"I'll be at Thanksgiving, but I'm bringing someone with me," I informed her.

"Not that dreadful girl, I hope," she chided. "She'll spoil everyone's appetite with all of that frowning."

My unoccupied hand balled in my lap.

"Evelyn." Daddy didn't seem to mind Raquel the way Mother did. Mother never attempted to mask her disdain toward her, but Daddy looked at Raquel like he wasn't sure what to do with her.

Pity her and write her a check or thank her for keeping me out of too much trouble.

"Raquel, Mother. Her name is Raquel. She's my best friend, and I'd appreciate if you demonstrated a modicum of respect when you mention her name." I gritted my teeth. "And no, Raquel will *not* be joining us. She has a prior engagement with her mother." I wished she would come to Connecticut. I'd only met Pauline Flannigan once when Raquel dropped money off for her. She was a piece of work who made my best friend's life hell.

Admittedly, I hated her.

"I thought her mother was dead."

"That's her sister and dad," I corrected.

"Right," she said absently. I knew she'd be looking for the Ambien after this call. Nighty, night. "Who will you be bringing then?"

I took a fortifying breath, my spine snapping ramrod straight. I squared my shoulders, even though she couldn't see me. Now was as good a time as ever to tell them. They may as well brace themselves. "My boyfriend."

Mother was quiet.

But not as quiet as Daddy.

I pulled the phone away from my ear just to confirm the call hadn't disconnected.

"Boyfriend?" she finally asked. "What's his name?"

"Doug—" I paused. "Douglas."

"Douglas, who?" I could envision her looking at Daddy, wide-eyed. "Do we know a Douglas in Boston?" The question wasn't for me, it was for Daddy.

"William Forbes' son?" Of course, they'd immediately rush to their Rolodex to confirm who they were connected with of what remained of the Boston Brahmins—Boston's antiquated elite WASP society on steroids.

"They don't have a son, just the daughter," Mother informed him. "Beatrice. Lovely girl."

They were silent for a moment until Mother's unhinged gasp ripped free. "Penelope, not Lincoln Chafee's son." She dropped her voice to a whisper, as though there was a threat of someone hearing the next words leaving her mouth. "He's a *democrat*."

Newsflash, so was I. They just didn't know that. More importantly... "Who the hell is Lincoln Chafee?"

"Enough of this," Daddy interrupted, trying to modulate his tone. "Douglas *who*?"

"Douglas Patterson."

"Patterson isn't part of the Brahmin." Mother huffed.

"Because Dougie," I began, "*isn't* a Brahmin."

"Don't begin a sentence with 'because', Penelope," she admonished, pausing. "If he's not Brahmin, what is he?"

You could have heard a pin drop. "Hedge-fund banker?" Daddy asked.

"Lawyer?" Mother suggested when I didn't reply. She was fidgeting now, her pearls shifting with her every move. Fixing her hair, no doubt in its signature polished chignon, smoothing out the invisible wrinkles in her dress, anything to keep her from bouncing her leg. Proper ladies didn't bounce their legs, they maintained the illusion all was right as rain and had a prescription when they couldn't get it under control that no one was to ever know about.

She should consider therapy—I still maintained my bi-weekly

sessions with someone in the city—or go on one of those yoga retreats they'd shipped me off to.

"A doctor?" My parents' hopes were deflating and fast.

No, none of those things.

Douglas Patterson was a construction foreman from Fall River, Massachusetts with a well-endowed cock, a deviated septum that jutted in the same direction, with dark green eyes the shade of a pine tree who I might be falling in love with. He was kind, made me laugh, and didn't care about things like my parents' wealth.

And I was currently sitting in his bed, in his sparsely furnished apartment.

Was that an impressive enough resume? Would that satiate their curiosity? Could I have their blessing? I knew better, but…

"He's from Fall River."

"Fall *where*?" she asked, her voice tremulous.

I dragged my knees up to my chest, draping my arm over the valley. "Fall River. It's near the border of Rhode Island."

"You cannot be serious!" She cried out as though I'd told her I'd been diagnosed with a terminal disease. "Penelope!"

I pulled the phone away from my ear. What was wrong with Fall River?

"What does he do for work?" she demanded.

I flopped back on the bed, letting out a tight breath as I stared up at his ceiling. "Construction."

"Con-con—" she cut herself off, her breaths growing labored. "He's… working… working class…"

"Mother, this isn't a fucking class warfare. He's a good man who works hard. What's the problem?" She grossed me out. No wonder WASPs had a terrible reputation. It was because of shit like that.

"The Rochesters and Huntingtons will be here! You cannot bring him here."

Good, even better. "Then I'm not coming." I'd rather figure out how to make a turkey myself or one of those little hams that had twenty percent meat protein in it.

"Walter!" Mother was no doubt glaring at Daddy now, demanding he intervene—talk some sense into me, make me see reason. But I wasn't budging on this.

Dougie was my boyfriend, and I wasn't going to not bring him to Thanksgiving if they didn't welcome him. They could get fucked.

Daddy was quiet for a moment more before clearing his throat. "Cancel with the Rochesters and the Huntingtons. Let them know something came up."

"The scandal, Walter—"

"Evelyn, either cancel or accept that Pearl is bringing her..." Daddy paused, trying to find the resolve to say the word, "*boyfriend*."

Mother sniffled, and I said nothing.

"Fine," she spat. "I'll cancel."

I scoffed. Figures. "Whatever."

"Penelope," Daddy said, sighing. "A little compassion on your side would do you wonders."

"Compassion for what?" I asked. "I'm not the one behaving like my boyfriend is a disease. She is. She doesn't deserve compassion. She *needs* therapy."

Or a lobotomy.

"I think it's best we part ways for the time being," he suggested. I could hear him patting her back, no doubt attempting to console her. "We'll see you at Thanksgiving." I'd just opened a can of shit for him to deal with and the only remorse I felt was because he had to clean my mess up.

They hung up before I got the chance to say bye.

I tossed my phone to the foot of the bed, and then rolled over, finding Dougie's pillow to bury my face in.

I screamed.

I couldn't stand their shit—the burden of appearances, society, and expectations. I didn't give a flying fuck what they thought about Dougie. He was a good person, better than any of their artificial society members combined. Dougie was real. Sitting upright, I shoved the sheets back, testing the floor and my equilibrium with my feet before committing to standing up.

I was grateful the room didn't spin out on me. Padding over to the bathroom, I caught sight of my disheveled appearance in the mirror and let out a laugh. Mother would have a bird if she saw the state of my hair and yesterday's eyeliner smeared in the corners of my eyes.

Lifting Dougie's shirt over my head, I started the shower and prepared to wash the phone call and the sick away, mulling over what I'd make for dinner tonight. Grabbing a clean towel from the hallway linen closet, I headed back to the bathroom, the heat from the shower creating steam that fogged up the bathroom mirror. Hanging up the towel, I pulled the shower curtain back just enough for me to get in and got to work.

Squirting Dougie's five-in-one shampoo and conditioner into my palm, I worked it into a lather on my scalp, the invigorating albeit artificial scent of wood, citrus and bergamot from the Irish Springs hitting my nose, waking me up a little more.

What else was idiot-proof that I could cook?

One of those meal kits?

You know, with the pre-measured ingredients... oh, tacos. Yeah, there was that commercial for a taco kit on television last night that I'd seen when I was curled up on Dougie's lap in his recliner. Yeah, okay. Tacos. That seemed straightforward.

I needed one of those kits with the soft tacos and shredded cheese, lettuce, ground beef mixed with peanut butter. Stepping under the spray of water, I paused.

Peanut butter?

Peanut butter didn't belong on tacos, and yet, my stomach growled with approval, my taste buds salivating. That was weird. Rinsing the five-in-one thoroughly from my hair, I pumped the same liquid into my hand and scrubbed my body, running through my grocery list again. Slipping my hands over my breasts, I winced. They were tender, which meant my period was around the corner, too.

Better grab tampons, just in case.

Cutting the shower, I extended a hand for the towel to wrap myself up in. Searching the floor with my foot, I lifted my leg over the edge of the tub, clearing it until a thought slammed into me.

When the hell was my last period? Hadn't I just had it? My muscles tensed as I reached for my breast again, tweaking it hard.

Jesus, that fucking hurt.

Gritting my teeth, a tight breath left my lungs as I strode out of the bathroom, back into the bedroom where I'd discarded my phone on the bed. Thumbing my passcode in, I tapped the calendar app open, my eyes searching for the date of my last period. My stomach sank to the ground-floor apartment when I had to turn the calendar to the next page.

Fuck.

Dougie

I twirled my keys around my finger while whistling, taking the metal stairs two at a time, not caring that they wobbled under my weight. Fear was a weird thing. With enough exposure to it, its hold on you eventually waned. These stairs used to scare the shit out of me, my hand always gripping to the railing, just in case.

Clearing the last one, I turned on the landing, heading toward my apartment door, grocery bag in tow. Pen hadn't answered when I'd called to see how she was feeling, so I assumed the Dramamine had put her on her ass. I'd grabbed soup for her and saltines. I figured that would help her feel better, or at least be gentle enough on her stomach to hopefully kickstart her appetite again.

Unlocking the door, I pushed it open. Surprise greeted me when I found Pen sitting on the recliner in a daze, dressed in a pair of skinny jeans that looked a lot like the ones she'd worn on the day I met her and one of my Bruins sweatshirts. Her damp hair was scraped away from her face, held back by a clip, her eyes cast downward.

"Hey," I said, shutting the door and inching toward her.

She didn't look up at me.

"Pen?"

Finally, she lifted her eyes just a little, finding the grocery bag in my hand. "I got... a taco kit..." she trailed off.

I smiled, shaking my head to clear the worry percolating in the back of my mind that she was behaving oddly. "I grabbed you soup, but if you're up for tacos, we can do that instead." That sounded really good, actually.

She nodded absently, her lips parting on her next exhale. "And some peanut butter."

"You sound like you're feeling better, then." I laughed. "Did you grab bread?"

She shook her head. "No, I want it on my tacos, with some sour cream."

I blanched, my head jerking back. "Interesting combo, but okay."

"You needed more coffee grounds, so I stopped at that Portuguese bakery you like on Columbia Street that carries the fancy coffee and grabbed that, too."

Why wasn't she taking it easy? I was grateful, but that was a lot of errands for someone who had been yacking her guts out earlier.

"I called you earlier, and you didn't answer." I rocked my mouth. "When did you go out?"

"An hour and a half ago," she replied noncommittally, tugging on the sleeve of my sweatshirt. "You needed more bleach. It was on sale, so I grabbed two."

She was behaving robotically. "Just leave the receipt on the counter." I set the groceries on the floor, lowering myself onto my haunches in front of her.

"I went into the Stop & Shop," she added. "I've never been there before. I was going to go to this other organic store in New Bedford, but then I thought it was kind of bullshit that I'm shopping organic if all I've been making you is pasta lately."

Her hand was stiff and clammy in mine when I grabbed it, running my fingers over her delicate veins. "You feeling okay?" I asked. "Dramamine messing with you?"

Her eyes rounded with fear. "I don't know how to cook anything else, Dougie."

I smiled. "You're doing great." Not that big of a deal we'd eaten a lifetime's worth of pasta.

"I don't know how to cook or manage a household."

"Penny, it's okay. I've lived off sandwiches for years." I wasn't much of a cook, either.

"Or a baby," she threw in quickly, her eyes flaring. "I mean, I've always wanted kids, and thinking about it more seriously lately, but…"

What did that mean? Before I could ask, she launched into another monologue.

"I don't know how to take care of them. I don't have any siblings, and any of my friends' mother's growing up had nannies. A house-keeper raised me. Did you know that? Babies are accessories to WASPs. We grow up to be near carbon copies of our parents and perpetuate the cycle. I don't know how to take care of a baby, but maybe I could… I don't know…" She drew her hands back, shaking them out and flexing her fingers.

My chest tightened as my heart kicked up a shitstorm, heat burning in the tips of my ears. "Penelope. *What* baby?"

Her blue eyes rounded with terror, glossing over with a veil of unshed tears. "I don't have a bug or food poisoning," she panted. "I took a test. I'm…"

I lost my balance, my feet giving out from under me, my ass hitting the ground.

No fucking way. There was no fucking way.

But we'd played with fire.

Penelope rolled her lips together, shaking her head. "I'm sorry."

She didn't need to say the word. I heard it in her silence.

Pregnant.

Penelope was pregnant.

Chapter Fourteen

Dougie

Present

I'D SPENT A LOT OF TIME LATELY THINKING ABOUT OUR BEGINNING, TRYING to understand how Pen and I got here. For some reason, I thought a lot about when I crouched by her feet three years ago while she told me she was pregnant on a whispered apology.

I'd cut that off fast, swept her into my arms and cheered for fucking joy because in an instant, it became the best day of my life, the day that changed our lives forever. She'd stopped crying immediately, breaking into a fit of laughter instead. We ate tacos that night, and I watched in muted curiosity as she slathered her taco shell in peanut butter and munched away happily, her worries melting away. I didn't know the first thing about being a dad, but I promised her I'd be the best one. All she did was smile and told me, *"I know."*

We were gonna be parents. We were gonna have a family, and a life together, and I knew above all else I wanted to propose. I didn't care about anything else but her, our baby, and me.

Funny how things changed.

I hadn't said one fucking word to Penelope in days. If we'd been methodical in avoiding each other in the past, this was a new level. She left every room I entered and avoided my eyes when she couldn't leave. If the house had felt insufferable before, it paled compared to now. I felt like I'd hardly slept in that time, too. I kept getting flash-backs of her avoiding kissing me, yet trying to—what? Fuck me? Was that what she'd wanted? Or more importantly, how she'd wanted it? Like she was fucking a stranger. She could burn out the motor on her vibrator at that point, because I wasn't going to be her personal sex toy.

I wanted something more, something that was real.

My eyes burned with exhaustion as I wandered the hardware store, in search of…

Honestly, I didn't know what the fuck I was here for. When I wasn't reliving the last couple of years of my life, or the other night, I was out. This had been the trajectory of my week, escaping the house in search of make-work projects, anything to take my mind off my reality. Attempting to rake the yard, twice, which was completely futile, because more leaves seemed to hail down in an ultimate "fuck you." I took my truck to a do-it-your-self car wash back in Fall River, even though it was cold as shit. I'd begun the process of wrapping Pen's rose bushes in burlap to prep for winter, pricking myself twice in the process—karma, I assumed.

Now I was here, for a second time this week. Initially, I'd come here two days ago in search of shelving units for the garage. I'd found what I wanted, brought it home, only to realize it was cheaper to make the shelves myself.

I needed to be money conscientious now since I was *unemployed*. I'd texted Katrina an apology—not for telling her to mind her business, but for bringing up Adam. It was a low blow. I shouldn't have mentioned it, no matter how mad I was.

She told me to take my advice and shove it up my ass.

With the return receipt in my back pocket, I studied the neat shelves with screws in plastic packaging. The air perfumed with fresh cut wood—I missed that smell—classic rock droning in the background over the periodic intercom call for a price check or floor assistance.

I'd already marked the studs in the wall in the garage this morning and outlined where I'd install two rows of two-by-fours. I had wood projecting awkwardly in a cart to my right. I just needed three-inch screws, and some sandpaper and I'd be out of here. That was one way to kill an afternoon and thirty bucks.

"Dougie?" At the utterance of my name in that thick Bristol County accent that could have paralleled my own, my blood ran cold.

Fuck.

I didn't dare move, not even to adjust the bill of my baseball hat to mask my features, holding perfectly still like the source of the voice was a stinging insect and if I did nothing to provoke him, he'd leave me alone.

I suspected that only worked if you hadn't already provoked the beast. My silence only antagonized him. Hell, I thought the last few months had all but guaranteed he was gonna sting regardless of what I did.

Sean huffed out an exasperated breath, and even from the small distance between us, I felt the waves of anger emanating from him in thick waves. "I don't fucking believe it."

Every muscle in my body throbbed with the desire to run, dread fueling a buzzing in my ears. It was two in the afternoon. What was he doing here?

What day was it? Tuesday.

Right. Sean didn't work on Tuesdays. It was the one day of the week he wasn't bouncing between two of his restaurants.

"Hey, asshole," he snarled, his voice growing closer as he moved. I thought about ignoring him, but as though detecting my intentions, he stormed down the aisle, his sneakers gritting with each urgent footstep. "I'm talking to you."

My lids fell shut. For a split second, I considered ditching my cart and all. I could do this on another day. On a day that wasn't a Tuesday, where he'd be in his own little deep-fried dough-world paradise, where the sweetness matched the state of his entire fucking life.

Sean threw the package of paint roller refills and painter's tape to the floor, the roll of tape bowling to my feet. I lifted my eyes to his, trying to remain impassive, but the venom in his dark eyes stung my skin like a cobra had struck me.

He looked like hell. Worse. He looked like Maria.

Nah, I couldn't do this.

I darted around the cart, hurrying toward the end of the aisle, but he caught me by the back of my jacket, hauling me back. An "*oof*" escaped me as Sean shoved me against the wall of shelves, grabbing me by the neckline of my shirt, wrapping the material twice around his fist, and pinning me in place. "Coward. You think I won't fucking knock you out?"

I glowered up at him, my upper lip curling back. He had four inches on me, but I could handle him. I'd handled his bullies for him too, once upon a time. Of course, back then, we'd been eight years old, and he didn't understand a word of English, but that wasn't the point.

I enveloped his fist with my hand, tugging hard. "Get. Off. Of. Me."

He leaned forward, the notes from his cinnamon gum falling over my face. "I'm bigger than you, Dougie."

"Not where it fucking counts." I'd bet on that.

"Wanna put your money where your mouth is?" he taunted with a sneer. "My wife's not complaining."

Like I needed the reminder only one of us had a wife who wanted them. I shoved back at him, but Sean wouldn't let up. He had the strength of seven months of resentment fortifying him now.

Fine, he wanted to get a few punches in, I'd let him. "Not here."

I knew he'd do a hell of a lot more than just punch me if he knew half the shit I'd done.

"Then where?" Sean demanded. "Where do you want me to kick your ass for turning your back on us?" He twisted my neckline in his powerful fist, nearly cutting off my breathing as he doubled down on his anger. "Your wife made mine cry. She needed her."

Puh-lease. He wanted to compare a list of faults? His wife's list of infractions could extend over two states. She was far from perfect. I didn't care what rose-colored lenses he saw his little South Boston knock-off Disney princess through.

"Your wife did that to mine first," I tossed back. He thought I'd forgotten Raquel's disappearing act a couple of years ago. I hadn't. I'd had to deal with that mess, too.

It didn't matter that she cleaned up her act.

"And *my* wife owned her shit!" he yelled, his voice carrying to the exposed ceilings. Sean seethed at me, and I knew whatever he was going to say next was going to set me off. "*Yours* is acting like the pretentious little bitch I always knew she was."

Tunnel vision set in, swallowing my rationale as my elevated pulse kicked me into overdrive.

He could say what he wanted about me, but not about Penelope.

Never about Penelope.

My fist reared back, striking him square on his too-sharp jaw. He grunted, his grasp on me slackening enough for me to shove him back.

He could come at me all he wanted. He could bury me alive, but I drew the line at Pen. I'd kill him or die trying. "Don't you ever," I spat, heaving a breath. "And I mean ever, call my wife a bitch again."

He scrubbed his jaw to redistribute the sting of my fist, his tongue pressing into his cheek. His eyes flashed with contrition, like he too recognized he'd gone too far.

Going after women wasn't his style, we both knew that. His father had raised him better, not like mine. Mine hadn't raised me at all. He showed me you moved onto something easier when shit got too hard.

It didn't change that Sean was still rightly pissed at me. "Fine," he snarled back. "I'll call you one instead."

That was better.

I charged at him, sending him against a shelf, the store-displayed packaging rattling with the force. His hands flew out behind him to catch himself. "You motherfucker."

God, this felt kind of good. The adrenaline, the rush, the anger finally coming to a head with someone who I could throw down with. I wanted it. I needed it. The release, the escape, it felt like an act of penance on par with self-flagellation.

I needed him to fight me, to be as angry at me as I was at myself.

"What's wrong? You got a problem with being called a bitch, Dougie?" Sean taunted. He lunged forward, locking his arm around my thick neck, the familiar scent of his leather jacket and the clove in his cologne hitting me as he dragged me to him. For someone who had traded in his hard hat for an apron, he was still strong as shit. There was nothing doughy about him.

He was probably still diligently exercising and watching his diet, too, because that's what Sean did. He decided on things. He stuck to his promises, not like me.

I broke my word.

"This isn't you, and you fucking know it," he said through gritted teeth, clenching tighter against my throat, the blood rushing from my head. "What did she do to you, huh?"

"Nothing," I growled, pulling on the latch of his arm. He wanted someone to blame, but it wasn't Pen. This was entirely on me.

"You've always been a terrible liar. So, what is it? We're not good enough for you anymore?"

That wasn't it either.

He broke the band of his arm, jerking me into the shelf I'd shoved him into. The side of my face hit the display. The pain in my cheekbone making me wince.

Shit, that was gonna bruise.

It was a miracle my hat hadn't flown off, but then again, Katrina had nicknamed me "Big Head" for a reason, and I knew it only partially had to do with my ego.

Sean descended upon me, a vibrating mass of muscle and pent-up rage. "Tell me what the fuck we did!" he shouted as I nursed my cheek, gritting my teeth. "Tell me what we did that was so bad, you would desert us."

I didn't want to desert them. I... he had it all wrong.

My chest heaved, my short inhalations burning in my lungs. I didn't know how to answer him. I had nothing. Nothing but the burden of Pen's rings in my pocket, burning a hole. Not even a pound in weight, but they felt like a two-ton brick that would drag me to the bottom of the ocean that same shade of her eyes if I dove in.

The urgent rush of footfalls descended upon us, four sets of arms pulling us apart. "Break it up, guys. C'mon."

Sean staggered back, breathing hard. He shrugged out of their grasp, brushing their hands away. "I'm leaving," he assured them, dropping his voice, appearing every bit as contrite as I knew he was. "I'm sorry for the trouble." He bent over, picking up his items and handed them gently to a clerk who seemed confused by the about-face.

He was always the fucking good guy, even when he was a dick. He shoved his hands in the pockets of his jeans, glancing at me one last time, his mouth a thin line as he shook his head, expressing his disappointment.

Then he walked away.

Someone said something to me, but I didn't hear them. My eyes followed the tall silhouette of my former best friend's shadow as it disappeared from my line of vision. That inescapable ache of loneliness resounded in my chest, and without warning, my legs pursued him. My lungs burned as I followed him through the sliding glass doors, the bitter October air nipping at my exposed cheeks.

Sean fiddled with his keys in the pocket of his jacket, heading toward his Jeep Wrangler. If I knew anything about his routine, he'd probably still gotten up at five this morning, worked out until seven, showered, crawled back into bed with his wife for fifteen fleeting minutes, where he melded his body with hers. Made breakfast for her while she nursed their babies, gotten to at least four remedial chores before ten, and then left the house for a few hours to get to all the other things he didn't have time to do otherwise because he worked six days a week.

Did he have any new friends?

Who was he watching the Pats play with?

Did he see Brady's two-yard touchdown with Branch?

Did he miss me as much as I missed him?

Had he replaced me with Maria's boyfriend once and for all? I knew how much he liked him.

"What are you painting?" I called at his back.

Did he need help?

Sean stopped walking, glaring at me over his shoulder. His jaw flexed with warning, and for a moment, I thought he was going to charge at me again. Finally, he spoke. "The shed."

"You built a shed?" He hadn't had one before.

Sean nodded absently. "A ten-by-ten one."

"Where?"

He folded his arms over his broad chest. "End of the hill in the back, near the maples."

A snapshot of his perfectly manicured backyard populated in my mind. Seriously. I'd teased him in the past that he cut each blade of grass by hand. "By the firepit?"

"Yep."

I offered him a slight smile. He made no effort to mirror it. "How's Raquel?"

At the mention of his wife, Sean's wide, linebacker shoulders hit his ears. "Shove it—"

"Up my ass," I finished for him. "Yeah, I know. You're the second Tavares to tell me that in two weeks."

He scoffed, knowing full well what I meant. "You deserved it."

"I needed that job." *And the distraction it provided me with.*

"Funny thing about needs, Dougie," he began, turning his sharp profile to stare back at the hardware store, the muscle in his jaw jumping. "When you lose things, you realize most needs are just wants."

I watched my best friend get into his Jeep and drive away without so much as a second glance.

Message received loud and clear.

He didn't need me anymore, either.

Chapter Fifteen

Penelope

Three years ago…

"WHAT ARE YOU DOING IN MY CLOSET?" SEAN QUESTIONED LOUDLY IN THE background of the phone call I was on with Katrina.

"He's got a wool-blend suit jacket, but that's about it," she said, ignoring her brother. "Will that work?"

A wool-blend suit jacket?

Honestly, Sean.

Okay, it wasn't ideal, but it would have to do. I needed this to go perfectly.

"That's fine. And make sure he shaves," I added. "I don't want him photographing like some kind of caveman." Although, I wasn't sure the shave alone would help improve his vocabulary or need to communicate in glares.

"What the fuck is going on?" Sean demanded. I drew the phone back from my ear just as he erupted on Trina. "Why are you in my room, messing with my closet?"

"I'm helping you get dressed."

"Get out, Katrina."

She didn't acknowledge him, jumping straight into her next query. "Can you try this blazer on? I need to know if it's going to fit or if Pen and I are going to have to re-strategize." She sounded doubtful.

Oh, God. How old was this blazer?

"Re-strategize for what?" he demanded thinly.

"The interview," Trina replied.

"What interview?"

I opened my mouth to speak, but she beat me to it again. "To help promote the sale of the house."

"You've gotta be fucking shitting me."

To my left, in the driver's seat, Dougie grimaced, shrinking into his seat as we drove to said house.

Sean just needed to trust me on this. They all needed to trust me on this. He wanted to offload the house, and I knew exactly how to do it.

Raquel.

My best friend just didn't know it yet, but she was next on my list of phone calls. I needed to get Sean in order first, and then I could get them in a room together and pray to the church of Bruce Dickinson that they got on well enough to embolden me.

Okay, I had ulterior motives.

I wanted a preview of what Dougie and I could expect when we told them our pregnancy news. This seemed like the right situation to perform a social experiment of sorts.

"It fits him," Trina informed me. "Tight in the shoulders, but if he tucks his hands in his pockets, it should be fine."

I chewed on the corner of my lip while Sean complained in the background. Better than nothing. "Perfect."

"I don't know about this, Penny," Dougie said quietly. "He's all pissy now. I don't like him pissy."

I waved him off. Same shit, different day.

"What about his shoes?" Trina asked.

"What do you mean by my shoes?" Sean growled. "Is this shit not enough? I feel like a sardine."

"Not his work boots," I thought out loud. "Does he have oxfords?"

"What the fuck are *oxfords*?" Sean asked.

"No," Trina replied. She shuffled in the background, the hangers in his closet rocking as though she'd shoved them aside to find his shoes in the back, the sound drowning out Sean's grumbling. "He's got an unworn pair of derbies though."

"I'm *not* wearing those."

"The derbies will work," I said.

"What about his pants?" Trina asked. "He's got black dress pants but—"

"No!" Sean snapped. "I'm not fucking wearing those in front of the guys, c'mon."

I drummed my fingers against the armrest of my door. I was willing to negotiate. "Will you be agreeable if I concede on the dress pants?"

He said something under his breath I didn't catch, but I heard the soft "thwack" of Katrina hitting him, so I could only imagine. "*Fine.*"

I was going to get him to like me someday. One day, he'd be nice to me.

One day.

"The blazer, dress shirt and the shoes."

"And no pants."

"Clean jeans," I warned.

"Clean jeans," he repeated.

"And a tie."

"Penelope—"

I cut him off. "Trina, have him showered, shaved, dressed, and at the house as soon as possible. We're working with an extremely tight window of time."

"Can do," she crooned.

"And don't forget his tie!"

"Unbelievable," Sean said.

The line went dead, and I sighed with relief, sinking back in my seat.

"Do you really think all of this was necessary?" Dougie asked as he turned on his indicator, waiting for a break in traffic to turn left.

Alright, maybe I hadn't needed to turn it into a whole thing, but I couldn't stomach the idea of Sean and Raquel meeting for the first time and then dropping that kind of information in their laps all at once.

Plus, if I sprung another impromptu meet-and-greet on Raquel, there would be no way in hell I'd be able to control the narrative.

And trust me, I needed to control her as much as humanly possible.

I hooked my boots at the ankles, nodding slowly. "Yes." I was sure of it. Or as sure as I could be given the circumstances.

Picking my phone back up, I thumbed through my contacts list, finding Raquel's number. It was early for a Monday, but I knew her routine like I knew the back of my hand. She left her apartment in The Dot every day at twenty to eight, got to The *Eaton Advocate* within an hour, and then sat in her rust bucket Camry with her forehead on the steering wheel until at least a quarter to nine, sometimes with a crinkled packet of Pall Malls clutched in her fist. Today was Monday, which meant that her boss, Earl, a sweet cherub of a middle-aged man, although he was kind of goofy, was no doubt assigning their stories for the week today.

Actually, she was probably in that meeting now. Shit, I hoped I didn't miss her or my window of opportunity.

The phone rang twice until she answered. She didn't immediately speak, the sound of a push bar on a door squeaking when her exhaled greeting came out. "Hey."

Then I heard it—the spark wheel on a lighter. "Kell, are you smoking right now?" I shouldn't be surprised. I was still constantly nagging her to quit. Didn't she know that shit was going to make her wrinkle?

"Morning to you, too, dollface," she jested.

"Raquel."

"Penelope." She rolled the vowels in my name, her accent thick as her inflection headed upward the way everyone in her native South Boston neighborhood spoke.

I heaved a sigh. "You're going to look fifty before your time."

"Good. Maybe it'll put me in a hole a little faster."

Raquel was only half kidding, but the joke made my insides heavy. She was ambivalent to death the way most people were about the rain. I hated the idea of a world without her in it, which heightened my fear of how she would react to the news when I told her I was pregnant. She didn't like change, and here I was, changing everything.

I straightened in my seat. "That is morbid, even for you," I remarked drolly.

"You still wearing Iron Maiden T-shirts to bed?"

I held up my pointer finger even though she couldn't see. "Maiden is not morbid. Maiden is life," I declared. The fucking audacity to even suggest otherwise.

"Yeah, yeah," she teased. "So, what's up?"

I cleared my throat as my segue for the reason of my call. "I had the most brilliant idea." Inhaling through my nose, I held it in my lungs for a moment before releasing it through my mouth. Here went nothing. "Remember how I told you I was doing that design job for Dougie's boss?"

Dougie shifted uncomfortably in his seat just as he turned into the house's driveway, the gravel making the tires bounce under us. My eyes caught on the *For Sale* sign staked in the ground. I was going to get this house sold if it was the last thing I did.

"Yah-huh?" she purred. Well, at least she hadn't immediately said something nasty about Dougie.

"You think you could convince Earl to run a story on it?"

She coughed, her lungs wheezing. "Uh…" her voice carried.

Raquel was silent for a moment. Dougie was careful when he turned off the truck, his features twisting with concern, making the bend in his nose look more severe.

I held up a placating hand. He was way more worried about this than I was. Then again, he hadn't liked the idea of me "manipulating the situation." It wasn't manipulation, it was arranging things in a mutually beneficial situation for everyone.

Sean got free press.

Raquel got a real story.

Dougie and I got our best friends' blessings.

I didn't read into Raquel's prolonged silence. It wasn't necessarily indicative of her refusal. She just needed to process things at her own pace.

She would come around eventually.

Right?

And no, I wasn't just referring to agreeing to do a story on the house anymore, either.

Finally, she spoke. "You mean you don't want to read another story about the fire department's charity drive?"

I rolled my eyes, thinking about the story she covered nearly every year. "You can do so much better than that. C'mon."

She was silent again. I wondered if she remembered that Daddy would have gotten her into the *Boston Globe* if she weren't so concerned about how it would look. She wasn't a charity case. She was my best friend—of course I wanted the best for her, and I was willing to exercise all my resources.

"So, is this favor for you or for your boyfriend?"

"Both," I replied quickly. Probably too quickly.

Dougie rubbed the bridge of his nose. It was clear that he wasn't Raquel's favorite person in the world, but she needed to understand that when she helped him, she helped me... and herself.

And Sean. Okay, maybe Dougie was right, and this was a little calculating. I squirmed, uncomfortable that perhaps I was a bit like Mother after all.

Raquel interrupted my reverie. "I'm starting to think things are getting serious with you and Dougie. Look at you, trying to call in favors for him." I didn't think she really meant anything by the comment and was just trying to joke around with me.

If only she knew...

"What's in it for me?" she asked.

"Seriously?" I snorted. "You really want to write about the car wash drive *again*?"

"Not really," she conceded, the phone shuffling. I thought she might have tucked it between her shoulder and ear now, no doubt picking at her cuticles. "But I already came up with a catchy headline —'Blazing Charity Initiative Sounds the Alarm on Children in Need'."

Dougie rolled his lips to contain the laugh.

"First of all, that is a terrible headline," I began.

Raquel made a gasping sound, feigning insult.

"Second of all," I continued, lifting my eyes to the incredible house, "you don't give a shit about that. Trust me. You'll love this house. Dougie's boss does nothing but century-old home restorations." My heart sank as I looked at the house. I was going to miss this place when it sold. We'd made a lot of memories here in a few months. Creamy white clapboard hugged the four-thousand-square-foot colonial, plenty of sash windows, and a long gravel-filled driveway framed by beautiful maple trees.

Saying goodbye was going to be hard.

Raquel's silence made me think she might be considering it. "So, kinda like giving things a new lease on life?" she tested.

"Exactly!" I squealed. Okay, so I had intentionally left out the part that Sean was a surly asshole—really fucking surly. And he wasn't happy about this and would not make the interview easy.

What? She could handle it.

Besides, who didn't want to know what was happening to all the century homes in Bristol County and the people who fixed and flipped them?

But I was still nervous over how Sean and Raquel were going to handle each other, especially since Raquel didn't resist or give me any pushback the way I'd expected her to.

They were going to be in each other's lives for the foreseeable future. What was the worst that could realistically happen?

Plus, it wasn't like I had to worry about them dating. If Raquel had a type, Sean was not it, and I was certain Sean didn't date. Short of him piping in that he was an ass man when he'd been prompted by one of the crew to come up with an answer—but not before glaring at them first—he'd never mentioned women. If I didn't know better because of infrequent anecdotes Dougie had shared with me about their shenanigans in their younger years, I would have assumed he was as celibate as a Catholic priest.

Raquel cleared her throat, getting my attention, and I knew she was in. "If Earl agrees—"

"*When* Earl agrees," I cut in. "Head to five-eighteen Riverside Avenue. You gotta drive across the bridge on Main Street and swing a right past that Presbyterian church. It'll be on the left-hand side. You won't be able to miss all the crew. You do your interview, and then we can hit that sandwich place you like so much in town."

Food would get her. I knew it would.

"You're buying," she grumbled.

"Yeah, yeah. Just get your ass over here. And do not show up smelling like a pack of Pall Malls."

I hung up before she could argue. Honestly, she needed to just quit.

Or find a good reason to.

Sean hadn't shaved, and I pretended like it didn't tick me off. He was mad enough for the both of us. He glowered at me as I adjusted a pillow for what felt like the umpteenth time. I wanted this to go perfectly. I *needed* this to go perfectly.

"Sean, why do you look like someone just died?" It came out like a croon, but I hadn't intended it, too.

I just desperately needed levity right now. I was so nervous, I wanted to be sick.

Could he be amenable for an hour? Two hours, tops?

Nothing.

He didn't utter a goddamn word.

Not even the formation of a smile. Hell, I would have been satisfied if he flipped me off.

A bead of sweat slid down my spine, hitting the waistline of my pants. God, it was fucking hot in here despite the dropping temperatures outdoors as late mid-fall enveloped us. Or maybe it was just my hormones running wild.

"It's an interview," I stressed, flipping a lock of my hair out of my eyes. "It's good press."

We'd disregard the fact that I had other intentions, too.

If she took to Sean even two percent, then maybe she wouldn't lose her absolute ever-loving shit that not only was Dougie not just someone I was spending a lot of time on top of, but was going to be the father of my child.

Oh, God.

Who was I kidding? Raquel was going to fucking hate Sean. And then she was going to hate me.

I fought the urge to place a hand on my stomach to settle my nerves. Instead, I rushed to the fireplace to adjust a vase on the mantel.

Breathe, Penelope.

I was more concerned about her reaction than my parents, and somehow, I knew they'd say all the wrong things, too.

"Can you please lose the constipated look?" I asked Sean without looking at him. I shifted the vase three inches to the right, paused, then slid it back to where it had been. Settling my hands on my hips, I propped the tip of my shoe on the floor.

Shit, that still didn't look right.

Vase aside, this house was a showstopper. I'd chosen a dark color scheme, accented by white teakwood furniture. It created the impression of the different stages of day and night. To compensate for how dark paint could shrink a room, I'd balanced it with mirrors of various sizes on a gallery wall.

Trina and I thought it looked pretty, but Sean had rolled his eyes and remarked, "Whatever."

His opinion didn't matter. Sure, he was footing the bill, but he owned one suit jacket and it hardly fit his broad shoulders. What did he know about good taste? Turning on my heel, a small smile tugged at my lips. I couldn't wait for Raquel to see this house, to see what I did for a living. I was proud of being able to bring a space like this to life, to set the mood and create an environment that made you want to stay.

This was my outlet, and it made me happy.

I glanced at Sean. For fuck's sake, he'd untucked his shirt while I had turned my back to him and the ends were sticking out over his jeans, his tie lopsided as though he'd been pulling at it.

He caught my frown. "Now what?" he groaned.

"Your tie is all messed up." I didn't know what kind of knot that was supposed to be, but I could do a full Windsor knot with my eyes closed. I moved toward him, my hands extended.

He took a step back, as though I were coming at him with a kitchen knife, his thigh hitting the arm of the suede couch.

Just fucking hold still, damn it. "Here, let me just—"

He waylaid me with his hand. "You can stage the house, Penelope, but you can't stage me."

At that, I stilled.

Ungrateful asshole. Miserable, insufferable prick.

I pursed my lips, my eyebrows pinching together. "I'll have you know I pulled a lot of strings to make this possible," I warned.

And I had.

Sorta.

"I hired you. You work for me," he stressed, shoving his hands into his pockets. Trina was right—it almost disguised that it was too short at the wrists due to the breadth of his shoulders. When the hell had he purchased the ugly blazer? Nineteen ninety-five?

I harrumphed, my expression growing smug. "As of..." I made a show of tapping my bottom lip, "two weeks ago, when your checks started bouncing, I'm more of a volunteer." I sent him a smarmy smile. He wasn't the only one who could dish it.

But I felt for him all the same. Two-thousand-and-eight was proving to be one of the worst financial years the world had experienced in a long time. Even Daddy was complaining.

I suspected that was what was really contributing to the house not selling. It was beautiful, done up to the nines, but the recession had made the banks reluctant to award anyone with less than an eight-hundred-and sixty credit rating a mortgage.

Which was one of the other reasons I thought he had relented and hired me.

Okay, I'd own that maybe I'd had gone a bit balls to the wall when it was my turn to call the shots around here, but the features I'd implemented were "must haves" in order to get him an actual bidding war and not a lowball offer.

Or at least, that had been my intent. So far? Radio fucking silence. Sure, people wandered through for showings with hearts in their eyes, but we saw it in their faces when they left.

They couldn't afford it.

Sean knew it, too. He ground his molars together, his sharp jaw flexing. "I'll get my finances back in order," he said, his tone gruff but apologetic.

It made me feel bad for bringing it up at all.

"Don't sweat it," I replied, turning away. I crouched low to the floor in a squat, balancing on my ankle boots while adjusting an earth-tinted area rug with a geometric print on it. "Dougie told me you're good for the money."

Again, not that I was desperate for it, but I knew it was the principle. All he needed to do today to make it even with me was pretend like he had his shit together and, at a minimum, be polite.

That was worth twenty-five-thousand dollars to me.

"I hope to God she's not as annoying as you are," he muttered to himself, moving toward the full-length mirror in the adjacent foyer.

Sean examined himself in the mirror. He really could have afforded that shave, but at least his beard was neat enough, presentable.

"I heard that," I sing-songed. "But I wouldn't worry. Raquel's a fan of brevity." Seriously, after she'd met Dougie for the first time, I think she'd said all of fifteen words after she'd left the bathroom at O'Malley's, and we'd been there for over two hours.

Sean tugged on the ends of his shirt, untucking the rest of it. He was such a kid. I'd told him he looked "Very Wall Street" when he'd gotten to the house as a compliment, but he'd taken that as permission to make himself unkempt.

There was one other matter to attend to.

"Also, before you ask, she doesn't have a boyfriend." I kept my tone unusually business like as I rounded behind him, my hands coming to his waist. This time, he didn't fight me, but I felt the weight of his stare in the mirror. Like he didn't know why I would tell him that. I adjusted his shirt, tucking the tails back in place. "But you're one hundred percent not her type, so let me spare you the trouble and tell you don't even think about it."

He wasn't her type, but he would be attracted to her.

It was hard not to be with her heart-shaped face, soft brown eyes and long lashes, pale complexion with a dusting of freckles over the bridge of her nose and dark hair.

You just needed to overlook the cigarette permanently hanging from her lips.

And her bad attitude.

Sean let out a breathless laugh. "No problem, Princess."

A twinge of something replaced the urge to roll my eyes. I couldn't place the sensation zipping through me that made me not want to believe him. But maybe that was my nervous system just over engaged.

I needed to calm down.

The sound of what I knew to be Raquel's car in the driveway based on the rattle of her rusty undercarriage had my ankle boots thundering across the foyer, a whistle shriek on par with a dog's low whine leaving my throat.

Seeing her face would give me the reassurance I needed to know everything would be okay. When I heard her car door close, I swung open the deep, red-stained front door, allowing a cold draft of air to circulate across the foyer.

"Hi!" I called, my voice growing several octaves higher.

Raquel barked out a laugh, vapors of her breath leaving her mouth on her exhale as she shook her head. Her appearance wasn't any better than Sean's.

Well, at least she wasn't wearing her beanie, but her hair was a mess, like she couldn't be bothered this morning.

She lifted the camera around her neck up to her face. "Close the door, you're messing up my shot."

I obliged her ask, closing the door and beaming at Sean. My smile slipped when he greeted me with his death stare. My gaze tightened on his, my smile not faltering. I jerked my head for him to come closer, my beaded chandelier earrings swinging on my earlobes.

Honestly, I'd kill him myself if he fucked this up. I was pretty sure that threat was perfectly clear in my expression.

Raquel knocked once on the door, and I swung it open. My nose wrinkled, the stench of tobacco hitting my nose. She'd definitely had a cigarette or two on the way here. I fought the urge to sigh. I couldn't win every battle, now, could I?

I waved Sean forward with my hand in a cupped motion like I was scooping air before I stepped out onto the porch, my boots creaking on the wooden boards. What was his deal?

She wasn't going to bite him.

"Raquel," I began. I waited until I detected Sean was standing in the front door's threshold behind me. "This is Sean Tavares."

I thought I heard him suck back a breath.

I frowned, glancing between them.

Dead. Fucking. Silence.

Raquel stared, her expression indecipherable. And he stared right back—*smitten*.

I held in the snort.

Raquel broke the silence first, 'cause you didn't engage a woman from South Boston in a staring contest. "Mr. Tavares."

I shot a glance at Sean, but he looked like a fish out of water. His throat worked frantically but nothing came out. I couldn't get a read on him. One moment, he seemed like he'd momentarily plunged into an alternate universe, tossed flat on his ass, and the next, he seemed even more pissed off, if that was possible.

"I'm Raquel Flannigan. I work for *The Eaton Advocate*." She held out a hand for him, his expression remained impassive. He didn't accept it, which was funny, because she hadn't accepted Dougie's handshake at the bar a few weeks ago, either.

Regardless of what Sean's body language suggested about his clear attraction, his stupid mouth said otherwise.

His sharp features closed on him, that more familiar annoyance tacking back in place. "I know who you are," he said, his tone clipped. "Take off your shoes when you come inside."

Yep, I was going to slaughter him and turn him into artwork for the next Maiden album.

Raquel wasn't bothered. I supposed his demeanor was tame compared to everything else she was used to, but that wasn't the point.

Her eyes swung from me back to him, an amused look blooming on her face as she drew in her bottom lip to stifle a laugh.

"Sure," Raquel replied with a shrug of her shoulders. "Let's start the tour." She sidestepped him to enter the house, bending over to unlace her boots.

I wanted to smash the vase on the fireplace over his head.

Sean stared at the fireplace, and then without warning, his neck curved back, and his eyes dropped to appraise her while she was bent over.

I couldn't believe him. What had he told me when I warned him he wasn't her type?

"No problem, Princess."

Now the asshole looked like he was practically ready to take her on the floor in front of me. I cleared my throat, drawing Sean's attention back to me. Folding my arms across my chest, I tilted my head at him, reminding him silently that Raquel wasn't on the menu.

Not really... but if Sean took to her, then maybe there was hope for all of us after all.

Maybe she'd warm to the idea of being around him.

Maybe she wouldn't completely lose her shit when I told her I was pregnant.

"How was lunch?" Dougie asked me when I approached him, holding out his roast beef sandwich wrapped tightly in aluminum foil. My palm was sweaty when he accepted it from me, a combination of the heat of the sandwich and my own nerves. I shoved my hands into my pockets, slouching into the neckline of my camel-colored car coat.

My heart hurt, my chin tilting downward. "Not good."

His face fell. "Did you tell her?"

I shook my head. Even if I'd wanted to tell Raquel the news, the mood had sobered quickly, and any window of would-be opportunity shut fast.

"Sean pissed her off." Sean had gotten under Raquel's skin and come on to her during their interview. Or at least, that had been the impression I'd gotten in her recounting of their interaction together.

"He has that effect on people..." Dougie trailed off, glancing at the doorway. "Charming son of a bitch." He chuckled, his green eyes crinkling in the corner. "I think he might be a bit smitten."

"I think that might be mutual."

Raquel had gotten very flustered with me. When I brought it up to her at lunch, she hadn't cared to be called out on eye fucking him while we'd all been in the kitchen together when the tour first started. I mean, if she didn't want to be called on it, she shouldn't have made it so obvious. If she wasn't looking through the viewfinder on her camera, she was studying him.

Then I got the idea to suggest maybe she should broaden her horizons since she'd only been with one other guy, and maybe Sean might not be such a bad thing for her.

Honestly, it didn't even *need* to be Sean specifically. She could have fucked anyone.

Anyone *but* her ex. I hated that asshole. He was bad for her, a coping mechanism that kept her trapped to her monsters and a life she'd tried to leave behind.

Especially during this time of year. Her sister's death anniversary was coming up.

Raquel shut down on me after that, asking only to eat the rest of my salad even though she'd insinuated it was pretentious looking.

"Hey," Dougie said gently. He set his sandwich down on the edge of the kitchen counter, opening his arms for me. I stepped into him, burying my face in the crook of his neck, inhaling deeply. "It's going to be okay."

I felt so fucking overwhelmed. "She's going to hate me."

"She's not going to hate you, Penny," he reassured me, squeezing me tightly. "Who would hate you for something like being pregnant?"

Raquel.

That's who.

Chapter Sixteen

Penelope

Present

"You look awful, Penelope."

You would have thought after nearly thirty-one years of being at the receiving end of Evelyn Cullimore's bitter criticism that the familiar sting would fade, or at least dull with time, but it didn't.

It was ever present, just as caustic as she'd intended it to be.

I stared at the screen, slouched in my seat. Unlike me, in her window of our Skype call on my computer, she was as pristine as ever. Not even a single flyaway dared to step out of place. The background behind her polished and put together. I knew she was in her office, if you could call it that. Everything around her was too ornate, too fussy, kind of like her. Mother liked antiques and Tiffany. We shared that in common, but she wanted every room to feel like a period film. I preferred to marry vintage with something new. The wall sconces behind her were brass.

As a kid, I used to fuck with her for shits and giggles and loosen the bulbs a little, so they'd flicker.

I wished I could do it right now, just to inconvenience her with my disruption.

I didn't really want to speak to her, but this was... hard for me. And I was desperate.

At my silence, she extended the nude-polished tips of her fingers to the string of pearls around her neck, stroking the delicate beads, one by one.

"Where's Daddy?"

"Working," she supplied, offering me her best attempt at a dour look. God, her face barely moved anymore. There wasn't a natural expression to be found under all the Botox and filler. Her cheeks rounded and smooth, forehead flat, not even a wrinkle to be found near her eyes.

Pristine. Poised. Plastic.

"Did you brush your hair today?" she questioned.

I touched my hair out of reflex, the short ends tangled. No, brushing my hair hadn't made it high on my list of priorities today. Or this week. I'd showered at some point, though.

I thought I had, anyway.

Mother leaned forward, squinting her eyes as much as the atrophied muscles would permit. "I'm going to send you some under eye cream, too. I hope you're wearing SPF—"

Just rip the bandage off, Penelope.

"Dougie and I are getting divorced." I pinched my lips together to keep from crying. Saying the words out loud made them real. Telling her meant... meant we'd have to see it through.

Nothing would make my parents happier than this news. They'd never really liked him, anyway.

And now, now, he'd said the words back to me. The ones I'd callously thrown around at him all the time like a weapon when he pushed me too hard.

I waited for her to erupt into her controlled version of celebration, to listen to her prattle off about a party of some sort, a reintegration into high society.

Divorce parties were in now, weren't they?

Mother stilled, her expression indecipherable for a moment before that somber veil slipped back into place.

"No, you will not be."

I lost control of the garbled sound I released. "What?"

She offered me a curt smile. "When you're selecting an SPF, you want something without oxybenzone in it," she said. "It's very toxic."

An iota of worry zipped through me. Was she fucking senile?

"Did you hear me?" I slanted my head, my greasy hair falling into my face, my breath hitching. "Dougie and I—"

"I heard you the first time, Penelope Louise. I speak for Daddy and myself when I tell you 'no.'" I let out an unbridled laugh that went unacknowledged. "We expect you both for Thanksgiving next month."

Thanksgiving. Fucking Thanksgiving.

The dizziness set in, my mouth tacky as I wrapped my arms around myself. "I wasn't asking you for permission."

Mother attempted to raise her brow. "Then I bid you well in finding a lawyer to assist you."

"I wasn't seeking help with legal representation, either."

My gut tightened when she held up her patronizing finger. "Penelope, make no mistake when I tell you we will ensure that no lawyer in the northeast coast will assist you. Am I making myself very clear?" She slanted her head, her brows attempting to raise to drive her point. "Now, would you prefer turkey or ham?"

Turkey or ham? Was it really that easy being her? Did she ever feel inconvenienced by the realities of life, or did she simply shift into the next inconsequential item on her meaningless to do list?

I was getting divorced, and she didn't care, because in her eyes it wasn't happening.

I willed the anger to come at the abundantly apparent absence of her support, at the non-concern, at her fixation with moving along as though I'd asked her opinion on a bedspread—but some small part of me was relieved she'd make it difficult for us.

I didn't want a divorce.

No matter what I'd said to Dougie, regardless of how angry I was.

I didn't want to give up on him anymore than I wanted him to give up on me.

But it was the fucking principle. "You are incredible, Mother." *And cold.*

"We won't help you ruin your life."

Too late. I'd done that all by myself.

I watched in silence as she shifted in her chair, head held high, then crossed her leg over the other, bringing a delicate teacup to her lips with a floral and gilded trim around the rim. As predictable as ever, she wet her lips because Mother never slurped, nor sipped. She'd do that for hours on end until the teacup depleted, or she tired of it. Settling the teacup down, she touched her mouth with a napkin unceremoniously, then looked at me as though remembering I was there. "Unless you wish to call that woman who reviewed the prenuptial agreement. What was her name?" She touched her polished hair absently. "The best man's sister."

She had never slapped me before, but I felt as though she had just reached through the screen and struck me with an open palm at full force.

"Fuck. You."

Why would she bring her up? She didn't know what that woman had done to me, done to my marriage, but it hurt me all the same because my mother knew nothing about me. She never even tried. She knew what she wanted to know, and that was the extent. Everything else was inconsequential.

Her head snapped back. "Penelope," she admonished.

"Fuck you," I repeated, the muscle in my jaw jumping. "Fuck you, and fuck your money and pretension, and fuck your rules. I don't need anything from you or Daddy."

Just please be my mother, just this once.

Ask me what's wrong.

Ask me how Dougie and I even got here.

Ask me anything.

Instead, I got her criticism, just like always. "You're behaving like a child."

"And you're behaving like a frosty bitch," I seethed. "I wish you could be my mother instead of treating me like I'm some kind of extension of yourself."

She pressed an appalled palm to her chest. "You represent the family."

"I represent *me,* and you have never accepted that." My chest caved in as the tears came. I didn't fight them. She could give me hell about it, too, for all I cared.

"What has gotten into you?" she asked quietly. "I thought you and I were getting along."

She wasn't wrong. I'd been trying for the last couple of months. Trying to make her like me more in some way or another because I was lonely. I wanted her to care. I stared down at my wrung hands, my knuckles tight with tension, the pang of loss from my wedding rings ricocheting through me. "You're not even asking me why Dougie and I are getting divorced."

"Because the matter is done with."

"No, it's not!" I said, my voice rising. My head was swimming. I felt disoriented as a ringing set off in my ears. "It's not done just because you say it is. The only reason you and I were ever getting along was because I made the mistake of behaving just like you."

At the cost of my marriage.

She didn't even flinch. She just studied me, her gaze momentarily sharpening for a moment before she reached for that fucking teacup again. "I see."

I closed my eyes, shaking my head. "Why did you even want to have a child?"

She'd never behaved in a way that suggested she liked me, not really. Sure, there was the obvious maternal obligation, and the life box that required a check mark, but...

She'd never been warm. She'd never seemed to care at all.

When I opened my eyes, she was staring straight at me and for a moment, I felt like I was looking into a mirror of myself. But just as quickly as I saw a splinter of her vulnerability, it was gone. "That's what people do when they marry."

"Did you *want* a child?" That part had never been completely clear to me. Sure, I knew they'd tried and struggled after me, but my parents weren't emotional to begin with.

They didn't discuss their worries.

They discussed polo, tennis, stocks, and charity galas.

Meticulously and regimentally grooming their lives around their society and their country clubs. They tried to give me the best advantages life offered because that was what they believed was expected of them. It was their job.

But all I'd ever wanted was them to love me.

There was so much about life that they hadn't prepared me for—things I'd had to learn the hard way because there was no price tag on it.

All that precautionary therapy, and I still had no idea what to do with the messy parts of life.

Like getting divorced.

I knew nothing about my parents beyond what they wanted me to see.

The din of her teacup finding its saucer resounded, sharp and tinny. Then came the familiar brush of her sweeping palms over the hemline of her dress. "I wanted many."

I snorted. "So, someone else could raise them?" She had hardly been present for my upbringing.

Her face reddened, her jaw flexing as much as her atrophied masseter muscles would allow. "I think perhaps it would be best if we concluded this conversation."

But I didn't want to get off the phone with her. I wanted to fight her. I wanted someone to fight with, to fight for me. "When you accused me of putting on weight when we went to lunch the day before the wedding," I said, my voice quivering. "Did you know I was pregnant?"

Lunch that day had been a disaster—not just because Mother had antagonized me over my weight, but because Maria had been there with her boyfriend, and I'd... I don't know, tried to extend an olive branch to her in the form of my thanks for helping Dougie with the prenup. But all she'd done was stare at me like I'd taken something from her.

I supposed I'd had, and then life took something from me.

I was pregnant.

And then I wasn't.

An eye for an eye.

Mother stiffened, losing control. Her mouth fell open with shock, her stare working over my face. She cleared her throat, her posture shifting. "*Was?*"

"I had a miscarriage a few days later," I whispered, the emotional paralysis filtering through me. "I just thought you should know. You're my mother after all."

Someone should know.

Her self-soothing increased, each shift of her hand against the fabric of her dress louder than the last. "I'm sorry to hear that."

I nodded, my jaw quivering. "Me, too."

Mother allowed herself to slouch for a moment, hanging her head. "May I inquire how far along you were?"

I sniffled, swiping the tears away frantically, looking heavenward. "Not out of the first trimester." I was weeks away from the second trimester.

She slanted her head forward, remaining quiet. I'd never felt more hollowed out and numb in my life. I didn't know what I was expecting when I told her I'd lost a baby.

But it wasn't her mentally shutting down and freezing me out like she had every other point in my life. I'd never confided in her over anything, ever.

"You're aware Daddy and I struggled to have more children after you," she began. I lifted my head, watching as Mother tried to tack on false bravery. "We saw many specialists across the country, looking for someone that could tell us why, but then..." she trailed off, a flickering smile touching her mouth. "I was pregnant."

My heart thumped in my chest, my limbs tingling. "When?"

"Oh, you must have been three?" she said, thinking out loud. "Far too young to remember."

But for some reason, her saying that knocked something inside of me that recalled her dresses growing snug, and her wardrobe changing from her fitted dresses to looser floral prints that were more flattering on her figure, the glow in her skin, and the twinkle in her eye.

The only time I ever recalled Mother happy.

"We lost him at seven months," she whispered, bringing a hand to her mouth before she cleared her throat. "When you're that far along, you have to deliver." My heart thumped, a buzzing ringing in my ears as I grappled to process what she'd said.

But I remembered. The leather carry-on bag that Daddy had carried down the stairs, guiding her out the front door while she cried.

Frieda, the housekeeper and nanny, held my hand as I watched them pull out of the circular driveway by the sitting-room window.

"We named him Samuel, after my father," she volunteered. "The nurses were very gracious." She looked away from the camera. "I held him until Daddy said it was time. He was beautiful. His hair was gold like yours." Tears welled in my eyes, my hands twisting in my lap. "I remember running my finger along his hands. You forget how small babies are until they're in your arms, their tiny little nail beds, each delicate wrinkle in their fingers, and then..." her voice trailed off. "The agony of hearing the full, viable cries in the distance of another baby taking the breath Samuel never would."

I'd been awful to her over the years, and knowing that she'd harbored this, that my parents had suffered such a loss and I'd been brutal, and stubborn to a fault... "Mother—"

"I could still feel him kicking for months after that, phantom little juts of his foot against my stomach. Eventually it stopped, but sometimes I think about the kinds of trouble you two would have caused," she carried on, as though I'd never said her name at all. "Or if he would have been the staid one."

I wanted to be sick. "How could you have never told me this?" I whispered.

That she'd lost a baby. That she'd had to deliver him. That I'd had a brother.

Shame made my eyes sting, realization dawning on me. I supposed it was the same reason I hadn't told Dougie.

"I live my life very meticulously, Penelope, because it helps me maintain control of my person." She inhaled, squaring her chin. "Our loss breaks us. It challenges the strength of our marriage. It changes our view of ourselves and of the world. Some of us can compartmentalize, and some of us..."

Ended up like me.

Struggling to salvage the pieces. Some profoundly idiotic part of me wanted to compare our losses, our grief. She'd lost more than me. She'd held him.

She'd been able to look down at him, and see his tiny, mostly developed features, identify who he looked more like, plead with his heart to beat. My loss was an inch long and not quite one-third of an ounce.

But the wound felt like I'd been flayed alive, the torture on my mind unlike any other that I wouldn't wish it on my worst enemy.

"The grief can overtake us if we allow it." She gave me a knowing look. "Losing a pregnancy, a child, that kind of... suffering... it changes you forever. It adds a complicated strain to a marriage because you're left wanting to blame someone. And it's not anyone's fault, not even yours."

All I could do was cry, because that was exactly it. I felt an indescribable anger. I struggled to put it into words because of how tight of a grip it had around me. Every breath was a negotiation, every smile a challenge, every day required immeasurable strength.

"Now, Douglas isn't like Daddy... he's more *emotional*," she said, punctuating emotional. "So, I suspect this kind of grief is something more vocalized by him and that puts an immense strain on a marriage." Her mouth pulled a little. "Is he being cruel?"

Cruel? Dougie? Never. He'd never been cruel. That was me, all me.

Not telling him? That was another sin. I had blood on my hands.

I swiped the tears away, running my teeth along my bottom lip before I shook my head. "Dougie doesn't know," I offered her quietly. "I never told him."

She did nothing to contain the gasp, and it sliced through me when she said my name. "Penelope?"

"It just happened, you know? There was so much already going on, and I thought..." I bit my lip, trying to contain the sob. "I thought telling him I was pregnant while we were away on our honeymoon would bring us back together again."

"Back together again? I don't understand."

"We've been struggling a long time." I brushed my hair back. "The wedding got too big and out of control, and Dougie was just trying to be amenable and make everyone happy, but he... he never wanted such an opulent event." I looked up at her. "That wasn't him."

It wasn't us.

I'd never wanted a big wedding, either. And yet...

Her mouth tensed with understanding. "You did it because we asked you to."

I bit my lower lip, nodding my head. "I just... I wanted what I thought was easy, what would make everyone happy."

"I thought it was unlike you to be so agreeable," she breathed, letting out a little laugh. "Even when we asked you about him changing his last name." They really had asked that, and he'd been rightly offended.

I shook my head at her. "You know that was offensive."

"In hindsight, I suppose it was. We were just trying to make him one of us, completely." But it was still my fault for not fighting back, for even insulting him at all. "What are you going to do?" she asked.

"I don't know."

"He's your husband. He should know."

"It's not going to make a difference now."

"Penelope." She exhaled my name. I looked up at her, surprised to find her eyes glossed over and the back of her hand held against her mouth. "He deserves to grieve for his loss, too. Stop lying to yourself and to him."

I sagged back against the kitchen bar stool, my lungs tight as I buried my face in my hands. She was right. I knew she was, even if I didn't want to admit it.

I had to tell him, and I needed to own the repercussions of my decisions.

"What if—"

"If we based our lives on what-if's, nothing would ever get accomplished," she said, blotting her eyes with a handkerchief she'd produced from God only knew where. "Marriage is a union, and divorces are for lazy people. Despite your obstinance, you are neither lazy nor interested in getting divorced. You didn't fight Daddy and I about him just to get divorced."

No, I hadn't fought my parents and their perception of Dougie just so I could sign divorce papers.

"There's something else," I said, stirring in my seat. "The night Raquel went into labor." Mother didn't flinch when I said Raquel's name anymore. Now that my best friend had married, made a career and a name for herself, she was no longer something she scrunched her nose up over. "I found Dougie with..." my voice cracked at the end. I extended a hand toward the paper towel dispenser, tearing a sheet off. "With Maria."

Saying her name out loud took what little warmth remained in my body. I wanted to recede in on myself, to focus on anything but reliving this part year.

"Maria...?"

"The lawyer. Sean's sister... the best man."

Mother sucked back an aghast breath. "Douglas had an affair?" She sobered, straightening a little as though this changed things somehow. It was one thing for me to lose a child, it was another thing for my husband to embarrass me—embarrass them.

"I don't know."

"Well, what did you see?" She lowered her voice, glancing over her shoulder, despite being alone and her door being shut. "Was it compromising?"

It depended on her definition of compromising. What I saw was enough for me to surmise. "He was just with her in his truck."

"In his truck? Doing what?"

I stared down at the soiled, crumpled paper towel in my hand, running my finger along the edges I'd created. "She was crying. Her makeup was smudged."

"That doesn't mean they had an affair, Penelope."

I shook my head. "It's more complicated than that."

"Why?"

I wasn't about to tell my mother that my husband and I hadn't had sex in over half a year. That, of course, he'd want something from someone else. That I'd feel the same way, too.

Biology did not design us to be absent of affection for months on end with no explanation. It would drive any sane person over the edge, no matter how much they loved you.

Did I truly expect that he'd be able to handle it until I decided otherwise?

I never even gave him the opportunity. I never gave him the chance to understand, to grieve with me, because I was so fucking ashamed that I'd let him down.

That I'd gotten pregnant at all.

So, I got mad. I got angry. I got bitter. I said things I didn't mean to him, about him, about Raquel. I pushed, and I pushed, and he found someone familiar, someone who understood him.

Someone who could love him.

"I-I pulled away from Dougie when I found out I was pregnant. I was upset about the timing and frustrated. The wedding was over-whelming, and my hormones were raging and I..." I paused. I needed to accept responsibility for my role. "Mother, I, Dougie... we—" she held up a hand, stopping me.

I'd never spoken to my mother about sex. She'd been content to believe that a stork delivered Christopher.

"Yes, I see where this is going." I slumped over the counter, framing my forehead with my hands. "Have you spoken to Raquel for her opinion? It was her husband's sister, after all. Surely, she'd have some-thing of value to contribute."

Raquel would kill Maria. I knew she would. But there was still this seedling of doubt that existed, that perhaps I hadn't seen what I thought I had, that maybe Dougie had been honest with me. That the extent had only gone as far as he'd confessed—a thought.

But the thought still hurt, and he'd still gone to South Boston. "Raquel and I aren't speaking at the moment," I volunteered.

"Why?" Mother's influx of questions was out of character for her, but a small part of me bloomed with dull warmth every time she asked. Then she made a sound, as though filling in the blank herself. "She was pregnant."

"And I wasn't." *Anymore.* The keyboard of my laptop blurred on me as another fresh batch of tears spilled over. "I'm too ashamed to admit to her that I resented her for having what I didn't."

"Penelope, you have what she has." And more. I had more than her, and I had no right to be irrationally envious of her, but seeing her pregnant, knowing she'd never even wanted children to begin with...

I was awful for allowing my thoughts to go where they had. I was making excuses for myself, rather than just owning them.

"I know, I just..." I swallowed the lump in my throat. "It was hard being around her. I didn't want to spoil her happiness with my misery and I felt horrible about the things I'd said about her. So when she ended up in the hospital for her accident, wh-when..." I was struggling to speak, my nose running and my throat raw as I tried to conjure up the words. "When I thought she was going to die, I just, I didn't feel I deserved her anymore."

"She's your best friend," she reminded, but then she paused. Her face closed on her, making the connection. "You didn't tell her you were expecting either, did you?"

"I told no one." I offered her a dull stare. "You're the first one."

She sighed, her expression grave. "All that effort with therapists, and you're struggling to remain transparent."

"Because I'm ashamed."

"Shame is a useless emotion," she volunteered, her voice dropping. "Shame ruins friendships and marriages if you give it an opportunity to breed."

I nodded, sniffling.

"Do you honestly want a divorce?"

"No."

She turned her head, focusing on the window I knew was to her left. A strobe of sunlight streaked across the room. "You need to tell him, Penelope. If you have any hope of salvaging your marriage, you need to stop lying to him."

"It's not a lie."

"And stop lying to yourself, too." She glanced back at me, her eyes narrowing. "You didn't fight this hard for your independence and for our approval just to hand in the towel when it got hard."

I slanted my head. "He's going to hate me."

"You're his wife," she reminded, as gently as Mother could manage. "He's fought for you, too." At my silence, she added, "Figure out what brought you two together." She pursed her lips, no doubt questioning what exactly that had been to begin with.

But I knew.

I just wasn't sure if my husband still felt that way, too.

Chapter Seventeen

Dougie

Three years ago...

Raquel Flannigan was a piece of fucking work, and I didn't have the slightest idea why Sean was interested in her.

Especially as I blotted Penelope's tears from her ruddy face.

"Breathe, Penny," I murmured as she sobbed, seated on the closed bathroom toilet seat in her apartment.

"Sh-she ha-hates m-m-me," she gasped, another wail escaping her as her chest heaved, trying to find her next breath.

Tonight had been a fucking disaster. We'd invited Sean and Raquel to O'Malley's to tell them both about Penelope's pregnancy.

Only Sean knew ahead of time. I'd warned him earlier in the week after I'd gone over to his place for pizza, a couple of beers and video games.

Then he'd asked for intel on Raquel. Information I hadn't been all that interested in giving him to begin with, but Penelope had witnessed something between the two of them the morning they met at the house. She thought it was worth them exploring and had given me Raquel's number to hand over to Sean should he ask for it.

And just as Penelope predicted, after Raquel had rebuffed his emails, and his phone call to her work line—he had asked for her cell-phone number. Despite my better judgment, I handed it over to him because I trusted Penelope's instincts. If she said she saw something spark between them, then I believed her.

Except now I regretted it because that snarky, hardheaded harpy had gone and made my girlfriend cry. As Penelope feared, Raquel hadn't taken the pregnancy news well.

At all.

"Congrats and good luck." There was a finality to it that devastated the hell out of Penelope.

Sean hadn't helped in that moment when he told her, *"You don't owe her shit, Penelope."* Then he tossed his beer back. *"You need people who are going to be genuinely happy for you."*

I guess I hadn't helped either when Raquel snarled the remark that, *"I should shove it, Douglas. Ideally somewhere, you can't impregnate her again."* Which made me vault upright, and Pen begged me to sit back down.

Raquel was unbelievable. She hadn't said one nice congratulatory thing, and then, after making a mess, she had zero interest in cleaning it up. She stormed off.

Was she really that unhappy for us? I didn't get it.

I'd brought Penelope back to her place, and she'd been crying inconsolably ever since.

"If she's pissed, what are my parents going to think?" Truthfully, the thought had crossed my mind. If Raquel had flipped her shit, there was no way Daddy and Mommy Cullimore were going to be clapping their hands with joy or wheeling out a shiny new baby carriage.

But there was one thing that resounded in my mind every time that thought had whirred. I dropped to my haunches, tossing the tear-soaked tissue into the wastebasket and framing her knees with my palms. "Penny," I began, exhaling. "Does it matter?"

She swallowed the lump in her throat, sniffling. "What do you mean?"

"Does it matter what they think?"

She curled her fingers into her palm along her jeans. "This isn't exactly what they dreamed for me, Dougie."

"But what did you dream about for yourself?" I pressed, probing the inside of my cheek.

She rolled her lips together, making the connection. "A family."

I steadied myself against her left knee, extending my right hand to brush her matted hair away from her flushed face. "That's right," I murmured. "So, does it matter what they think? Any of them?"

So it wasn't on their timeline, or the way they had or hadn't wanted it, but it *was* happening. Why make it harder for her than it already was? She didn't deserve it.

We didn't deserve it.

Pen digested my question, finally shaking her head. "No, it doesn't matter. I guess, I-I just wanted her support, you know?" she whispered. "I could deal with my parents' rage if I knew that... that she backed me how Sean backs you."

Sean was an asshole, I'd never deny otherwise—but he was an asshole who stayed in his own lane and didn't make a habit of trying to tell people how to live their lives. Sean had lost a lot, too, but Sean had more sisters than I had friends. His support system was dependable.

Raquel didn't have any of that. She only had Penelope.

Of course, anything threatening that was going to set her off. *Argh, fuck it.* "You told me that Raquel's lost a lot, right?" I asked. Man, I couldn't believe I was about to defend her even an iota after the shitstorm she'd caused, but, in some regretful way, I understood it. "'Hurt people, hurt people'. She's probably terrified that she's going to lose you."

Her expression softened, a fresh batch of tears glistening in her eyes as her whole chin trembled. "She's not going to lose me."

"I know that," I agreed. "But sometimes, I think that's hard for people like her to see. She just needs time to adjust to the idea." I thought that was what she needed, anyway.

And maybe a daily dose of serotonin.

It was probably why Raquel hated me so much right out of the gate. I was a threat to her safety net. She didn't trust me to not take Penelope away from her, and now that she was pregnant, it guaranteed that their time together would become fractured.

But I wasn't trying to steal Penelope. I just wanted some of her, too. "It'll be okay." I repeated Sean's sentiment from the bar. "She'll come around."

Or at least I hoped she would.

"How do you know?" she asked, her glossy blue eyes searching mine.

"Because she's going to miss you too much." I tried for confident, but I wasn't entirely sure. Raquel was stubborn and a mean piece of work, but she was human, too. She wasn't as impenetrable as she wanted to pretend she was. She was just as scared and vulnerable as the rest of us.

Life had hurt that woman immeasurably, and she wanted to make sure everyone knew it, too.

She'd come back for Penelope. She just needed to grieve the loss of whatever fantasy she'd constructed in her head for them first.

"I was horrible to her," Penelope murmured, her brows furrowing in the middle as she no doubt played the memory back in her mind of tonight.

I didn't know how the fuck Raquel instinctually had figured it out, but she had trailed after Sean when they entered the bar, a chip on her shoulder, with fury already twisting her features. As soon as she spotted Sean joining us at the table, she looked as though she'd had the wind knocked right out of her as she put two and two together.

The surprise fled, and then there was just her familiar disdain. Her hackles were up, her fingers digging into the strap of her bag, and her eyes wide with mistrust as if she knew whatever we'd summoned her for would not be good.

"I called her foul," Pen recalled, sniffling. "And a fucking jackass."

Like I said, that was tame. "Well, she was being both things, Penny."

As far as I was concerned, she'd gotten off easy. Sean and I gave Raquel more grief than Penelope had.

As soon as Raquel walked away, disappearing to God knew where, Pen slouched in the booth like she wanted nothing more than to just disappear.

We left shortly after that, leaving Sean behind to finish the pitcher of beer by himself, his eyes scanning the bar. I wasn't sure what he was looking for, but so much for neutral territory. I felt bad for dragging him out there, only for the night to end in a disaster before it really began.

Pen released a helpless mewl, the tears freeing themselves. "She's never going to forgive me."

"I think the question you need to ask yourself," I started, cupping her cheek, catching an errant tear with my thumb, "is if *you* want to forgive *her*?"

Penelope sniffled, leaning into my hand before she nodded. "Always. She's my best friend."

I smiled. That's what I thought. "Then give her time. We're adapting, but so is she."

"Sean didn't seem surprised," she observed, glancing up at me wearily. "You told him beforehand, didn't you?"

"It might have come up," I confessed.

"You lied," she whined.

"I omitted," I corrected. "It came up, so I told him the truth."

She heaved a sigh, her shoulders slumping. "No wonder he was so amenable."

"Sean wants kids," I supplied. "This kind of thing is normal in his mind."

"Raquel doesn't," she said, reaching for the toilet paper, wrenching her hand to free a couple of squares. "We were supposed to travel the world and I just shit all over her plan."

"Her plan, not yours," I said. "Plans sometimes change."

"Maybe Sean will sweep her off her feet," she said, trying to brighten.

"Let's be realistic, Penny." No one swept women like Raquel off their feet, not even God himself.

"I *am* being realistic," she replied, watching me through her matted lashes, tacky with her wet mascara from crying. "It could happen. I'd support it. She deserves to be happy, too."

The only thing that would make Raquel happy, I was certain of, was if Sean and I exited stage left and never came back.

I blew out a breath. I wasn't sure I would support any kind of romantic venture between my best friend and hers. That had *recipe for disaster* written all over it even if he was interested in her.

It was time to get her off the subject. "How about we wash your face and get you into bed?"

I helped her up, then patted her countertop, lifting her weight up onto it. I fiddled in her drawers, pulling out fresh cotton squares and the bottle of makeup remover I'd seen her reach for dozens of times before.

"You don't like her, do you?" she inquired as I soaked the cotton square in whatever the hell was in the bottle.

I cleared my throat. "She's an acquired taste."

"She's my best friend."

I dragged the cotton square over her cheekbone, watching it leave a clear track against her skin as her makeup melted away. "I'll never come between you two."

"Promise?" she asked me, her eyes dropping as I brought the pad against the smudge of black on her eyes.

"I promise."

"I need her support more than I need my parents'," she confessed, tipping her head back to give me easier access to her face. I didn't know why she slapped all this shit on. She was pretty without it. "She keeps me grounded in a way I can't explain."

"She's supposed to," I said with a sigh, reaching for a new cotton pad. "That's what best friends are for." I repeated my motions on the other half of her face until all that was left for her to do was to wash her face and use the other shit in her drawers.

Toner, or whatever. All I knew was that it had an artificial floral scent I didn't like because it was vaguely reminiscent of a funeral parlor.

As I was stepping back from her to create space for her to slide off the counter, she hooked her fingers around my belt loops, drawing me back. Pen parked her chin on my chest, watching up at me through her lashes. "Can I tell you something?"

When she looked at me like that, like she was taking a dozen pictures rapidly to immortalize a moment in time, my stomach always lurched, my heart swelling.

"What?"

She smiled at me shyly, and despite her red-and-blotchy face and swollen eyes, she was still the prettiest fucking thing I'd ever seen. "I love you."

She always said the kind of shit that brought me to my knees. I bracketed her face with my hands, lowering my forehead to hers. "I love you, too, Penny."

"You do?" she whispered.

"I do." And the next time I said 'I do' to her, she'd be in a dress that would never match her beauty, with a bouquet grasped in her hand, and a wedding officiant running us through our vows.

'Cause I was gonna marry the hell out of Penelope.

She feathered her lips against mine, her legs circling my waist. Her hands snaked up my chest, arms looping around my neck. I braced one hand against the lip of her bathroom counter, the other cradling the back of her hand, pinning her to me.

Pen opened her mouth, brushing her tongue against mine as her hips rolled against me. "Let me bring you to bed," I suggested, shifting my arms to pull her off the counter.

"No," she argued. "Here."

"Penny." I wasn't interested in fucking the mother of my child on a bathroom counter, even if it was in the ritziest neighborhood in the state. It felt wrong.

She seemed to know where my thoughts had gone, too. "I may be pregnant, but you're going to continue to fuck me in every conceivable place possible when I ask you to."

I gripped the back of her head, earning myself her little gasp as our breathing mingled. "You've got a mouth on you."

"A mouth that's equipped to do many things if you don't treat me like some kind of trophy." She shifted her hands up my shirt, the blunt edges of her nails dragging upward. "Nothing changes between you and me, baby or not." She studied me, her eyes half-lidded. "Promise me, Dougie. It's always you and me, just like we were in your truck."

"I can't treat you like you're disposable."

"You never have," she assured. "Even when I wanted you to."

That was the closest thing to a confession I'd ever gotten out of her. She had wanted a cheap and dirty fuck back then, and she'd wanted someone that she could keep on the line, someone that she knew would hurt her.

But not me. I couldn't hurt her. I wouldn't hurt her. No, I'd spend the rest of my meager existence worshipping her, wanting her, loving her.

I let her tug my shirt upward, my arms rising so I could help her pull it off. When it cleared my head, I tossed it to the floor, practically preening as she examined me.

She always lost control of her mouth when I ditched my shirt, her explorative hands moving along the planes of my abs, roving inquisitively along each delineation there. I bent back as she fiddled with my belt, the buckle squeaking as it came undone, the waist of my pants growing slack.

Well, mostly slack. The only thing keeping them up was the pitching of my hardening cock. "You wanted me to use you back then, didn't you?"

She pressed her lips against my chest, her head weaving in a barely there nod. My skin grew hot under her mouth, her teeth grazing against my nipple. "I got more out of you than I bargained for because of your rules."

"What rules?" I murmured, sweeping her hair to one shoulder.

"You wanted to date me."

"I'm gonna want to date you for the rest of your life, Penny." She stopped, leaning back. "Even when I put a ring on your finger someday, even when you're old and gray, I'm never going to stop dating you."

Her bottom lip and chin quivered, but this time it wasn't from sadness. No, that was the realization that no matter what happened, there would be a constant in her life that she could always rely on.

Me.

I slipped my hands into her hair, needing her to know just how much I loved her. I licked her bottom lip, demanding access back into her hot mouth. Pen fumbled with her shirt, struggling to get it over her head when she broke away from me long enough to push it over her head. I helped her pull it over the length of her lean arms, tossing it to meet my shirt.

Then I was back on her mouth like she was the source of all my oxygen. And in a way, she was. She gave me a reason to believe that despite my shortcomings, someone could want and love me enough just for who I was.

That I could be enough without accolades, without money, without a legacy.

I could be the reason for her next breath, too.

Pen undid the button and zipper of her jeans, lifting her ass to get them over the small swell, and shimmy the denim and the lace of her thong over her thighs. She kicked them off her legs, and then parted her thighs wide open until the sweet scent of her arousal hit my nose.

My eyes flared when I glanced downward, the welcoming shade of rose pink of her glossy bare pussy beckoning me. I dropped to my knees, my hands pinning her thighs wide open as I buried my mouth against her.

Pen cried out, my tongue flicking against her clit. She kept herself propped with one hand slammed against the counter, the other hand twisting in my hair as she rolled her pelvis against my face and her body bowed.

"Dougie." She chanted my name as though it were a prayer, and whatever God was listening right now, I wanted them to know I'd never take her for granted. That I'd cherish her for the rest of my fucking life if they let me keep her.

And if I didn't? If I somehow fucked this up?

They could take her from me, and I'd know I'd deserve it.

But I'd never stop trying to fix it.

Pen tugged on my hair; her eyes hot. "Fuck me," she demanded breathlessly.

I stood back up on jelly legs, wiping my glossed mouth with the back of my wrist, then tugged my waistband down, my hard cock snapping free. She fitted one hand against my waist, pulling me to her, the other hand slipping between us to guide me to her entrance.

Need and desire spiraled through me as I inched forward, her melodic, satisfied moan hitting my ears as I flexed my hips. Pen trembled under me when I found my rhythm, her ass precariously close to the edge of the counter, one of my arms banded around her waist to support her.

She cupped my face with her hands, pressing her nose against mine, her warm breath fanning my face.

"Harder, Dougie," she goaded on. Her legs tightened around my waist, her pelvis bearing down on me, searching desperately for friction. She hardly gave me room to move, but Pen rocked herself against me, the shifting of her movements allowing me to drive my hips in a series of short strokes, giving us what we both wanted.

"Gimmie your mouth," I commanded. She slanted her head up to meet mine, her lips parting. I flicked my tongue against hers, heat swelling in my balls as her movements grew jerky. She cried into my mouth, lust bursting in my body as she came, her body quivering under mine. My orgasm chased after hers, my cock kicking, my small thrusts slowing as I plunged forward one last time, losing my load as my skin tingled and my vision blurred momentarily.

Our panting filled the quietude of the bathroom. We looked each other over for what felt like an eternity until my cock softened inside of her and I retracted my hips gradually. Pen closed her thighs, containing my release, as the plug of my cock left her.

The toilet paper roll spun as I tore away a few sheets, holding them against her. She twitched under the aftercare, her skin tender. Pressing a kiss to her cheek, I dragged my nose along the length of her jaw. "Do you want a shower?"

She shook her head. "I like smelling like you when I fall asleep."

"Why?" I asked with a chuckle. "You can smell the real thing right beside you."

She lifted her shoulder in a half-shrug. "I don't know," she confessed. "It's always made me feel safe." She turned her head, kissing me gently. "I gotta pee, though."

I laughed. "Okay, I'll see you in there, then I'll come brush my teeth." I signaled to her adjacent bedroom, helping her slide off the counter.

Shutting the bathroom door behind me, I padded over to Pen's made-up bed. She had too many goddamn throw pillows for one person, in various shades, sizes, colors, and textures. I made quick work collecting the pillows, stacking them on the upholstered bench she had at the foot of her bed. Pulling the crisp sheets back, I sat on my designated side, listening as she flushed the toilet. She washed her hands, then opened the door, beaming at me, her hair still tussled.

I slid off the bed, walking back into the bathroom, my pants still loose around my waist. She had lined up our toothbrushes on the counter, toothpaste already on the head. I'd never had an electric toothbrush in my life, but Pen had made sure I'd not only gotten one, but that I flossed nightly. She'd told me good oral health was something WASPs didn't negotiate on.

We brushed our teeth in silence, save for the vibrating hum of the toothbrushes whirring, her eyes finding mine in the bathroom mirror. She bumped her naked hip against mine playfully, leaning her head against my bicep as she glided the toothbrush along her teeth.

Was I really going to get to do this for the rest of my life? After everything, did I finally get the girl?

She leaned forward over the counter, cupping a polite hand around her mouth and spitting into the sink. Pen rinsed her toothbrush head, and then her mouth, settling the toothbrush back on its charging stand and fiddling with the box of floss. I mirrored her movements, flossing alongside her, then I accompanied her into her room.

I ditched my pants, sliding into bed as she turned off the small nightstand lamp on her side, the room growing dark. Leaning over, I pressed my lips against her bare shoulder. "'Night, Penny."

"'Night," she replied, her timid voice rushing out to add, "I love you."

"I love you, too." I gave her another chaste kiss, this time on her cheek, before I allowed myself to roll back, resting on my side. A content sigh left me, loving the way the pillow cradled my head and the satiation in my body as exhaustion and sleep came to claim me.

But then her voice filtered into the darkness.

"Dougie?" she murmured, throwing her leg over top of mine. I stirred, glancing at her over my shoulder.

"Mhm?"

She was quiet for so long, I almost thought I'd imagined it. But then her voice came through once more. "I want to buy the house from Sean."

I stiffened a little, taken aback by the statement. There was no way in hell I'd ever be able to afford my half of that house. I knew Sean was being realistic that he wouldn't get full asking price after everything, but I wasn't even in the realm of being able to afford it at a fraction of the cost. No bank was ever going to give me a mortgage, not with my debt load. My face flushed hot, embarrassment making my tongue thick until I found my nerve to speak and let her down. "Pen, my money situation—"

"You've got some saved, right?" she asked, ignoring the concern in my tone. Well, yeah. I did, but that didn't mean my debt-to-asset ratio wasn't laughable. "I'll put down what we need, and you can take care of our living expenses and put down what you can." She'd given this thought.

I shifted onto my opposite side, facing her. "But then it's your house and not mine."

"No," she disagreed, placing her palms on my bare chest. "Then it's our house, our place to raise our family."

I thought it over for a moment, battling the war of my ego and my pride. Of course, I knew inevitably, we'd have to figure out our living arrangement sooner rather than later, compromise somewhere or another. But I worried about the contrast in our financial situation. I didn't want to feel like a burden to her or create the impression that I couldn't take care of her or our kid.

Especially to her parents when they found out.

"Please?" She loved that house. I knew she did. Her eyes lit up every time we were there, this kind of childlike wonderment lingering in her gaze whenever she got out of her SUV at the start of the workday to look up at the pretty edifice.

But it was fucking huge.

I hesitated but found my argument slipping away. "That's a big house," I observed, brushing my fingers along the column of her throat, her pulse throbbing against my touch. "A lot of bedrooms."

"More bedrooms for us to fill up with more babies," she suggested, her tone growing flirtatious.

She was too much. I chuckled. "Haven't you had enough for one night, Ms. Cullimore?" I flattened her on her back, settling myself between her parted legs, my cock rousing when I brushed myself against the heat of her slick pussy.

Damn her.

"Never," she replied, her legs banding tight around my waist like they'd always belonged there. "I'm insatiable for you."

"Well," I started, lowering my lips as close to hers without kissing her. "I guess I'll have to fill you back up."

"Is that a yes to the house?" she asked between kisses she impatiently claimed, her fingers trailing along the disks in my spine.

"That's a yes, Penelope."

And some day, I hoped she'd give me a "yes" of another kind.

Chapter Eighteen

Penelope

Present

I NEARLY JUMPED OUT OF MY SKIN WHEN I HEARD THE FRONT DOOR OPEN, my eyes darting to the clock on the kitchen stove.

Five-thirty.

He'd been gone most of the day. Now that he wasn't working, I had no idea where he went most of the time. Sometimes, I'd watch him leave from the family room window, my arms wrapped around myself in a hug. But I never asked him where he was going, or what he was doing.

Or who he was with.

He didn't ask me questions, either.

After my failed attempt at seducing my husband a week ago—if we could call it that—we'd seemed to double down on dodging each other. He didn't speak to me when he brought Chris to me to say good morning, and he said nothing to me when he passed me in the house, his eyes trained anywhere but on me.

I'd successfully ensured my husband, whose love I once thought unwavering, despised me.

The front door opened, Chris's excited shrieks hitting my ears, making my chest hurt. A lump formed in my throat as he announced his father's presence. "Daddy!"

On cue, Dougie conjured up the enthusiasm that would never tip our son off that anything was ever amiss. "Hey, Little Man!"

I heard him blow a raspberry against Chris's cheek, earning him a sharp and happy giggle. A tear hit the knuckles of the hand curled around the handle of a knife.

I didn't know how I had it in me to cry anymore.

Sniffling, I lifted my head to survey the room. The kitchen perfumed by the aroma of a chicken I'd spent the better part of the afternoon trying to figure out how to cook after I got off the phone with my mother. I'd taken Christopher to the grocery store, making a point of buying enough food for all of us.

All three.

Christopher, Dougie, and me. Because my mother was right.

No matter how angry, how hurt, how devastated I was—Dougie was my husband. I'd never given him a chance to grieve with me.

I'd harbored the worst secret and grieved in a way that I thought would suffice for the both of us at the cost of destroying my marriage.

Dougie was wrong for whatever had happened with… *her*.

But I was wrong for fostering an opportunity for it to happen at all.

I wasn't innocent.

"Come!" Christopher demanded.

"Where are we going—ah, nah, Chris," Dougie said, clearing his throat. "How about we go play?"

I took a shuddering breath, willing my vocal box to cooperate. "D

—" the first letter in his name sounded weak. *C'mon, Penelope.* "Dougie?" I tried again. I set the knife down, brushing the lingering tears away.

I felt the frigid chill travel from the foyer right over to me in the kitchen. Dougie's familiar footsteps hit my ears, clipped yet even, accompanied by Christopher's as he led him into the kitchen.

Dougie avoided looking at me as he entered. His profile stippled in his scruff was tense, his jaw flexing as he waited for me to say what I wanted. His T-shirt under his plaid shirt was wrinkled.

He'd probably left it in the washer overnight and threw it in the dryer anyway.

I used to do his laundry for him. I used to be his wife—more than just in title and vows and promises we'd both made and had no intention of keeping.

My eyes found my left ring finger, absent of his rings, the indentation still present and hollowing my insides with my cruelty. I'd thrown them at him without hesitation, and now all I wanted was for him to give me my rings back.

"Are you hungry?" I asked, looking from the chopped vegetables for a side salad to him.

Please look at me.

Even though he didn't dare gaze my way, his eyes flared, his brows slamming together like he couldn't reconcile what I had just asked him. My heart hammered as I observed him ground his molars, fighting to contain some rapier-like remark that I rightly deserved after everything.

"I'm hungry," Christopher babbled, playing with his dad's fingers, still clenched in his own. "Daddy, too?"

Dougie glanced down at him. My throat felt like it was closing in on itself, the burning tightness in my chest distracting me from my urge to cry.

"I'm..." I paused. I was what?

I was sorry.

Sorry that I'd slapped him the other night.

Sorry that I'd turned into this unrecognizable person.

Sorry that I'd deprived him of me, of the truth.

"I'm trying out a new recipe, and there's a lot of food," I volunteered instead.

He nodded. "Thanks, but I'm not hungry."

I squeezed my eyes shut, my body trembling. I wanted to argue that I knew he was hungry. Dougie hardly ate. He picked at food in the fridge. My husband, who'd always had full, filled-in muscles and a body that was as thick and sturdy as a tree, had withered right before my eyes.

His cheeks were too sharp, his face too gaunt and ashen, his body too lean.

"Okay," I whispered, my eyes stinging. I had no right to cry in front of him.

"Hungry, Daddy?" Christopher asked again, eyeing his father hopefully. He was two, but he was perceptive. He knew his dad never ate with us, because he had never been home.

But Dougie used to be home. He used to arrive at five fifteen on the nose, leaving the jobsite as soon as he could. He could never get home fast enough in the past, eager to be reunited with us again.

"You could sit with us," I suggested. It was then he turned his face and looked at me dead-on and I gasped. He had a bruise forming on his face that hadn't been there this morning. "What happened?"

He looked down at Christopher again, playing with one of the golden locks of his hair. "Saw Sean at the hardware store." His accent was hard.

My sharp intake hit my ears, my stomach coiling with nervous knots. "He hit you?"

"I got one in, too," he assured me, sounding stilted. My eyes dropped to his tightening fingers. His knuckles were split. But then he asked a question that nearly knocked me on my ass. "It was Raquel's birthday last month. Did you call her?"

I hesitated, but I knew he knew.

No, I hadn't called her. I never called her. I never returned her messages or her emails—even the stupid chain ones she forwarded me because she knew I liked them.

Send this to ten people you know by midnight, or your life will be ruined.

Joke was on the email—my life already was in shambles.

Dougie let out an agitated laugh, shaking his head. "Nah, I definitely don't want to sit with you."

Because I was a cruel, entitled bitch.

"Then don't do it for me," I implored, giving him a nervous smile. I dropped my gaze to Christopher. "Do it for him."

"You wanna give me that now, Penelope?" he asked in a snarl, gaping at me. "You want to play house with me now for *his* sake?"

I flinched, clamping my mouth closed. "Our son is not some kind of bartering chip for you to use when you feel like it," he growled at me. "Wake up and smell the coffee, sweetheart. I'm not trying to live a lie anymore. Neither should you."

"I don't... I don't want a divorce." I dropped my voice, the D word feeling so permanent—because it was. I'd wielded it like a weapon, over and over again.

The longer he said nothing, the faster my hope slipped away from me, moving so quickly I felt as though I couldn't reach out and intercept it even if I tried.

I didn't want a divorce, but that didn't mean he didn't want one now.

My body tingled with a warning that I needed to keep breathing, but my lungs felt as though they wouldn't cooperate, growing smaller with each protracted minute. "I—" I blurted out loud, fidgeting where I stood. "I need to tell you something."

"And short of it being about where to sign," he uttered coldly, "I don't want to hear it." He bent down, scooping Christopher off his feet. "There's a pile of leaves outside with our names all over it," he chirped, sounding artificial, beaming at Chris. "Let's go play until it's time for you to eat."

"Play!" Christopher's giggle didn't work its way through my shattering heart this time. It didn't fill in the cracks the way it always had. But it was the only thing that kept me from collapsing on the floor.

I watched numbly as he fitted Christopher's hat and jacket on him. The back door opened and closed, allowing a gust of cold air to enter the kitchen.

I shivered, but it wasn't from the elements. Mother Nature's coldness paled compared to the one pervading inside of me.

My husband was done with me.

I'd lost him for good.

I couldn't sleep. I'd tossed and turned for nearly two hours, listening to every creak and groan of our house, my breath hitching every time I heard Dougie.

Some stupid part of me held on to the hope that he'd brush his knuckles against our bedroom door. That he'd climb into bed with me and wrap his arms around my waist.

We didn't need to talk. I just missed him. I missed us, the old us.

But I'd ejected him to the other end of the house. Anything that I'd ever asked him for, Dougie had delivered on. Why would a divorce be any different now?

Oh, God. I tugged at my hair, my elevated body temperature making my skin sting as I sat up in our bed.

We were really getting divorced, weren't we? He was going to leave me. The room felt as though it was spinning, my pulse pounding in my ears, panic making me tremble.

Releasing my hair, I frantically searched the nightstand in the dark, my fingers brushing against my iPhone as I desperately struggled for my next breath.

I had no right to call her, just like I had no right to ask my husband to change his mind. My hands shook violently, nausea making my cheeks swell as I struggled to keep the weight of the iPhone against my ear.

When the first ring resounded in my ear, the acid ripped up my tract, the need to vomit suddenly so intense that I nearly hung up.

But then the familiar click of the phone being answered kept me grounded in place.

She didn't speak, but I could hear the unevenness of her breathing, trying to determine whether I had pocket dialed her in error.

"Just hang up," Sean grunted in the background. "I'm over their shit."

It was late, but his voice had never sounded more alert.

Raquel swallowed tightly, the sound coming out like a gulp. "Pen?" I pulled the phone away from my ear, my finger hovering over the "end" button. "Don't hang up," she implored, as though she could see me. "Just," she exhaled, defeated. "If you didn't accidentally call me, don't hang up."

I didn't think I had anymore tears to produce, but I was wrong. My tired eyes ached, my skin burning as the familiar sting of salt coated my cheeks.

"I don't know what happened," Raquel said with controlled desperation. "You don't have to tell me, but..." I heard the familiar shuffle of her hair being tucked behind her ears. "I'm here, okay?"

"O-okay," I managed, clutching at myself, my free arm a tight band around my waist.

"Dougie knocked Sean good," Raquel offered, her voice breaking a little like she was trying to hold back a laugh.

"He hits like a bitch," Sean grumbled in the background.

"The bruise on your jaw says otherwise," she replied in a murmur, earning another agitated response from her husband I couldn't make out.

"Why did they..." I trailed off. "Was it..." What was I even trying to ask?

But she understood. "Because they're two hotheaded assholes who don't know how to use their words," she suggested.

"I'm not the hotheaded asshole, and she has no right—" Her hand came around the talk piece of the phone, cutting her husband off. When she removed it, the sound of a door closing gently behind her filtered through. "Ignore him, he's cranky."

Some things never changed. "But he's right," I offered softly. "I have no right to call you."

"Of course you do," she whispered back. "You're my best friend."

How could she still call me that with confidence after everything? I'd abandoned her at the most vulnerable point in her life. I'd done the very thing I'd scolded her for years ago when she'd left Sean after he'd lied to her. After she'd left me while I was pregnant, I'd done worse to her. I'd turned my back on her after she delivered.

After she'd nearly died.

Because I had been envious. I was envious of my best friend, who finally had the life she deserved. It was me who didn't deserve her. I'd become this version of myself I hated.

I hated myself.

When she made it through the other end of her delivery, when they'd stopped the bleeding after her accident, when I knew she was going to live? I pulled away, because I had no right to be anywhere near her. God, I'd made Dougie stay away from them, too.

I felt responsible, like I'd willed horrible things to happen to her.

I clenched my teeth, fighting the urge to cry, but it was no use. The uncontrolled tremors racked through me, the sob escaping my pinched lips.

"Pen," she soothed. "It's okay."

"No," I said, weeping. "It's not."

She was silent, listening as I tried to regain control of my breathing and stop the tears from coming.

"Where are you?" she asked.

"Home."

"Do you want me to come—"

"No," I cut her off. No, I didn't want her anywhere near my house. It was bleak and miserable. No one deserved to be tainted by this place.

"Do you want to come here?"

This time, it was me who was quiet. "What time does Sean go to work tomorrow?"

"He'll be gone by five tomorrow morning," she supplied. "Come over."

"I'm sorry, for not—"

"How does ten sound?" she interrupted, ignoring my attempt at an apology.

I squeezed my eyes shut. "Okay."

Dougie didn't ask me questions when he came down the stairs the next morning, taking them one at a time with Christopher on his left, clinging to the railing.

"Mommy, you go?" he asked, his feet searching the next riser.

"Yes," I replied, freeing my hair from under the neckline of my car coat. "I'll be back soon, okay?"

"'Kay!"

I studied Dougie as they cleared the last step. "Can you put him down at—"

He huffed. "Despite what you think, I know how to take care of my kid, too."

I cringed, huddling into my jacket. I deserved that. "Alright." I fiddled with my keys, running my finger along the grooves. "I'm going to—"

"Yep, bye." He turned his back on me, leading Christopher away.

Dougie didn't care where I went.

He didn't care who I saw.

He didn't care about me.

After everything, could I blame him?

My knees nearly buckled, watching them until they were out of eyesight. Until the singing of *Sesame Street* hit my ears, and Dougie's synchronized whistling pulled me out of my trance.

I ripped my feet away from the foyer, the October cold slamming into me when I opened and closed the front door, making my nose run as I walked to my SUV, the gravel crunching under my feet.

The car door felt heavy in my hands when I slammed it shut, my fingers fitting around the steering wheel, my knuckles tensing as I flexed out my fingers.

And then I did the unthinkable. The kind of thing I'd been raised to refrain from doing.

I screamed.

In the cabin's safety of my clean Range Rover that my parents had bought me, that Dougie had maintained, with our son's booster seat in the back, I emptied my lungs until my throat shredded from exhaustion and my lungs stung.

I slumped over the steering wheel, my hands dropping into my lap, the pain in my vocal cords so raw it hurt to swallow. After another moment, I straightened in my seat, and looked up at the front window. My heart stuttered when I found Dougie standing there, his arms folded over his chest. Controlled concern tightened his face, and I knew it then.

It wasn't that he didn't care.

It was that he didn't want to.

And somehow, that hurt more.

Raquel and Sean's house wasn't far from ours. Even driving under the speed limit in a complete and total daze, I got there in under eight minutes.

Pulling into the smooth half circular drive, my heart lurched as I parked behind Raquel's Jeep. The structure was familiar and different from how I remembered it. The dark gray brick a stark contrast to the redbrick found throughout the rest of the neighborhood.

It wasn't quite Halloween yet, and Sean had already lined the gambrel roof with a string of even unlit Christmas lights. The lavender bushes by their steps wrapped carefully with burlap, the garden beds overturned, the lawn free of debris. I'd bet he'd had both chimneys that flanked either side of the roof cleaned, too.

A decorative bale of hale by the front door on their portico housed two plump, uncarved, bright orange pumpkins.

Pumpkins. Raquel bought pumpkins now, and bales of hay with no intent other than for a decorative purpose.

The house was new construction after a fire a few years ago leveled the original First Period English American colonial to the ground. This had been the last project Dougie and I had worked on together before I'd had Christopher and had become a stay-at-home mom.

The house had been the thing that brought Raquel and Sean back together.

I wished Dougie and my house had been able to do that for us, too.

Realizing I could torment myself no more, I tucked my hair behind my ears, opened the car door and carried myself up the porch steps. I almost laughed when my eyes dropped to the doormat that read *Welcome* in an ornate scrawl.

Never in a million years did I believe there would be a time where my hardened best friend would ever welcome anyone.

But she did. Before I could raise a hand to knock, the locks on the front door released—one, two, three—Sean was paranoid. She opened the door, and my insides immediately ached.

All I could do was stare at her, taking her in.

She'd cut her hair again recently, to her shoulders, evidently not by her own hand. The brunette ends layered, hugging her heart-shaped face, her bangs long and falling into her line of vision. She blew them out of her eyes, her throat bobbing with a swallow.

"Hi, Pen." She modulated her tone, but I heard the familiar inflection of her South Boston accent on my nickname.

I pressed my trembling lips together, but it was no use. I broke.

"I'm sorry," I whispered, stepping toward her as the door widened and she met me halfway. She wrapped her arms around me, the citrus vanilla of her shampoo, absent of Pall Malls, infiltrating my sinuses as she clutched at me tightly. It was her unexplainable strength that stole my next breath, that energy, that life force that promised to keep me upright despite everything that I'd done to her.

"I've got you," she assured me, pressing her lips against my cheek. "I promise, I've got you."

"I'm so, so sorry." I tucked my face against her cheek, feeling the warmth of her tears against my skin, her fingers stroking the back of my head.

"It was because we left the wedding early, wasn't it?" she teased, laughing through her sobs at her joke.

"Definitely." I choked out a laugh. I wished we could have left early, too. Breaking from her embrace, I framed her face while she extended her hands out and swiped my tears away. "Look at you," I murmured, giving her the once-over. She wore a plaid button-down shirt that billowed at the waist over a black nursing tank top fitted tight against her ample nursing chest, black leggings and wool-blend socks that hugged halfway up her calves. "You're so stylish now."

"*Now?*" Raquel stressed with a laugh and a roll of her eyes.

"That's not what I meant, but..." I snorted, smiling at her.

"I know," she agreed, shrugging her shoulders. "Giving up cigarettes means I can afford to budget a wardrobe, and a professional haircut." She touched her hair, then reached out for my hand. "Come inside."

I hesitated, staring at the open door, discomfort working through my bones.

"He's not here," she assured. Not that I was afraid of Sean, per se, it was that I didn't want to be yelled at right now. "But," she gestured to the discreet camera tucked in the portico's corner, a faint red light indicating it was recording, directed at the front door. "He definitely knows you're here."

I wondered if she had told him I was coming. Based on how nonchalant she was acting, I suspected she hadn't.

"Is he going to be pissed?" I didn't want to look up at the camera, but out of reflex, my eyes lifted.

"Do I care?" she deadpanned. She glanced up at the camera, blowing a kiss to her husband, then pulled me inside. "Ignore the mess. I just got the twins down." She shut the door behind me, my eyes moving around the foyer. The air was fragrant with the lingering sweet scent of baby powder, mingling with the heady aroma of freshly brewed coffee and faint traces of dryer sheets coming from the adjacent main floor laundry room to the left of the foyer.

She held out a hand for my coat, and then I watched, mystified, as she opened the closet door, tucked my coat on a hanger and then hung it up.

My best friend used to just toss her clothes wherever they landed, but not anymore. She cared. The mess she'd warned me of made my stomach twist. A nursing blanket draped over the back of the couch, a half drunken glass of water on a coaster, a crumpled tissue next to the television remote.

Their house was cozy, like Dougie and my house used to be. Sure, I'd designed the finishings here, and it had been me who decided on the barnacle-gray engineered-hardwood floors that ran throughout their foyer and living room. It had been me who encouraged clear sight lines for their floor plan. I saw myself in the married elements of modern aesthetic and the subtlety of eighteenth-century hints peppered on the dentil work over the fireplace, the trim of their windows and the archway into their kitchen.

I was here, even though I wasn't.

But they'd given this house a pulse. They'd made it into their home.

"Coffee?" she asked. "I just put the pot on."

I nodded, taking off my ankle boots and following her into the kitchen. They had a massive kitchen island, evidence of their life seated there. A bowl of apples from their tree in the back sat in the middle, next to a paper towel dispenser on a decorative matte-black roll. The cabinets were snow white, the countertops a deep black granite with creamy vanilla swirls in the middle. They had a floating hood vent that was practically commercial grade and an oversized apron sink that had a neat pile of dishes stacked, waiting to be loaded in the running dishwasher.

There on the nook of the chef's desk, next to their refrigerator, sat a baby monitor hub. The camera trained on two small bodies with a headful of dark hair, respectfully, sleeping away in their beds.

I'd missed out on so much.

"Two sugars and a splash of cream still?" Her voice pulled me out of my reverie. Raquel flexed on her toes, reaching an extended hand out to grab two matching black mugs from a shelf.

I nodded, watching as she navigated around her space. It surprised me when she added a spoonful of sugar to her cup. "You drink your coffee with sugar now?"

She smiled a little, stirring the innards of her mug with a spoon. "I've learned that it's okay to indulge ourselves on the sweetness life offers."

I felt sad for her for a moment. She'd always taken her coffee black —it had never occurred to me it wasn't because she enjoyed it.

Raquel handed me the mug, then gestured with her head to follow her back into the living room. I knew in the past, she favored her shabby armchair, but she settled into the middle where the groove on Sean's worn-in furniture from his bachelor days existed. Their throw pillows were mismatched, but that kind of thing had always been inconsequential to them.

My eyes found their wedding picture nestled in the middle of their fireplace mantel. They'd had the wedding Dougie and I should have had—simple, no bullshit.

An impromptu courthouse event. She hadn't even worn a traditional wedding dress. It was a simple white blazer dress, loose in the waist to disguise the small pregnancy bump. There had been no suit for Sean, just gray slacks and a white dress shirt.

They'd been so happy that day—and all I could do was stare at them both with longing because even then, I knew the wedding my parents forced on us wasn't what Dougie and I wanted.

It was already breeding a wedge between us that I was struggling to contain.

"How are you?" she asked, tucking her legs under her on the couch.

"I feel like I should be the one asking you that," I confessed. I hadn't seen her since she delivered. After I'd gotten the assurance that she was going to be okay after coming out of her emergency C-section, I'd fled the hospital.

"Tired." Raquel laughed, blowing on the hot mug in her hands before taking a small sip. "I didn't think it was possible to love someone so much. Sometimes I look at them and I feel like my heart's just gonna explode." She stared down at her coffee mug, her lips pressing together like she was almost ashamed of what she was going to say next. "But I cry a lot." She chewed on her lip. "Don't get me wrong, I love being a mother, but nothing anyone says, nothing you read, ever really prepares you for any of this."

"I know," I sympathized. "The first four months with Christopher, I was..." I trailed off. "Exhausted to the point of anger. It's a hard adjustment."

"Exactly," she exhaled. "And it's not anger directed toward them, it's the overwhelm of feeling like you can't handle it. That frustration that you're fucking up at every conceivable turn."

"And then..." I began, smiling a little. "Then you adjust, and you find your routine and it's rewarding as hell."

She mirrored my smile, nodding her head. "And you look down at them and think you'd do it all over again in a heartbeat."

My insides twisted, my face crumpling a little. "Yeah." I brushed my thumb along the handle of the black mug. "How's Sean and fatherhood?"

She brightened, her mouth slanting with an asymmetrical smile. "He's obsessed with them, calls six times a day. He'd spend all day on FaceTime with them if I allowed it."

I laughed. "He's quite the softy, isn't he?" It was hard to reconcile that the guy yelling at me from the top floor of a jobsite with the permanent scowl etched on his face was the same guy who was head over heels in love with my best friend.

If I could still call her that after today.

"You have no idea," she stressed, snorting out another laugh. Her smile slipped a little. "I have Christopher's birthday present upstairs."

It was Raquel's birthday last month. Did you call her?

Shame, all I felt was shame. "I'm sorry I didn't call you for your birthday," I blurted.

Raquel flinched, looking down at her mug. She lifted her shoulder in a half-shrug. "It's okay."

"It isn't, Kell," I replied, my tone soft. "None of what I did, none of what we did, was okay." She tried to hide her expression, but her eyes betrayed her.

"If it wasn't my shoe choice, or ditching the wedding early," she began tentatively, raising her eyes. "Can I ask, what... or why?"

I put my coffee mug down on a wood coaster on her coffee table, folding my hands in my lap. "I don't even know where to start, but..." I studied her, trying to savor every moment, because it all felt short-lived, "I'm going to confess some things to you that might make you hate me."

She shook her head, clucking her tongue against the roof of her mouth as though what I'd said was silly. "I could never hate you, Pen."

The lightheadedness and rising fair hairs on the back of my arms under my shirt told me otherwise. "You might."

Her face fell as she struggled to reconcile with herself that there would ever be something I could do or say to her that would make her that upset with me.

But I'd said things that were unforgivable. Things that maybe I wasn't obligated to confess to her, but my need to be transparent, to be honest for once, overwhelmed me.

I was tired of telling lies.

"You know that the wedding…" The words wedged in my throat.

"Got out of hand," she finished for me when I couldn't. She'd gotten caught in the shit storm of helping me organize it and managing the seating chart.

I nodded.

Some couples on the path to divorce could distinguish the moment the first hairline crack appeared in their marriage, where their relationship waned or displayed signs of trouble.

I could readily identify three.

There had been a night, the first of what felt like many, where Dougie had reached for me in the darkness. I could still feel the brushing of his heated knuckles against my bicep, his warm breath falling over my face, the spearmint from our toothpaste touching my nose.

I had pulled away. It wasn't a graceful shuffle with a polite, "Not tonight."

It was a harsh recoil, as though his touch might kill me.

My easygoing husband hadn't made a thing of it, but I knew it had hurt him. I felt it in the way the mattress recoiled alongside him, heard it in his tight exhale.

After building a relationship focused on communicating, we didn't discuss it. It was the first time we didn't talk about it.

Which made the unescapable sting of my rejection that night linger between him and me because it wasn't a one-off. It was the beginning to a string of steady dismissals that drove us further apart when we were already struggling to remember who we were. And things only got worse.

A lot worse.

My parents' involvement in our wedding planning was a mistake I still regretted with every fiber of my being today. Initially, I was adamant it wasn't going to happen. I hadn't left Connecticut just to get sucked back into their cesspool of shit.

Mother came in strong with the guilt. *"You've embarrassed us enough by having a child out of wedlock."* I was unmoved.

But Daddy was the one who got me where it hurt. Daddy, who'd always been as understanding as he could be and compassionate toward my desire to be different. *"All I've dreamed about since the day you were born was giving you away on your wedding day in front of my friends. Please reconsider your decision, Pearl."*

So, I caved, if not to make Daddy happy, then to once just be agreeable in a way that Dougie always was toward his mother.

But I seriously underestimated how much of a pretentious circus our wedding would turn into. And Dougie?

He didn't argue.

He *never* argued. It seemed like being amenable was his way of attempting to extend an olive branch in my parents' direction, too.

After all, in their eyes, he'd taken something from them without asking first—me. He always tried to appease them because he felt responsible for getting me pregnant.

What was supposed to be an intimate affair between us and our respective families as we exchanged vows saw our guest list go from fifty to four-hundred-and-fifty. There were names scrawled on invitations we didn't recognize, an A-list and B-list of guests just in case. All the tables needed to have the same number of guests, no matter what.

It was unlike anything I'd thought our wedding would be. I'd wanted a simple outdoor wedding, an off-the-rack dress, and no cake.

Dougie was happy to just sign a marriage license.

But that wouldn't do for Mother and Daddy. Our tiny fifty people affair grew nine times in size, and it was no longer our wedding—it was a Cullimore *event*.

We'd become nothing but over-glorified real-life Sims overnight. A pie-menu full of actions we had to fulfill, every move driving us further from the things we'd wanted.

Further from each other.

My parents heard our asks and ignored them or interpreted them into having a larger-than-life meaning. When I argued we said, *"Small and quaint"*, they rebutted that *"four-hundred-and-fifty was conservative."*

There were four hundred members at the country club, after all.

They'd only invited half. The rest of the guest list consisted of their society friends, distant relatives I'd never met, the well-to-do doctor who'd delivered me at birth, Dougie's family, our friends and some of their family, and *her*.

My eyes roved Raquel's living room, finding a framed photo of Sean with his sisters tucked close together with a tall and wide decorated Christmas tree behind them.

Katrina made a goofy face, her tongue jutting to the right, her left eye closed in a wink.

Olivia, their middle sister, posed like she was receiving an Academy Award.

Sean served the camera a shit-eating grin, Raquel no doubt on the other side of the camera.

And then there was Maria, staring dead at the camera, her lips lifted slightly to the right in a smirk.

Smart, sexy and completely fucking aware of it, Maria Tavares.

Dougie's first love.

Truthfully, ever since I'd met her, I'd never liked her—and it had everything to do with the fact that while Dougie was mine, she would always be his first.

It hadn't mattered that because of her missteps, because of her role in our meeting, that I'd won. She was still the one who got away, because she'd never wanted to belong to anyone but herself.

Maria was frustratingly beautiful. Gorgeous, really, with her long, lush chestnut brown hair and her hourglass figure. The sharp and classical features that made her appear as though she'd strode right off a runway during Paris Fashion Week. Her complexion was that enviable natural-bronzed shade that soaked up the sun, golden like her brother's. Her eyes dark, and her mouth always painted in that shade of oxblood red.

She was the closest thing to a femme fatal I'd ever seen in the flesh.

But while I was the one in the wedding dress, and I'd been the one Dougie had said, "I do" to, Maria Tavares stole his attention on our day, because there had been an anomaly in the form of Maria's new boyfriend he hadn't accounted for. One that threw him right off kilter and left him silently wondering, "what if?"

What if he'd been patient with her when she said she didn't want a boyfriend?

What if she'd given in to him and agreed to be his forever?

What if it had been her standing in my place?

It hurt, realizing on the most important day—second to the birth of our child—that I had created an opportunity for what-ifs to breed in my husband's mind.

It was excruciating, but could I really fault him after the way I'd been treating him? Maria had always been exactly who she said she was. She hadn't sold him on a different version of herself like I had.

A version I thought didn't exist anymore.

In my haste to make my parents happy, to ignore the fact that I was unexpectedly pregnant again, I'd become enraptured by the idea of perfection, gotten sucked back into the toxic world of being the dutiful daughter of Walter and Evelyn Cullimore.

I wanted everything to be pristine on our wedding day, and it was clear Dougie just wanted to get it over with.

Which brought us to moment number three, and this one, perhaps, haunted me the most, because the prior would have been avoidable had I just played my cards differently.

If I'd remembered to be the woman he'd fallen in love with, the one who wasn't combating heightened pregnancy hormones, and stress, and a latent desire to get this day over with, too.

Dougie had called me the night before our wedding, from his room in the hotel down the hall. Why we had gotten two rooms despite having already had a child together, I didn't know—but again, Mother had said, *"it's tradition"*, and I caved to spare myself the argument.

"Pen," he said quietly, followed by an audible swallow. *"It's just you and I, right? After all of this, it's just you and I?"*

In hindsight, I should have interpreted that as cold feet. I'd ignored the underlying panic lacing his query and focused on my annoyance. I should have left my room and padded barefoot down to him and given him the reassurance he needed. Melded my body with his for the first time in ages, kissed him and told him we were going to have another baby, but I didn't.

I scoffed and acted flippantly toward his concern. *"What kind of ridiculous question is that, Dougie?"*

Ridiculous. My husband had needed me, and I wrote him off.

So, was I surprised that when he saw Maria—the woman he'd previously engaged in a clandestine friends-with-benefits relationship with—that he'd be having a case of buyer's remorse?

No. Not at all.

Raquel offered me an encouraging smile that didn't reach her eyes, but I felt the palpability of her worry. The buildup and the anticipation of what was to come, the trepidation filling the room as she tried to determine what I would say to her that would give her something to hate me for.

"Pen?" she probed.

I tore my gaze away from Raquel, from the photo, my eyes shutting as I tried to find my nerve. "There was something I didn't tell you, something that was..." My chest rose as I tried to take in a breath. "An unintentional secret."

"An unintentional secret?" Raquel threaded a hand through her hair, her eyes falling to her knees, mouth pulling to the right with thought. "What secret?"

I'd never kept anything from her before, but I'd kept this. My vision went fuzzy for a moment. I saw the blood on the back of my eyelids again, splattered on my clean bathroom floors, the squelch of my crimson-stained underwear puddled at my feet while I slumped forward on the toilet. The cramping and the accompanied blinding pain that made me want to vomit.

But the tears, they were absent this time. "I was pregnant," I whispered. "I was pregnant during the wedding."

She stared at me, transfixed with horror. Her shallow breath left her as her shoulders sagged and her back fell against the couch.

I didn't have to explain the rest.

Her mouth opened and closed, questions forming on her tongue that she'd never let free.

Why didn't I tell her?

When?

How?

"Your honeymoon," she mumbled, her voice haunted. "That... that was why you didn't go."

"Yeah," I whispered, hardly recognizing my voice.

She squinted, her face crumpling as she held a hand to her mouth. "I'm sorry." She glanced up at me, tears clinging to her lashes. "I'm sorry that I—"

"You couldn't have known, Kell." I reached for her hand, folding my fingers around hers. "There was no way that you could have ever known." Even when I was pregnant with Christopher, I'd been on the smaller side until the second trimester. This pregnancy had been on the trajectory to be no different.

Except for Mother. She'd noticed my changing body, but that was because I was always under a microscope with her.

Raquel held my hand to her face, her brows sad as they pulled inward. "God, how did Dougie take it?" My face dropped, my skin tingling as sweat broke out. Raquel tensed at my prolonged silence. "He wasn't an asshole, right? Because that isn't your fault."

I shook my head, pulling my hand carefully from hers. I rubbed my palms along my jeans, every hair on my scalp beading with sweat.

"Pen?" She exhaled my name, her freed hand curling around the hemline of her shirt, tugging it.

My lips rolled together as I struggled to find the words and avoided her eyes. "He," I took a shuddering breath, flexing my trembling fingers. It never got easier to say. "He doesn't know."

"What?" Raquel sounded incredulous. "What do you mean he doesn't know?"

The truth dangled in the air between us, the weight of my secret threatening to strangle us both. "I never told him."

I waited for her anger, for the shock to paint her face, for the judgment to come. But all she did was lean forward and wrap her arms around me, holding me tight against her. "I'm so sorry you had to go through that alone."

I broke. Completely, utterly shattered in her arms, because it was more kindness than I deserved from her. It was the hug I wanted from my husband. My hollowed insides lurched, my heart beat wildly in my chest as my adrenaline rushed through my veins. I held on to her, letting her rock me as she ran her hands over my hair, murmuring her apologies.

She released me tentatively, her hand reaching for mine, squeezing. We said nothing for some time, the silence working its way through the room. "That's why you pulled away from me," she murmured, understanding for the first time in months. "Because I was..." she trailed off.

"I'm sorry," I whispered. "It was..." My self-loathing crashed into me, the familiar curdles of rage I'd experienced back then greeting me like an old friend. "I was jealous."

She inhaled sharply, her neck bending to avoid the line of my vision. Her hands shook in mine, but she never withdrew them. "And then you fell, and I just... I felt like I brought the accident on."

Raquel glanced up at me, her throat shifting with the emotion she was struggling to gulp down. My chest caved in, my ribs tightening. "I know that sounds crazy, but I became someone I didn't like while you were pregnant, Raquel. I was jealous in a way I'd never been toward anyone, especially..."

"Especially me," she finished for me, her voice cracking. She'd never had an enviable life, but this... this was a jealousy I'd never been able to understand.

"I always had everything, and you never did, and... and when you fell, I really thought I'd wished that into existence." Saying the words out loud paralyzed me in my fear, as I waited for her to erupt into a justifiable fit of rage.

I'd envied her. I'd spoken poorly of her. I'd questioned why she got to be pregnant with twins.

Why she got to be pregnant at all.

"Do you still think that way?" she asked, her thumb trailing over the valley of my knuckles.

"No," I insisted, shaking my head while looking at where she clasped my hand in hers. "I didn't mean it then, either. I was just..." I struggled to find the word.

Raquel lifted her head, her brown eyes shimmering with a fresh batch of tears. "Grieving, Pen. You were *grieving*." I didn't know how she could be compassionate and understanding when I'd just confessed that I'd felt responsible for what had happened to her. That my resentment of her pregnancy had turned me into someone who didn't deserve her. "We're not true reflections of ourselves when we're mourning." She thumbed at the thin stack of rings on her left ring finger. "I know it's not quite the same, but when Holly Jane died…" she looked toward the ceiling, thinking of her late sister. "You know my entire world fell fucking apart. I said things, I did things…" she looked my way. "I was hard on you back then, too."

I stared off at nothing, remembering that cold Thanksgiving Day, thirteen years ago, when Raquel's sister had flipped her car on The Pike. It had been her unraveling, and if she'd been a hardened person before, Holly Jane's unexpected death threw her into an abyss I never thought she'd crawl out of.

But I'd held nothing against her. How could I when the center of her being, her purpose and motivation, had just been ripped away from her?

I'd understood Raquel's anger, but for some reason, I believed she'd never be able to understand mine. "I'm sorry," I whispered. "For envying you. For abandoning you."

I'd never even given her a chance, just like I hadn't Dougie.

Raquel didn't speak. A brick sank in my stomach. I was mired in my shame, waiting for her to explode, anticipating her dismissal from her home, from her life.

Forever.

"Not that long ago, I abandoned you," she supplied instead. "When you needed me while you were…" she hesitated, fear drawing her brows together before she tried the word again. "While you were pregnant with Christopher." When I didn't flinch, she continued, "I ran away, too."

Three years ago, Raquel had broken up with Sean and left the state without so much as a word. For nine months, she hid out on the West Coast, only returning when I was getting ready to deliver. For a long time, I didn't think our friendship would recover, but she'd been steadfast, patient with me, willing to work at proving she'd changed. That she wasn't the same girl from college, the one she thought so little of.

But what I'd done was just plain cruel. I didn't think they could compare. And pleading for her forgiveness, committing to being a better person—none of it would change anything.

I wanted her to know that I recognized that, too. "It was different—"

"It really wasn't," she interrupted absently, tipping her head back against the couch. "Maybe the circumstances were, but it was still done with the belief that no one could understand what we were going through that drove our actions, Pen." She uncurled her legs from under her, propping the instep of her sock-clad feet on the coffee table. "When we're hurting, it's next to impossible to see beyond that. It drops a weight on top of us so heavy, it's a battle just to keep our heads above water." She draped my hand in my lap. "When I fell," she began, pressing an open palm against her stomach, "the only thing I kept praying for was that they'd be okay. I didn't care if I didn't make it. I just wanted them to have a chance. I wanted to do something good for once."

"You *are* good."

She shook her head, her lips rolling together. "I wanted to leave behind something good." Her fingers curled against her stomach. "Because if I couldn't be here, I wanted Sean to have something that would give him a reason to keep going." She tilted her head, staring at the site of her accident. "Every time I go up or down those stairs, I relive it. It doesn't matter how often I process the emotion, there's always this fleeting moment that passes through me, even if it's brief, that wonders what would have happened had things gone differently. If I hadn't had my phone in my hand when I fell. If I'd hit my head. If I hadn't tried to break my fall to avoid landing on my stomach. It knocks the wind right out of me."

I pressed my hand to my mouth, trying to avoid seeing the visual she'd laid out for me, but it was impossible. "They say your life flashes before your eyes when you're about to die," she murmured, biting her bottom lip for a moment. "And as the paramedics were fitting the oxygen mask over my mouth, and the red-and-blue lights were blurring, I remembered meeting you." She shook her head. "You and those *stupid* Mary Jane shoes." Raquel let out a laugh. "And I remembered you telling me you were pregnant." She looked my way. "That was the night I kissed Sean for the first time. The night that changed my life. My life as I know it right now? It's because of *you*."

My mouth felt chalky and dry as I listened to her speak, watching as her expressions shifted as she ran through her memories. "I thought about the precious time I spent away from you, and from him. When I believed I could never forgive him for lying to me back then, for making an error in judgment." She glanced my way, her expression softening. "Because it was time wasted. We burn time because we think we have a lot of it. We never consider what will happen when the universe decides our time is up." She closed her eyes for a moment, the tears escaping, and I wanted so desperately to brush them away. "But you know something?" she asked in a breathy whisper, opening her eyes. "I asked whoever was listening to let me live." She exhaled, sniffling. "I wanted a chance to be better than my parents were, to give my kids the life that my sister and I never had. I wanted to stay."

She glanced at her wedding picture. "I wanted to love him a little while longer, and maybe that makes me selfish," she confessed. "But I wasn't ready to die." She swiped her cheeks with the heel of her palm, offering me a small smile. "So no, I'm not mad at you. Not for feeling how you felt, or for doing what you did. If there was anything nearly dying taught me, it was that some things don't matter in the grand scheme of things, Penelope. I don't submit to my emotions anymore. They're meant to teach us, not lead us."

My lips parted, a small, agonized sound crawling up my throat as I leaned forward, planting my forehead on her shoulder. "I'm sorry, Kell. I'm so fucking sorry." The warmth of her lips pressed into the crown of my head. She laid her head against mine, the two of us sitting there, processing what we'd said.

"I forgive you, Pen," she whispered. "But you need to forgive yourself, too."

How could I, when I knew now more than ever, if I'd just done things differently, my marriage wouldn't be on the brink of total and complete collapse?

I sniffled, pulling away from her. "Kell." She glanced my way. "There's more." Raquel clutched at herself, her expression tightening.

"What is it?"

"Dougie, he…" I stumbled, trying to find the words. Dougie, what? He was adamant he hadn't slept with Maria, but the desire had still been there.

"Pen?"

"We were in a really awful place," I said, then shook my head. "We've been in a really terrible place for a while." I kneaded my shoulder, drawing in a sharp breath. "The night of your accident, I, I found him with—"

Something flashed across her face, her eyes dropping. "Maria," she finished for me.

I stiffened, my head snapping back.

"She told me," Raquel said quietly as she dragged her teeth over her bottom lip. "She knew there would come a day where you might want answers, her side of the story…" she trailed off, the muscle in her jaw jumping. "But she's adamant that they didn't… do that."

"And you believe her?" I didn't know why but hearing that she took her sister-in-law's word over mine made something bubble in my stomach. Some sliver of me seethed internally, wanting to demand she pick between us. I couldn't handle ever having to be in a room with Maria Tavares again, never mind the idea of Raquel spending any time with her.

But before I could say anything, Raquel's voice came through. "Honestly?" she asked me. "As much as you don't want to hear this from me, I do." Raquel flexed her feet, folding her arms over her chest. God, she knew me too well. "Maria's a lot of things." She met my eyes, confirmation that she knew what my ask would be living there. "But she's not a liar—even if she is a lawyer." I heard what was unspoken, though.

Please don't make me choose between you two.

It wasn't that I didn't think she wouldn't choose me, it was that the expectation was unrealistic.

I disappeared, and life continued. I didn't get to make demands now. It would be cruel and unfair.

I released a long exhale, feeling unsatisfied by her absolution of Maria, but it didn't change that even if it was true—Maria hadn't pursued my husband—and what I saw might not have been accurate after all. "He shouldn't have gone there."

"He shouldn't have," Raquel agreed. She glanced my way, appearing uneasy for a split second. "Intent is still wrong, Pen. And I don't fault you for struggling to forgive him." There was something she wasn't saying. I caught her chewing on the inside of her cheek.

"But?" I probed.

She let out a resigned sound. "But Maria said despite what his intent had been by being there, all he wanted was you."

"What do you mean?"

Raquel's shoulder slumped, her mouth rocking. "He talked about you the majority of the time, about…" She seemed uncomfortable for a moment. "About the struggles you guys were having."

"I can't believe he went there to tell her that," I uttered numbly, my face heating, every hair on my neck standing upright.

She wrung her hands together. "And then he cried."

My head snapped back. He what? "*Cried*?" I echoed.

Raquel nodded her head. "That's what Maria said, and she's kind of uncomfortable with emotionally regulating for other people, so…" She blew a flyaway out of her face, falling quiet for a moment more before she added, "I think he was desperate to talk to anyone, Pen. Maria was just the convenient choice."

"Why not Sean?"

"Because Sean would tell me, and if Sean told me, then I wouldn't give you a choice but to talk to me." She scratched at her cheek. "Plus, I think with Sean and Jordan getting closer, Dougie felt out of sorts."

Raquel shifted on the couch, looking at me seriously. "Look, I'm not absolving Dougie. I still want to dropkick him in the throat." I laughed at the visual, pressing a hand to my mouth. "But I'm not sure if any of what happened was because he didn't love you or want you, if I'm being honest. I think, much like you, he was grieving, too."

"Grieving what?"

She slanted her head. "Losing you."

"He didn't lose me."

"Didn't he, though?" she asked quietly. "You can't do an about-face on your husband and expect him not to believe that he's not the problem. You can't shut down or become obsessed with busying yourself with your wedding and expect that he's not going to think that it's him you don't want."

I looked away from her, my eyes finding the window, watching as gray clouds formed in the sky. God, more fucking rain. "I never thought you'd become such a Dougie sympathizer."

Then again, despite their earlier animosity toward each other, Dougie had been her olive branch to me when she'd run away. Her one connection to the life she'd turned her back on. "I wouldn't call it sympathizing so much as recognizing that even though you didn't... you didn't tell him what happened, or what you were going through, you were trying to ensure you didn't lose him, too."

That had been what I'd been trying to do. I was trying to hide my defect, the flaw. My body had failed me, but I'd failed him, too. I thought about the grocery store so many years ago, when he'd whispered his fantasy into my ear. A house full of babies, and I'd—

"Dougie isn't going to blame you, Penelope," she assured me. "You know he never would."

"I'm scared," I confessed. "I'm scared that we're too far gone to get back on track. That he'll hate me for keeping it from him, that he won't understand."

"In sickness and in health," she murmured.

I wanted to laugh. Was she really reciting wedding vows?

She nudged me, waiting for me to say the next line. "In sorrow and in joy."

"So long as you both shall live." She looked at me long and hard, her eyes tracing over my face before she offered me a soft smile that spurred hope inside of me for the first time. "Give him a chance to prove he's still the man you married, and," she brushed my hair back, "give yourself the chance to remember who you are, too."

Chapter Nineteen

Three years ago…

"You okay?" Dougie kept his tone easy, but I picked up the nerves in his query.

That made two of us in the anxious department.

I shifted with unease in the passenger seat, watching as the blur of canopied autumnal trees and dense thicket of overgrown bushes hugged the edge of the road we were driving along.

Thanksgiving had come too quickly.

I rolled my knotted shoulders, offering him a forced smile. "Yeah."

We'd been driving for over two hours, oscillating between listening to the radio play another song I was too anxious to appreciate and engaging in light conversation.

I'd be fine. I just needed to stretch my legs, pee, and get my mind off how the last couple of weeks played out.

Dougie flittered his stare in my direction, seeming uneasy as he drove. Before he challenged the integrity of my single-worded response, I noticed where we were and said, "My parents' house is your next right." I pointed at a group of tightly clustered, centuries-old pine trees that acted as a lush barrier, concealing the monolithic house seated on acreage beyond its green fortress.

His foot touched the brake, slowing down as he indicated. Dougie squinted, nearly missing the small clearing in the road. He made a jerky turn, approaching the opened metal gates. The large, cursive C for my family's last name split down the middle in half. Ornamental trees lined the gray asphalt driveway, their leaves long since given in to autumn's kiss, limbs bare.

He inhaled sharply, drawing my attention. I studied his tensed profile, eyes flaring.

I didn't need to ask why. My parents' house had that effect on people. The first time Raquel had been here, she'd sworn and accused my parents of being richer than Satan and God combined.

Personally, I thought it was a ridiculous house for two people.

My childhood home was a pretentious and massive white-brick Georgian mansion with rows of even windows framed by subtle gray shutters, seated on two-and-a-half acres of rolling hills that backed onto an orchard I used to walk through when I was a teenager visiting from boarding school, with my headphones pumping out loud music that would have made my mother furious, a cigarette I'd flirted to get my hands on tucked between my lips, and a glossy red apple clutched in my hand.

My parents' front porch was respectable and boring, with two columns carrying the weight. Boring and impersonal unlike the porches I'd fallen in love with back in Massachusetts.

A mortared gabion fence enclosed the property, fringed by trimmed hedges, the grass still green despite November's chill twirling in the air.

"You ready?" I stretched in the passenger seat of his truck, my question hanging between us.

He stared at my parents' house.

I caught the hint of worry flickering in his uneasy stare. He was out of his element, and despite my best efforts to prepare him for the interrogation that awaited him beyond those doors, it was different when we were facing what was once a future problem.

Dougie puffed out his chest and extinguished any worry, offering me a staid smile. "Yeah." He turned the truck off.

Admittedly, I had felt as tense as an overextended rubber band most of the drive, and it had nothing to do with telling my parents we were expecting and everything to do with Raquel. She'd apologized for what had happened the night of our announcement at O'Malley's, then confessed that she'd kind of hooked up with Sean.

Kind of.

In the house that Dougie and I had officially bought from Sean. We were moving in before Christmas. I supposed I needed to tell my parents that, too.

While things were fine between Raquel and me, I couldn't shake the feeling that I should have demanded she joined Dougie and me in Connecticut for Thanksgiving.

I knew she had a long-standing commitment to her mother—if we could call Pauline Flannigan that—but I hated the idea of her being anywhere near Southie. It brought out the worst in her. It always had. Being within Pauline's grasp was one thing, but the added element of Raquel's ex-boyfriend sniffing around now that he'd realized Sean was in the picture...

I could see the writing on the wall.

Her ex was unpredictable, moody, and irrational. Always had been, and getting older encouraged him to double down on his behavior in a way that scared me but didn't scare Raquel.

And that, that was the part that worried me. While Sean might have pumped the brakes on them after his little all-you-can-eat Raquel buffet on the desk in Dougie and my new place, I wanted nothing to throw her back on the wrong path.

Was it horrible of me to wish her ex would just disappear?

"Pen?" Dougie's voice encroached on the fog of my messy thoughts. The heat of his palm closed around my fingers, squeezing gently. "You sure you're good?"

I nodded, ignoring the quickening of my heartbeat as my racing mind warned me something was going to go wrong. "Just worried about Raquel."

"You really think it's gonna be that much of a shitshow?"

My stomach churned in affirmation. Unfortunately. "It always is with Pauline." Where Raquel's ex-boyfriend Cash was mercurial, Pauline was as predictable as snow in winter. She only ever called for money or to dig her fingers into an unhealed emotional wound or two.

It didn't help she wasn't above putting her hands on her daughter, even if Raquel was twenty-eight.

With all this worrying, it was almost as though I didn't have enough on my plate.

As though the universe had heard me and reinforced my observation, the huge front door opened. That should have been my first tipoff this trip was going to be a clusterfuck.

Mother never opened the door for anyone. I used to think that short of a house fire, where she would insist that the fire department come to the door properly and wait to be announced, she'd never do anything she believed was beneath her.

No, Evelyn Cullimore insisted on everyone being completely fucking aware that she was the lady of this grand *maison* and left the tedium and tending to the housekeepers.

But there she was.

Unimpressed and proud. Pale blond hair perfectly coifed at the base of her neck, not an eyebrow hair out of place, the string of pearls at her wrinkle-free neck, the most delicate thing about her, laid against the high neckline of her deep-purple sheath dress.

If the Connecticut cold bothered her, she didn't show it. The tapping of her impatient high heel disturbing the otherwise quietude of the property was surely keeping her warm. She riveted her hands on her hips, that sour look deepening on her face as she craned her head as much as her commitment to remaining furtive would allow.

"You look like your ma," Dougie remarked, releasing my hand to press down on his seatbelt. His head slanted in my direction as he stared at her through the window.

I scowled at him, scoffing. Not that my mother wasn't pretty, she was, if you were into ice sculptures, but I also didn't like the idea of believing I shared any similarities with her, either. Physical or otherwise.

That we shared DNA was a minor issue.

I didn't want to be anything like her.

"I'll grab the bags." Dougie opened the driver's side door.

It was now or never. Throwing open my door, I searched for the truck riser, sliding out when I found it.

Mother sighed, her arms rising to cross over her chest, a terse huff leaving her. "Honestly, Penelope—" Yeah, yeah, I had the mannerisms and posture of a barn animal.

"Hi, Mother," I cut her off as I climbed the wide stone portico steps, not really in the mood to be chastised already. "Nice to see you again after so long. The drive was long and the traffic horrid. Thank you for asking."

She rolled her eyes as I tilted my cheek at a forty-five-degree angle and touched my cheek to hers in polite greeting.

"Jeans?" She glanced over at my attire when I stepped back, sighing.

I gave myself a once-over. What was I supposed to wear on a road trip? A cocktail dress and Louboutins? There was nothing wrong with jeans, sensible black ankle boots and a white button-down shirt under my camel-colored car coat.

I tsked, curling my mouth. "More Botox?"

She'd started using Botox in her early thirties, calling it preventative. But I wasn't sure anything was preventative anymore as much as it made her look borderline expressionless, no matter how hard she tried to move her face.

I didn't have a problem with cosmetic procedures of any kind, but if she was going to come at me over jeans, then I was going after her for irrelevant details, too.

Anything to keep her from going after Dougie. I'd rather be her target.

She tapered her eyes at me, then decided she wasn't interested in continuing this pissing contest with me, as Dougie rounded the bed of the truck, our weekend bags clutched in one hand. He tested the portico steps, looking on edge for a moment before he tacked on his best smile.

That kind of smile earned him my heart.

She stared at him agape, appraising him as if I'd dragged him in from the curb. Her eyes nearly distended out of her head when she zeroed in on the thin denim around his jeans.

Then came her stupid gasp.

Oh, for fuck's sake. Here we went. "Mother," I said through clenched teeth, because apparently, she'd developed a case of amnesia and those manners they'd ensured I'd had drilled into me fled the estate's premises.

That snapped her back to attention. She righted her rigid posture. "Hello, Douglas."

He swallowed hard, extending a hand in her direction. "Mrs. Cullimore, nice to meet you." He glanced up at the house, his hand still outstretched. "You got a beautiful home."

Mother blanched as she accepted his hand, clearing her throat. "Oh, my," she remarked, holding one hand to her chest, the other hand stiff in his. "That's quite an accent."

"Ah, yeah." He chuckled. "Fall River will do that to you."

"I see." I didn't miss her swiping her palm on the outside of her dress when she extracted her hand from his.

Neither had Dougie. His jaw flexed, his eyes dropping for a moment to mask the shame.

I was going to kill her. She didn't get to do this to him.

I glared at her, telepathically imploring her to be nice, but she ignored me.

She wasn't even this rude when I brought Raquel around and she hadn't pretended to like her, either.

Mother bristled, then gestured to the house. "Shall we?"

I just hoped Daddy wouldn't be like this. I couldn't handle a concerted effort.

Clearing the threshold, my insides twisted. The house still smelled the same—like too much of the artificial almond-scented wood polish Mother liked and insisted was wiped on all the furniture every two days. Over the sickeningly sweet scent lived the distinct mustiness of antiques mixed with the natural fragrance from the fresh flowers seated in a wide, clear vase set on a round wooden table in the middle of the foyer. I drew my eyes to the stately grandfather clock with the ornate enclosed face against the wall near the impressive, curved stairs. The heavy brass pendulum swung back and forth, as hypnotic now as it had been back then. I had spent much of my childhood looking at that clock, wishing time would hurry so I could escape.

The red oak floors gleamed in the stream of muted sunlight afforded by the transom window over my parents' front door, strobing a bright path my eyes followed, toward the woman who'd been my heartbeat in my youth.

The only person who'd kept me sane here.

Frieda offered me an affable smile. "Penelope." Her German-accented voice worked its way into my chest, easing the tight knots living there.

She opened her arms with invitation despite Mother's narrowed gaze and I sped toward her excitedly, throwing my arms around her neck and sinking into her pillowy embrace. She still smelled the same—like clean linens, fresh cut roses and safety.

"Hi, Fri." I kissed her soft cheek gently. Frieda was a silver-haired woman well into her sixties with kind blue eyes, deep laugh lines around her mouth, and the only member of my parents' staff who'd been able to tolerate them for all these years.

Which was why Mother didn't argue when I hugged her, despite the loud clucking of disapproval behind me.

Frieda had raised me, as far as I was concerned. She deserved more than some bullshit cheek-to-cheek air kiss.

"Look at you." Frieda drew me back by the biceps to look me over. Something flashed across her face, an unspoken question in her raised eyebrow as though to ask, *is there something you're not telling me?* Instead, she said, "You're glowing."

The blush crawled up my neck, burning my cheeks. I'd noticed it, too.

But I couldn't confess the why, not yet.

Before Mother's suspicions were aroused prematurely, Frieda continued her praise. "Don't be shy." She chuckled. "You know you're pretty, too."

I let out a little laugh, ignoring the heat of Mother's rapier stare burning a hole in my cranium. Stepping away from her, I gestured at Dougie. "Fri, this is Dougie."

Frieda nodded politely at him. "It's a pleasure to meet you, Mr. Patterson. Welcome."

"Ah," Dougie said nervously, scratching the back of his neck. "Dougie is fine. I don't need any of that formality sh..." he paused, catching himself. "*Stuff.*"

No, he was right. It was shit.

Mother was on the verge of cracking a molar. "Welcome, Dougie," Frieda replied. She straightened, glancing Mother's way. "I'll take their things to their rooms."

"Rooms?" As in, more than one?

I glanced at my mother.

She clucked her tongue against the roof of her mouth. "Don't look at me like that, Penelope."

Thou shalt not be given any opportunity to fornicate in thy parents' home. Noted.

Rolling my eyes, I breezed by her. I'd sneak into his room after she took her Ambien for the night. The element of sneaking around made me kind of giddy.

"Where's Daddy?" I strode down the hall, the eyes of historical figures in ornamental picture frames following me from their station above the chair railing and the pale gold walls

These pictures had been creepy back then, too.

"In his study." Mother raced after me, as urgently as her shoes would allow her. "But don't go in there, he's on a—"

I turned the handles of the double doors, throwing them open.

Daddy didn't startle behind his austere desk. Instead, he smirked at me as he leaned back in his chair, his gray eyes twinkling, the phone tucked between his ear and shoulder.

"Bill, I have to go." Daddy shook his head just as Mother appeared behind me breathlessly. "Yes, she's home."

I twirled on the spot, pretending to curtsy, earning Dougie's chuckle in the short distance, while Mother let out a controlled snarl.

"We'll do lunch at the club on Tuesday." He drummed his fingers against the glossy desktop. "Happy Thanksgiving to you, too." Daddy leaned forward, setting the phone down on the receiver.

Pushing his seat back, he stood up, swiping his palms against his blazer jacket. He wasn't a man of impressive stature, but he dressed respectfully in suits and kept his graying hair neat and combed back. He always had a brightly colored pocket square in his blazer pocket. He rounded his desk, approaching me with his arms extended. "Welcome home, Pearl."

"Hi, Daddy." He hugged me tightly, letting out a content sigh.

"Has she started with you already?" he probed under his breath, pressing a kiss to my forehead.

I kept my response just as hushed. "Do we expect anything else from the venerable Evelyn Cullimore?"

Daddy laughed a little, letting me go. He cleared his throat, tugging on the folds of his blazer, tacking on a serious expression. "And where is—"

"He's here," Mother announced, folding her arms over her chest, reminding me of a pouting child. She glanced in Dougie's way, beckoning him over in frustrated silence with her eyes.

Dougie stepped into the door's threshold, offering Daddy a polite head nod.

"Mr. Cullimore."

"My…" Daddy straightened. "Douglas." He held out a polite hand, doing better to mind his manners than Mother had. "I'm Walter Cullimore, pleasure to meet you."

Dougie shook his hand, appearing a little more at ease with Daddy than he had Mother. "Nice to meet you, sir."

Daddy smiled politely. "Walter's fine."

Mother tutted. Frigid bitch.

"Shall we sit in the drawing room with a libation until dinner?" Daddy asked her.

She nodded stiffly, turning on the ball of her heel and strutting off.

"I'm going to kill her." Or, at least, ensure I ruined her weekend the way she was already ruining mine.

"Pay her no mind, Pearl," Daddy said. "She's just upset about not hosting the Rochesters and Huntingtons."

"She could have." There was nothing stopping her. This house was eleven-thousand square feet. She could have invited the entire state and still had room to spare.

Daddy smiled tightly at me, and any happiness I'd felt at seeing him immediately evaporated. Right. Of course. They couldn't afford to be the source of gossip if anyone discovered their daughter dared to date off their preferred menu.

Well, fuck them. I reached for Dougie's hand, pulling him hurriedly after Mother.

I wished I could say my parents' drawing room was functional, but it was an over-the-top and showy room wrapped in decorative wood paneling, and a gilded fireplace with careful dentil work as the focal point. Despite how spacious the room was, it was easy to feel claustrophobic in here, given how crammed full it was with antique pieces. Your eyes didn't really know where to focus and it could knock the breath right out of you.

In the corner sat a walnut grand piano and peppered throughout the room were highly impractical and ugly Victorian furniture that was uncomfortable as hell, settled on an oversized Persian rug I'd once spilled nail polish remover on.

Frieda helped me rearrange the room and the rug to mask it under the foot of the sofa. The secret had been going on for thirteen years and my parents were never the wiser.

I didn't believe everyone needed to know everything. It wasn't really a lie.

Mother accepted a crystal highball glass from Frieda. Her legs were pressed together and slanted slightly to the right as she brought the shaking glass to her lips, wetting her lips.

I settled into a high-back English Regency armchair opposite of the fireplace, kicking my legs out in front of me. I was intentionally goading her on, but she just continued to pretend like she hadn't carried me in her womb for nine months. No, I didn't exist.

I never wanted to be like that, ever.

"Thank you, Frieda," Daddy said, accepting a double old-fashioned glass from her.

Her hands met in the middle of her lap, looking Dougie's way. "What can I get for you, Mr. Patterson?"

"It's Dougie." He adjusted his weight from foot to foot, uncomfortable being put on the spot, his eyes darting to me helplessly like he didn't know the etiquette.

"He'll take a beer, please, Fri."

"He can speak for himself, Penelope," Mother chastised, her lips pressing with displeasure. "And we do not serve beer in this house. It's a beverage for paupers."

Dougie tipped his stare to his shoes, his brows meeting in the middle.

My blood curdled. How many times had she insulted him now? We shouldn't have come. I seethed at her, something nasty crawling up my throat. But before I could launch into a venomous tirade on par with something that would have come out of Raquel's mouth, Frieda intervened.

"Forgive me, Mrs. Cullimore." Frieda touched her chest, appearing remorseful though I knew she was anything but. "Penelope mentioned some time ago that Mr. Patterson's palate was for beer, so I took the liberty of ordering some during our last inventory order."

I fought the urge to beam, grateful Frieda had remembered that when I'd called home, a few weeks ago, and she had answered.

Mother made an indignant sound.

"Wonderful, Frieda," Daddy announced, ignoring Mother. "Will that work for you, Douglas?"

"Uh, y-yeah," Dougie stammered, his face flushing. "Thank you."

Frieda left the room, returning with a pint glass she'd conjured from God only knew where without anyone having noticed much sooner.

I met Dougie's eyes and kicked my chin at the armchair opposite of me. He looked like he wanted to wither in place as he settled into the chair stiffly, his posture awkward as he surveyed the room from the corner of his eye, trying to take it all in.

Frieda handed him the frosted glass that he eagerly accepted, taking three hurried and exaggerated gulps.

She innocently handed me a whiskey glass, her eyes curious. Too curious.

Shit, I hadn't thought this far.

Well played, Fri. I smiled politely, bringing it to my mouth and dampening my lips, feigning a swallow while I held her gaze.

Her eyes flared, but all I could do was smirk at her.

She was on to me. Winking, she moved out of Mother's line of vision, who practically had steam coming out of her ears as she nursed her gin and tonic, her knuckles whitening as her grasp tightened around the glass.

At this rate, she was going to wrinkle beyond the extent of Botox's power. She was just lucky I wasn't sitting in this chair sideways like I did at home.

I rolled my wrist, the contents of the glass spiraling, creating weak, miniature tornadoes in the glass.

Dougie gaped at me as if he wanted to snatch the glass from my hands. I flashed my eyes knowingly his way, giving him as much tacit reassurance as I could in my silence that I wasn't drinking it.

No, this was part of the illusion.

"So, Pearl," Daddy started, crossing one leg over the other, revealing golden-striped socks under the leg of his pants and shoes that made me smile. He always wore ridiculous socks. "How's the city?"

"Dreadful, I imagine," Mother volunteered, glancing at her fingernails.

"It's amazing actually, but..." I straightened, deciding it was better to just get on with it and clear the air. "Dougie and I—"

"That's a beautiful piano," Dougie blurted.

I sagged in my seat, tossing him a look. Why had he done that?

Mother startled at the intrusion, as though she hadn't just interrupted us moments earlier.

Daddy followed Dougie's stare, his mouth curving to the right with a faint smile. "It's Pearl's."

I waved the comment off. "It's *not* mine."

"I didn't know you play piano," Dougie said, his brows raising as he brought the pint glass to his lips, studying me carefully over the rim.

"*Played*." I hadn't in years. "And just a little." I rose my shoulder in a half-shrug. It wasn't a big deal.

"Just a little?" Mother echoed, swiping a piece of invisible lint from her dress. "That's what you would call playing at a grade eight level?"

"I don't play at a grade eight level," I bit back. And I didn't, at least not officially. "I didn't take my exam."

"No, you didn't show up for your exam," she corrected, holding up a pointed finger. "You were off doing God knows what."

I'd skipped it as a big ol' fuck you to them.

"Pearl," Daddy said, before Mother and I could launch into a full-blown argument. "Why don't you play something?"

I brought the glass back to my lips, simulating another swallow. Lowering it, I stared at the amber contents. "I don't feel like it."

Mother sighed, pressing her lips together. "You used to love playing. You'd sit in here for hours and hours."

I ground my teeth. She wasn't wrong. I used to spend a lot of time in here because piano distracted me from the fact that I was bored and alone. While Frieda was saddled in housework, Daddy was working in the city, and Mother was busy with who the hell knew what—I'd sit in here, with my fingers fitted into a claw shape and play until my wrists burned and my spine ached.

"No one plays Debussy like our Pearl," Daddy assured Dougie.

"Well, other than Debussy himself," Mother tacked on, tittering loudly at her own joke.

Debussy… I huffed out a laugh inwardly.

Fine, they wanted me to play something I would.

I slid off the armchair and stood up. Jutting my chin, I stormed toward the ostentatious piano, then placed my glass on a nearby table.

Thirty-five thousand dollars of walnut and ivory sitting in the corner of this room, untouched over the years. The polished wood of the Steinway Model C was in pristine condition, and I almost felt bad that it had sat here, unloved since I'd left.

"We had the pins tuned and strings redone in the summer," Mother said, surveying her glass.

Such a pretty piece in a house that lacked the love and warmth it deserved. This piano had been my outlet, my escape from myself. The only reason I stopped playing was because I realized being exactly who they wanted me to be, it wouldn't change anything about the relationship I had with them. I'd always felt like a slab of modeling clay on a pottery wheel, spinning in place, with their fingers running over me, trying to smooth out all the imperfections and abnormalities in their eyes.

They'd never seen me.

Piano wasn't going to make Mother love me more.

It wasn't going to make Daddy stay home.

My parents' marriage wasn't perfect, but they'd committed to perpetuating that lie to everyone and themselves. I never wanted that.

It was what made falling in love with Dougie so easy.

Untucking the plush piano bench, the black leather creaked under the addition of my weight.

What to play, what to play.

I fought to contain the grin as an idea struck me. Settling into a comfortable position that kept my back and neck aligned, just like my former Russian piano teacher had instructed me, I relaxed my spine. A decade later and I could still sense the weight of a ruler at the base of my neck. That crotchety old bitch used to tap it there just to remind me how to sit. Training my elbows so they weren't floating, and preserving a ninety-degree angle, I relaxed my shoulders, found the core muscles I hadn't engaged in over a decade, then hooked my hands as though holding a softball and found the cold, familiar ivory keys.

Memory was all I had to go on.

"I don't recognize this piece," Mother said as I set off.

I played the song between an E minor and an A minor, resolved on a G, and then immediately jumped back between an oscillating E minor and A minor to create that familiar rhythmic drumming reminiscent of Lars Ulrich.

She'd figure it out soon enough.

I didn't have to look her way to know she was worrying the inside of her mouth, frantically trying to discern where she'd heard this song before.

And she'd heard it. She'd yelled at me to turn that drivel off more than once over the years. I couldn't help the smile claiming residence on my face.

Daddy cleared his throat, his legs uncrossing as he adjusted the button on his suit jacket, buying himself some breathing room. "I don't believe this is Debussy, dear."

Not even fucking close.

"Well, who is it?" Mother trilled, her embarrassment on full display. She was either too far gone in her humiliation to figure it out, or she truly didn't want to admit she recognized "Enter Sandman" in any capacity.

Whatever would her friends think of her if they knew?

Dougie broke first, throwing his head back and snorting out a laugh before his open palm drummed in time with the music against his thigh. "Metallica."

"Me-Metallica?" Mother clutched at herself.

I looked their way, the breathless laugh breaking out as I increased the tempo.

The music did something to my insides, a kind of overwhelming, triumphant freedom pumping through my limbic system that made me want to chase after it. Serotonin washed over me, excitement heaving my lungs as my uncontrolled breaths came out of me faster and faster.

If I didn't know better, I'd say our baby flipped excitedly.

Maybe I had missed this—playing the piano. Not necessarily antagonizing Mother, although that was a plus, but that feeling of creating something, of putting my all into it and just letting go.

Under my dress shirt, I could sense the horripilation of my skin, the hairs on the back of my neck rising as tingles raced down my spine.

Any anxiety I'd had vanished with each urgent and light stroke of my fingers against the keys.

My soul was vibrating, and all I wanted was for Dougie to feel it, too.

And he did. His depthless green eyes softened as he rubbed the corner of his mouth to mask his shit-eating grin. *Troublemaker*, he mouthed at me.

"Who is Metallica?"

"One of the biggest heavy metal bands in the world," I called to my mother over the increasing rhythm. There was no need for me to play it this fast, but I'd committed now.

She looked like she was on the verge of a nervous breakdown.

And Daddy... Daddy just stared at me like I'd lost it.

Hell, maybe I had. But this was the most fun I'd had playing a piano in years.

I got through the first chorus before I pulled my fingers back. I grinned at my audience, taking a lazy bow with a bend at my waist and a flourish of my hand. But while Mother and Daddy watched me like I was someone they knew they'd created but didn't recognize, Dougie clapped, shaking his head.

He saw me. He always had.

"Yeah, you definitely play only a little," he observed.

The remark set Mother off. She lurched to her feet and stormed out of the room.

Her bedroom door rattling above us when she slammed it shut was the first hit of dopamine I'd gotten all day.

"Was that necessary?" Daddy asked with a frown. He still thought this was about her, about being surly and kicking up a fuss just to get under her skin.

But it never had been. This had always been about me. "Abso-fuck-ing-loutely."

Mother didn't come down for dinner, which suited me just fine, because I'd had enough of her nagging for one night. Daddy was terse with me, but he relaxed eventually when I suggested we have dessert in the parlor while watching golf.

What could I say? Even at twenty-eight, I still knew which buttons to push—good or bad.

That hadn't stopped him from asking me to be a little kinder to her tomorrow.

At around ten, he suggested we all retire for the night, so we followed him up the stairs—where he ensured Dougie went his way and I went mine.

Thirty minutes later though, I was inching carefully across the hallway, footsteps light and nimble as I passed my parents' bedroom, the transom from the front door illuminating a pattern on the hallway floor from the silvery moonlight pouring in.

My hand wrapped around the knob of Dougie's room. I didn't open it all the way, slipping inside with the small amount of space I'd created. He stirred as I was closing the door behind me. I tiptoed across the bedroom to where he laid with his back turned to the door, the moonlight a spotlight from the parted curtains.

He always left the curtains open. He called it a free alarm clock.

The mattress hardly shifted under the addition of my planted knee. Why Mother insisted on firm mattresses, I'd never know. Dougie rolled over, parting his legs to create room for me to lie between them. I blanketed his body with my own, tucking my head under his chin, inhaling deeply.

"Hi," I whispered. He'd showered before he'd gone to bed. The air in here still damp, notes of his bodywash touching my nose.

He lifted his head, meeting my eyes as his mouth pulled with mischief. "You're not supposed to be in here."

"Goody two shoes." I shot him a smile he didn't reciprocate.

"Think we've annoyed your parents enough for one night." He tilted his head toward the window. "Plus, I'd like to be respectful while I'm a guest in their house, Pen."

"We're having a baby, that ship has sailed." His stomach hardened under me, his exhale leaving him tightly. After a beat of a second more, Dougie banded his arms around my shoulders, seeming reluctant at first. "Do my parents scare you?"

"Your mother's intense, but no," he replied, lifting one arm to tuck behind his head.

"And my dad?"

He sighed, his fingers tracing faint patterns against my shoulders. "Just wants whatever's best for you. I can respect that."

"You're what's best for me." I tried to ignore the whirlpool of worry spiraling in my gut. He lifted his eyes to meet mine, something I struggled to place flashing in his face. "You know that, right?"

But the unarticulated question lingered there, his face saying what his mouth wouldn't. *Am I?*

"Dougie," I pleaded, squeezing him harder around the middle. "It's too late for regrets."

"I regret nothing." He said it with certainty, but I couldn't ignore the gravel that had entered his tone. "I just... this isn't how I would have liked to have done things, that's all." His brows muddied in the middle, his mouth pinching. "And I don't need you defending me like that."

"Like what?"

"In a way that's more about you than it is about me."

I focused my gaze on his neat pile of clothes on the bench at the foot of the bed, this afternoon coming back to me. "The piano."

He took up so little space in this room, and that made me sad.

"The piano," he agreed. "You're talented, Penny, and I loved hearing you play." He brushed his knuckles along the back of my arms. "But that stunt to stick it to them, just reinforces that I'm the problem in their eyes."

"But you're not," I insisted sharply, my body heating. "I've always been like that." It was a running remark that I was the source of Daddy's gray hair.

"That intensely?" He cocked a brow at me. "You didn't even try to speak to your ma."

"Why should I?" I sat up, folding my arms over my chest. "She was awful to you. If she gets rattled over Metallica, then she doesn't have any actual problems."

He propped himself up on his elbow, giving me a careful once-over. "Look." He took in a tight breath. "I'm trying to keep the peace as much as possible to ensure that tomorrow goes smoothly. Can you meet me halfway?"

Why was he so fixated on making it easier for them? "You wouldn't let me tell them about the house."

Dougie rubbed his forehead with his other hand, as though he was massaging away the onset of a headache. "These things need to be done delicately."

"You're an expert on my parents suddenly?"

"I'm an expert at not being good enough," he rebutted noncommittally.

I flinched on top of him, my head snapping back. How could he say something so untrue about himself with the casualness of asking for the pepper shaker?

Dougie tensed, then rolled back on his pillow, regarding the ceiling. His throat contracted, a bob weaving there like he was refraining from saying something else.

He was wrong. "You're good enough." I swathed my body over his, wanting to expel all his doubt. I found the crook of his neck, my favorite place, as my arms tightened around him. I'd never feel close enough to him, no matter how tightly I held him. I just only hoped he'd let me keep him. "You're better than me."

He chuckled, but there was an edge to it that left me unsettled.

"I mean it, Dougie. You're better than all of us."

My heart thrummed in my ears. I pressed my mouth against the stubble dusting his jaw, his body relaxing unwillingly under mine.

His arms banded around my waist, his strangled inhale coming from his nose. "What am I going to do with you, hm?"

"Love me forever?" I drew heart-shaped designs on his chest with my fingers. "Is that too much to ask?"

"Hmm," he mused. "Big ask."

"Hey!" I whisper-yelled.

He laughed this time. Not the full-bodied one that I would have loved to have heard in this moment, but the kind that shook his chest and spurred calmness through me. "Yeah, I can do that." He tilted his head to kiss the top of my head. "But be nice tomorrow."

I scoffed. "I'm *always* nice."

"Penelope." He squeezed me tighter. "I mean it. They're about to experience an enormous life shock tomorrow that's going to destroy every dream they ever had for you, and I'm going to be the asshole who did that to them. You need to prepare yourself that you may not get the fanfare or enthusiasm you're hoping for."

"You think they're going to take it badly?" Apprehension rocketed through me. I knew they wouldn't be happy, per se, but I'd hoped that seeing me happy would matter.

He hesitated, threading a hand through his still-damp hair. "I do."

Man, that was the last thing I wanted to think about while trying to fall asleep. I blew out a sigh, trying to collect myself, as my mind wandered back to something he'd said earlier. "How would you have done it?"

"Properly."

Not good enough. I wanted to know what he would have done had things been different, had we had the time to go slow.

"Describe it." I dropped my voice, my hand dragging down his exposed chest, the tips of my fingers brushing against the band of his sweats.

"Pen," he husked out in warning, trying to snatch my curious hands, but I avoided capture. He groaned, throwing his head back in defeat against the pillow. "Not here, c'mon."

But he didn't fight me. He seemed drunkenly resigned to let me have my way.

"Describe it." I inched forward until my palm wrapped around the thick shaft of his hardening cock, twitching in my hand. I loved I did that to him, that all it took was the slightest gesture and his body came to life for me.

"Fuck me," he muttered.

"I might do just that." I fortified my statement by stroking him, his member jerking in my palm. I swiped my thumb along the crown, gathering the bead of precum, massaging it into him. "I'm waiting."

Dougie squeezed his eyes shut, his jaw flexing as he fought for some semblance of control while I stroked. "We would have dated a lot longer." His hot eyes opened, singeing my skin as he stared. "We would have gotten married before we had a kid."

"Do you want to marry me?" I released him to hook my fingers around his waistband. He lifted his hips to help me, giving up the fight. His cock sprung free, hard and proud and desperate for attention.

But he hadn't answered me.

My eyes found his, an ache setting off in my chest as he fixated on me. I'd never been this aware of my heartbeat before, but the longer he looked at me like that, like he couldn't imagine a world without me in it...

It made me want to cry. Dougie gripped my shoulders, pulling me to him. He brushed the tip of his nose against mine, his warm breath fanning my face. "I do, Penelope. I want to marry you."

He pulled me to the floor with him, neither of us trusting the headboard, the strength of Mother's Ambien, or Daddy's determination to keep us in separate rooms.

My boyfriend, the father of my child, made love to me on the floor like I was his wife, with a tenderness that promised me our forever. I wasn't sure what the future held for us, or what tomorrow would even bring, but I didn't care.

'Cause as long as I had him?

I had everything that money could never buy.

Chapter Twenty

Dougie

Present

THE TWO BODIES ON THE MUTED SCREEN MOVED IN A FRENZIED TANDEM. Their desperation palpable as they clawed at each other, mouths parted, eyes narrowed with lust. The woman's head tilted back, her co-star's needy fingers digging into her parted thighs until his knuckles whitened, his hips slamming into hers as his head fell back and he let out a muted roar of release.

Only I couldn't get there with them.

"Fuck," I bit out, releasing my chafed length and throwing my head back on the pillow, my chest rising and falling with frustration. The blood rushed through my forearm, my bicep heavy with deadweight.

There was only one of us in this house who could apparently routinely get off without the other, and it wasn't me.

Reaching for the remote, I turned off the television as I fought to regain control of my breathing, rolling onto my side as pins and needles set off in my hand.

I'd always been successful at this part, getting myself off quickly.

But lately, I'd been too wound up, too stressed to achieve anything close to a release. I laughed to myself as a thought whirred through my brain about whether Penelope was experiencing the same struggles.

Probably not.

She had been checked out of our marriage for a while. I was sure getting herself off was easier now than ever.

I winced, both from the realization and the sharp discomfort of blue balls setting in. My cock still engorged and stiff, pulsating with the reminder that we hadn't achieved what we'd set out to do, but the ache in my wrist told me it was a no-go. I tried to swallow, but my mouth was too dry from panting so heavily.

I needed water. Searching the floor for my pants, I slipped them over my legs and headed for the door. The hallway was dark, save for a small nightlight that illuminated a path bright enough for me to wander down the stairs without eating shit.

Wincing, the friction of my pants against my balls painfully uncomfortable as I made my descent down the stairs, the heaviness getting worse as I moved. The faint purr of the dishwasher running in the kitchen hit my ears when I cleared the last step. Padding barefoot to the kitchen in the darkness, I extended a hand out in front of me to avoid the risk of smashing into anything until I cleared the kitchen threshold, feeling for the light switch.

The pot lights ate the obscurity of the kitchen, revealing a small, hunched over figure sitting at the kitchen island.

"Jesus Christ," I hissed, jumping back as my stomach fluttered.

What the hell was she doing down here?

Pen lifted her head, her eyes weary, the dark rings of her under eyes closer to bruises. Her slender fingers toyed with the string on a tea bag. She tipped her chin back to the steamless mug. "Sorry."

How long had she been sitting there for?

Don't ask, Dougie. "Why are you sitting in the dark?" Of course I asked, because despite how frustrated I was over last week, for forcing herself to do something she didn't want to do, she was still my wife.

I still loved her. I knew I always would.

She shrugged halfheartedly. Pen pitched her elbows on the edge of the counter, framing her forehead with her hands, her spun gold tresses falling forward. "I spoke to my mother yesterday."

Wonderful. My hackles rose, my molars finding each other. I'd be up sitting in the kitchen in the darkness for days on end too if I'd spoken to Evelyn. That woman was wound up tighter than a coiled Yo-Yo. And based on how things had been as of late, I could imagine how great that conversation had gone.

But I kept myself from asking if Evelyn was hosting her an "I'm getting divorced" party that would establish her newfound status as a rich, single heiress back on the dating market.

Frankly, thinking about her being with anyone else but me...

Someone with my wife, with my son...

I couldn't allow myself to go there. I wouldn't. The infecting thought polluted my mind, each muscle in my body knotting with silent fury.

Giving her my back, I moved for where we kept the drinking glasses, grabbing one, then ambulated with discomfort in my groin and anger stoking an inferno in my stomach over to the fridge. Pressing my glass against the lever, I watched as the water dispensed.

Despite my better judgment, I couldn't stop myself from the query freeing itself from my tongue as I pulled the glass back. "And?"

I watched as Pen traced her finger over the rim of the mug, her brows inching together. "She mentioned us going to Connecticut for Thanksgiving."

Thanksgiving... she hadn't told them about us? And now we were supposed to pretend? Just like we had been here? Perpetuate the lies some more because the truth looked worse.

Unbelievable.

Chortling, my shoulder blades snapped together. Funny. "I'm not going."

"I..." her mouth trembled, her waist leaning forward in her seat. "I understand why you wouldn't." She raised her nervous eyes to mine. "If you want us to spend this year at your mom's—"

Us?

There was no us.

Not anymore.

"You can go to Connecticut." My stomach hardened at the brute force of the statement as I brought my glass to my mouth, guzzling it back. I had zero interest in participating in anymore illusions for her family or for *us* like some kind of circus performer. "We'll figure out where Christopher is going this year."

We'd alternate holidays.

I guessed, anyway.

I didn't know how co-parenting worked, how holidays were shared. When my dad walked out on Ma and me, I'd never heard a word from him again. He was as good as dead to me, but I would not repeat that pattern.

No, that part of the cycle ended with me.

But it didn't change that my insides were shredding when Pen stared at me with this hollowed-out desperation in her eyes to salvage what remained of *us*. I swore her eyes would haunt me for the rest of my fucking life. I'd known that the day I'd met her, but I always believed it would be under different circumstances.

The hues of blue and green around her irises could have drowned me in her devastation and loss.

That was the face you never forgot, and I'd see it etched on the back of my eyelids every time I thought of her. We'd never spend another Thanksgiving together. This house would never smell like artificial pine come December, and I wouldn't find her candy cane wrappers everywhere. I'd never eat anymore of her cinnamon candy hearts come Valentine's Day or witness her painting hard-boiled eggs with Christopher at Easter. No more holidays. No more us. There would only be fleeting moments that would pass through my memory when I thought of her, stolen moments that I never thought to savor a little longer because I thought we had forever.

Forever was another lie.

"What?" I questioned, my ribs tightening as I struggled for my next breath. "Did our divorce not come up?"

She flinched.

It must have come up. I couldn't see why it wouldn't. So, was she surprised I'd questioned her?

No more lies, no more bullshit, no more playing house.

No more doing this to her.

She wanted out. I'd give her an out.

Pen rolled her lips together, shaking her head as both hands found the island as though she were stabilizing herself. "We're *not* getting divorced."

My hand flexed around the glass, my head shaking a little. Why the fuck was she still trying to convince herself of this? She was killing me —or was that what she wanted?

Exhaling, I wandered to the sink, downed the rest of my glass and set it down in the sink to deal with tomorrow when the dishwasher finished its clean cycle. "'Night, Pen."

Turning away, she stopped me in my tracks when she dropped something else in my lap, her voice soft, but the statement stabbing me all the same. "I saw Raquel today."

My blood ran cold, the shell of ribs closing in on my lungs.

Why now? Why was she trying to do all the right things *now*? Was it enjoyable for her to watch me squirm? Evelyn was Mary Poppins compared to Raquel. Raquel would feed my nut sack through a paper shredder and then cater it to me on a baby spoon while cooing.

Shit, that understood threat was one way to cure blue balls.

Penelope dropped her head, her lips pressing tightly together, her eyes trained on her mug. "The twins, th-they," guilt entered her stammer, my free fist clenching at my side, "they have a lot of hair." She'd seen them when she was the reason I hadn't. The smile she attempted didn't take on her face, her brows raising a little at her next observation. "They look like Sean."

I could imagine them almost perfectly—head full of dark hair, soft plump features that would sharpen with age, bronzed skin, and curious russet-brown eyes.

I gave her my profile, the bruise on my face pulsating, as fresh as though he'd only shoved me moments ago.

If they looked like him, it meant they looked like Maria.

Lord only knew why my mind went there.

Right, because Maria Tavares hadn't wanted to fuck me either, and I'd messed up my marriage in my desperation to find someone who *did*. The reminder at my attempt at an indiscretion stung.

Hopefully, the twins grew up to punch better than their old man.

I tipped my head back, my expression flinty, while I stared at the ceiling as though it were the source of all my anger. "What brought on that change of heart?"

"I'd love to tell you, if you'll let me," she whispered. Her sad eyes drew my unwilling attention back to her, my insides constricting. "I'd like to… to tell you everything."

I didn't utter a goddamn word.

But I couldn't find the will to walk away from her again, either.

She accepted that as permission to keep going. Turning in her seat, one of her bare feet pressed against the rung of the chair, the other dangling.

God, she looked so small.

Her shoulder-length flaxen locks were a mess, like anytime she hadn't been fingering her tea bag, she'd been threading her fingers through at the roots and tugging.

I wanted to fix it, brush her hair out for her. Pin our anger and our hurt and hold her for just a little while, to remember what she felt like in my arms. Tuck her head against the crook of my neck and bury the tip of my nose in her soft hair.

How did we get here? The heaviness in my body demanded I take the seat opposite of her, but my ego kept me right where I was, my feet forming roots like a sentinel tree that would guard this place forever.

She didn't beg me to sit down, but she resigned herself to talking without it.

A first.

So many delayed fucking firsts.

"I've accepted that… that in telling you this, I risk losing you forever," she began tentatively, sounding as though it were taking a goddamn miracle to keep it together. Pen tugged on the edge of her soft pink sleep shorts, her fingers curling against the fabric. "But I want you to know, despite how I felt about it at first, I didn't want it to happen, okay?" Her chin trembled with the promise of another release of emotion. "I've been trying to fix it, I—"

I interrupted her, hating the impatience coursing through me. "What is it?" I clenched my teeth. What was she going to say that would induce this much fear within her? That would justify all of this after so long?

My eyes dropped to where she'd gripped her sleep shorts, her hands rattling against her thighs as the foot propped against the rung of the chair bounced with nerves.

Pen's mouth opened and closed, her jaw flexing as her chest caved in. "Dougie, the night of our honeymoon, I..." she released her shorts to flex her fingers out in front of her. "The bathroom—"

"You got your period," I said.

But when she didn't nod or confirm it, dread entered my veins. The furnace vibrated beneath us in the basement, the roar of life loud. A dog barked in the distance, once, twice, three times. My heart, my fucking heart, squeezed, and all I could do was wince and plead with her to say something.

Penelope shook her hands out in a way that was too familiar, her tell that whatever she was going to say next was bad.

Really bad.

Her next shuddering intake marked itself in my brain over the furnace, the dog barking, and my heartbeat. It was a sound so permanent that genuine worry assaulted my insides. "That wasn't my period."

I frowned, searching her face.

"I-I," she let out a pained, garbled cry crawling up her throat. "I was pregnant... and I lost it."

Time seemed to stop, my skin erupting into painful goosebumps, every hair on my body upright and on guard.

What? She had been what?

Pregnant?

My mind kept tripping over the word. Every time I tried to digest it, it was like a needle skipping a track over a lint-laden record—the sound familiar, yet so foreign.

How could she have been pregnant? We hadn't.

But then the timeline came back to me. We had.

She stared down at her knees, her arms wrapping around herself in a hug to try to keep her quivering under control.

New Year's. The front door. The last time.

Shit. My expression slackened, growing pale as my heart jackknifed in my chest to the point of pain, my breathing frantic as the pieces of the puzzle snapped into place.

That had been why she pulled away.

That was why she'd buried herself in wedding planning, why she'd wanted to rush through it.

Why she'd withdrawn herself from me.

She'd kept this from me. *Why*?

I staggered back, catching myself against the trim of the kitchen threshold, my fingers digging into the molding until an ache exploded in my nail beds.

Numb.

White noise set off in my ears, a sharp, tinny ringing, robbing me of every conceivable thought as I watched her. Her elbows found the edge of the counter once more, her head slanting forward weakly as her shoulders quaked and a shuddering sob ripped from her throat.

She was pregnant.

She was.

Was.

Lost it.

She'd kept that from me. Me. Her fucking husband.

Penelope glanced at me, her face marred with tears, cheeks ruddy. "I'm sorry," she croaked. "I'm so sorry."

"Why?" A single word with so many meanings. Why the lie?

Her pregnancy, her mis—fuck, I couldn't even get the word out.

I settled on loss. *Our* loss.

Why didn't she tell me she was pregnant at all?

"I didn't want you to hate me. I-I," her throat worked, "but I did."

"Why?" I demanded again, grit entering my tone as the overwhelming wave of emotions threatened to suffocate me.

I wanted to yell, hit something, anything. But all I could do was stare at her, this stranger who'd always told me everything, while every muscle in my body jumped.

"I didn't..." she trapped her bottom lip between her teeth, releasing it as she swallowed another cry. "I didn't want to be pregnant, and then, I did, and by then..." the confession died.

I squeezed my eyes tightly, tension building from my jaw to my temporal lobe, the promise of a headache throbbing in warning.

By then, it was too late.

She hadn't wanted to be pregnant again, but she was.

Now it made sense. All of it. Why she had detached herself from me. Why she'd been adamant about staying away from Raquel and Sean.

Why that feeling had intensified after Raquel's near-death experience.

It was too hard for her, the guilt and shame overwhelming.

"My body failed us, and I-I-I made you hate me," she gasped, her voice trembling. "I pushed you away. It's my fault you went to..."

The insinuation of Maria's name made me sick this time, my anger edging away. This was on me.

I released the trim, pivoting away. My wife had lost a baby. My wife had kept a pregnancy from me, and I...

I wasn't supposed to be that guy, the clueless moron who didn't fight for her, who gave in when it got too hard.

But I had been.

I hadn't broken any cycle, any behavior. No, I was my father through and through.

I was the asshole, so unaware, so ignorant of his wife's behaviors and about-face that he couldn't even figure out that she was pregnant.

The signs had all been there, rushing at me—her unreasonable irritability, the nausea, her need to get every detail of our lives sorted as though she were nesting again.

Because she was in a way.

Shoving my fingers through my hair, I clawed at my scalp, the shock and denial making my head spin. I was struggling to breathe, my lungs refusing to balloon as the looming threat of a panic attack charged at me.

Then the brute force of the repulsion twisted my stomach and raced up my throat. She'd been grieving, and I'd been thinking with my cock the entire fucking time.

I ripped away from the kitchen. I couldn't even look at her.

"Dougie?" She called my name brokenly, but I didn't stop walking, no longer concerned about walking into anything. If I got lucky, maybe I'd walk into something and seriously hurt myself.

I would deserve it. A concussion might be one way to forget I'd ever done this to her.

But it wouldn't change that she'd never forget, and I'd never be able to fully undo it all.

My eyes found the front door. The memory of exactly what we'd done against it in January punched me. There was no smile to accompany it. All there was, was the intense urge to hurl because we'd made a baby that night in the darkness and I hadn't known. I shoved the powder room door open, dropped to my knees and attempted to heave the contents of my stomach as the thought resounded with a merciless brutality.

I'd watched my wife lose *our* child in our bathroom, and she said nothing. My stomach lurched again, my tract burning as I retched, bracing myself against the toilet seat.

I couldn't even vomit right. I spit saliva into the toilet, my insides still roiling with the mess of my memories.

God, she'd cried that day.

I couldn't purge the image of her bleeding all over the bathroom floor, nor the betrayal and agony flooding in her face.

That had been why she was bawling her eyes out—not over her fucking period, not over a canceled honeymoon.

And what the fuck had I done?

This time, the water I'd drunk came up, my guts heaving with the tasteless contents. I wiped my mouth on the back of my wrist, panting hard.

There was so much I wanted to say to her, answers I was desperate for, yet all I could do was stare at the clear remnants of what had been in my stomach twisting with the saliva and bile, looking back at me from the toilet bowl.

Leaning back on my haunches, I extended a shaking hand out to the toilet seat, closing it and then pressing down on the lever, the whirr dull in my ears.

Pen's shadow emerged against the wall in front of me. I avoided her eyes, my hot skin tingling with shame, sweat licking up my spine. There was a persistent ache in my throat, and I wasn't confident if it was the aftermath of throwing up, or my own fucking disgust with myself, trying to claw its way out. Bracing myself against the wall, I forced myself upward. With my back still turned to her, I turned the faucet on, rinsed my mouth out twice, and then washed my hands.

"Dougie." All the vowels in my name left her in a whimpered apology.

I wished she'd stop saying my name like that, like she had something to be sorry for. I'd been such a prick to her this morning, trying to punish her back. She'd lost her shit in her truck, and I stood and watched through the living room window.

She'd needed me, desperately, and I hadn't fucking realized it because I was in my head, focused on what I needed from her.

The extent of my regret wouldn't change a goddamn thing now.

I found my nerve to face her, and whatever she saw in my stare shattered her. Tears glistened in her eyes, her forehead puckering as her dwindling self-control vanished.

Her spine found the wall, her legs giving out on her as she sagged to the floor. "I'm sorry," she pleaded. "I'm so sorry. Please forgive me."

Not as fucking sorry as I was.

She had done nothing wrong.

But I? I'd...

I'd missed all the fucking signs. Her avoidance of Raquel, the way she'd been suffering internally, in silence. Her hyper fixation on Christopher and doing everything perfectly. How she'd withdrawn from me.

My burst of sunshine was hurting.

And me? I'd been the asshole desperate for—God, I was gonna be fucking sick again. I pressed the back of my hand against my mouth until the skin pulsed under the pressure, my throat working to swallow the bile back down.

Pen dragged her legs to her chest weakly, her forehead finding her knees as the weeping ripped through her.

I'd nearly cheated on my wife.

The mother of my son.

My perfect, gorgeous wife.

And she'd kept a miscarriage from me.

Who the fuck were we?

We weren't these people—the ones who pathologically lied, who kept secrets from one another. Pen never had qualms around me about anything. She peed with the door open, head banged in the kitchen, and didn't hesitate to pick something out of my teeth for me in public when I didn't notice.

Penelope wasn't demure. She wasn't like her upbringing.

She'd never kept a secret, even when she should have. Pen said what she thought, as she thought it. She lacked a filter. She was brave, and strong, and loving.

And I'd destroyed her. I'd made her fearful of me, and that fear had mutated and twisted us into something unrecognizable. My actions hadn't just added fuel to the fire, it burned our fucking world right down until it consumed us both. All that remained were the lingering curls of smoke and ashes of what we'd been.

There would be no Phoenix rising here.

She leaned her head against the bathroom wall, her eyes squeezed tight enough that her features pinched. "This wasn't supposed to happen to us."

No, it wasn't.

Because somewhere along the way, we'd lost sight of what mattered.

Us.

I sank to the floor in front of her, draping the back of her calves with my hands. She jolted, her body shuddering as though it startled her, I'd touched her.

I guess I'd stopped trying to touch her, too.

The back of my lids stung. She looked so small and frail on the floor, defeated and aggrieved by what she perceived as being her fault. Pen had suffered immensely, torturing herself for what she deemed a defect.

This wasn't her fault.

It had never been her fault.

She hadn't pulled away from me before our wedding because she'd hated me, or because I could have been anyone, or she regretted her decision.

She'd withdrawn because she was stressed out about planning a wedding and being pregnant—because the timing felt wrong.

But how did you voice that to the man you loved? How did you express you were uncertain about another unplanned pregnancy because your lives were hectic when you'd always tried so hard to be the person he'd idolized?

And what happened when you accepted you were pregnant—hell, even got a little excited—and your body came and robbed it from you?

She'd been rife full of shame and grief, and I hadn't dug hard enough for an explanation because I'd been scared, too. I'd let her pull away, and I'd gotten angry and desperate.

I hadn't asked the right questions. I'd made it too easy for her to recede into herself because I'd been afraid of the consequences.

And for what?

For us to end up here, anyway?

I felt her frantic hands on me, pleading, clinging to me in a way she hadn't in forever. Like if she let me go, she might sink into whatever lifeless, dark place existed in the abyss of her mind.

"Say something, please." Her chin trembled. "I feel like my heart's going to rip out of my chest."

There was only one thing I could say, and the words would never be enough.

"I'm sorry," I whispered, releasing her thighs to frame her face, lowering my forehead to hers. "I'm so fucking sorry."

For not seeing it, for not trying hard enough, for taking the easy way out.

For nearly ruining us.

Because there was an us. There'd always been an us.

She shifted her face, the tip of her nose brushing mine. "I didn't want it to happen."

"It's not your fault, baby," I assured her, my voice breaking. "It's never been your fault."

Vignettes of Pen's happiness played in my mind in sepia. The first time she'd shown up on a jobsite, completely out of place and determined.

The heat of her inquisitive eyes on me when she tripped and landed in my arms.

The assertive brushing of her soft and confident lips in my truck that first time, that kiss alone claiming her spot in my heart permanently.

How she'd demanded to be invited into my world, a world she'd never belonged in because she was too good for me.

And her inclusion of me in hers, despite the odds stacked against us.

How she'd accepted my proposal on bended knee in front of her parents that fateful Thanksgiving three years ago, after we told them she was pregnant—moments after I'd overhead them in her father's study that they'd believed that this thing between us was temporary—only for Walter to demand I marry her.

But that had always been the plan, the dream come true, hadn't it? Make her my wife. Spend the rest of my life being by her side, supporting her, and loving her.

Building a family with her.

Pen guided herself closer, her head tilting back, her throat working with a nervous bob. She kissed me—so gently at first that I felt the timidness coursing through her, seeping deep into my bones, reawakening a part of my brain I'd thought I'd lost.

She drew back, her lips parted, breath ghosting all over my face as her red-rimmed eyes traced over me. "I don't want a divorce, Dougie." She brushed her teeth over her bottom lip. "I just want you to love me again."

I broke. The mournful, deep howl so unlike me I didn't know I could experience a grief like this. I felt it in my bones, every muscle in my body heavy, a tightness in my chest that would never break. I released her face, binding my hands around her waist to drag her to me because she was my calm in the storm. Pen came willingly, her body pressed as close to mine as our skin and bones would allow.

"Please, just love me again," she asked on a sob, her fingers curling around my sweater, her hot tears stinging against the crook of my neck as they fell.

"I love you." My fingers sank into her hair, cradling the back of her head. "I've never stopped loving you."

This time, when she kissed me, there was no hesitation. This kiss was urgent and expressive of all the things she wanted to say but couldn't. The pleat of her lips firm, her fingers releasing my sweater to weave through my hair, pinning me to her. Pen dragged her teeth against my bottom lip, her leg draping over my parted legs on the floor, nestling herself into my lap in a straddle and pressing her lithe body against mine.

She drew back a little, looking down at me through half-lidded eyes, searching my face for a sign. Satisfied by whatever she found, her hands left my hair, traveling to slip up my sweater. And even though my cock stirred to life against her hot core, I seized her hands.

"Slow down."

She shook her head, her chest caving in. "If I slow down, then I'll think," she confessed on a hard swallow. "I don't want to think anymore."

My stomach sank as I searched her face for a sign, my mind rushing to weigh the pros and the cons, but Pen decided for me. She was done waiting for me to get on the same page as her when I'd always been chapters behind. She tugged her hands free from my grasp. Finding the hemline of her shirt, she lifted it over her head.

Even if I wanted to look away, I couldn't.

Just like she had banked on, because unlike last week on the couch where it had felt forced and awkward, a do-or-die effort, there was desire tangled with her remorse in her eyes, a silent apology swaying between us because she needed me.

This time, her exposed skin pimpled and her pink nipples pebbled without ever having touched her.

This time, when she rolled her hips against me, the heat of her damp arousal clung to the fibers penetrating through my clothes, seeping into my cock.

This time? She wanted me the way I'd always wanted her.

Pen twined her arms around my neck, my mouth fastening against hers with an aching hunger, my tongue darting into her eager mouth. She met my tongue stroke for stroke. Her hands fumbled with the zipper on my sweater, tugging it down and then helped me peel it off my arms. My hands only left her long enough to take my T-shirt off.

She pressed her naked chest against mine, vocalizing her content- ment into my mouth on a breathy moan that made blood rush to both heads and my skin heat. Wrapping my arms around her waist, she helped me climb to our feet before I hoisted her from the floor, her legs encircling me.

"Bedroom," she instructed, her mouth finding my ear. Shit, hers or mine? Did it matter? Detecting my hesitation, she filled in the blank, nibbling on my earlobe. "Ours."

With one brawny arm braced against her waist, Pen's face dipped into the crook of my neck, sampling my stubbled jaw, making my mind swim.

Was this actually happening?

The thought kept me from clearing the doorway of her bedroom —*our* bedroom.

"Dougie?" She anchored her hands around my face, searching my eyes. "Are you okay?"

I glanced up at her, my gut souring for a moment before I asked the burdensome question, "What did you mean you've been trying to fix it?"

Her throat bobbed with another swallow, her eyelids lowering for a moment.

But then it hit me. The doctors appointment. "You were telling the truth last week." And I'd accused her of... Not only had she been upfront, but I'd twisted it. No wonder she'd hit me. I would have hit me, too—but I'd gotten off easy.

Too easy.

Her shoulders lifted in a half-shrug. "Yeah."

"Fuck, Pen." I set her down on her feet, shame robbing me of this moment.

"Don't," she pleaded, banding her arms around my waist. "Don't do that to yourself."

After everything, how could I not?

I hissed when her palm closed around the outside of my cock, squeezing when my hips shifted forward out of reflex. She left a trail of kisses against my exposed chest, following the column of my throat, no doubt sensing the pounding of my pulse there. She flexed on the tips of her toes and tested her mouth against mine again.

"We made mistakes," she observed in a whisper. "Both of us." I didn't want her to shoulder any of this. This was all on me. "Can you forgive me, Dougie?"

"There's nothing for me to forgive you for," I replied, chewing on the inside of my cheek as I brushed her hair out of her face.

I'd missed her so goddamn much.

She smiled sadly at me, and though she didn't voice it, I heard it.

There was plenty to forgive her for—it just would never compare to what I needed to forgive myself for.

But for tonight, for her, I could forget it for just a little while. I could use that time to love her the way she'd always deserved.

I trailed my fingers down the center of her chest, reveling in the thrumming of her urgent, familiar heartbeat, and brushed the back of my knuckles against her attentive nipple. I watched as they turned into tight peaks, and her breathing shifted.

Her back curved in response, the shudder ripping through her. My fingers journeyed further down her flat torso, tripping at the thought that there would have been another baby in our house right now.

Clearing my head with a quick shake, my fingers hooked around the band of her sleep shorts, tugging them off, while keeping my eyes riveted on hers. Such pretty, depthless eyes I wanted to spend the rest of my life losing myself in.

Hundreds of times we'd done this before, and yet, this time felt unlike the rest. I was apprehensive about touching her because I knew I'd been right back then.

I'd never deserved her.

The soft whisper of her shorts landing on the floor hit my ears, jostling something familiar in my mind. A tremulous quake rocked through her when I didn't immediately descend upon her in a ravenous lust. I just wanted to savor this moment—'cause in a few hours, things would change.

I knew they would, because I had to change.

In order to be worthy of being her husband, I had to become someone she'd forgotten existed.

I'd always been consumed by Penelope. I'd never taken my time with her. I was always hurrying to the next stage.

At my inaction, she folded her hands across her breasts, her thighs clenching together as the flush crawled up the column of her throat. Her chin dipped into her neck, the need to hide taking over her motor movements.

"Drop your arms, Penny."

Her head snapped back with attention, her eyes flaring. "I'm scared you'll see something you don't like…" She chewed on the inside of her cheek. "I'm self-conscious."

Self-conscious? A small, agonized laugh I'd never release ripped through me. My wife wasn't self-conscious, but I'd made her that way, hadn't I?

I'd sown doubt and worry, that the reason I'd toed the line was because there was something she was lacking, but it was never about that.

"You're nothing like her," I said quietly, looming closer.

She seemed so defeated; her exhale pained as it ghosted across my exposed chest.

"You're better." I flattened my palm against her stomach once more, guiding her backward until the calves of her reluctant legs hit the edge of her—our—mattress. "In every single way." Her chin trembled, her eyes rounding as she found her nerve to look at me.

"It was never about her or about you." I gritted my teeth to keep the emotions in check as I made my confession. "It was about me."

She bowed her head, and I accepted that there was a chance she'd get upset. But I couldn't, in good conscience—whatever that was worth now—crawl back into bed with my wife, without her understanding that it was never about Maria Tavares or about her.

It was about me.

It had always been about me.

My weaknesses, my insecurities, my worries.

If she didn't drop her arms, I wouldn't push it. I didn't blame her. How could I? I'd fostered those insecurities. I'd fertilized them. I'd taken the spark out of her eyes and plucked the very sun out for her sky.

I'd ruined this confident, bright, shining light in my desperation for something.

Her arms fell to her sides slowly, her hands flexing against her thighs. Her voice came out in a whisper. "The light stays off."

My smile came out flimsy and sad, because it wouldn't matter if we were in complete and utter darkness. I knew Penelope's body better than I knew the back of my hand—every dip, every beauty mark, every strand of hair on her head. I'd memorized the details like she was my religion.

I fastened my hands around the curve of her hips, guiding her back on the bed. The mattress shifted a little under the addition of our weight, her chest rising and falling. "We'll take it slow," I said against her cheek. "And if you want me to stop at any time, I'll stop."

"Okay."

Her scent was the strongest under her ear. At that small slope of her neck my mouth fitted upon easily, her heady pulse throbbing in homecoming. I was going to take my time with her, I wouldn't rush into any of it—not like the paid actors in the pay-per-view movie I was gonna have to explain to her in about two weeks' time when the bill came in.

Her body elongated in a curve, giving me more access. My callused hand stroked her side, her skin dimpling against my exploration. Pen turned her head, seeking my mouth in the darkness, her hands clutching my biceps, and pulled me on top of her.

She squirmed under me, her hands bracketing my jaw, her eyes studying mine. "I don't hate you, Dougie." But I hated myself. "You know that, right?"

I kissed her instead, my lips skimming over hers, tracing my tongue along the dry groove running down the middle of her bottom lip. Pen opened her mouth for me, her tongue darting out to greet mine, her legs wrapping around my waist, rolling upward in search of contact.

She mewled when she found it.

The charged connection rushing between us was all-consuming, reminiscent of an easier time in our lives. Before we'd hurt one another. Before life and expectations had gotten in the way.

Pen pulled at the waist of my sweats, and I broke away before she could get them off. "Dougie," she complained breathlessly.

"Slow." The reminder was as much for me as it was for her, because left untethered, I could devour her with the hunger of almost one full year. My mouth left hers to fasten against one of the beaded points of her supple breasts, my hand closing around the other.

Pen moaned in approval, her legs falling wider apart in offering. The moonlight strobing across her face cast soft shadows against the pretty, aristocratic arches. She was ethereal like this, something out of this world, and I'd taken her for granted.

But I wouldn't anymore.

Never again.

My cock swelled in my sweats, my stomach twisting with anticipation as I shifted to the other nipple, and then licked a trail down her stomach, right down the trimmed apex of her pussy. My knees found the floor. I hooked my arms under her lean thighs, dragging her closer to the edge, lust swirling inside of me as I prepared to worship her in the way she'd always deserved.

Her potent arousal hit my nose, the gloss of her pussy beckoning me closer. My body tingled when my mouth closed around her clit, her taste erupting on my palate, need making my head spin. She quivered before that familiar eager and musical whine of hers hit my ears and etched itself into my memory, sending more blood flooding to my already throbbing cock.

I'd forgotten what she'd tasted like—an earthy sweetness that goaded an insatiable fire inside of me. One of her hands fisted my hair, the edges of her fingernails grazing my scalp, the other snapped to one of her thighs, fingers curling. I hummed against her, the gesture causing her to twitch against my mouth before she fell back again. My taut tongue dipped lower, testing her opening, my lips tugging into a wolfish smile when she whined.

Thrusting my tongue forward, my head swam when she bore down, rocking her hips. She'd always liked this. I wasn't sure if she still would, but she'd responded eagerly, her body moving in time with each plunge of my tongue, vibrating with need.

I unhooked one of my arms from under her thighs, one of my thick fingers replacing my tongue as I penetrated her slowly. She clenched tight around my finger, my lids dropping to a close to concentrate on the sensations of her warmth flexing around my finger before I added a second. I skimmed my tongue over her clit and her hips jacked upward under the relentless pleasure when I sucked her and hooked my fingers inside of her.

My heartbeat pounded in my ears when she fastened both hands possessively in my hair, riding my face frantically. The thigh still slung over my arm tightened, her frame seizing against me as she came on my enthusiastic tongue, her head tipping back as I lapped at her release leaking out of her.

She twitched when I soothed her with one final lave of my tongue along her sensitive clit, her grasp on my hair slackening. Releasing her thigh gently, I stood up. Her hair was a golden crown spilled out behind her, highlighted by the moon, her forearm draped against her forehead as she fought to control her breathing.

Pen shifted her arm just a little to peer at me through one opened eye. "You still do that tongue and finger thingy," she commented indolently.

I smirked, playing coy. "What tongue and finger thingy?"

She dropped the shield of her arm to her side, slanting her head with a sheepish smile, sloping the corner of her mouth. "You know what tongue and finger thingy." She raised a brow.

"Ah," I conceded with a chuckle, sitting down on the edge of the bed. "I wasn't sure if you'd still like that."

Her hand wrapped around my bicep, tugging me back. Pen shifted on her side, curling against me the same way she used to. "Why wouldn't I?"

"We're not the same anymore, right?" I ran the pads of my fingers along her smooth, sweat-slicked skin. "We're different."

Different people, different tastes, different lives. Two passing ships that used to be on the same trajectory, somehow, passing by each other, despite sailing on the same choppy sea.

She was silent for a moment, digesting the observation. "We are different, but I think some part of us is still just the people in your truck." She slid a sticky, lean leg over my body. "Just trying to forge their own world where no one else existed."

I held her waist as she came to a seated position on top of me, my eyes trailing over her frame until they settled on her face. "Is that what we were doing?"

Pen nodded. "It's what I want to do now," she confessed. "It's what I always wanted to do."

She leaned forward, her hands flanking either side of my head on the mattress, her mouth grazing curiously against mine, tasting herself on my lips.

"How did we get here, Pen?"

Pen drew back, studying me carefully. "I don't know," she whispered. "I didn't want to feel responsible, but I couldn't help but wonder if I'd just told you..." her throat bobbed. "Things might have gone another way."

"I would have pushed back on the wedding." And that would have caused shit with her parents, without a doubt. "I understand why you didn't."

We were both guilty of trying to keep the peace.

She snorted a laugh I didn't think she felt. "That wedding was a joke."

It had been—a pretentious event for the plutocratic to show off their wealth while attending the event of the year. I hardly remembered it, and the parts that I could recall? They just made me sad.

"I wish I could do it over again," she said, leaning back, fitting her hand against my chest. "Our way... the way we had wanted to."

"Like Raquel and Sean?"

She rolled her lips together, nodding. "They didn't give into his mom." She lifted her eyes wearily. "I just felt bad, I'd..."

"*I'd* gotten you pregnant out of wedlock." Twice. "You felt obligated to do that because of something—"

"*We* did," she corrected. "It takes two, Dougie. I was equally irresponsible. What did we expect?" She swallowed tightly, her focus finding the window. "I didn't want to let anyone else down anymore, and I just ended up letting us down instead." She threw her hands up in the air with defeat. "None of it was worth what we lost."

I grasped her hips, a sigh leaving me. "I let you down."

"I let you down, too." Her form shrunk in my lap, her head shaking. "I read about the statistics. Twenty-two percent of couples who experienced a miscarriage ended up divorced, and I didn't want to be part of that statistic. I avoided it, and I don't know how to come back from that."

She'd been trying to protect us. In her own fucked-up way, she'd been trying to prevent her biggest fear and most utilized threat from coming to fruition.

I just didn't know what came next. Now that our cards laid spread out on the table in front of us, I didn't know whether we folded our hand or drew new cards.

"I have no idea where we go from here," I admitted. "Some part of me feels like I shouldn't be here." Her brows knitted together, worry stabbing the air. "And other parts of me can't fathom not being here."

Her nose crinkled, realization dawning on her. "Don't."

I ground my jaw, fighting the intrusive thoughts that entered my mind, demanding that I do that very thing. Because how could I be what I needed to be for her and Christopher if we were constantly in each other's faces?

"Dougie?" She scrutinized me, not trusting my silence. "Don't. We won't figure it out that way."

Was she right? If I left for a little while, could we not come back from that? Would that solidify the beginning of the end? If that were true, why wouldn't it drown out the voices in my head that told me it was the only way to get us back on track?

We needed to fold, to come down like a house of cards, to rebuild something new. I didn't want to be like my father, but I didn't want to pretend that any of this was okay, either.

How did we move on from here if I felt like I couldn't think because our hurt existed like a living, tangible thing in this house? It lived in our arguments trapped in the walls, and the pain grouted to the floors. It was the foundation of everything we'd become, and everything I didn't want us to be anymore.

Pain.

Hurt.

Shame.

Pen decided she wasn't interested in allowing me anymore opportunity to think on it. She shifted off my waist, her knees settling between my legs. Her deft fingers hooked around the waistband of my sweats, tugging. Despite my better judgment, my hips lifted with concession, my cock jutting outright when she got my pants over the curve of my ass. She stepped away from the mattress to pull them off my legs, tossing them to the floor. The bed moved with her return, her soft hands skimming up the length of my legs.

Her golden tresses fell forward when she came face-to-face with the head of my length, her tongue jutting out to lap up the precum at the tip. The chafing from earlier was a distant memory as the unsuppressed groan ripped from me. Her fingers dug into my thighs as her mouth opened to envelop the tip.

My body tingled, the familiar-yet-foreign sensation of her hot, deft mouth working over me, flooding me with both pleasure and guilt that I wasn't deserving of this gorgeous creature licking the length of my cock.

Pen's body leaned forward, accepting more of me and in a rapturous daze, I thrust forward. Her throat twitched against me, and I retracted my hips. "Shit, I'm sorry."

I was still just a prick.

She held up a hand, then reached for my hand and fitted it against the top of her head, commanding me in silence. Pen leaned forward again, accepting more of me down her throat, going as far as biology would allow her to. Her expert tongue stroked me, her heady mouth sucking as she bobbed. My head spun as pleasure took over my senses, ripping every cognizant thought clean from my mind.

Withdrawing, the absence of her warm mouth swathed my cock in a chilled blanket, but the cold didn't last long. Pen slung her legs over my waist, her knees nestling on either side of me. Her hand closed around my swollen length, stroking tentatively to gather her arousal until she guided the tip to her entrance, her molten eyes finding mine in the darkness.

"Pen." The tightness of her body accepting me as she sank her weight down snatched the words away, her hands slamming against my chest as I slid into her.

God, she felt good clenching around me, my senses coming back online after being dormant for so long in a ceaseless winter that wouldn't end. The whole thing made me kind of fucking emotional.

I wasn't gonna cry, but I was gonna watch her and cherish this moment like it might be my last.

She rolled her hips, lifting herself to acclimate and then slammed back down, the ecstasy bubbling in my gut as I watched her move atop of me, her chest rising and falling as she took what she wanted from me.

Gripping her sides, I helped her ride me, my hips flexing to meet her every time she descended, burying myself to the hilt, her core muscles tight. I couldn't think straight, my only focus on her, and how good she felt after all this time. I wanted her closer, so much closer than she could ever physically be.

After my failed attempt at getting myself off earlier, I wouldn't last much longer. My fingers dug into her thighs, keeping her pinned against me as she drove herself against my pelvis, capitalizing on the friction. Her mouth fell open as she chased after her second orgasm. Her skin hardened against my hands as the pleasure snatched her, the sweet, controlled sound of her release hitting my ears as she shook atop of me.

Holding on to her, I pulled out of her to roll her under me. Draping her legs over my shoulders, I tugged her down, my hips angling forward as her pussy accepted my punitive cock once more. Pen shivered, a small gasp escaping her when I thrust deep inside of her. I kissed the inside of her soft calve, her lidded eyes twitching, body shifting up the mattress as I pumped.

She held out her hand, her fingers flittering like they used to in the grocery store, until I accepted it. Giving my hand a squeeze, her eyes opened a little, a single, glittering tear escaping. "I love you," she murmured.

I grounded my teeth, blinking fast. Sliding her legs from my shoulders, I butterflied her thighs, folding my body atop of hers. My mouth fitted against hers, my heavy balls jerking in warning. "I love you, too."

My hips pistoned quickly and just as my skin tensed and pleasure came to claim me, I pulled out, painting the taut stretch of skin on her stomach with thick spurts of warmth that left me in delirium.

Pinpricks of light blurred my vision as I came down from my high. My slick forehead found her shoulder, my frantic breathing fanning over her skin. She smelled good, like me, like her, and I wanted to do it again after I caught my breath. Kissing her cheek, I collapsed to her side, trying to even out my harsh intakes as exhaustion claimed what was left of my energy.

"You pulled out."

My chest heaved, her question percolating in the room. "Of course I did."

"Why?" There was a weight to her question that robbed me of my next thought.

She couldn't possibly be thinking about... we were so far from being ready for that. What the hell?

I sat up, glancing at her over my shoulder. "*That* isn't what we need right now, Penny."

She turned her head, giving me her profile as she stared ceiling-ward, but I caught the flexing of her jaw, sobering the mood.

How could she possibly think otherwise? I shook my head, sliding off the edge of the mattress. Padding to the bathroom, I opened a drawer and pulled out a hand towel. Running it under hot water, I wrung it free, then walked back into the room.

I knew this was a bad idea. Too fast.

Again.

She flinched when I wiped her stomach off. "We're not ready, okay?" I said gently, wanting to soften the tension brewing between us once more. We were a long way from that.

"But we were ready enough to fuck, right?" she bit back.

The muscle in my jaw jumped, my eyebrows finding each other as I stared down at the soiled, damp washcloth clenched in my fist. "I didn't fuck you. I made love to you."

"Give me a break," she muttered, sitting upright. She threw the decorative shams on our bed to the floor, frustration tightening the muscles in her pretty shoulders as she moved. Tugging the sheets back on her side, she slid in, her back turned to me.

"You think we're ready for another baby?" How could she not see how mad she still was with me after everything?

She didn't look at me as she replied, "I'm ready to move on with our lives."

Move on? When this had been the crux of her secret?

How was I supposed to move on when I had just learned that she'd had a secret, too? "And I just found out that there was a part of our lives I wasn't even a part of," I seethed.

"If I can forgive you for having an affair, you can forgive me for—"

Any headway we'd made in the powder room, on this bed, vanished, glaring a spotlight on the chasm between us. The riven was too deep, and I knew then...

We might not recover from this.

"I *didn't* fuck Maria." And I wasn't blaming Penelope for what happened with the pregnancy, either.

Pen shot up in bed. "And thinking about it," she hissed, stabbing the air, "is still just as bad, so don't martyr yourself for me." Her face fell as I paled, my chest aching.

This was a mistake.

Rushing into bed with her again was a mistake.

But as per usual, just like everything else in our story, we were always rushing to the next thing. Someone needed to fucking be the one to hit the brakes, and I knew in that moment, it had to be me or we were going to destroy what was left of the other until nothing remained.

"Dougie." The fight was absent in her voice this time.

I shook my head, clearing my throat. Gathering my sweats from the floor, I hastened for *her* bedroom door, ignoring her when she called my name again. Closing the door behind me, I kept my footsteps light against the hallway floor as I inched toward the guest room.

Throwing my pants to the floor when I got in there, I shut the door behind me and then collapsed face-first into bed, exhaustion making every muscle in my body ache. I pulled the pillow under me, laying my cheek against it as I stared at the full moon from the window, high in the inky sky.

The satiation from the physical reconnection was long gone, the hollowed emptiness returning with a brute force. We shouldn't have done that, but I never learned. I allowed myself to become re-consumed with Penelope because she was fucking intoxicating to me, a drug I could never ween myself from.

Pulling the duvet out from under me without getting up, I slid into the sheets, then punched the overstuffed pillow and dropped my head in a defeated huff.

I should have trusted my instincts and not let things get that far, but I'd gotten swept up in the moment with her—*again*. Dropping my eyelids, I focused on the expansion and deflation of my lungs, drawing air through my nose and expelling it through my mouth.

But then I heard it.

My ears craned at the sound of bare feet padding against the hardwood. I sensed her on the other side of the door, but she didn't rush to open it, as though she were contemplating her next move. Finally, the knob of the guest room door turned slowly, opening only wide enough for her to slip in.

Pen's ginger, peaches, and vanilla shampoo hit my nose first, my chest constricting with frustration and adoration. I didn't turn to look at her, and she didn't dare utter a word to me, either. The sheets shifted as she slid in, her forehead finding my back, her arms sliding around my waist, her naked body pressed against me.

Her heartbeat hammered against my back, trying to draw the melancholy from my body and absorb the pain into her own. "I'm sorry." She massaged her lips against my shoulder blade, then dragged her nose along the disks in my neck.

Pulling away from her, I rolled over. Her eyes were wet with a fresh batch of tears. My throat worked over a lump. "I'm not trying to hurt you, Penelope. I'm trying to give us a fighting chance."

She squeezed her eyes shut for a moment, the tears falling when she opened them. "I know."

"We're not ready."

"I'm—"

"*I'm* not ready," I corrected. She looked downward, her head weaving with a quick bob. "I'm still trying to process." It was a big thing she'd kept from me, and I couldn't help but consider how things would have changed had she just been up front with me from the beginning.

I never would have... if I'd just known...

I wouldn't have stopped fighting for us.

"I understand." Her eyes lidded, more tears spilling over, but she would never open them again for the rest of the night. Kissing her forehead, I ignored the agony in my chest as I silently implored her to forgive me someday for everything.

A few minutes later, Pen's breathing evened out as sleep came to claim her. But for me?

It was the beginning of another sleepless night.

Chapter Twenty-One

Dougie

Three years ago…

THE FIRST THING THAT HAD OCCURRED TO ME WHEN I WOKE UP WAS THAT my back felt like shit.

The second thing was that these sheets were really itchy, like someone had starched them to holy hell.

The third thing was that we were fucking screwed.

Lurching to attention, I blinked the sleep back, a ray of early morning sunlight pelting me in the eyes when I lifted my head.

We were at Pen's parents, and this mattress was as hard as a slab of concrete. The stirring to my right cleared my sleep-addled brain.

This was the guest room.

And the warm, naked body pressed against me was not supposed to be in it. To my right, she whined, burying her face into my side to block the sunlight.

"Penny," I said, shaking her gently. She clearly didn't realize we weren't in her apartment. "Wake up. You're in the wrong bed."

Penelope stirred, her brows meeting each other in the middle while her eyes squeezed tighter together to remain in dreamland. "What are you talking about?" she groaned, rolling onto her back. "Close the curtains." She licked her parched lips, swallowed, and then opened one eye halfway.

"We fell asleep," I murmured, my ears craning to the hallway. "And I'm almost ninety percent certain your parents know you're in here."

That did the trick.

Bewilderment snatched whatever lingering sleep had remained in her body. She shot upright, her golden hair a mess. "Oh, fuck."

She turned her head to the door, urgent footsteps charging down the hallway to our door, and then pivoting back the other way.

Mr. Cullimore's voice filtered through, attempting to mollify the storm brewing. "Evelyn."

"How dare they!" her mother trilled. "They're not married!"

I winced, massaging my temples. God, this weekend needed to end.

Pen's head fell forward, the stiff sheets shifting with her as she pressed her forehead to the valleys of her knees when she brought her legs to her chest. She wrapped her arms around her shins and smirked at me over her shoulder.

She'd already accepted we were up shit's creek without a paddle.

"Wanna get married today?" she asked, batting her lashes. We'd discussed it last night—not getting married today, per se—but at least she knew my intention was to marry her.

She just didn't know that I intended to get a ring on her finger before the weekend was up.

My eyes bounced from my duffle bag back to her. I knew she was kidding, but my heart couldn't distinguish the difference and was on the verge of punching its way out of my chest to grab the ring for her right now.

Her mother's charged, plummy voice came through from the other side of the door. "I'm going in there."

"Evelyn, you are *not* going in there."

"What if the Huntingtons find out?"

"That our twenty-eight-year-old daughter shared a bed with her boyfriend while they had to ship their thirty-year-old son to a rehab facility in Maine for a pornography addiction because his fiancée can't handle it anymore?"

"Walter," Evelyn whispered. "It's a *wellness* facility."

Pen snorted at the rumor, shaking her head.

At my extended silence, she fell back on the mattress, the springs not even bouncing. This bed was worse than my own—too firm, with sheets that were intended to feel luxurious but were uncomfortable, and a bed skirt with ruffles in it.

Rolling to her side, Pen's fingers traced over my exposed pec. She definitely felt how frantic my heart was pumping. "I was kidding about getting married today, y'know." She lifted her eyes, the blue, green, and yellow sparkling in the early morning sunshine as the corners of her mouth twitched in an almost-there smile. "Don't panic."

"Who said anything about panicking?" My mind was swinging between thinking about the ring box tucked at the bottom of my duffle bag, shoved into a roll of socks, and whether her father would give me their blessing.

She lifted the shoulder she wasn't lying on in a shrug. "The color drained from your face."

"Sorry," I replied, planting a kiss on her forehead. "Probably nervous about today."

Pen nodded, expelling a breath. "I know they've had the tendency to infantilize us since we got here, and I haven't helped things, but," she slid her head upward, cupping my scruffy cheek, "I just want you to know, however they react today, I don't care."

I was less concerned about their reaction to her pregnancy than I was proposing to her. Not that I thought there was a chance that she'd say no, but it felt like there was a lot happening at once, too.

Part of me worried it was too much, too fast.

We were getting the keys from Sean next week for the house. Pen had already started building a mood board for a nursery, and the conventional guy in me wanted to marry her. Not just because she was pregnant, but because, well, it was all I'd thought about since she strutted into the yard this summer.

The timeline just hadn't been what I thought it would be.

Pushing the worry away, I got my head back into the game. There was no time for what-if's now. "You remember the plan?" I asked. We'd gone over it right before we'd passed out.

"Yep." She popped her lips on the 'P', grinning at me. "Not a word until after dinner." She brought a single finger up to her lips as if to say, *secret's safe with me.*

But I didn't trust her temper. Penelope was levelheaded on a good day, but something about her mother brought out the worst in her.

All it would take was one snide, backhanded remark from Evelyn, and the entire plan would go to shit. I'd need to keep her calm today until it was time.

"Let's try to make today a good one," I suggested, recalling a joke Sean had made a few weeks ago about telling Pen's parents about the pregnancy. "And maybe they won't try to stick my taxidermic head above their mantel."

"Oh." Pen brightened. "It would look so good next to Mother's riding ribbons."

I snorted, dragging her against me. "You're a brat."

"Only on Thursdays in Connecticut."

"What was your excuse for yesterday?" I quipped.

She examined her nails, then gave me a shit-eating grin. "Full moon, and Mercury was in retrograde."

Rolling my eyes, my hands twitched with the urge to tickle her sides, but the mood sobered as the door rattled with a strident knock, followed by her father's clipped voice. "Penelope."

"*Penelope ist nicht da,*" she called out to her father, then threw a hand over her mouth to suppress the laugh shaking through her.

"You speak German now, too?" Any other secret talents I needed to know about the woman I wanted to marry.

Mischief twinkled in her eyes. "Nope. Just picked up a phrase or two from Frieda." She rocked her mouth from side to side. "I think that means I'm not here… maybe."

"Just open the door, Walter."

"Do not just open the door!" Pen hollered, lifting the sheets to look herself over. "Trust me, you do *not* want to do that."

"Penelope Louise!"

Pen dropped her voice to a whisper, pride settling in the corners of her mouth. "My mother's on the verge of a nervous breakdown." She sat up, scraping her fingers through her hair. Her body shook with a laugh. "We're *so* dead."

"No, no," I corrected, faking complete and utter innocence in all of this. "You're dead. I'm where I'm supposed to be."

She popped her mouth open, holding a hand to her chest. "Are you suggesting I took advantage of you?"

"I mean," I rose my brows, "my lower back feels like shit."

"Aw," she said, her lip dropping with a pout as she extended a hand to my cock. Out of reflex, my hips rocked into her hand, a salacious growl bubbling in my chest that earned me her sultry smile. "Did I ride you too hard?"

She had zero scruples. Literally didn't have a fuck to spare for her parents standing on the other side of the bedroom door. When Pen got horny, she got tunnel vision.

And this pregnancy so far seemed to leave her in a permanent state of turned on. No complaints here.

"You're asking for it—" The door flung open, rattling against the stopper, cutting me off and causing Pen's hand to snap back.

Evelyn brought in a blast of cold air with her, akin to a gale of wind billowing through the arctic tundra, her arms crossed over her chest. She was already ready for the day. Her navy-blue dress hit her at the knees, her creamy blond hair back in its signature chignon, tiny heels on her feet and an unimpressed look carved into her expression. I was getting the impression that she wasn't capable of smiling—ever.

"You have zero respect, young lady." She tried to frown, but her face wouldn't let her. Which was fine. Her eyes could penetrate you just by remaining in her line of vision, though it didn't escape my notice she was avoiding looking at me.

"Morning, Mother." Pen sat up, stretching her arms. She yawned dramatically as though nothing was amiss, patting her open mouth. "What's for breakfast?"

"Mr. Cullimore?"

Walter kept his back turned to me, his hands conjoined at the base of his spine, attention directed out the oversized bay window. "Hm?"

He donned a three-piece suit, hair perfectly combed back, but his expression was somber.

I inched into the drawing room, scratching the back of my neck. "I just wanted to apologize about this morning."

He offered me a sober, tight smile without looking my way. "It's fine."

"Nah," I began. "It was disrespectful."

He huffed out a laugh that lacked any warmth. "Douglas." He turned and faced me. "May I inquire the source of your guilt?"

"The source of my guilt?" I echoed. Ma had raised me better, that's what it was. I wouldn't have pulled this stunt in her house, and I owed him an apology.

He gave me a casual once-over, his head weaving in a nod. "Yes, for some, it's because they've been caught. For others, they recognize they possess a proclivity to do things they know they shouldn't."

I wanted to stagger back, but I remained rooted in place, processing what he'd said. I was getting the impression that even though he'd indulged me yesterday, what happened this morning ensured he was done pretending. There had been a double meaning in his statement that wasn't escaping me. A proclivity to do things they know they shouldn't...

Like being here?

Dating his daughter?

"Are you of the latter or the prior?" Walter asked, pressing the tips of his fingers together, steepling his hands in front of him.

"It wasn't his fault, Daddy. It was mine," Pen said, padding into the room barefoot with a steaming, hot mug in her hands. Her hair was still damp from her shower, the roots drying naturally in a soft wave. Her dark jeans were cuffed at the ankles, a loose oversized plaid shirt buttoned up over her upper body.

She pressed a kiss to her father's cheek. "He didn't even know I was coming."

I mean, if she skulked into my room like that, she was definitely coming. Clearing my throat, I ignored the inward joke. I didn't think that would go over well.

"Your mother doesn't like it, Pearl," he said, rankled and sounding toneless. "And frankly, neither do I."

She drew her brows together, rounding her eyes, appearing innocent though she was the furthest thing from it. "I understand."

"I suggest you both exhibit self-control for the duration of your time here."

"Of course." I'd barricade the door if I had to. Evelyn had stood in our room until we'd both gotten out of bed with our arms and hands situated on our respective bodies to maintain some level of...

I think the word she'd used was "decency." She'd thrown a housecoat at Penelope, then jutted a finger that could double as a weapon out into the hall, slamming the door dramatically behind her.

I showered quickly and sought Pen's dad. This day was already not going down the way I wanted, but I wasn't hopeless that we couldn't try to get the day back on track.

Assuming Pen stuck to the plan.

A bell chimed in the distance, my ears tracking the sound. "Breakfast," Walter announced, striding by us until it was just Pen and me. I wasn't sure if he was just starving or if he was just as over this Thanksgiving weekend already as we were.

"What's in the mug?" I asked.

She glanced down at the mug. "Tea." She propped the instep of her foot against her ankle, chewing on the corner of her mouth. "I'm sorry."

"You should be," I replied, screwing up my face. "I think my sciatic nerve is fucked."

"Not for that." Pen snorted. She sighed, glancing at the piano in the corner with what I thought might be want. "I know I'm making things harder than they need to be."

"Self-reflection before food?" I gasped. "Who are you and what have you done with my girlfriend?"

She rolled her eyes, her cheeks flushing. "My mother brings out the worst in me. Every time I'm here, I feel like I'm fifteen again and need to assert myself or she'll steamroll right over me." She folded her lips together, eyes flashing with pain. "I used to love playing that piano but as soon as I realized me playing was more for her, to give her some-thing to brag about to her friends, I never wanted to play anymore." Her eyebrows muddied in the middle.

Feathering my lips against her forehead, I sighed. "We won't do that to our kids." This house, the people in it, tried to force her to conform. She just wasn't that type of person. She was creative, sponta-neous, and curious—traits that were all frowned upon here. While I was sure her parents didn't realize they were doing it, or hell, maybe they were, they had tried to make her someone she wasn't.

I never wanted us to be like that.

"Definitely not."

The plummy voice I'd hear in my nightmares filtered through the house. "Penelope."

Pen's hackles rose at the sound of her mother's voice, her eyes rolling.

"Be nice, Penny."

She gave me an unconvincing smile, despite how melancholic her energy still felt. God, I just wanted to wrap my arms around her and take her home. She was unhappy around them, and I hated it. Still, I followed her out of the drawing room and into the dining room. We settled into high-back button-tufted dining chairs that were about as uncomfortable as the mattress. There was a massive centerpiece on the table, a cornucopia made of horn-shaped wicker with a neat burlap ribbon wrapped around the base. An assortment of varying gourds, multicolored corn husks, moss, leaves, and flowers delicately assem-bled inside and outside of it. Fixed breakfast plates were already on the table, some kind of wet egg concoction and a sad piece of toast.

"Eggs Benedict," Pen whispered.

Guess there were no sugary cereals for me over the next few days. Evelyn stormed into the room, sullen as ever, with Walter trailing behind her. He untucked her chair for her, guiding it back into place when she settled in.

"So, Douglas," Walter began as he sat down, his forehead pinched with concentration as he cut into his eggs. "Explain your line of work to me."

Jesus, straight to business before I was even caffeinated.

I swallowed the mouthful I was chewing. Whatever was on those eggs was a little too rich for my tastebuds, but I'd eat it. "It's primarily century home restorations."

"Fascinating," he said. "And do you..." he searched for a word, "perform the restorations yourself?"

Penelope sniggered to my left.

I nudged her lightly under the table. He was just curious. I could respect that, under-caffeinated or not. "I'm a foreman."

"What's that?" Evelyn asked, bringing the teacup to her lips while her eyes narrowed.

I frowned. Was she even drinking it?

Clearing my throat, I answered the question. "I mean, I get my hands dirty." Pen's ma tensed in her seat. "But I also do up the schedules for the crew, manage task lists for the day, quality control and work with my best friend on keeping track of the budget." Which was a bit ironic.

"Your best friend?"

"Sean," Penelope added, picking up her tea mug. "I told you about him."

"But Sean is your boss," Walter said, quirking a quizzical brow.

She set her mug back down, picking up her fork. "Sean is my client," she corrected, pushing her eggs around as she sat up straight in her seat. For someone who had been so hungry a half an hour ago, she wasn't eating.

"Penelope doesn't have to work, you know," Evelyn pointed out, staring dead at me. I was pretty sure if she was physically capable of snarling, she would. "We've been trying to coax her to come back home."

Pen set her cutlery down with a clatter, her mouth pinching. "Penelope doesn't want to come home because this *isn't* her home. Penelope enjoys her work and the business she's established on her *own*."

Evelyn rolled her eyes, appearing a lot like Pen had in the drawing room. "And I suppose," she waved a hand out in front of her dramatically, sounding as snide as ever, "*Boston* is your home now?"

Oh, fuck. I felt the bluster of Pen's temper rising, the hand on the table curling into a tight fist. "Boston's busy," I intercepted. If I could align with Evelyn for a minute, maybe I could get us back on track. "It smells sometimes, too."

"It does not," Pen argued, her jaw setting. "It smells like a city."

"Like exhaust fumes, a bad night out and the Red Line."

She paused, mulling it over, jutting a resigned finger out at me. "Okay, I'll give you the Red Line."

"What are you doing riding the Red Line?" I questioned. Seriously, out of all the lines in the city, that was the sketchiest one next to the Orange Line.

She shrugged, cutting into her eggs with the side of her fork. "I take it home from—" she caught herself from saying 'bar'. "From client meetings."

"What's the 'Red Line?'" Walter asked.

"A subway line."

"You ride a subway?" Evelyn gasped. "But the Rover!" Yeah, I was with Evelyn on this one.

"Do you know how hard parking is to find in the city sometimes?" She had a point, but I'd still prefer to just drive her and pick her up if that was the issue. "Anyway," Pen continued, "I like the city, but I won't be living in it for much longer."

Evelyn brightened, sitting upright. She glanced hopefully at Walter. "You're coming home?"

Had this woman experienced a case of amnesia?

Pen scoffed with disgust. "No." She straightened in her seat, her posture mirroring that of her mother's. "Dougie and I—"

Nope. The plan, Penelope. Stick to the fucking plan. "These eggs are wicked good," I interjected.

Pen kicked me under the table—hard, scowling. I lost control of my facial muscles, the cramp in my leg throbbing.

Deciding she'd had enough of everyone, she said what she needed to say, and I didn't fight her on it because fuck it, you couldn't stop a Nor'Easter. You just took cover and hoped it blew over... *eventually.* "Dougie and I bought a house."

You coulda heard a pin drop from a house four doors down that was twice the size of the Cullimores.

"Why on earth would you do that?" Evelyn demanded, losing control of her slackened jaw.

"Pearl," Walter began, picking up his napkin and pressing it against either corner of his mouth. He draped the napkin back on his lap, inclining his head and trying for stern. "We asked that you discuss any major purchases with us first."

She folded her hands together, sitting up straight, meeting her father's eyes. "I'm not a child, Dad."

Walter paled. Dad. Not Daddy. "I'm old enough to make my own decisions and my own choices, and if your intention of issuing my trust fund was to keep me under your thumb, then I'd prefer to give you your money back."

"Penelope," they said in unison.

But she didn't care. "Dougie and I bought a house in Eaton because we're expecting a baby."

Oh, double fucking fuck. She'd gone rogue.

My balls were on the floor, and my stomach was in absolute knots, the urge to keel over, battering through me.

No one uttered a word.

"Did you hear me?" Penelope asked, her eyes bouncing between her parents. Evelyn released her grasp on her cutlery, the sharp clanging resounding throughout the dining room as stainless steel kissed good china.

She was transfixed in horror, her jaw falling open.

This was not how we discussed telling them.

I fought the urge to shake my head, instead fixing Pen's profile with a hardened stare. All she'd had to do was get through Thanksgiving dinner at a minimum, wait until the tryptophan from the turkey settled in and her parents were as close to sedated as serotonin could make you be—then drop the bomb.

Not tell them at eight a.m. over... what was this again? *Eggs Benedict.*

Why had she steered away from the plan?

"I'm pregnant," Penelope repeated. "I'm due in July, next year."

Yeah, I was sure they'd heard her the first time.

The burden of her dad's wrath could have strangulated me from his place at the head of the table. He looked as though he were on the verge of tossing his customs and respect out the goddamn window and launching himself over the dining table and squeezing my thick neck with all his might.

Evelyn's eyes rounded to the size of the breakfast plate she'd be eating from. "What?"

Penelope sighed. "We were going to tell you later, but my stomach is off, and rather than risk having you insult me for chasing my food around my plate, I thought I'd be forthcoming." She glanced at me, remorse entering her voice. "I'm sorry. I know we discussed doing this in another way."

Fuck. The nerves had me wanting to shovel more of my breakfast in my mouth just to give me something to do, but the man in me... it demanded I meet her father's eyes dead-on.

His hand tightened around his fork, the cords in his scrawny neck compressing. Walter broke eye contact first, but not before I witnessed the disappointment flash in his gray eyes.

Setting his fork down gently on the plate, he grabbed the napkin from his lap, pressing it against his mouth once again. Clearing his throat, he untucked his chair from the table and rose to his height. "A word in my study, Penelope." He looked at his shell-shocked wife, her breaths wheezing out of her as she clenched the pearls at her neck. "You, too, Evelyn."

Evelyn nodded absently, her body swaying as she rose to her feet. "This is a-a-a d-d-disaster," she stammered, throwing a trembling hand to her mouth, her breaths coming out in short huffs.

Disaster was a stretch. Not as any of us had planned? Definitely. A disaster? No.

Christ, Pen was pregnant. I hadn't given her a fucking incurable venereal disease. But I was the disease to them, wasn't I? I'd always be the disease in their eyes. The man who came in and tainted their little girl and dashed all their hopes and dreams with my presence and my seed.

There would be no changing their minds.

I didn't move, although every part of me wanted to chase after them. Whatever they were going to say to her, I deserved to be a part of, too. How could I protect Pen otherwise? This was my fault.

Sure, this hadn't been what I'd envisioned for us, either—at least not this quickly—but shit happened, and I was going to make it right. The ring in my back pocket was practically burning a hole through the denim. I'd been planning this for weeks, and when she'd described the apple orchard abutting her parents' estate, I knew it would be the perfect setting to propose.

But I'd had a plan—*we'd* had a plan.

Pregnancy announcement first, then after the shock wore off, I was going to find an opportunity to ask her dad for permission to marry her, just like I was sure custom demanded.

Then we'd tell them about the house.

But Pen had completely thrown our entire fucking plan in a lurch. She hadn't even mentioned she was feeling off this morning. She tossed me an apologetic glance over her shoulder just before she cleared the dining room threshold.

The study door slammed shut, the pictures in the hallway shaking.

Frieda popped her head into the dining room, a small sigh leaving her. "*Die katze ist aus dem sack.*"

I blinked at her, wondering if I was officially losing my mind.

"The cat is out of the bag," she translated. She folded her arms over her black capped-sleeve uniform, her mouth pulling to the right. "How far along is she?"

My molars connected, my brows softening. "Couple of weeks. Did she tell you?"

"*Nein,*" she said with a soft laugh. "She usually sucks back her whiskey when she's here."

Laughing through my nose, I nodded. "Yeah."

Frieda was quiet for a moment more. "May I ask you a question, Mr. Pat..." she trailed off. "Dougie?"

I shrugged. "Go for it." Might as well practice, since I was sure I was destined for the third-degree questioning whenever they got out of that study.

"Do you love my Penelope?" she asked, her tone gentle and warm in a way that was practically maternal. She was warmer than Evelyn was, that was for sure. Then again, a meat freezer was the tropics compared to her.

"Yeah," I said softly. "I do." With everything in me.

"*Gut.*" She straightened, holding a finger out in warning. "Make an honest woman out of her, *ja?*" I patted my pocket, earning her head nod of approval. She beckoned me forward with her hand, jutting toward the kitchen. "Come with me."

The kitchen was predictably massive and buzzing with people—none of which looked my way. Someone was at the stove, whisking at a pot frantically, another, at the dishwasher, loading the cooking ware from breakfast. The tiles in here were a surprising Mediterranean influence—the only pop of the color in this entire mansion, laid in a patchwork style in a bright cobalt blue and white that brought out the deep cherry mahogany of the kitchen cabinets. The appliances were massive and stainless steel, with the infamous Wolf logo and red knobs on the stove. There was a huge, uncooked turkey on the counter, another staff member elbow deep with the stuffing.

Frieda brought me into a pantry flanked by floor-to-ceiling shelving filled to the brim with canned goods and baking ingredients. She hit the light switch and shut the door behind us.

"What are we doing in here?" I looked at all the neatly arranged canisters, jars, and canned goods. I wasn't trying to go all seven minutes in heaven with the woman who raised Penelope.

She pointed to a single opening at the wall. "Listen."

"Listen?"

She nodded. "The other side is the study."

Wait a minute. "You want me to eavesdrop?"

"Best you know what they think of you, so you know what you're working with." She'd done this a few times.

My tongue thickened in my mouth. "That feels sneaky."

She sighed with pity. "If you want to win, play their way."

"I'm not trying to win anything." Outside of Penelope's heart. I couldn't contain my bewilderment. What was so wrong with what we were doing?

Frieda placed a hand on my shoulder, giving me a gentle squeeze, but her eyes said it before her mouth did. "You're not in your world anymore. You're in theirs."

Penelope

"I knew you were a tart, but this is simply unacceptable!" Mother shouted at me.

God, she was on the verge of popping a blood vessel.

"Evelyn."

My smile flickered as I wrung my hands out in front of me. "I believe the word you're looking for is 'whore', but I'm not one."

"Penelope."

"How can you say such despicable things about yourself?" Mother questioned.

I flung my hands up in the air. "You just called me a 'tart!'"

Daddy's fist pounded on his desk like a gavel, making the contents jump. "Both of you be quiet!"

Mother visibly startled, but I just stared at him, daring him to push me. I was looking for any excuse to get out of this shithole, and this might be it.

"I've had enough of this ongoing feud between the two of you." He shoved his chair back, breaking out into a crazed pace across his study, playing with his bow tie as he flexed his jaw.

Daddy never paced, but he also rarely lost his temper, either.

Something told me I needed to gird myself for whatever was coming next.

"This is your fault," Mother said, her voice quivering as she stared at him. "You spoiled her and look what's happened." Her chest hitched, a handkerchief she'd gotten hold of from Daddy's pocket pressed to her thin lips. "She should have gone to Yale."

"Fuck. Yale."

He whipped around; his upper lip curled back. "I've had just about enough of you."

"Then I'll leave." I stood up, but he charged at me, his pointer finger stabbed in my direction.

"You will sit down, and you will listen to every goddamn word I have to say. Am I making myself very clear to you?" Spittle freed itself from his mouth, his eyes rife with rage as sweat broke out against his hairline.

"I am *not* a child," I spat back. "Look at you both, freaking out over something so natural—"

"This is not natural. This is a deviation from the plan!" Mother erupted, malice polluting her eyes. "He is an inferior, unsatisfactory choice."

"Fuck you!" I screamed back at her. "You're the inferior one, you pretentious bit—"

"Penelope, she is your mother!" Daddy's voice reverberated throughout the house.

I didn't care that she was my mother any more than he was my father.

"That doesn't give either of you some kind of God-given right to talk about Dougie however you feel like. He is the father of your grandchild."

They both stiffened.

My chest rose heavily as I tried to regulate my temper, but I couldn't. They were disrespectful, cruel and entitled. Dougie was better than any of us combined.

"And what plan?" I demanded. "Huh? What plan? Puppeteer Penelope's life? Give her a little rope to explore what life is like away from you both and hope she eventually trots back home like a well-behaved lapdog?"

I wasn't a fucking bichon frise, for fuck's sake. And if I was going to be compared to a lapdog, I was closer to a miniature dachshund—stubborn as fuck.

"What kind of life do you think he's going to provide for you?" Daddy asked, dropping his voice as defeat touched his weary features. He looked like he'd aged ten years in a thirty-minute window. "Have you considered that?" The question seemed to suck all the life out of the room for a moment. "What does life look like for you and *our* grandchild?"

I drew my eyes from his, taking in the opulence of his study before I dead bolted my glare on his again. My chest expanded with the first full breath I'd taken since we'd arrived here. "Hopefully nothing like this."

Our house would be warm.

We'd respect our children and their choices.

And love them harder when they skinned their knees on those choices, too.

It wasn't about the money, because I'd sooner live on pasta for the rest of my goddamn life if it meant we were happy.

"Nothing like this?" Daddy uttered, pulling me from my thoughts. His throat thickened, his lips pursing. He turned away from me, striding back to his desk and settled in his chair once more. Slanting his head, he held me in his sharp gaze. "What do you see, Penelope?"

"A lie." A cold one at that. I didn't need to think about it. It was what I'd always known to be true. There was no warmth in my parents' marriage. It was closer to a business transaction than it was a blissful martial union. Two people who'd agreed to marry themselves to the same code of values, who believed combining their fortunes made them a well-suited match. They valued money, society and whatever gave them their next reliable hit of dopamine.

They tolerated each other just enough to perform their roles. They had no shared interests beyond me and their assets. Daddy was in

Manhattan most of the time, and Mother was riding or at brunch. He only came home when it mattered, when people would see.

But there wasn't love there. I could remember singlehandedly the number of times I'd seen my parents exchange any kind of affection amongst each other.

It was an arrangement that suited both of their life goals.

It wasn't what I wanted.

In a marriage, I wanted someone to dance with me in the kitchen after a bad day to late nineties Brian McKnight. Someone who didn't squawk when I played something unconventional on the piano, who didn't care that I was a terrible cook, or that I ate peanut butter directly out of the jar while sitting on the counter in my underwear and a crop top. I wanted laughter, and private jokes, and memories that would stay with me until my very last breath.

That was what I wanted our children to see—love—and to know what to do when they found it, too.

I didn't care if I had to give up everything I'd ever known just to have it, because that kind of relationship, that kind of love? Was worth its weight in gold. I'd marry myself to that in this life and in the next.

Daddy drummed his fingers against the desktop. "Your mother and I are a partnership."

"Exactly," Mother agreed. "And we've given you an impeccable life." They still weren't getting it.

How fucking sad and clinical. "It sounds like a business deal." I looked between them. "Did it ever occur to you that maybe the money you spent on trying to give me that impeccable life wasn't what I wanted from either of you?"

"That's what marriage is, Penelope." She ignored the latter half of my statement. Figures.

I shook my head. "No." My limbs tingled with fatigue, processing my parents' clinical viewpoint. "It's really not."

Mother scoffed. "You're so incredibly ignorant."

"I'm the ignorant one?" I challenged. "You two look artificial to everyone. Do you realize that?"

"*Artificial?*" Mother questioned. "To whom?"

My laugh came out high-pitched and curt, as I held up an apologetic hand. "Sorry, you're right. You don't look artificial to your equally fake friends, perpetuating the same lie."

"You have a lot of opinions, Penelope," Daddy said, clearing his throat.

"The luxury of the bird escaping her cage," I muttered.

Daddy leaned back in his chair. "What are you going to do when he can't pay the bills at your new house?"

"I'm not concerned about the money," I replied.

"You naïve, little girl," Mother said, her profile closing up on her as she shook her head. "You've ruined your life. Do you understand that?"

I smiled at them, climbing to my feet. "My life's only just begun."

Moving for the door, they didn't argue with me this time. With my hand wrapped around the brass knob of the door, I paused, regarding them over my shoulder. "I hope you two experience this feeling someday, too." I swallowed. "Either with each other, or someone else."

Daddy's eyes flared.

"He's going to marry you," Mother called at my back. "I won't hear anything otherwise."

I rolled my eyes, my shoulder blades meeting in my back, pain smarting. "I don't need you to perpetuate some illusion of maintaining my womanly virtue."

"It's not up for discussion, Penelope," Daddy replied just as I closed the door behind me. "Our grandchild will not be born out of wedlock."

Dougie

I was back in the dining room when Pen came charging in. I folded my hands in front of me on the table, my head heavy. "Hey."

She just stared at me, and all I could wonder was if she was seeing me the way they saw me.

"Where are your parents?" I asked.

Inferior. Were they right?

I rolled my lips, trying to suffocate the pain away.

She shrugged, snapping out of her trance. "I don't care." She shoved her hands in her hair, pacing. "Do you want to leave?"

Yeah, I wanted to get the hell out of this place, but that was what they'd expect. I shook my head. "We should try to ride this out." I still had an apple orchard on the brain. The weather was nice.

What if she said no? What if they'd gotten into her head and she was realizing the gravity of our situation, that maybe I wouldn't be able to provide her with the life she was accustomed to and deserved?

We could sell the house, and... fuck, I didn't want to lose her.

"I don't want to ride this out," she said, her voice full of moxie, her posture stiffening. "I want to leave."

The study door opened down the hall, Walter and Evelyn's footsteps falling in perfect harmonization with each other. Pen's expression clouded over as she turned her head toward the sound until her parents appeared.

She snarled, her shoulders nearly hitting her ears.

"Douglas," Walter said, tacking on the best smile he could manage. He tugged on the lapels of his suit jacket, his knuckles flexing. "A word."

A word? I had a lot more than just a word to say to him.

I shrugged. "Sure."

Evelyn threw daggers at me with her eyes. Pen brushed her fingers helplessly against mine when I passed her. Such a slight gesture, but it carried the weight of a thousand words.

Nothing had changed between us. She still wanted to be mine.

I didn't know what this fucker with his bow tie and his shiny loafers had to say to me, but all I knew was that I had only one thing to say to him. He just needed to agree.

After I'd heard them call me inferior, I'd left a horrified and apologetic Frieda standing in the pantry by herself. I didn't need to hear the rest. Hell, I wasn't sure if it had really been to my benefit to hear what they thought of me at all. I understood she believed it would have given me the upper hand to fortify myself, but fuck, it had stung.

Shoving my hands in my pockets, I followed him wordlessly down the hall to his study. The door closed on a quiet snick. I stood a few feet away from his stuffy desk, keeping my eyes trained on him when he rounded it, and settled in his desk chair.

He gestured to one of the opposite leather-clad seats. "Sit." He steepled his fingers together, his intake of breath sharp as his eyes found an ornate, wooden picture frame with a photo of Pen no more than twelve years old, mischief alive in her eyes and a mouthful of braces with red ligatures and a clementine orange power chain.

"She was a precocious child, a very clever little girl."

"She still is," I replied, hooking my legs together at the ankles to keep me from bouncing my leg. He didn't need any tells that I was nervous as hell.

He nodded absently. "I fear our efforts to keep her well educated failed her after all."

May as well just spit it out. "Because she ended up with me?"

"What would you have us do, Douglas?" He leaned back in his seat, dropping the facade of a shrewd businessman, showing me his hand—vulnerable, and legitimately afraid. It was an offensive overreaction. "If you were us, how would you feel?"

"I love your daughter." It really was that simple, so why couldn't that be enough?

"And in our world, love isn't enough," he informed me, his head turning toward the window. "We don't marry for frivolous reasons. We marry to forge better alliances, keep bloodlines intact."

"It's two-thousand-and-eight, and this isn't a medieval faction." Although, I was sure in their eyes, I was Robin Hood and Penelope was Lady Marian. I had indisputably stolen her from them.

He swung his gaze back at me, his brows furrowing. "I am aware of the year, but you are ignorant of how things work for girls like Penelope."

I was ignorant of how things worked for girls like Penelope? Nah, I was more than aware of how things worked for girls like Penelope. It was why I'd always been hyperaware that she was out of my league, that there was no universe in which I got the dream girl. But the dream girl had wanted me, and I'd made it my life's work to know everything about her, to understand her as well as she understood herself, to ensure not a day went by where she didn't know that she was loved for who she was, not what she had.

I knew what their expectations were for her, but I also knew that their expectations didn't match her. They'd deluded themselves into believing that all this micromanagement of her life had been for her own good, and that caused them to miss out on the opportunity to really get to know her.

I scratched at my cheek, before leaning back in my seat to mirror his posture. "What's your daughter's favorite color?" I asked.

His eyes sparked with fury. "Blue."

The palpability of his annoyance might have scared me a few weeks ago, but after everything I'd witnessed since we got here, it just emboldened me.

Her parents were pathetic. "Orange," I corrected, glancing at the photo of her as a kid once more. The evidence was obvious even when she was a kid, and he'd missed it. "Like the sunset." I drummed my fingers against my thigh. "What's her favorite food?"

"This is nonsense."

"Then it shouldn't be a problem to answer the question, right?" I asked, cocking my head. "You know her so well, answer the question."

He gritted his teeth, outrage exploding from him. "Are you accusing me of not knowing my daughter based on arbitrary things like her favorite color or food?"

"No, I'm accusing you and Mrs. Cullimore of not knowing your daughter. *At all.*" I paused, before adding, "Sir."

They didn't know a goddamn thing about her, and no, I didn't just mean the random details like her favorite color or favorite band. They didn't know what motivated her, what inspired her, what was the source of her happiness, or what even scared her. Pen didn't want to share with them the things that were important to her because she didn't trust them not to shit all over her. She didn't yearn for her parents' support. She didn't miss them enough to call on her own accord. Maintaining a relationship with them was a chore.

And could I fault her? How did you miss people who made you feel like garbage about yourself?

They saw a mess with Penelope that needed to be cleaned up and polished to be presentable for a society she didn't care about, but I saw Penelope as she was.

As good as goddamn perfect, flaws and all. Sure, she was stubborn and bratty, quick-tempered at times, but she was passionate, eccentric, and alive. She saw the good in everyone. She wanted to make the people she loved happy, even at the expense of herself.

I mean, no one put up with Raquel and Sean's shit for no reason other than love.

Penelope knew how to love with everything she had in her and all her parents had taught her was that love was flawed and wrong.

I wouldn't let them do that to her anymore.

Walter was silent. He extended a hand to his bow tie, adjusting it to busy himself as he thought on a response. "Colors and food don't make for a marriage, Douglas."

"Probably not," I agreed, leaning back in my seat. "But understanding what makes the person you love happy, remembering the small details like how she hates peas because of the texture, and she has a scar over her knee from climbing a fence while running from the cops when a kegger she attended got busted and she was underage, or that she loves Iron Maiden? Those things matter."

It wasn't about Yale or marrying the right asshole. It was about understanding her motivations, what made her bloom, hearing her stories, and writing new ones with her.

"And what happens when they don't?" he asked, sounding earnest. His hands collapsed in his lap with defeat. "What then?"

My stomach twisted, my lungs heaving. "I can't answer that," I confessed, ignoring the way my muscles jumped with uncertainty under my skin. It was the truth. None of us could say what the future looked like. I wasn't ignorant. I knew there might come a day where the road would feel bumpy, where things might not seem linear or easy. All I knew was that was a road I wanted to be on with Pen.

She was my person, and come hell or high water, it was her and I, always.

Maybe I was inferior, and maybe I wasn't good enough for Pen, but I wanted to spend the rest of my life trying to be.

"But I can tell you we're having a baby." He shifted in his seat uncomfortably at the reminder. "And I'm sorry I'm not who you would have chosen for her. I can't play tennis. I don't know the first thing about stocks, and I don't bring a lot to the table in terms of what you value."

He looked down at his hands, a palpable sadness saturating the room.

"But I love her," I continued. "I love her, and I promise you, I will make sure not a day goes by where she doesn't know it. That what I lack in achievements and titles, I'll give her back twofold in memories and happiness."

"Memories and happiness aren't the foundation to a marriage, Douglas," he said, his tone sober. "Financial stability is. It provides safety. It's a guaranteed life."

"I'm not going to pretend to have money," I replied. "But what I do know about your daughter is that those things aren't important to her."

"So she says," he murmured, his eyes growing weary. "But can you handle it?" I frowned. What did he mean? He gathered my confusion, expelling a tight breath. "Can you handle that when the sun sets and doesn't rise again for some time, when the clouds roll in, and the novelty of forbidden love has worn off... can you accept that what you have left is the basis of your marriage?"

"As long as I get to be by your daughter's side, I'll go to hell and back for her."

Walter's silence ate up all the air in the room, and for a moment, I thought he might laugh at my answer. I wasn't trying to wax poetic or blow smoke up his ass. It was just how I felt.

I wasn't the best pick on paper for Penelope, but I also knew I was the only one for her. The only one who didn't give a shit about her family's wealth, who wanted to use his last breath ensuring she had a smile on her face. That had to be worth something to the Cullimores.

Walter rose to his feet, then wandered over to an antique cart with a crystal decanter with amber liquid in it and two glasses. He poured two knuckles worth in separate glasses. Facing me, he extended the glass to me.

I stood up, inching over, and accepted his olive branch.

"You will amend this situation and propose to my daughter." He nodded, deciding on it before I'd even asked, while swirling the contents of his glass. "We expect it to happen as soon as possible." He stared at his glass. "Evelyn and I will not be the butt of our friends' jokes." He lifted his eyes, peering at my coldly. "Do you understand me?"

My heart jackknifed, and I had to fight the urge to smile. Yeah, I understood him loud and fucking clear.

Tipping the glass back, I set it on the cart, lumbering toward the study doors. "Douglas?" Walter called as I turned the knob. "Where are you going?"

"To propose." It was taking everything in me not to fucking skip.

"You don't even have a ring."

I snorted, shaking my head. *One step ahead of ya, Walt.*

Pen's voice hit my ears as soon as the doors were open—urgent, irritated and promising another volcanic eruption if her mother kept provoking her. "We don't need to get married just to spare you and Daddy the scandal."

The heat of their argument billowed toward me, especially when Evelyn added kerosene by snapping back, "You will do as your told for once, Penelope Louise."

"Hey," I said, defusing their argument.

Pen straightened in her seat, her eyes uneasy. The table had been cleared, no traces of breakfast remaining.

"Hi," Pen whispered back. Her face was a mix of emotions—regret, worry, fear. "I'm sorry." Her chest caved in, her hands balling in her lap, and I knew she wanted to launch into an explanation.

But there was nothing left to say.

"Douglas?" Walter called, entering the dining room.

Fuck the orchard. I shoved my hand into my pocket, walking around the dining table. "Pen." My mind went over the worst-case scenario.

She might still say no. After everything, and her joking around, she might tell me to take a hike.

"What are you doing?" she asked, watching as I dropped on one knee and fished the ring out of my pocket. She gulped, her stare fixating on the ring.

"The first time I saw you, I knew I wanted to marry you. Did you know that?" Pen held a hand to her mouth. She tried to mask a smile as tears filled her eyes and she shook her head. "I think the universe, or God, or someone musta heard me."

"Must have," Evelyn corrected under her breath, but I paid her no mind.

As far as I was concerned, she and Walter weren't even in the room with us right now.

"'Cause they gave us something I've been dreaming about since I was a kid." I reached for her hand. "You, and our baby."

I ran my thumb over the thin gold band of the round opal ring, the sunlight catching on the stone from the dining room windows, sending iridescent streaks across the wall. She'd told me in passing once she loved opal, and I'd remembered. "I love you, Penny. I don't know what our story has in store for us. All I know is I want to write every chapter of my life with you."

Pen broke, a choke of a laugh and a cry shooting out of her as she nodded her head. "Me, too."

I grinned. "Wanna get hitched?"

"*Married*! Do you want to get married!" Evelyn hollered in frustration.

Pen laughed harder, throwing her arms around me, ignoring the ring all together. "Yeah, I wanna get hitched," she murmured in my ear. "And make a dozen more babies with you."

"Is that a yes?"

She found my lips, kissing me hard. "That's a hell yes."

Chapter Twenty-Two

Penelope

Present

I STIRRED IN MY SLEEP, MY EYES OPENING SLOWLY AS EXHAUSTION STILL swirled in my head. A crow cawed in the distance, the dim-morning autumn light touching my skin.

I couldn't remember the last time I'd slept that deeply.

The dormant muscles in my body ached with satiation, used for the first time in months. I waited for that hollowed feeling to weave its way back into my chest, for the familiar squeeze of my lungs to arrive.

But neither came, and for the first time in what felt like forever, I had hope that things might get better—that we had a fighting chance to start over.

I'd told Dougie everything. Part of it had been a do-or-die, but most of the driving force had been because Mother and Raquel were right. He deserved to know, after everything that had happened, he deserved to know why we'd ended up where we did.

It wasn't all his fault.

I should have told him sooner. It shouldn't have come down to us being on the verge of a catastrophic dissolution for the words to finally leave me, but I'd been so worried that after everything we'd both gone through just to get here, that it would destroy his perception of me irreparably.

I wasn't perfect. After all the years I'd spent on the shiny, coveted pedestal he'd placed me on, I had a flaw that I'd desperately tried to keep out of sight at the expense of hurting him on my terms.

But I'd missed him.

I'd missed his warmth, the safety of his arms and the weight of his body moving in tandem with mine. The way he expressed himself in a way his mouth couldn't.

Dougie still loved me. And as long as that was true, we stood a chance.

Rolling over in the guest room bed, a frigid chill settled in my bones when I found the spot next to me vacant. Brushing my hand against the spot where he had laid, the cold trapped in the fibers of the sheets.

Where had he gone? Sitting upright, my pulse whirred in my ears. I pinched the bedsheet under my chest, my eyes spotting the alarm clock on the dresser. Why was he up so early? It was ten to seven in the morning, and he didn't have anywhere to be.

I listened carefully for any sign of him in Chris's room next to the guest room, getting ready for the day, but there was nothing. Momentarily transfixed, my mind raced through all the explanations.

He was in the bathroom.

He'd gone downstairs for a glass of water.

He went for a walk.

But there was one persistent, harrowing thought that kept nagging at me and twisting my insides, too horrific to put into words because it scared me unlike anything else. Pulling the flat sheet free from the mattress, I wrapped it around myself and padded toward the bedroom door on wobbling legs.

I inched out of the room on light feet, not daring to even swallow despite my dry tongue's desperation for my saliva glands to cooperate.

It was fine. Everything was fine.

Maybe he was getting dressed, or he was...

The sound of the dresser door closing on a controlled whisper evoked the sense that it was furtive in a way he'd never been. It nearly brought me to my knees, extinguishing any remaining optimism I'd had.

Frozen in the hallway, I listened with the crescendo of my heartbeat thumping painfully as each of his movements grew more deafening by the second, despite being restrained.

The teeth of a zipper opening and closing.

An empty hanger creaking on a closet rod.

The soft shuffle of clothes being neatly folded.

I held my breath, my insides shrinking as understanding hit me.

No, no, no.

Why was I being punished now, after everything? I raced the rest of the way down the hallway, not interested in perpetuating his illusion of calm because it was another pretty lie meant to deceive.

My husband had the audacity to appear devastated when I cleared the threshold, my chest rising and falling while my chin jutted sharply, meeting his plaintive eyes. His Adam's apple weaved excruciatingly slow before my eyes took in the rest of him and our room.

Dougie had showered, the air faintly damp from the steam coming from the adjacent bathroom and the clean mint notes of his beloved five-in-one hitting my nose. His clothes were loose on his gaunt frame, the bags under his eyes more pronounced. He stared down at the fistful of socks in his hand, his knuckles flexing for a moment before he ripped himself from where he stood by his nightstand drawer and placed them into a brown leather overnight bag on our bed. The sheets were still a mess from last night.

I could see where we'd laid.

"What are you doing?" I heard the question. My ears picked up that it was my voice that had spoken, but my mind screamed why I'd asked at all.

I knew what he was doing. It was perfectly fucking obvious.

"I've been thinking—"

I cut him off with a dry laugh, forcing his forehead to knit.

He was thinking?

When?

When he kissed me?

When he told me he loved me?

When he came all over my stomach?

When?

Oh, God. I clung tighter to myself, clawing at the bedsheet. I wanted to be sick. "You fucked me, and now…"

"Please stop calling it that," he implored, his gaze growing flinty.

"But you *did*," I countered, staring at the bag, wishing I could set it aflame with my eyes alone. "You got what you wanted and now you're leaving." I didn't care what word he wanted to describe last night as to make himself feel better.

I wasn't interested in mollifying his guilt.

"I'm *not* leaving."

How could he say that to me as he put his socks in the bag, next to his neatly folded boxer briefs? I could see the plaid from his favorite shirt, the threads loose around the first button. It belonged in the closet with the rest of his long-sleeved shirts I'd color sorted. Instead, it was piled on top of his jeans, the ones with the worn-out threads in the knees that lived in the bottom dresser drawer.

None of his stuff belonged in that bag, away from me.

My blood pressure rose, the tightness in my chest making it hard to breathe as my temper spiraled out of control. The realization of the situation sank its claws into me, drawing blood and penetrating me with its poison.

He fucked me, and now he was leaving.

This was really happening. "Looks like it to me."

"It's not like that."

I snorted. "You have things packed, right?"

Dougie stared at the addition of the socks in the open bag, the cords in his thick neck flexing with a swallow, but he said nothing.

I controlled the urge to scream at him, my voice coming out modulated and thin. "Then it is like that."

He stepped away from the bag, scrubbing an open palm over his face, his eyes tipped downward. "Pen, you need to trust me on this."

But that word. That ugly five-lettered word, an integral part of our marriage vows, eroded what remained of my self-control, of my desire to keep myself in check.

"*Trust?*" I trilled, resenting how much I sounded like my mother as I stormed toward him with my finger jabbing the air between us. "Trust *you?*"

Dougie turned away from me, pressing his lips together to prevent himself from launching into another tirade about how it wasn't like that with her.

"God, I can't believe you." I pushed down on my stomach, fighting to keep the vitriol in check when all it wanted to do was projectile launch right out of me.

"Last night shouldn't have happened," he said, dropping his voice as his eyes fell shut.

My head snapped back, ugly laughter spilling out of me. "When did you have that epiphany?" I demanded, my tone scathing. My body was vibrating, sweat licking up my spine. There was a buzzing filling my ears, eating up what was left of my calm, the distortion of my thoughts taking over.

Nothing.

He gave me nothing but that silence I was convinced was designed to put me over the edge. I shook my head, every hair on my body standing upright as reality penetrated through each blood vessel in my body.

My husband was leaving me, and that unescapable thought made the trembling in my body uncontrollable and the sting in my eyes feel like acid that would rob me of my vision.

At least then, I wouldn't have to witness any of this unfold. I wouldn't have the memory of him leaving me tattooed on the back of my eyelids forever.

"I know you don't want to hear this from me," he began, inhaling sharply. "But if we have a fighting chance in hell, we can't rush through the steps, Pen. And we went from one to five."

The steps? The roadmap to recovery? What kind of deluded bull-shit had he been feeding himself? The pain in my jaw intensified, my molars threatening to crack as the statement ricocheted in my mind.

I didn't want his explanations—there was no one who understood the odds stacked against us better than me. I'd spent the last few months trying to keep our marriage together. I'd swallowed my lies, while his lived on display.

I'd done that for us, and what was he doing for us?

Leaving me.

I resented the remorse alive and brimming in his eyes. The meeting of his regretful brows, or the thinning of his mouth, did not move or assuage me.

I wanted a fight.

Nodding my head, the punitive surge of rage entered my blood-stream and I let it go, untethered. He didn't deserve me in control. He deserved the maelstrom. "Right, so after you came on my stomach. I got it."

He gritted his teeth. "Stop. It."

"Stop it?" I echoed. "That's what you should have done if this was your plan all along."

He shook his head. "It wasn't, Pen." His hands found his pockets, sliding forward. "Last night," he hesitated, thinking of how to word it.

"You got what you wanted," I finished for him. I felt like I might shatter under any more pressure, that I might do something as uncouth as beg him to stay. "You're punishing me now for everything I did to you, right?" I couldn't stop rewinding the thought repeatedly, my head spinning.

"That's not it, not at all."

"Then don't leave," I whispered, my bottom lip betraying my

anger. "Don't leave me." The vise in my lungs squeezed, my stomach twisting with nausea as reality took over.

I couldn't believe I was begging him to stay, that I was being left behind for telling the truth.

My body sagged. Panic threatened to buckle my legs as I struggled to hold myself up. This couldn't be happening.

Blistering white pain exploded in my chest when his arms wrapped around me, and he pulled me close. I sagged into him, hating myself for being so goddamn weak. I dissolved into sobs, fighting with the urge to cling at him with desperation.

"I am not leaving you," he insisted. "I need time to process, Penelope. Not because of you." He exhaled into my hair, pressing a kiss against my crown to disguise the shaking in his limbs. "But because of *me.*"

"You promised," I cried, losing my resolve. My fingers clawed at his shirt, pinning him tight to me. "You promised me you wouldn't stop loving me."

"And I *do* love you, Penny. So much that I need to become the man you fell for again, okay?" He relaxed his grasp on me, drawing me back to look at me. Dougie's eyes were red rimmed, his jaw flexing as he struggled to keep it together. "This is *not* about you."

It sounded like another lie, painted in gold, intended to lessen the blow. Swallowing back the sob, the strangled query left me. "Then why does it feel like it is?"

How could he do this to me? After everything, after I found the courage to tell him the truth, confronted how much it hurt. How could he strike me down once more?

"Give me a chance, Pen," he whispered, "I need you to please…"

Trust.

I knew that was the word he wanted to say, but the way his lids fluttered shut and his nostrils flared, he wouldn't let that word free. "I need you to give me a chance to redeem myself."

"But you don't have to." I cupped his face, trying to commit the way each coarse hair of his unkept beard tickled my palms in memory. I was so afraid I'd forget how his skin would feel against mine, that I wouldn't remember which direction his nose deviated in, or how ethereal his green eyes could be. "You don't need to prove yourself to me. You just need to stay by my side."

He stared into my eyes, and I watched as tears pooled in his ducts, turning the pine green into a jeweled emerald. The calluses of his fingers wrapped around my wrists, tugging me away gently, my insides shredding. "I'm sorry, Penelope."

I sniffled, turning my head from him.

He kissed my cheek, his chest quaking against me. "I promise, I'll come back."

But if he left now, I didn't want him to return. He'd humiliated me for the last time. "If you leave, don't bother," I threatened, my anger refortifying me.

An anguished sigh left him, his arms falling to his sides. "Pen, don't make empty threats like that."

"I'm not threatening you," I gritted, my anger making my limbs buzz. "I'm telling you, if you leave, I'll file."

Dougie sniffled, then held out a hand to me. "This is my point." I stared at him, finding myself rendered quiet, waiting for the next axe to fall. "You are," he looked me over, rubbing the corners of his mouth, his brows bending in the middle, "so fucking angry with me." Dougie shook his head. "Any opportunity to fling mud at me, you're going to take it."

I squeezed my eyes shut, my body temperature rising. "Because you wanted to fuck someone else."

"I did." His admission made my whole body rack with pain. "I considered having sex with someone else, and you kept a pregnancy *and* a loss from me." He scraped a hand over his face. "This is not the basis of a healthy marriage, Pen. This is not what we wanted."

The grit in his voice hurt as he continued, "It's a whole lot of pain that we need to sort out as individuals if we have a chance in hell of coming through this on the other side."

But I was still too angry to be reasoned with. He didn't get to decide for us.

We weren't playing house. This was a marriage.

He didn't get to run away.

I didn't run away.

"You don't get to take a time-out on a marriage when it gets hard," I bit out, my mouth twisting into a sneer. "That is *not* a partnership."

Partnership.

That word.

We both froze. Had I said that? My throat closed up on me, my tongue thickening as I raced to digest the words I'd allowed free.

To anyone else, that word wouldn't have been bad. It would have suggested we valued each other as equals in a loving relationship.

But to us, to me, that word described something that had never reflected who we were. That transactional noun my parents had used to describe themselves to justify the lack of warmth shared amongst them. I'd accused them once of being artificial, but somehow along the way without warning, Dougie and I had become the fake ones, because I'd kept everyone out. I'd ensured no one could see or hear what we were going through because I'd wanted to perpetuate the illusion that we were better than my parents, better than Raquel and Sean.

And the only way I'd been able to do that was by keeping them out.

I'd told my parents their marriage was a lie once.

But as it turned out? They weren't the only liars. They'd raised one, too.

Somehow, Dougie found his nerve to speak again. "I don't want to rush this, Pen. I don't want to go back to being who we were, because those people don't exist anymore. This is you and I now, and I want…" his voice broke, "I *need* our next chapter to work, okay?"

My tears fell, burning a hot tract down my cheeks, dribbling off my chin.

I didn't want to acknowledge the small voice inside of me that assured me Dougie wasn't leaving me despite the thought distortions.

He needed to think. He was trying to give us a chance. The chance I'd been determined to deprive us of for so long until fear propelled me into action. We couldn't rush through this, because he was right. We weren't who we'd once been, we were different.

And we'd hurt each other, and those wounds wouldn't heal when the reminder constantly existed—when I couldn't let my anger go because Dougie was right.

I was angry with him, and anytime he so much as stepped a toe out of line, I was ready to level him to the ground without remorse.

That wasn't love. That was chaos.

It wasn't us.

Reluctantly, and despite the raging protests in my heart, I nodded.

"I need to become someone worthy of your love again. Someone you can be proud to call your husband." He placed this thumb like a button on my lips, knowing I'd interject. "I hurt you, and I need you to let me work at earning you back."

Dougie dropped his hand slowly when he was sure I wouldn't try to argue with him.

The numbness swept over me as I watched him zip up his bag, then hoisted it over his shoulder. He studied me carefully, before leaning in and pressing a kiss against my cheek that I knew I'd feel the pressure of for hours. My heart had the audacity to stammer, but I didn't beg or plead this time.

I wouldn't.

"You just have to trust me."

I was certain there was going to be water in my ears, and I didn't care.

Any discomfort the clog would provide me would pale compared to everything else. The ginger notes of the lingering soap from my bath perfumed the room. The bath water had long since gone cold, the steam no longer a blanket of condensation against the mirror.

The ending notes of No Doubt's 'Don't Speak' rang out, silence pervading only long enough for me to catch the brassy notes of Sean's baritone voice below in my family room, though it was too indiscernible for me to make out specifically what he'd said.

The familiar guitar plucking hit my ears once more as the song started again. I had no idea how long I'd been in here for, or how many times I'd listened to the track on repeat.

I didn't resurface when the subtle knock echoed on the bathroom door, nor when Raquel's shadow bounced against the wall in front of me when she pushed the door open.

"Your fingers are going to turn into raisins," she warned, padding toward where I'd discarded my phone. The music cut. "I think that's probably enough No Doubt for the day."

I laughed. I didn't want to, but I did.

Lifting my hands out from under the tepid waters, I examined the wrinkled skin that had formed along the pads of my fingers.

Her citrus and vanilla scent comforted me as she sat on the edge of the soaker tub, her concerned brown-eyed stare giving me the once-over. I didn't think I'd ever adjust to her maternal instincts, though it was a welcomed change. "How you feeling?"

I gazed up at her through my lashes. How had we ended up in a role reversal?

Two years ago, it had been me in her place. Coaxing her to make amends with her then estranged ex-boyfriend, now husband, who was busy downstairs playing uncle with my oblivious toddler. Now, she was as poised as a South Boston expat could be, strong and even keeled.

I watched a droplet of water fall from the tub faucet. "Like I want to die."

I was an awful wife. A terrible mother. And an even worse friend.

She snorted, shaking her head. "Over that busted-nose asshole?" She was trying for levity, but even she had sounded bewildered when I'd called her. "Your baby needs you."

I knew that, and I would never.

But it hurt all the same.

"Kell," I replied. I knew the intent was good with her jab, but he was still my husband.

She picked a strand of damp hair caught on the perspiration on my face, tucking it behind my ear. "I'm kidding. Bad joke."

I didn't trust myself not to cry if I looked at her, so I avoided her eyes at all costs. Parts of me couldn't reconcile how badly I'd hurt her, too. She'd gotten caught in the crossfire of my judgment error this year, and I'd punished her mercilessly once for doing the very same.

She hadn't hesitated to come right over when I'd called after Dougie left. She hadn't fixated on rhyming off my wrongdoings or sticking it to me.

Raquel had been who I couldn't be back then. She knew what I needed and, like a chameleon, became it.

Concentrating on the turbulent bath water as I extended my legs, I plucked up the courage to say the words. "I can't believe he left."

Even saying it out loud didn't feel real, but the tightness constricting my chest assured me it was true. He'd walked right out on Christopher and me without any hesitation.

She leaned back against the wall, bringing her legs up to her chest. Raquel played with the edges of her thick wool-knit socks, her mouth pulling to the right with thought. "As someone who did the leaving once, it's not always about you, but about them."

This time, I couldn't help but look at her. Her profile was tense, gaze fixed on the subway tile lining the bath wall behind me. "I needed to catch my breath back then."

"But you hurt Sean."

"I devastated him," she agreed, her throat weaving in an obvious swallow. "But it wasn't about him, or you. It really was about me, needing to regain my footing and figure out who I was again, and whether I was worthy of this life."

"You always were."

Her legs extended as she draped her hands in her lap, letting out a restrained sigh. "Sometimes, you can tell someone that over and over again, and until they believe it themselves, it's pointless."

Dropping my gaze, I studied the ripples in the water. Had that been what it was like for Dougie? Trying to convince himself he deserved me?

"I don't know if I can forgive him for this." I swiped the tears away. It was one thing to need space, it was another thing to methodically pack a bag and leave. It was premeditation. He'd known last night, and he still made love to me.

I felt like my entire world was falling apart. Christopher got out of bed moments after I got off the phone with Raquel, as happy as could be, and all I could do was stare at Dougie's carbon copy despite my hair color and wonder how I'd fucked this up so badly. I'd driven his father right out the door, destroyed our marriage and ruined our family.

Would my son someday resent me, too?

What if his dad never came back?

I dropped to my knees and pulled our boy close and bit the inside of my cheek until I tasted blood to keep from crying. His little voice calling for his dad lacerated my insides, and I swore to God I'd get strong, so he'd never have the memory of his mother falling apart at his feet in his mind.

He didn't deserve any of this. He was the one pure thing we had.

Less than twenty minutes later, the doorbell rang.

I hadn't been prepared for Raquel to show up *with* Sean, but when they'd appeared at the door as a fortified unit, bundled close together to stave off the chill of October, my face crumpled. It was impossible to read either of their expressions. Based on his attire and the faint dusting of flour on the front of his shirt, Sean was supposed to be at the restaurant, not on my front porch with his wife, studying me for the first time in months. He had stepped forward, pulling me into the most crushing hug I'd ever received from him.

I cried all over his chest while he rested his cheek on my head and smoothed a palm over my upper back while murmuring apologies. For someone so grumpy in a past life, he really gave the best hugs, and somehow, it was exactly what I'd needed. In that moment, I discerned he knew enough. Not everything, but enough.

Raquel had left the twins with Sean's ma with a blanket explanation that she needed to run some errands for a couple of hours to ensure nothing would get back to Dougie's ma. Then she picked up Sean and raced over here.

Her voice pulled me out of my reverie. "We're not judging you guys, Pen."

"Just the knowledge that you both know, I'm just..." *unsure how we could recover from that.*

"You just need to take it one day at a time and go from there." She offered me a soft smile. "You don't need to have all the answers right now."

I nodded my head, my back squeaked against the tub as I slid further in, my hair floating around me. Where had he gone... "He stopped talking to Sean because I asked him to." I hated the idea of him alone, isolated.

Being alone never did anyone any good.

The admission quieted her.

I flitted my eyes to her, taking in her pensiveness. "I was so... ashamed over everything, over finding him with Maria that night, that I just..."

She didn't need me to finish the statement. She climbed off the bathtub's edge, unhooking my terrycloth bathrobe from where it hung. "What do you think about getting out of the bath?"

"Do you hate me?" I asked. "I wouldn't blame you."

Raquel shook her head. "Never. You're my best friend, nothing will change that." She parted the bathrobe. "C'mon, out."

I sighed, the enduring guilt and shame flooding my veins. Getting out of the bathtub meant having to face the world, and I wasn't sure if I wanted to just yet.

She shot me a smirk. "I'll brush your hair out for you."

Damn her. She'd played that card. When we were in college, we used to brush the others hair out when we were feeling down.

Reluctantly, I conceded with a nod.

The water sloshed over the edge as I stood up, allowing her to fit my arms through the sleeves. I knotted the robe closed while Raquel unplugged the tub and then rummaged through my drawers in search of the paddle brush. Finding it, she closed the drawer with her hip and disappeared into the bedroom. I paused as I passed the bathroom fogged mirror.

But even the steam did nothing to disguise the woman looking back at me. I ran my palm across the lingering condensation, hating everything I saw. The dark circles under my eyes, the lines that had appeared within hours near my mouth and forehead, how ashen my skin had grown.

Where had my light gone? My hopes, my joy?

My dreams?

How had I become this weak? This afraid to be vulnerable and honest?

When had I stopped being real with myself?

"Pen?" Raquel called as the gurgled eddies worked their way down the tub drain.

My insides cut through the vines shrouding who I was, the ones I'd allowed to keep me safe at the cost of myself and my marriage.

I made a vow of another kind right then and there.

I was cutting those vines down and setting myself free.

With or without Dougie.

Chapter Twenty-Three

Penelope

Three years ago...

"Run me through this guest list again," Dougie called out to me over the rush of water in the shower. I released the strand of hair wound tightly around the wand of the wide curling iron, watching as the shaped wave bounced as it came to a rest against my shoulder.

Appraising myself in the mirror, I tilted my head, fingering the wave. "Raquel, Sean, everyone from work, their spouses..." Maybe I should brush it out. I didn't like how perfectly put together they looked. Reminded me too much of the polished little bitches from Hotchkiss. Setting the curling iron down, I tugged open the bathroom drawer on the right—my side—and reached for the paddle brush. The countertop in our primary bathroom adjoining our bedroom featured a gorgeous double vanity with deep drawers and a generous amount of room in the cabinets. My side was mostly full, but Dougie's... I glanced at his side of the counter. His toothbrush, a comb, and the cologne I'd given him for Christmas.

We didn't make it to Connecticut for our first Christmas together—I know, *darn, better luck next year!*—but I was grateful for the opportunity to finally meet Eileen, Dougie's mom. She was nothing like Mother. There was a kind of palpable immediacy in her warmth as soon as she opened the front door before we'd even climbed out of the truck. There'd been no hesitation as she raced to my side of the truck and pulled me in for a hug before my feet even touched the ground.

It had been a simple Christmas, more toned down than anything I'd ever experienced before, and I'd adored every minute of it.

I loved that Eileen had an angel on top of her tree rather than a star or stylish bow or whatever the latest trend was as per Mother's inner circle. Eileen's decor was a combination of things she'd scavenged outside over the years like pine cones, or plastic baubles that were worn out, accented by fistfuls of cheap tinsel that reflected the candy-colored strings of lights. I didn't think I'd ever seen tinsel before in real life prior to that moment, but I hadn't been able to resist plucking a strand from the tree and rolling it between my fingers curiously. She'd kept a large candle in the bay window of her tiny Cape Cod, explaining to me it signified that should Mary, Joseph and baby Jesus require a place to stay, they were welcomed.

And while I hadn't considered myself religious by any stretch of the word despite my Protestant upbringing, it made my insides swell with happiness.

It was the perfect Christmas to mark Dougie and mine's first one together, and I'd had such an enjoyable time with his ma that I'd insisted we come back the following day and go to church with her.

I didn't even like church, but there was something about Eileen that made you want to spend more time with her—I understood why she and Dougie were so close. I couldn't wait to make her a grandmother, I knew she'd be the best kind.

"That's it?" Dougie called, pulling me out of my silver bell and tinsel-filled memory.

"What do you mean, 'that's it'?" I snorted, running the paddle brush through my hair. "That's already twenty people."

He barked out a laugh. "Fair enough."

I chewed on the inside of my cheek while I brushed out my curls into waves. That had been in it, hadn't it? It was getting harder to remember things. I thought baby brain was a myth, but I was wrong. Running through the list inwardly once more, I recalled there had been people I'd forgotten to mention "Oh, I remembered a couple of others."

He laughed. "Oh, yeah?"

I spun around, facing the glass-enclosed shower, the notes of his mint 5-in-1 hitting my nose—I hadn't been able to convert him off that in the move despite the array of shampoos and bodywashes I'd left in there for him to try. He wasn't interested in the loofah either. *"Shit feels weird against my balls."*

Dougie turned in the shower, his fingers scrubbing at his scalp as he attempted to meet my eyes through the thick haze of steam and condensation building on the glass. "Who else?" he asked.

"I told Trina to extend the invite to Olivia and Maria." Sean's other sisters.

I wanted to meet Maria formally in person. I'd only ever conversed with her via email, briefly, and it was important to me to not only thank her personally for the way she'd changed my life with this job reference, but also polite to invite her and Olivia. The covert WASP in me deemed it rude to have two out of the four Tavares siblings here, and we had the space for a few more.

"You what?" he asked thinly.

I frowned, setting the brush down. Why had he seemed flustered? "You just said, 'that's it' about the guest list—what's wrong?"

Dougie peeled his stare from mine, stepping into the stream of water. The shower floor clouded with the suds from his head, twisting into eddies that dipped down the drain. The water cut out, the seal on the shower door creaking as he pulled it open. His mouth set in a hard line as he extended a hand to the clean towel I'd hung up for him when he'd forgotten to grab one because he was still used to just sticking his hand out from the shower at his old apartment and snagging a towel from off of a shelving unit above his toilet.

It probably didn't help our bathroom was the size of his bedroom in his old apartment. He wasn't used to everything being so... big. He seemed afraid to even take up space sometimes.

He towel-dried his hair harder than he needed to, sending beads of water everywhere before he wrapped the towel around his waist and stepped onto the bathmat. "I really would have appreciated if you had discussed that with me first." His tone took on something sharp, carrying an edge to it I wasn't used to from him.

Setting my hands on my waist, I lifted my chin. "Discussed *what* with you first?"

"Inviting all of Sean's sisters." I couldn't tell if he was red in the face because of the heat of the water from his shower, or...

"I don't understand. What's the issue?" My skin prickled with the sense that there was something he wasn't saying, and the longer the silence extended between us, the worst I felt.

There *was* something he wasn't saying. He spaced out for a moment, his arms hanging loosely at his sides, eyes glassy like he'd transported himself elsewhere.

"Dougie?"

He shook his head, knocking whatever thought he'd had percolating in his mind away, his spine straightening. "Can you sit down a minute?"

My body heated, my insides fluttering with warning. I didn't miss the pinched expression tacked onto his face or the stiffness in his posture as he flickered his eyes from me to the edge of the soaker tub.

Sitting down, I crossed and uncrossed my legs twice before I settled on keeping them uncrossed with my legs slightly parted to accommodate the growing, albeit small, baby bump. I placed my hands on either side of me, intensifying apprehension making every hair stand up on my body.

Dougie fiddled with the closure of the towel around his waist before his head tipped down, his teeth dragging across his bottom lip with thought. "This past summer, you asked me," he hesitated, and the wave of wariness slammed into me full force, "you asked me if I got hurt."

My restless legs wanted so desperately to bounce as I took in the tightness in his eyes and the smoothing of his palms against the towel. "I did get hurt, Pen," he whispered, avoiding my stare for a moment more before he found his nerve, his green eyes brimming with guilt. "Maria and I had a..." he searched for the word, shifting his weight from foot to foot, "a thing."

"Oh." My face heated as I shifted on the edge of the tub, leaning forward to drape my hands in my lap. "I didn't know." I swallowed hard, my chest tightening for a moment as I digested what he'd just said.

I didn't know if I was upset that I'd invited her without knowing, or mad that she might have the audacity to show up.

Fuck.

"I didn't think you needed to," he confessed.

I gaped at him, my eyes flaring. He didn't think it was important that I knew he... had a thing with his best friend's sister? It didn't occur to him that at some point, our paths might inadvertently cross?

What an absolute jack ass.

He detected the errant nature of my thoughts. "I didn't mean it like that, Pen."

"Well, what did you mean it like, then?" I demanded.

Dougie turned away, his cheeks inflating as he blew out a long breath. "I just meant, I don't know everyone you've hooked up with."

"Because I don't continue to associate with anyone I've hooked up with in any capacity."

Dougie blanched at my outburst, his jaw rocking. Finally, he nodded. "You're right." I folded my arms across my chest. "It's a complicated situation."

My jaw rocked. "Did you..." I swallowed. "Did you love her?"

His silence spoke volumes. He didn't make any excuses for himself, but he didn't rush to assuage me either.

Which gave my mind permission to run wild.

He'd loved her, and now she was coming over. This changed everything.

What was Maria like? Did she look like Trina with her animated, cartoon-like features, or was she sharp and angular like Sean?

All I knew was that she was a lawyer.

Was she impossibly beautiful, or was there a chance that she wasn't pretty at all?

Was she kind? Why hadn't they worked out?

Did it matter?

My lips pressed together in a tight line, my mouth parched as a wave of disorientation came over me. I couldn't believe I was tripping myself up over this, but I'd never had to meet a boyfriend's ex before.

"The part that makes it complicated is Sean doesn't know," Dougie added with a wince, "and I'd appreciate if you didn't mention it to him."

Great. He was making this so much worse. He'd loved his best friend's sister, and it was a big ol' secret.

I wondered if that meant Raquel was oblivious, too. She and Sean were back on despite a falling out a little before Thanksgiving. I'd had to call on him for a favor when Raquel found herself in a precarious situation while Dougie and I remained trapped in Connecticut trying to smooth things over with my parents and since then, things had been looking up for them.

But right now… I couldn't reconcile with what Dougie had just divulged to me. My mind was tripping over every additional tidbit, contending with the need to understand how he found himself in this position to begin with, never mind why he felt the need to keep it a secret.

And sure, we couldn't fault ourselves for having lives before each other, but it didn't change that there was a pummel of inadequacy hammering through me that made me want to create space between us for a moment because he kept this from me. He knew eventually I'd find out, and he never thought to tell me.

Was that because he was still harboring something for her, even now?

I braced myself against the wall, pulling myself to my feet, staring at the floor as I headed out of the bathroom.

"Penelope?"

"I need a minute," I breathed. My skin was on fire, embarrassment tightening my gut as the licks of frustration burned a path up my neck that threatened to turn into anger.

God, did Trina know when I'd invited her?! I felt so stupid.

It wasn't that Dougie had slept with Maria. I didn't care about that. It was that he slept with his best friend's sister, didn't tell him, and left me in a position to do something like this.

And he'd *loved* her. I had to stare at the woman I replaced all night.

I didn't want her here anymore. I didn't want to thank her for shit.

"Penny." His voice echoed from the bathroom. "Can we talk about this, please?"

"I don't trust myself to say something I don't mean right now," I confessed from our bedroom, letting the back of my knees hit the bed as I sat down. Glancing to my right, I stared at the modest outfit I'd laid out for myself and saw nothing but the inadequacies in it. I needed to find something else to wear. Nothing was fitting me right. I had gone shopping a month ago with Raquel, but anything I'd grabbed then had been prepared to accommodate my soon-to-be changing body, and that suddenly felt very irresponsible.

I hadn't planned this right, because I'd found myself preoccupied with moving and unpacking, and meeting Dougie's mother and trying to turn this house into a home, and now...

God, I kinda wanted to throw up.

Dougie's shadow hit the bedroom wall, his footsteps light as ambulated toward the bed. "Pen, I wish I'd..."

He wished he what? Told me sooner? Knew beforehand that I was going to do this? He'd been so ambivalent about who was invited, told me to do whatever I wanted, that he supported whatever menu decision I made, right down to the stupid oysters.

Oysters. I ordered fucking oysters for a bunch of construction workers who probably didn't care because I was a pretentious little bitch from Connecticut, desperately trying to fit in with them or at a minimum, make them like me.

Ugh. Why had I canceled my therapy appointment with Henry before Christmas?

Placing a hand on my belly, I took in a deep, calming breath. "Why did you two break up?" I resented how small my voice sounded.

"We didn't break up," he said, the mattress creaking with his addition. I couldn't find the nerve to look at him, and he knew it, too. He touched the underside of my chin, directing my eyes to meet his. When I kept my gaze pointed downward, he tipped my head back, not giving me a choice but to look at him lest I strain my eyes. "We weren't ever really officially together. Things just fizzled out. Maria's a workaholic, and she doesn't do relationships." His lips pursed, his throat weaving with a noticeable swallow. "Once I suggested to her that we tell Sean and take things further, she called it off." He blinked rapidly, as though he were trying to obliterate the memory.

But we never really forgot things like that, did we?

We never forgot the people who left us behind.

My stomach knotted as my pulse kicked up a furious storm. What the fuck had I been thinking telling Trina to invite her sisters?

I folded my arms across my chest, squeezing myself hard to control the nervous quivering racking through me. "When was this?"

"A year? Maybe a year and a half ago?"

Trina hadn't RSVP'd for her sisters, but I knew she and the new guy at work, Adam, were coming *together*, much to Sean's chagrin.

But if Maria showed up after all? What if… what if he looked at her like he was supposed to look at me? "Are you… over her?" I couldn't believe I was asking him that, but I didn't want to lie to myself that I wasn't bothered.

"Completely," he insisted, blanketing my shoulders with his hands, squeezing. "I don't feel that way about her anymore." His hands left my shoulders to cup my cheeks. "The only one I'm crazy about is you."

Dougie kissed me, brushing his nose against mine, and when he smiled, I mirrored it.

He said the right thing, but I didn't trust it.

The best lies told came out the prettiest.

But at that moment, I lied to him, too. "Okay."

Gorgeous.

Maria Tavares was frustratingly fucking gorgeous.

It had momentarily stunned me when I'd opened the front door to the Tavares sisters, huddled together closely to fight off the late December cold. Trina, bouncing on her toes excitedly with a cheeky grin and heavy eye makeup, explained Adam was on his way. She stood next to a brown-sugar-haired woman who I discerned was the middle sister, Olivia.

And then... Maria. I knew it was her instantaneously.

She was an unmistakable beacon. Your eyes couldn't help but lock on her, and even if you wanted to look away, you just couldn't.

She was surprisingly tall, pushing at least five-foot-nine out of her heels with a trim, hourglass figure. A headful of lush dark hair and classically pretty features that made her look like a European goddess. That golden, enviable complexion, and an oxblood red-painted pout I knew women back home paid good money to emulate through fillers.

Her dress when she slipped out of her winter coat made me feel inadequate despite finally settling on a stormy gray Merino wool dress with a fringed caplet that ended above my knees. I'd paired the dress with black leggings and gold-plated chain-linked earrings.

But looking at Maria, it perpetuated this resounding thought in my mind that I felt and looked like a beached whale, while she was...

Perfect.

Her timeless blood-red pencil dress clung to every dip and curve of her body. And without even trying, every head in the room turned and looked her way. She commanded a room effortlessly, and all I could do was look to Dougie with my heart hammering, and hope he didn't look her way, too.

He didn't.

Dougie offered me an asymmetrical smile, an assurance flickering in his eyes as he held my stare. It should have culled the anxiety inside of me, but it didn't.

She was here.

And she hadn't uttered a word to me, outside of a curt, "hello."

There was a terse, unspoken awkwardness filtering between us because instinctually, something told me she knew I knew.

And I hated her instantly for it.

But not as much as I hated myself for breaking down into tears over what everyone thought to be hormones and frustration over the sparkling apple juice Dougie had handed me in a champagne flute an hour later.

It wasn't about the fucking sparkling apple juice; it was about that... that she-wolf was in our house, surreptitiously staring at me while drinking expensive wine Dougie had accidentally opened sent to us from one of Daddy's friends as a congratulatory present. I hated how goddamn flawless and brazen she was for showing up at our house, for our New Year's Eve party when she'd fucked my fiancé.

She fucked my fiancée who had loved her, and all three of us knew it.

There was a two-ton brick on my chest and nothing I did could abate it, so I cried instead.

I stared at the mess of my reflection in the powder room mirror, sniffling. I wrenched my wrist against the toilet paper roll, dabbing under my eyes to save my eye makeup.

What a mess.

To my right, Dougie sat on the closed toilet seat, studying me carefully. Taking a shuddering inhale, I swallowed back the next cry.

I was being stupid about this. Completely fucking irrational. Why couldn't I just calm down?

"What are you actually crying about?" he asked gently. "'Cause I'm not buying you're this upset over sparkling apple juice." It was a stab at a joke, but I couldn't find it in me to laugh.

I sniffled again, trying to concentrate on the revelry of the New Year's Eve festivities taking place beyond the bathroom door. They were all so happy out there and I was in here with him, ruining our night. "It really makes me nauseous."

So did meat lately, which was a shame, because I'd really loved burgers.

Dougie's eyes thinned, mistrust muddying his brows. "Penny."

Staring at my hands, I squeezed the balled-up squares of soiled toilet paper in my fist. I needed to be honest with him, even if it was all in my head. I didn't want to be like my parents, telling the other what they wanted to hear to avoid confrontation.

"She's," I tried to clear the blades in my throat, "she's really pretty."

I hated how rattled I was by her being here. Even if it was brought on by the pregnancy, or my raging hormones, I hated she made me feel this way. How insecure her presence alone made the ground under my feet feel when I knew I had no reason to be worried.

But she had discarded him, and the way her eyes had followed him left me wondering if she was experiencing buyer's remorse.

And whether Dougie might feel the same.

Had she loved him back? No. She couldn't have... she wouldn't have let him go. I knew I never would.

"Who's really pretty?" The confusion in Dougie's voice was annoyingly genuine. Sometimes, I hated how clueless and naïve he was.

"Maria."

He scoffed, and even though I wasn't looking at him, I could tell he'd rolled his eyes. I rocked my mouth, not wanting to say the words, but uttering them anyway. "Don't do that, Dougie. Not for me." Sure, I tore her apart in my mind, but he didn't need to do the same for my ego's sake—it came across as disingenuous.

He made an incorrigible sound, interrupting my thoughts. "She's not you."

"But she *is* pretty." Her hypnotic dark eyes, and her shiny blowout, and her massive fucking tits and perky ass.

Ugh.

"And she's frigid and prickly."

I squeezed my eyes together, not wanting to cry again. "Just say she's pretty." Then I could move on with my night, secure in my knowledge that he thought she was pretty, and to give me something to pick myself apart over in this dress that was unflattering, and my swollen fingers reminiscent of tiny, canned sausages. I could justify my insecurity without having to acknowledge it was me, and me alone, who was responsible for my errant thoughts, not my pregnancy.

And then I could cry about it to Henry in January when his office opened, and I booked twice weekly appointments for the rest of two-thousand-and-nine, or at least until I delivered.

"What fucking for, Penelope?" Dougie demanded in a growl, inciting my shock. My eyes flared as I kinked my neck back to regard him. He was pissed. "Why do you need to hear me tell you she's pretty?" He recoiled away from me, his hands coming to his hips while he gritted his teeth. "Maria's pretty, so what? She also fucked me over." He stroked his chin, huffing.

Even now, it was clear it still hurt him. My bottom lip trembled, the threat of more tears stinging.

Dougie dropped his hands, licked his lips. "And you know what?" I held my breath, waiting for him to break my heart and tear my world apart. "It was the *best* thing that ever happened to me because it meant I met *you.*"

I clenched my molars, but it was useless. The tears came, hot and furious.

God damnit, these hormones.

"Penelope, you're beautiful, baby." He closed the distance between us, cupping my face. "I swear to God, I haven't thought of her or anyone else since I met you."

"I feel..." Insecure, small, scared. "Unattractive."

He placed his palm on my knee, squeezing me gently. "I find you pretty fucking sexy pregnant."

"You do?"

His forehead found mine, his eyes falling shut. "Definitely."

I wrapped my arms around his neck, leaning into him, trying to slow my thoughts down as I inhaled his scent. There had been nothing errant in any of his responses, only an indisputable honesty. He really hadn't noticed Maria, and if he had, all he'd felt was ambivalence coupled by a tinge of gratitude.

He was right. If things hadn't panned out the way they had, if she hadn't decided that he wasn't worthy of her, if she'd kept him to herself?

We wouldn't be here. There wouldn't be a party raging beyond us, eagerly waiting to ring in a new year and celebrate our new home.

I should feel thankful she'd made the decisions she had.

"I love you." He offered me a tender kiss, running the back of his fingers against my cheek to mop up more of my tears. "And I'll tell her to leave in a heartbeat if that makes you feel better."

"No, don't do that." I laughed, dropping my arms. "It's rude." I didn't want her ringing in the new year alone. I wasn't that cruel. Although it was weird she didn't have friends of her own or something better to do tonight.

"Fuck rude," he intoned seriously. "I want you to be happy and comfortable, always, especially in *our* own home. You know I don't give a shit about anything else." I liked his emphasis on our.

"I know." My lips lifted with a tiny smile. I felt a bit better now that we'd talked about it. "I'm ready to get back to the party now."

"You sure?" He ran his thumb over my cheek, my face leaning into his warm palm. "I could tell all these assholes to beat it. We could..." he trailed off, leaning closer. "Turn on the fireplace and eat those fancy cheeses all by ourselves?"

I swatted his chest.

"No go?"

"No go, Mr. Patterson."

"Okay, one last attempt..." The hand on my knee slid forward, brushing the hemline of my dress. "*You* could eat the fancy cheeses, *I* could eat you."

I sucked back a breath, my mouth growing momentarily parched as the lewd thought installed itself in my brain. That was a nice thought, actually.

"What do you think?" His fingers grazed the panel of my panties, my core aching with desperation for more, white noise filling my ears chasing any lingering doubts away. "My lips sucking your clit, my tongue in your pussy, you coming all over my face with the fire crackling in the background... sounds pretty good, doesn't it?" he husked, turning my nipples into hardened points under my bra.

It did. It sounded superb, and despite my legs parting as far as the dress would allow me to, what came out of me again was, "No go."

He broke out into a hardy laugh.

"But I think I'd like that for breakfast." I winked.

Dougie shot me a shit-eating grin. "I like the way you think, Penny." He extracted the hand from my thigh, curling my fingers. He brushed the pad of his thumb against the stone in my engagement ring, bringing it to his mouth. "I can't wait to marry you."

"I can't wait to marry you, too." I tilted my head back, looking up at him through my tacky lashes. He was lessening the weight in my chest where the insecurity had bred, and slowly the dulling of my senses faded away.

We had everything. Who cared about Maria or anyone else?

"I promise you I'm going to spend the rest of my life making sure you smile every single day," he assured, kissing the tip of my nose. "You just watch."

I smoothed a hand over the slight swell of my stomach. "Things will get hectic when he gets here."

His nostrils flared, his eyes dropping to my stomach. "You think it's a he?"

I nodded. "I don't know why, but something tells me it is."

"A son…" he trailed off, crooking a smile that flipped my insides. "We're gonna have a son."

"I was thinking Christopher."

"Christopher?" he repeated.

An impatient knock sounded from the bathroom door. "I gotta take a leek."

"Beat it. Go upstairs," Dougie called out. "First door on your left."

I wasn't even sure who was on the other side, but at that moment, I didn't care about being polite. "For his name." I swallowed. "I like the way Christopher Cullimore Patterson sounds."

Dougie took in a deep breath, appearing momentarily tongue-tied as he struggled to string his words together. "That's a strong name."

"Do you like it?"

He nodded. "Love it." He fitted his hand over my own, and I knew someday when he did that, there would be a powerful kick against his palm in greeting. "We should get back out there so we can hurry them home."

"You just want breakfast."

"I just want you to myself," he countered with a laugh.
And the funny thing was? That was all I wanted, too.
Dougie, Christopher and me.
Everything else? It didn't matter.
As long as I had my little family, I had everything.

Chapter Twenty-Four

Dougie

Present

NEVER IN A MILLION YEARS DID I THINK I'D EVER FIND MYSELF BACK HERE, like this. But as I stood at my ma's front door, my key in one hand, the overnight bag in the other, and the chilly October wind stinging my skin—my instincts told me to get back in the truck and go home to my wife and our son.

What the fuck had I done?

You don't deserve her.

That thought had kept me up last night. While Pen curled into my body the way she used to, with her forehead pressed against the side of my chest, her arm and leg slung over my frame, I thought about all the ways I'd meant to protect her and our life.

I thought about our first new year together, about all the promises I'd made to her in that bathroom while our party raged, about the insecurity she'd expressed toward Maria after I confessed that we'd had something once.

And when I had felt insecure, when I'd had doubts, I...

I took a shuddering breath and shoved my key in the door, twisting the lock.

The scent of baked bread hit me as the door creaked open, revealing the neat foyer. There was an end table older than me near the door with a tidy catchall bowl containing Ma's car keys to her beat-up Honda Civic alongside her bright orange frame bag purse. Voices from the television in the adjacent living room caught my ears, my head turning to the source. Was she in there?

"Douglas?" Ma's Irish lilt came from the kitchen. "Is that you?"

I cleared my throat, attempting to brace myself for her disappointment. "Yeah, it's me."

"Good!" Her enthusiasm made my stomach lurch. God, I wanted to be sick. "I've just pulled a soda bread out of the oven, come get it while it's still hot." That's what I'd smelled when I'd walked in the door, something innately yeasty and freshly baked had wafted over the normal familiar scent of Ma's place.

It was Thursday. That's what Ma did on Thursday's. She baked. Bread or scones, or whatever her heart desired. Normalcy existed here. In Ma's innocence beyond this foyer, I held onto the fleeting seconds where I was just a dutiful son, visiting her in the morning. I'd glazed over what had happened between Katrina and me a few weeks ago, telling Ma instead that the project Trina was overseeing was running on a tight budget and I'd volunteered to do the thing I'd once suggested Sean do a long time ago—temporarily laid me off.

The trouble with lying was once you started, you had a hard time stopping. The truth wasn't the first thing that touched your tongue when you opened your mouth. No, it was a steady stream of embellishments meant to betray the person listening.

I was fucking tired of lying, of being deceitful.

My fist found my rib cage, kneading hard, wishing like hell I could massage my lungs. I couldn't breathe, I just kept seeing Pen's face from this morning in my head.

I wished I could take it all back.

Ma stuck her head out of the kitchen, her smile collapsing immediately when she stared at the bag. "What's happened?"

Where the fuck did I start?

I opened my mouth, but nothing came out, not even a fucking garble. My mouth closed, my molars working under each other as I tried to keep my emotions in check. But the more she gaped at me with worry overflowing in her eyes and her mouth twisted in horror, the faster I lost the war.

What was the rule about crying in front of your ma?

Were you allowed to do that after the age of ten?

Did I care?

The bag slipped from my hands, colliding to the floor, bringing my weak knees with it.

I did this to us. I fucking did this.

I'd had everything.

Ma was on the floor with me in seconds, the rug under us shifting with the force as her arms came around my thick neck. She drew me closer to her with a herculean strength. "*Mo mhac,*" she urged in Gaelic, her soothing hands sweeping my back. *My son.* "Tell me."

But I knew. I knew once I started talking, when the embellishments washed away, what remained would change everything between Ma and me, too. There was a lot of ugly I'd concealed from her, and I wasn't sure I was anymore ready to see it than she was. "You're never gonna forgive me, Ma."

Hell, I lacked the confidence to believe I'd ever forgive myself.

I didn't know if her heart could handle it, literally. And I couldn't deal with losing anyone else right now—especially her.

"Forgive you for what, Douglas?" I knew she was trying for calm, but her voice quavered.

I drew back, taking a rushed breath as my insides twisted and my head spun. I didn't know if I wanted to have a fucking panic attack with the way my chest grew tight and my extremities shook against her, or vomit all over the low-pile rug under us she had by the front door.

"Come on," Ma said, encouraging me up from the floor.

I couldn't even look at her dead-on as I hauled my pathetic ass up. Ma had always been fairer, her hair a boxed orange-blond shade reminiscent of the skin on a butternut squash. She'd pulled it back in a clip, her bangs frizzy around her lined face, traces of gray catching on the light coming from the sidelights of her front door.

Her and Sean's ma had a reoccurring date every couple of weeks where they'd take turns mixing boxed dye and coloring each other's roots to mask the gray.

Which was funny considering Sean's ma hadn't liked my ma when we were kids—hell, I wasn't sure she'd liked me much, either. My ma was boisterous and had a lot of opinions she didn't keep to herself. I was the kid with the flaky dad, who eventually was completely out of the picture a couple of years after I'd met Sean. But damn, was I determined to be a part of the Tavareses brood.

Not because I didn't love my ma, but because their family seemed so complete and picture-perfect.

We were different, and Connie Tavares didn't like different. She'd had enough of that to contend with after emigrating here. But when Sean's dad died? My ma knew what Connie needed because, in her own way, she'd experienced that grief, too.

A friend.

And despite Connie's misjudgment, they'd founded an unlikely kinship with each other that guaranteed neither of them would ever be alone again. That used to comfort me, but ever since my stupid fucking mistake, I'd always held my breath with worry that someday soon, my ma or Connie would find out what had happened.

That day had never come.

Not until today. But at least it was on my terms.

Ma clutched onto my arm as she led me into her kitchen, the heat of the oven blasting against me as we passed it. The weathered nineties-esque green tile countertops mostly tidied, save for a squared cue card with curled edges containing the recipe Ma had gotten from my nan before she'd left Ireland in the early eighties. The loaf of bread sat next to the open recipe tin, cooling on a wired rack with steam wafting from it.

She only let me go when I settled into a honeyed farmhouse style kitchen chair, the tired padding under me decorative at best, seeing as it wasn't comfortable, and the wood still ate into my bones. My elbows found the table, my open palms a resting place for my face. I just wanted to sleep and when I woke up, not be living this nightmare.

Ma didn't speak as she stepped back. From the corner of my eye, I caught her appraising me as her arms folded over her chest. "Douglas." I winced, because she had made that face—the one that used to warn me as a kid that the jig was up. "Your clothes are hanging off your body. I know you're not well."

I shook my head.

"And, you haven't been for some time," she hesitated, her arms slipped as her hands found the front-facing pockets of her apron. "I haven't seen Penelope in a while... not since I told her things would be okay, with whatever's been going on between you two." And she was sad about it. I caught it in the brittle way she'd said my wife's name. "Have I upset her?"

Guilt.

So much fucking guilt.

Another person trying to share the burden of our lies with us.

Sean.

Raquel.

Ma.

Who'd be next?

How many more casualties would there be now that our house of cards was tumbling down?

Pen used to come here all the time just to hang out with my ma, especially when Raquel had fucked off after her breakup with Sean. Pen had needed someone, and Ma was there. They'd watch *Coronation Street* together, or Pen would take her to run errands. She'd enjoyed spending time with my ma in a way she hadn't with her own parents, and while I'd wished that her relationship with Walter and Evelyn was better, I was grateful that she had something special with her.

But Ma was right. Pen hadn't been here in months, and that was on me. Not her.

I tried to control the trembling in my jaw, dropping my gaze as I leaned back in my seat.

She closed her eyes, her chest caving in. "Bread first, Douglas," she decided. "And a tea before you tell Mam what's happened."

My elbows found the kitchen table once more, my head bowing as I hooked my hands on the back of my neck, staring at the knit placemat she'd made herself, the stitches once tight, fraying a little like I was. I let my lids drop for a moment, listening intently as she futzed around the kitchen—the seal on the fridge opened and closed, the shuffling of a carton of milk, and a jar and dish grazing against the shelf, followed by the snick of a drawer opening and closing and the metal din of her searching the cutlery, cut through the silence of the room.

But I still couldn't look at her. No, if my eyes remained shut, I didn't have to confront the clusterfuck my life had turned into this year. I wouldn't have to see the shame.

My eyes opened when Ma settled the plate in front of me. The sweetness from the jam mixing with the bread she'd spread on the still hot slices drifted into my nose, nostalgia flanking me from when I was a kid. The whistle of the kettle on the stove drew her away. She cut the heat, the soft pouring of milk in a mug and the plop of a tea bag followed by the boiled water hitting my ears.

Her worn-in slippers clipped against the kitchen linoleum floors as she returned to the table, setting one mug in front of me and the other in front of her. "Eat."

"I'm not hungry."

She jabbed the table with her pointer finger twice. "Your clothes are wearing you. *Eat.*"

There was no point in arguing. I picked the slice of hot bread, biting into it. I wasn't sure if it was because I hadn't eaten out of pleasure in a long time, but the combination of the rich butter and the sweetness from the jam burst on my palate, almost overwhelming my senses.

"Good?" she asked.

Chewing, I nodded.

Ma offered me an amiable smile. But I didn't miss it. The worry flickering in her gaze like whatever I was going to tell her was going to change everything, and she wasn't sure how she was going to handle it.

The kitchen was quiet, too quiet. Ma was normally the type to rush to fill the silence, a motormouth who always had too much to say about nothing and everything. Her need to maintain the silence was as jarring as it was out of character.

When I got through the first slice, I pushed the plate back. My stomach wouldn't let me eat the second slice, not until I tried to get the words out. "I did something."

"Drink your tea," she replied, pushing the mug forward.

"Ma, I don't want tea." I wanted a whiskey. Four knuckles worth. Fuck, gimmie the bottle at this point.

"Tea."

I scratched the space between my brows, blowing out a breath before I indulged her and took a sip. It was too fucking hot, burning a path down my tract.

"Okay." She drummed her fingers along her own mug with a floral print on it. "Tell me."

She leaned over the table, staring at the contents of her mug, and I knew with the surety of my last name that this would change the way she looked at me irrevocably.

'Cause I'd almost done to Penelope what my father had done to her. The memory of their arguing back then greeted me. I'd been too young to understand what Ma had screamed at Dad about, but I remembered him coming home late, reeking of someone else's perfume with his shirt misbuttoned and his hair mused.

He hadn't tried to be discreet about it, and when I was old enough to understand, I realized it was because he hadn't cared about hurting Ma—he wanted to. But in the process, he'd hurt me, too. Ma hadn't deserved it, neither had Penelope.

I could blame Dad. I could point the finger and say childhood trauma installed a broken system of beliefs in my mind, but it hadn't. That had been me. I'd always sworn to do better, and all I'd done had become another washed out version of him.

I had to own that.

"Pen and I have been in a rough place this past year," I began, a timid shake trembling through my hands as I played with the crumbs on my plate.

"I suspected that," she whispered, her grip tightening around the handle of the mug.

Of course, she had. She wasn't stupid. "And back in May, I,"

She closed her eyes, bracing herself.

I exhaled the words in a rush. "I almost did something stupid."

Her green eyes nearly leveled me. "With whom?" She knew. Without me needing to spell it out to her, Ma had already filled in the blanks of my near indiscretion.

Her disappointment was a two-ton slab on my chest, but I knew I needed to see this through, even if it killed me. "Maria."

The chair jerked back as Ma shot to her feet. "You did *what* with *who*?"

"I didn't do anything with her," I rushed out. "I just—"

"Went there and made a mess, did ya?" Her accent always grew harder and thicker when she got pissed off. "Douglas, you've gone too far this time."

I'd never been much of a troublemaker. A periodic shit disturber, sure, but what teenage boy wasn't? I'd learned to talk myself out of things, but I never brought my shit to Ma's door.

Not like this. No amount of talking would fix it, either.

"Ma, *nothing* happened." I was tiring of saying that.

I still thought about it, had still wanted it at the time.

And I might have done it had Maria reciprocated when I'd put my hands on her waist and drew her close to me. I touched the ends of her hair like I did with Pen, and for a split second, I almost convinced myself that it was my wife standing in front of me and not her.

It was Chanel No. 5 and ginger, peaches and vanilla I smelled, not Maria's creamy coconut. I wanted to turn off the lights and convince myself she could be Penelope for the night.

Maria broke the illusion when she told me she wasn't the solution to my problem, and I fell apart in her arms because she was right.

She wasn't the solution to my problem, but being there, when I knew I shouldn't, on the verge of ruining Maria's new relationship and destroying my marriage, knowing that my wife didn't want me anymore? It killed me.

If only I'd known that what was truly keeping Penelope from me back then was because she was mourning a loss on her own. My throat expanded, my cheeks momentarily swelling as nausea rushed at me.

I could keep saying nothing happened, but something had happened. Our lives as we knew it crashed down all around us into a million jagged little pieces and there was no way of gluing them back together again.

"What do you mean nothing happened?" Ma demanded, her face flushing red as she sat back down. "If nothing happened, then you wouldn't be in this situation." She shook her head. "I knew Maria fancied you when you were younger, but this is disgraceful." A long time ago, hearing those words would have jostled something inside of me.

Excitement, hope.

Now, they just annoyed me.

Years ago, I would have given my left nut just to be on Maria's radar in any capacity, but she'd never been interested in giving me the time of day. I'd always been a nuisance, her kid brother's annoying friend who was arrogant and pushy.

Hell, she'd broken my fucking nose when I'd asked her out at fifteen.

She would never give me a chance, didn't matter what I did to make her see that there could be a her and me if she let her guard down a little. So sure, I'd had girlfriends, I'd had one-night stands, I had reliable fuck buddies that put out without a second thought—but none of them had lived up to what I thought Maria would be like in my head.

I always believed that was the only place Maria would ever exist for me—my mind—at least until that faithful day a year and a half before I met Penelope. I'd gone to pay my respects on the anniversary of Sean's father's death, just like I did every year.

Maria had been there, on the ground no less, completely out of character, yelling at her father's tombstone. I'd hesitated to approach her, but I did anyway.

Call it stupidity or brass nuts.

I figured I already knew what the worst thing she could do was. The evidence still existed on my face from when she'd struck me as teenagers and broken my nose. When I lowered myself to my haunches next to her, I expected to be confronted by the gale of her rage. But she sucked back a surprised breath, her chest caving in while her bottom lip trembled. She tried to mask it with the back of her hand, but something quirked in her expression.

She surprised the hell out of me and launched herself into my arms and sobbed into my neck.

Which was a shock in and of itself.

Maria Tavares didn't cry in front of anyone, *especially* me. No, she had a facade to maintain, the one where she was beautiful, cold, and in control. But that shock paled in comparison when she lifted her weary eyes to me after the sobs finished racking through her, studying me through her soot-black lashes, and her dark gaze dropped to my mouth.

I took that as my invitation, lowering my forehead to meet hers.

But she'd been the one to decide to kiss me when she was done crying all over my shirt. And was I really gonna say no when her swollen lips invited me back to her place, and her coffin-shaped fingernails dug into my thick thighs and dragged upward?

You didn't tell your fantasies 'no', you bargained with them to stay in dreamland a little while longer. Except that was all Maria was supposed to be to me—a fantasy, a wish made from a fifteen-year-old kid a long time ago.

She was never meant to be mine. I knew that now. Hell, I knew it when I got into my truck a couple of months ago and drove to her place in a daze. I was just...

Confused.

Hurt.

Unwanted.

Desperate.

"Maria didn't do anything." I stared out the window, watching as a leaf fell from the branch of the birch tree in the backyard. "It was all me. "

"Oh?" Ma folded her arms, unimpressed and in disbelief. "It takes two, and that girl was always bad news."

The laugh that left me was dry, earning her glare. Ma was trying to shift the blame, just like she had with Dad's side piece decades earlier, but I could see it in her face. She didn't want to believe I'd turned out like him after all. We all had to accept things about ourselves we didn't like.

"And what's so funny about that?" she demanded, her fists balled at her sides.

I shrugged, not really knowing how to articulate it. It was odd thinking of Maria being the one pegged as trouble when, in actuality, it had always been me.

"You were always sniffing around her, waiting for her to offer you a crumb."

My mouth set into a hard line, staring at the very crumbs on my plate. "I know."

Ma leaned back in her seat, and for a split second, I felt as though she was trying to create distance between us. It made my heart ache. "Tell me exactly what you did," she said thinly.

"We didn't..." my features collapsed. I wasn't going to say 'sex' in front of my mother, that was too much. Hell, I was pretty sure we'd skipped this conversation entirely. She'd left that responsibility to school yard boys and high school health class.

Impatience had Ma filling in the blank. "*Fuck*?"

My nostrils flared, my jaw growing slack. "Ma!" I blurted.

She rolled her eyes. "I'm a God-fearing woman, but I'm not a stupid one."

"No," I snapped back, pressing a palm against my stomach to settle the contents. "We didn't do *that*."

She shifted uncomfortably in her seat, her teeth gnashing as she found the will to ask her next question. "Were you intimate with her in other ways?"

"No."

Confusion swept over her face. "Then what happened?"

"I was somewhere I wasn't supposed to be, and if Maria..." The tingling set off in my chest, the heart palpitations fluttering as I remembered that night. "If Maria had been interested, I might have." Instead, I'd held another woman in my arms and cried for the wife who didn't want me.

Ma couldn't even look at me. "I could knock your pan in right now." Yeah, I'd want to violently beat me up, too. "After everything." She was talking to herself now, her voice quivering. "You went and lost your head and did something so foolish to your wife." Her eyes darted around her quaint kitchen, looking anywhere but at me.

She'd raised me in this house, but my upbringing hadn't been enough to prevent me from becoming the very person who destroyed her.

Probably didn't help I looked a whole lot like him, too.

My skin was hot, my face flushing as the realization that the relationship between Ma and I was changing right before my very eyes.

But I'd known this was a real risk as I'd driven over here. I knew there was a chance we might not recover from this, that I might ruin another relationship.

"Your face," she asked. "Penelope's handy work?"

"Nope." I popped the 'p', clearing my throat. "Sean's."

This time, Ma snorted. "You've told him what you've done, have you?"

"Not quite."

But I was sure when I did, the current state of my face would pale in comparison. He'd take another cheap shot at me, only this time, I'd allow him to land more than one strike.

Ma's face wrinkled, contempt touching her mouth. She untucked her chair, taking my plate from me and moving toward the compost tin on her counter. "You can stay the night, Douglas. But tomorrow, you'll wind your neck in and go home to your wife."

I didn't dare argue with her.

"Ma." My skin heated as I prepared myself to say the last part, the patent tremor working its way through me, my limbs feeling momentarily boneless. "There's more."

Glass hitting the stainless-steel sink rung out in the air as she tossed the plate into the sink. It was a miracle the thing hadn't broken.

She glowered at me, her hands planting on her hips. "What?"

I stared at my socks, my big toe pressing against the thinning layers. "Penelope told me yesterday that…" I tried to swallow the lump that had formed in my throat, but I knew I'd have more success trying to swallow a fistful of sand with cottonmouth.

"She told you what?"

I couldn't do it. I squeezed my knee weakly, my stomach heaving as the words left me and the involuntary tears came. I couldn't lie to the woman who raised me anymore. "She lost a baby, Ma. I-I-I didn't know."

I slouched at the waist, the wound ripping open again as I leaned into my knees, fisted my hair and I let myself break again. My shrunken ribs made it impossible to breathe, my heart pounded in my ears and every part of my skin burned as the shame slithered through me like a snake.

How had I been so blind to her cry for help? My Penelope wasn't like what she had become. The woman I fell in love with hadn't given a shit about a big wedding. She'd been prepared to marry me in a hospital gown with her hair a mess, six stitches running from her vagina to her asshole, and the sweat from giving birth still spread on her skin. She didn't care about Michelin star chefs or designer wedding gowns because she spread peanut butter on her hamburgers and tacos and wore my boxer briefs to bed. This was a woman who stole my deodorant and razors because they 'worked' better.

And I'd missed it all. She'd been hiding behind the pretension and the poise because she didn't want me to see.

After last night, after… taking this time to myself, to get my head on straight, I didn't know where we went from here, or how she could still love me when I despised myself.

Pen had given me everything I'd ever wanted, and I'd destroyed it, just like that.

I didn't deserve her forgiveness.

The urge to cower away in disgust recoiled through me when I heard the shuffling of Ma's slippers approaching me. I prayed like hell she would just hit me, give me something to distract myself momentarily from the pain shredding my insides.

Releasing my hair, I pressed a fist to my mouth just to keep the agonized sob in check. I deserved this.

But then I felt her hands on my shoulders, squeezing with all her might—not to inflict pain, but to remind me she was still here. I let the sob out. Ma wrapped her hands around my neck, my face burying against her fleshy abdomen, soaking in her warmth and losing myself in the sensation of her hands smoothing my hair out just like she'd done when I was a kid.

"This isn't how I raised you, Douglas." She quivered against me, and I knew she was crying, but I spared her dignity as much as my own, keeping my head tipped down.

"I know." My voice shook as I snuffled. She'd done everything in her power to ensure that I'd be the opposite of the man who'd fathered me, and I... I'd become just like him, hadn't I? The apple hadn't fallen too far from the tree after all.

"I raised you to be a man who honored his vows and stayed true to his word, even when things got hard." Her arms tightened around me. "You have a son to think about. That boy deserves his parents to honor their vows. You don't get to run away when it gets hard."

She let me go slowly, her hands settling on my cheeks as she forced me to regard her. Tears clung to her lashes, forcing me to squeeze my eyes shut before the snapshot memory could etch itself in place—but no matter what I did to erase that memory, I knew I'd never forget it.

I couldn't.

"Tomorrow."

"Tomorrow," I echoed.

Tomorrow, I needed to go home.

But today? Today, I could just be the guy who needed his ma.

Chapter Twenty-Five

Penelope

Two years ago...

When we talked about love, we didn't consider its weight.

How could you equate the thrumming in your veins and the stutter in your chest to a number measured on a scale?

No, we'd been led to believe that something as transcendental and indescribable as love could never have a sum at all.

But it did.

It was nine pounds and four ounces, with rosy cheeks and tiny fists. It had a mighty, helpless cry, and promised to be the source of my heartbeat for the rest of my days.

And his name was Christopher.

Christopher Cullimore Patterson.

I watched my fiancé with our son, the adoration sweeping over me, expunging every lingering trace of discomfort in my body. It momentarily made me forget the soreness between my legs, the ache of the stitches in my perineum from the tear of delivering our love.

The IV in my hand itched as it pumped fluids meant to rehydrate me back into my body, the sterility of the room causing my nose to itch. The table near the hospital room window was covered in bright blue gift-wrapped boxes, a soft brown bear, and flowers and cards I'd yet to read. In the corner, a foiled balloon with *Welcome, Baby Boy!* affixed to a sparkly weight at its end danced in the current of air coming from an overhead vent. Beyond the closed hospital room door, a distorted intercom paged a doctor over the squeaky wheeling of a cart passing.

None of it mattered to me. My sole focus was on the overwhelming love in this room.

Any doubt I'd felt leading up to this moment that I wasn't equipped to be a mother despite my desire to be one had been replaced at the sound of that viable, healthy cry ringing out in the air. While I was too numb from the epidural, I'd felt this all-consuming whoosh rush through me at his hearty roar of life and I knew there would be no moment greater than this one in the entirety of my existence as I'd lost myself to this near out-of-body experience.

Seeing his face felt like I'd taken my first full breath in nearly twenty-nine years. Dougie had turned into a bleary-eyed mess, his face full of wonderment and reverence as they clamped the umbilical cord and handed him the scissors. Any anxiety he'd expressed, any doubt he'd had, vanished at the epochal snip that changed our lives forever.

Every insecurity and worry melted away when they placed Christopher against my chest, his head pressed against my hammering heart. All I could do was cry as my memory emptied itself of the recollection of morning sickness, the discomfort in my swollen extremities, my unpredictable mood swings, my insecurities—gone—creating room for new feelings.

Some had warned me to not worry if I wasn't immediately taken with my newfound role, but looking upon his small features, trying to determine who he'd grow up to look like, how could I not be completely and helplessly in love? I'd felt overwhelmed in the immediate aftermath, that all I could do was sob inconsolably.

How could I love someone this much? How could our bond be this instantaneous?

We'd made a baby with ten perfect fingers and toes, and round, curious blue eyes fringed with fair lashes that would turn color with time.

I hoped his eyes would turn into my favorite shade of forest green, a little lighter near his irises. That his plump, rosy cheeks would melt into the arches of my bone structure. That when his smile took form, he'd have a mouth that crooked to the right and promised mischief and adventure.

Just like his dad.

I hoped he'd never spend a moment of his life wondering if we loved him. I hoped he knew he could be whoever he wanted to be, that we would love him in this life and in the next.

That he was our son, our forever.

Dougie's face filled with love and pride; his thick brows relaxed as he brushed a thick finger over Christopher's tiny digits. His Adam's apple bobbed, throat weaving as he tried to clear the emotion from his voice, his accent thickening as he spoke. "He's real perfect, Penny."

I smiled, wincing as I shifted up the mattress and adjusted my back against the too-soft hospital pillows. It was surreal seeing them together, never mind trying to comprehend the incredible thing my body had done for us.

"How are you feeling?" Dougie asked, meeting my gaze.

"Like I'd love nothing more than to watch you with him forever." Truthfully, I felt like I'd been fucked dry, but that wasn't the way I wanted to recall this memory when I was old, and Christopher grew up. I was sore, my lower body burning, and I was desperate for a sedative and twelve hours of sleep.

But beyond all that? I was content and overwhelmingly elated.

Dougie chuckled. "Well, lucky for you, you can." He stepped closer, settling on the edge of my bed. "You really are incredible." I waved him off as if it was no consequence, but he shook his head. "I mean it, Penelope. You are."

Beaming at him, the blush settled on my cheeks. "Lots of women have babies."

He was silent for a moment, consideration softening his features. "Not every woman can be in labor and still find compassion for their friend," he replied, staring down at Christopher again as his profile tensed. Dougie's mouth pulled to the right, his teeth worrying his lip. "I ripped into Raquel pretty badly."

The tight sigh left me. I couldn't fault him, not entirely. A few months ago, on New Year's Eve, during our hybrid housewarming and New Year's party where I'd had a mini breakdown, Raquel had broken up with Sean and up and left without so much as a word to any of us. To make matters worse, she'd made it impossible for any of us to contact her until she reached out in February.

My blood pressure had gone up. Dougie blamed her for my preeclampsia, but to be honest, even if her absence had exacerbated my stress levels, I still didn't blame her. It didn't change that it hurt me. She couldn't confide in me of all people before she left.

Raquel was my best friend. She could tell me anything and everything, and I'd never fault her for it. But some part of me recognized she knew I would have tried to make her stay.

And as someone who felt as though she'd lived her formative years in a cage, I knew how desperately she needed to fly and find herself.

Sighing, I observed Dougie's face close up, as though he were trying to choose his next words wisely.

"She's fu—" he paused, glancing down at Christopher. "She's *messing* with Sean's head."

There was some degree of truth to that, I supposed.

"She doesn't mean to." I ran my fingers along the stiff hospital sheets where Raquel had sat hours ago, confessing everything to me through a flurry of apologies.

She loved Sean—I knew she did. But I also recognized firsthand that... "She's just scared."

Terrified of the weight of her love for a single person after experiencing so much loss—someone who could hurt her if she allowed herself to fall into him the way he wanted her to.

But he'd love her forever, if she'd only let him.

Fearful people were reactive people. Hurt people pushed away the people they loved the most, like a fucked-up defense mechanism. They thrashed in shallow waters and swallowed lungful's of water even though all they had to do was stand upright.

Love made us forget parts of ourselves. Sometimes, we let go of who we were, other times, we held onto these traces and kept them clutched close to our chest as if they were the only thing that would keep us buoyant and safe.

But I understood. We all had choices to make, a unique path to carve out that was ours. I'd once told her to get into the driver's seat of her life instead of sitting idly in the passenger's seat. And this time? I trusted her to drive.

But Dougie wasn't convinced. "Well then, she needs to either get un-scared, or leave Sean alone."

"He hasn't exactly left her alone, either," I volleyed back. And he hadn't. Sure, Raquel had broken up with him, but it hadn't stopped Sean from traveling across the country in a do-or-die attempt to get her back.

Dougie's jaw flexed. "He's in love with her. What do you expect?"

"And what do you expect from a girl who's only ever been loved by *me*?" Raquel didn't know any better. Of course, she was going to flee at the first sign of trouble. Sure, I'd been angry about that at first, but now…

Some part of me understood it.

It was hard to believe you deserved love after never having it, to question and not trust it. To look for inconsistencies and pick at it until you uncovered a half-truth and run with it to justify your instincts, however wrong they might be.

Dougie's stare fell back on Christopher. "I guess I'm having a hard time feeling compassionate toward someone who can hurt people like that."

"Weren't you the one who's been secretly taking calls with her since she left?" He thought I wasn't paying attention, and while I didn't think he'd continued to engage her to be deceptive, I knew he'd done it because whether he wanted to admit it—he understood it, too.

"That's not the same," he insisted, his eyes growing flinty. "I did that for you."

"Or were you doing it for her?" I asked softly, raising my chin a little.

He flinched at the accusation, a sharp inhalation whistling through his deviated septum.

"Is it because some part of you aligns with her, Dougie?"

I thought back to the night she'd reached out that first time. I'd been too angry to have a full conversation with her, short of demanding her to return home, but Dougie... I'd picked up parts of their conversation from where I'd eavesdropped in the kitchen, and I couldn't help but believe part of what he was saying to Raquel was just as much for him as it was for her.

He'd told her by running away, she was reinforcing the cycle of shame, and she was perpetuating everything she hated. And while he was here at my side, I worried sometimes that he didn't fully believe he was worthy of this life, of our forever.

I played with the starched sheets, my fingers journeying over the little valleys that had formed with my shifting. "Sometimes, I get this sense that there's a part of you who questions whether you deserve all of this, too." I gesticulated toward Christopher. "Our life, our son..." my voice dropped off into a whisper, "*me*."

I could tell he was marinating on my observation while Christopher yawned in his arms, his eyelids dropping as sleep came to claim him again.

"Last Thanksgiving," Dougie began, his mouth rocking from side to side. "I overheard some stuff I wasn't meant to."

My stomach sank as I cringed, my face falling. "You were listening," I murmured.

"Yeah." He let out a dry laugh. "The pantry's got great acoustics and thin as fuck walls."

I squeezed my eyes closed, blowing out my cheeks. "Frieda."

He'd heard what my parents called him.

Inferior.

An unsatisfactory choice.

"Your parents aren't even here, Pen," he murmured, looking around the room and taking in their noticeable absence. "Who goes to the Cayman Islands knowing their daughter was days away from delivering their grandchild?"

It was on brand, and I expected nothing less from them. "I don't care," I replied. I was happy they weren't here. They would have stressed me out. They were already pissed that I hadn't wanted to see any of their recommended doctors, that I wouldn't deliver Christopher in Connecticut, or at least Boston.

I delivered Christopher in the same hospital Dougie had been born in. It was important to me, like adding another layer to our little family's roots.

"I do, Pen," he replied, grit entering his tone. "I care that there might be merit to what your parents said, and that they avoided this monumental moment in our lives because of *me*." His jaw clenched, and even though he was less than a foot away, I could sense his heart beating wildly in his chest. "I'm scared that I'm going to mess this up, that I'm not going to be a good dad, or," he faltered, his expression growing pained. "A good husband."

"Of course you are, Dougie," I said, tilting my head. "Do you know why I fell in love with you?"

"I mean…" He bent his neck, making a gesture with his chin to his groin, raising his suggestive brows. His asymmetrical smile rendered me quiet for a moment until I couldn't control it anymore.

I snorted out a laugh. It was the best I could do. My lower body hurt too much to laugh. I shook my head. "That part is very nice, but no." I extended a hand to him, flitting my fingers. "It's because you make me feel rich."

His brows muddied in the middle, confusion filtering in his eyes as he stared down at my hand, the one he'd held in stores, on car rides, on the couch. The hand I wanted him to hold for the rest of my life.

"It's not about money to me, Dougie. I've had money all of my life, and I've seen what money does to people." I rolled my lips together as he reached for my hand, scissoring our fingers together. "It buys them short-lived happiness, but the dopamine fades and they're searching for their next hit." We locked eyes, and I watched as his jaw turned to granite, trying to hold it together. "They're never going to understand what you and I have because the concept is too big for them to grasp. They don't know what it's like to wake up in the morning and feel well rested and content in a room that had little in it. Or how delicious pasta tastes even though it's all we've had to eat in days, or the joy in even washing my hair with your 5-in-1 shampoo... they don't know how much those moments meant to me, because I was experiencing them with *you*."

His foot jiggled against the ground, his leg bouncing a little as his face crumpled.

I got this sense he was beginning to finally understand. "I don't care how they perceive you, Dougie. They're never going to have what we have."

Dougie sniffled, releasing my hand slowly. "Hey, little man," he let out a shuddering breath, his fingers sweeping across the blanket Christopher was wrapped up in. "You mind if your old man cries? Real men cry, y'know."

I broke out into another laugh, wincing at the pinching and burning sensation between my legs. "Ow."

"Stop laughing," he scolded, flashing me his red-rimmed eyes. "You're gonna hurt yourself."

I shook my head. "Hardly feel it," I lied.

Crooking my finger at him, I beckoned him closer. He shifted on the edge of the mattress, clutching Christopher close to his chest like he'd let no harm come his way. Framing his bearded cheeks with my hands, I studied every detail on his face. Every line near the corners of his eyes, the distinct twist in his nose, the way the shade of green in his eyes grew lighter closer to his pupil. "I don't want a manufactured life, a duplicate of the ones my parents have. I don't need you to provide for me." My chin lifted. "All I want from you is for you to spend the rest of your life loving me."

Dougie leaned forward, pressing his forehead to mine. "I can do that."

I swept my thumbs over the arches of his cheeks. "Stay with me, Dougie. Even when it gets hard, even when they say and do things they shouldn't... know I'm always in your corner, and how I feel about you? It's never going to change, okay?"

He nodded against my forehead. "Okay."

"We're in this together."

"We're in this together," he echoed, the words penetrating my insides.

"And that's all that matters to me."

"I promise I'm gonna be the man you deserve, Penelope." He kissed the tip of my nose. "And the best fucking dad I can be." He paused, his eyes crinkling in the corners with a wince. "Aw, shit, I swore."

I smiled. "I think we've got some time before that's a real problem. Until then..." I leaned back against the stack of cheap pillows. "I can tell you how much I fucking love you."

He grinned at me, my insides dissolving into a puddle of mush once more. God, what he did to me. My heart soared.

"I fucking love you, too, Penelope Cullimore." He winked at me. "And I can't wait to marry the hell out of you."

That was all that was missing now, wasn't it? The permanence of a piece of paper to solidify that he was mine, and I was his. "We should just do it this week," I suggested, touching my lips. "When we leave."

Dougie's smile collapsed a little, confusion touching the corners of his mouth. "Do what this week?"

It was crazy, but... "Get married."

His green eyes distended. He shook his head, staring down at Christopher. "We can't do that."

"Why the hell not?" I mean, aside from the fact that I was still here for at least one more day until my blood pressure levels were back up and the room wasn't spinning now and then.

He made a noncommittal noise, then gave me the once-over as though to remind me of my current state. "Your parents aren't around, you don't have a dress, and I—"

"I would marry you in this hospital gown with stitches running from my vagina to my asshole." Dougie shook his head, rolling his lips tightly together, trying desperately not to laugh because he knew I'd dissolve into a fit of laughter, too.

I'd never considered that my vagina felt laughter. Then again, I'd never given birth before. Every muscle in my body hurt, but that pain had all been worth it. "I mean it, Dougie. I don't give a shit about what my parents want. It's just about you, Christopher and me now."

"Our family," he murmured.

"Our forever. That's all that matters."

And I meant it.

Chapter Twenty-Six

Dougie

Present

I'D HAD AN IMPOSSIBLE TIME FALLING ASLEEP, SPENDING MOST OF THE night tossing and turning or fiddling with my phone, trying to fight the urge to call Pen. My finger hovered over the dial button, my thumb moving across the screen. I ran it across the arches of her cheeks in her contact photo that undermined her beauty.

If I called her, what would I say?

I'd insinuated I needed space, and I couldn't even do a proper night of separation right without her. I missed catching traces of her somewhere in our house. Her tinny, uncontrollable laughter when Christopher did something silly, or the soft pads of her feet moving across the hardwood floor. Every action, every word, every laugh, was my life source.

My wife and my son were the beat of my heart.

I didn't belong here. I belonged at home.

Ma and I hardly uttered a word to each other. All I could do was sit in the well-worn, floral print recliner in her parlor, with daytime television playing in the background eventually waning into prime-time TV until Ma suggested I go to bed if I wasn't going to eat anything.

I didn't have an appetite, so I did just that. Grateful that for once, she hadn't forced me.

Nah, that was her residual anger. She'd send me to bed hungry if it meant I learned my lesson, anyway. I think some part of her struggled to look at me, and knowing that I was under her roof, a man who'd nearly done to his wife what her husband had done to her?

That shit was hard.

My childhood room was tidy. Not even a single mote of dust dared to touch the varnish on the furniture, lest it meet its maker at the hands of Ma's feather duster. The room was painted in a dingy and tired shade of blue, and had always been too cramped, with too many pieces of mismatched furniture for a room the size of a shoebox—a dresser, two nightstands, and a bookshelf. White particleboard made up the twin bed frame that was just as unremarkable as it had been before I'd moved out, and the mattress was still as uncomfortable as hell as I had remembered it.

No foam mattress here. The pillows didn't cradle my neck, and the quilted, plaid comforter had long since lost its fluffiness factor sometime between the winter and spring of nineteen-ninety-two when Ma gave it to me for my fourteenth birthday.

Yep, I'd returned to my childhood home to take a miserable trip down memory lane, because it wasn't just enough for me to commiserate with myself in my own house with Penelope just down the hall. I needed to put myself through the wringer here, too.

So yeah, it was no surprise I hadn't slept—the unfavorable sleep conditions aside, I was emotionally and mentally fucked. I'd spent more time staring out the window, and in particularly weak moments, allowed my eyes to wander over to the slightly parted closet doors, where my old high school football jersey hung, mocking me.

I thought that was where all my problems started. High school.

I'd wanted to be someone important, someone worthy of Maria Tavares, so I signed up for the football team after weeks of the coach hounding me to try out because of my stocky build and the assurance that it would likely get me scouted for college. And with the way Ma's finances were looking? I'd needed all the tuition and scholarship help I could get. She was concerned about brain damage, but that hadn't been what she needed to worry about in the long run.

I tried out, and I made it.

It seemed like the stars had aligned and I had a good chance of getting into college on a scholarship and simultaneously injecting myself front and center on Maria's radar. She couldn't ignore me if the stands chanted, "Patterson!" in unison. Back then, she'd had a thing for football players—hell, Maria had a thing for anyone with just the right dash of power. Not that she ever stuck around. No, that girl had a reputation that proceeded her even in high school.

There was nothing more dangerous that a beautiful teenage girl who knew it—and Maria was exactly that. Dangerously beautiful. A wicked smart budding man-eater in the making who hadn't given a shit that the team called her easy in the locker room because somehow, she'd grown numb to that word. She wielded it like a weapon, and she used that strength to bring a handful of sixteen to eighteen-year-old boys to their knees. Sure, they called her names, but that didn't mean they wouldn't have eaten their left nut just to make her theirs.

But I wasn't like them. I genuinely cared, and I wanted to make the most of this opportunity.

It hadn't mattered that despite being the shortest on the team, that I was still the strongest, the most agile. I worked harder to make myself seen by her. And when she graduated, I bulked up, and I trained harder to ensure I was scouted by a D1 school—hell, I even got a scholarship.

My life was going to change, come hell or high water, and football was going to be my meal ticket. Until I fucked my knee up during a scrimmage and in the blink of an eye, it was all over. The stands stopped chanting my name. I spent more time benched than on the field, and eventually, I hung up my jersey and lost my scholarship, too.

I wasn't enough.

Anger, I should have felt anger, but I didn't. I still had this fleeting thing called perspective and mettle. I pivoted, I did what I had to do.

But I never felt sorry for myself or grew surly.

At thirty-three now, I never thought I'd have something to learn from a younger version of myself. I flung the sheets back, stormed to the closet, and closed the goddamn door with more force than necessary—because I couldn't stand it.

The jersey.

My past.

Myself.

My need to be someone I wasn't, created an inferiority complex that I spent the rest of my adult life trying to mask by becoming cocky and so blindly self-assured that there were moments I wasn't sure which parts of me were real and what parts were fabrications.

Well, that wasn't true. I knew which parts were real.

I knew after Maria broke my heart four years ago when I'd asked her to be my girlfriend after six months of sleeping together that the fantasy was over. I could overlook the NDA she'd made me sign, and how cold she could be—but she couldn't overlook what I wasn't, my inadequacies or my shortcomings.

It wasn't love, it never had been.

It was a fascination, a fantasy, a lie.

I wanted someone to care about. I wanted someone to love me the way I loved them, who saw me for who I was, not what I didn't have.

And I got it. My burst of sunshine stumbled unexpectedly into my arms one day, literally—and looked up at me like I was the best damn thing she'd ever seen in her entire life.

But rather than holding Penelope tight, I pushed her away when it got too hard—when she needed me the most.

We hurt each other.

We said things we didn't mean.

We lied.

Now that the truth was out, I couldn't give up on her or us.

I might not be able to repair the sun, but that didn't mean I wasn't going to fight like hell to bring back her light.

She deserved to shine again.

Ma was still asleep when I left her house a little after six thirty in the morning with my overnight bag in my fist.

The still dark and tawny lit streets were empty as I drove home, taking the long route from Fall River back to Eaton. There were only a few other solitary cars on the road at this hour, the falling leaves littering sprawling rain-soaked lawns as I turned onto my street twenty-five minutes later.

Pen and I needed to talk. Properly.

Without one of us trying to rush the process, without the other trying to silence us. Figure out what our lives looked like from here. It was opposite from what we'd both thought, but that didn't mean that there couldn't be hope. Hope didn't imply more sameness. It meant change, it meant coming to our relationship with only the truth and a willingness to be honest, no matter how ugly or hurtful the things we had to say were.

My stomach wrenched at the sight of the Jeep Cherokee covered in wet leaves in my driveway.

Shit.

My heart stuttered, my skin prickling with a heated awareness that my problems just got a hell of a lot worse.

Some part of me knew that before my keys were in the truck's ignition, Pen would call Raquel. My hope momentarily unhinged itself as I considered the brute force of the harpy's rage.

Was I still allowed to call her that, even if we'd developed a sort of kinship that compared to a sibling relationship?

God, I could remember the day she met me at the bar years ago, as clear as if it had just happened yesterday. I'd told Pen that Raquel had reminded me of Sean, but in a way, I felt like I aligned with her more than I cared to admit. It hadn't changed that Raquel had hated me unequivocally, but over the years, I'd liked to believe that we'd grown to understand each other, because she and I weren't that different, were we?

We both knew what it felt like to be overwhelmed by the screaming in our minds that told us we weren't enough. We knew what it was like to want something we didn't believe we deserved.

But this?

There was no understanding of any of this.

Nothing I'd ever done could compare to anything Raquel had done.

And there was a good chance that when I walked through that door, she might not be prepared to welcome me back to my home, either. That she'd wage a war unlike any other just to keep Penelope far from me because that was how deep the roots of her loyalty ran.

I pulled the truck into the driveway, the gravel crunching under me, lulling an unexplainable calm through me. I needed to face the music, come hell or high water.

If Raquel gave me the chance to talk to my wife without her interference, then maybe we stood a chance to get back on track.

Leaving, even for a night, had been wrong. It sent the wrong message to Penelope, and it was fucking hurtful. But I'd needed to process. I'd needed to ask myself what I would have done if I had been her? Would I have closed myself off, or would I have spilled my guts out?

The cold October air enveloped me as I flung open the truck door, my overnight bag in tow. The tree branches swayed above me, more leaves twirling in the gale in a kind of interpretive dance before they met their brethren on the ground. I stuffed my finger in the keyring, my eyes working over the leaf debris filled yard. Didn't matter how often I raked this shit, there was still going to be more. Only last year, it had looked pretty and picturesque speckled all over the lawn with our porch made up for the fall. Now it just made the yard looked unkempt, the porch neglected. It was a big fucking spotlight on us that something was amiss.

I hated it.

Uncertainty greeted me when I got to my front door, my house key pinched between my thumb and pointer finger. There was no going back after this, no more running away.

I had to be the man my ma had raised.

I had to fight for my family.

The lock turned easily as I twisted it, then pushed on the handle. The sweetness of black cherry merlot touched my nose, the distinct aromatic notes of coffee brewing in the kitchen mixed into the fold. I heard the coffee maker sputtering at its conclusion, my attention drawing in the sound's direction.

That wasn't Pen.

A coil of worry winded through me. I hadn't taken Raquel for an early riser, but maybe this was a good thing. I looked at the cleared floor mats. No evidence of her shoes or belongings. Some small part of me wondered how Sean had fared for the night without his wife while caring for two infants. Shit was hard with just one. I couldn't imagine two.

My jaw flexed. Who was I kidding?

Mr. Perfect probably had no problems at all. Everything always had come easily to him, never had to try real hard at anything. Just got to show up and throw his obnoxious height and weight around.

He wasn't even that tall, just compared to me... I blew out my lips with frustration.

Setting my overnight bag down on the floor, I shucked off my jacket, hanging it up on the hallway tree before I kicked my shoes onto the mat. Where were my indoor sliders? Frowning, I padded toward the kitchen fully prepared to grovel and ask my wife's best friend for mercy or a lifeline.

They'd had a whole day and night to talk, and if anyone had insight into what was running through Penelope's head right now, it was Raquel.

Only it wasn't Raquel fixing herself a cup of coffee in my pristine kitchen.

I gritted my teeth, my hackles rising as Sean's stupid fucking sculpted face sneered at me, his dark left brow lifting with a challenge as he noisily slurped his coffee.

The son of a bitch was drinking coffee in *my* coffee mug.

Sean glared at me over the rim of my Patriots mug, the one Pen gave me as a stocking stuffer last Christmas. It literally was personalized, my name scrawled on one side. It was taking everything in me not to knock the mug out of his hand, 'cause fuck him.

The steam billowing from the mug contended with the steam practically coming from his ears. "What the hell are you doing here?" he demanded, setting the mug down on my countertops with enough force he could have chipped the mug.

I flinched. If he broke it, I was breaking his face. Plain and simple.

His dark hair was a mess under the hood of his green Celtics hoodie, the shade enhancing the tired, heavy bags under his russet-brown eyes. He didn't know what a fucking barber was? The state of his scruffy, overgrown appearance made him look like a vagabond.

I glanced to the living room, now realizing that part of the sectional opposite of my line of vision from the foyer had been made up into a bed.

What the fuck? I left for *one* night, and they fucking moved in?

Now I was pissed. Forget calm.

All traces of humility and desire for mercy fled my body, rage and frustration rushing to fill the void. I had prepared myself to deal with Raquel. I was not ready to deal with this oversized asshole who had the balls to look at me like I was the interloper in my house. Like that wasn't my coffee he had brewed, was drinking, and…

My fucking indoor sliders. He was wearing my fucking sliders with his enormous fucking sock-clad feet! His heels hung off the edge of the shoe, the middle straining to contain the width of his foot. This was vaguely reminding me of the time I had pissed him off in the eighth grade and he intentionally overwrote my game save file of Final Fantasy IV.

Alright, I was still a bit pissed about it twenty years later.

"What the hell am *I* doing here?" I snapped, baring my teeth. "What the hell are *you* doing here?"

Sean made that face. The one that told me he was going to say something that would put me over the edge. "Being the man of the fucking house since you're clearly too much of a pussy to be one."

Yep, he'd said it. My ego howled as my blood kicked in my veins, heat exploding in my face. I charged at him with my fists clenched into tight balls against my thighs.

The smarmy smile brightened his features, the exhaustion seeming to leave him. "Bring it on, asshole," he called, beckoning me closer with his hand. "I've been dying to get back at you for that cheap shot."

"Fuck you!" I exploded.

Raquel raced into the kitchen, her dark, disheveled hair flying out behind her as though she'd literally woken up because of us and promptly scrambled out of whatever bed she'd been sleeping in. She darted past me, sliding in my trajectory, her arms wrapping around her husband's waist, the bare heels of her feet sinking into the kitchen tiles as much as they could to find traction.

"Sean," she murmured, her shoulders rising and falling as she fought to regulate her heart rate. "Please. It's too early for this."

"*Move*," he gritted, his murderous stare fixated on mine.

She pressed her forehead to her chest, shaking her head. "You know I can't do that."

"Hemingway," he growled without looking at her, his hands planting on her shoulders.

Hemingway. I rolled my eyes. What kind of stupid fucking nickname was that for his wife? I'd always thought it was dumb. I didn't give a shit that she was an author, or what his angle had been with that nickname when he'd first met her.

He forgot he owed me for his picture-perfect little life.

He only got her number because of my wife.

We'd made them.

Now they were hanging out in my house like the quintessential couple, weren't they? In what fucking alternative universe did these two become the embodiment of a solid marriage?

She'd left him once too, for fuck's sake. She'd left him, and he went crawling after her like…

I swallowed thickly, my TMJ muscle screaming in agony when I clenched my jaw as the thought occurred to me. He crawled after her like I was trying to do with Penelope, too.

He hadn't given up when it got hard.

Raquel's exposed forearms flexed as she applied more force to his middle, her profile tensing with her struggle. "You can't go around punching him every time he pisses you off."

"He deserves worse," Sean said unceremoniously, flicking his eyes up and down at me, a sneer twisting his mouth. "A hell of a lot worse."

This prick had a hard-on for me the size of his forearm. "Don't you have a job to get to?" I spat, waving my hands in the air. "A business to run?"

Wouldn't know what it was like to have to hurry off to work anymore.

"Dougie," Raquel warned, her shoulders stiffening under her sleep shirt that hit her at the knees. "You are *not* helping."

"I'm not trying to," I announced, shooting Sean a simpering smile.

The band she held around Sean's waist broke as she pivoted on her heel, malice polluting her features.

I'd done it this time.

"Let me tell you something," she stabbed the air between us, her accent punctuating her next statement, "he might knock you out, but I'll make it impossible for them to find you. Do you understand me?"

I stepped back as she lunged forward. Somehow, my fight-or-flight senses were more aware of her than they were of my best friend, because Raquel was the byproduct of a criminal and that not only made her a liability because of neurotransmitters and shit, but pretty fucking unpredictable.

You could take the girl out of Southie, but you couldn't take Southie out of the girl.

She didn't get far before Sean hooked his arms around her waist, her legs kicking out in front of her as he lifted her right from the ground and held her against him as she squirmed.

But she wasn't done saying her piece as she clawed at the sleeves of Sean's hoodie, fighting to break the hold he had on her. She looked deranged. "We are trying to help, you ungrateful son of a bitch!" Her face flushed red. "You *never* deserved her, and you *still* don't!"

I tilted my chin downward, shame tainting my cheeks. "Then why are you trying to help me?"

She seethed at me when I glanced back up at her expectantly. "Because for some fucking insane reason, she loves you, and regretfully—so do we!" I ground my teeth together. She was pissed, but she didn't realize how badly I'd needed to hear that. They didn't hate me.

No matter how mad Sean was at me, Raquel's thirst for violence, or the damage I'd done to my marriage… they all still loved me.

Sean pressed the tip of his nose against the crown of her head. "Easy now."

"Put me down!" Raquel demanded on a growl, clearly dealing with a bout of amnesia given only moments ago, she'd been trying to apprehend her husband. She tugged at the tight circle of his arms, her face tensing as she struggled, but he wasn't relenting.

"No can do." He nuzzled her. "You can't go around punching him every time he pisses you off," he parroted.

Maybe the oversized asshole was good for something after all. Keeping his pit bull of a wife on a leash. Raquel's ire seemed to be all Sean had needed to remember that there had been a time when he and I could have a conversation with one another without drawing blood.

We used to be brothers.

Raquel gave up, her chest heaving in her oversized and tired Red Sox T-shirt. I was pretty sure the shirt was his.

"If I put you down, are you going to behave?" Sean asked her lowly. There was something heated about the last part of his question that I'd rather drive a screwdriver into my ear canal than ever hear again.

Her nostrils flared, her head falling back against his chest with defeat. "No."

Sean snorted, murmuring something in her ear that got a smug smile out of her. Somehow, I suspected I was the source.

I pointed at my mug. "That's my mug."

Sean set her down gently, slinging an arm over her shoulder—just in case. "Ah," he said, reaching for the mug with his free hand, bringing it to his lips. "That's why this coffee tastes like shit."

My molars gnashed together as I prepared to hurl another insult in his direction, but the scent of ginger peaches entered my nose, robbing me of all cognizant thought and my next breath.

I turned my head to the kitchen archway.

God, how could I have missed someone so much in twenty-four hours?

"What are you doing here?" Penelope asked quietly. She didn't look at me, her shoulders stiff under her sweatshirt as she stared at the floors. She'd pulled her hair away from her face in a low ponytail, and intentionally avoided meeting my eyes.

For a moment, Sean and Raquel weren't here with us. In my mind, we were still just two people who found themselves under unlikely circumstances.

Outside of this house, two strangers fell in love.

And inside of this house, they'd destroyed each other.

But that didn't mean they wouldn't find each other again. That they wouldn't take the broken pieces and create something new.

"It's my house, too, isn't it?" I asked, my tone coming out hoarse.

The burst of annoyance erupted from the other side of the room, reminiscent of a volcano. "You *left*," Sean bristled, his shoulders punching to his ears as he stepped forward.

Penelope flinched.

A four-lettered word had done that.

I'd done that.

Her arms folded over her chest as the words suspended in the air, too high for either of us to snatch back.

"I didn't—"

But he wasn't having it. "You left your fucking family!"

It hurt. He was right, but it felt like I was being stabbed.

"Sean!" Raquel shouted, holding her hands against his chest. "*Enough.*"

His eyes flashed with betrayal, nostrils flaring. "Fuck this," he muttered. He broke away from Raquel, breezing by Penelope like a six-foot-two live wire of rage as he stormed out of the kitchen.

Raquel threaded a hand through her hair, looking at the kitchen archway where he'd disappeared through. "We'll be upstairs, Pen. I'll get Chris ready for the day." She pegged me with a hard look that spewed her conditions without her uttering a word.

Fix it or die.

Penelope nodded, dropping her arms to brush her fingers against Raquel's as she passed. But as soon as she was out of the room again, those arms of hers formed a half wreath around her chest once more, like a barrier intended to keep me out.

"They stayed the night?" My voice filled with grit.

I just wanted her to look at me. I needed to see what was in her eyes.

Penelope wouldn't give me the satisfaction. "I think that's obvious," she replied flatly, plucking up the courage to rip herself from where she stood and pad over to where the mugs were kept. She gave me her back as she futzed with the coffee carafe, pouring herself a cup. "Where'd you go?" There was something in her query that made me think she hadn't wanted to ask at all, but her curiosity was too much.

"My ma's."

Her back tensed. "Oh." Such a benign response.

I rubbed my eyes with the heels of my palms, my posture slumping. "I told her everything, Pen."

Her shoulder blades met in the middle. "Everything?" she questioned weakly, still not looking at me. Something heavy swirled in the thickening air. Her shame or... her anger. It choked me all the same.

"Yeah." I nodded, resisting the urge to rush to her and cleanse every bad thought echoing in her mind. "Everything."

She set her mug down, oscillating as she glanced back at the open cabinet. She extended a hand, her fingers curling back for a moment, then made a firm decision and pulled out another mug. Penelope didn't speak as she busied herself with fixing two cups of coffee.

It was the first time in a long time she'd done anything for me at all.

She opened the cutlery drawer, withdrawing a spoon and stirring the cream and sugar she'd put in a mug, sliding it in my direction.

"Thanks."

There was something she wasn't saying. It was like an insufferable black hole in the room, drawing everything toward it. "I'm sorry I left."

Pen grimaced, drawing a breath. She lifted her stare, her eyes swollen as though all she'd done yesterday was cry herself into a delirium. My heart wrenched, any misdirected anger I had toward Sean channeled toward myself. I'd done that. I was the source of her lowered shoulders, of her slightly bowed head as though she wanted to recede in on herself. Her tears were because of me. I was the thief of her joy, of her rest, of her happiness.

Of her hope.

I wanted to fix it, I *needed* to fix it. There was no other option.

But then she found her will to speak and robbed me of every single thing I was prepared to say.

"I'm not," she replied, her voice scratchy as it hit my ears. Pen's hands flexed in front of her, the same way they always did when she got anxious. Disbelief swept over her face, as though she couldn't reconcile that she'd said that either.

I blanched. Instincts had me touching my wedding band to ground myself, trying to desperately seek hope, needing to cling onto it as the creeping despair infiltrated my insides.

"I needed it, in some way." She nodded her head, lifting her shoulders in a weak, half-shrug. "It was a reality check."

Perspective.

I rubbed my lips with two fingers, digesting the statement. But no matter what I did to break it down to comprehension, all it did was install the resounding thought that I was too late. "What kind of reality check?"

"We're never going to be who we were, Dougie." She wet her lips, rolling her bottom one into her top one. "Those people are..." she rested her hands on her hips, raising her head, "they're dead."

Dead? Had she intended for the adjective to sound as cold and permanent as it had come out in her posh lilt?

Time seemed to slow as I staggered toward the kitchen island, bracing myself for what was to come. My limbs were an uncoordinated mess as I fought them to cooperate and get my weight on to the bar stool.

Dead. Were we dead?

Picking up the mug, I brought it to my lips. My throat still hurt from scalding it yesterday, but I didn't care. I wanted the pain. Anything to remind me that this wasn't a dream, this was my fucking reality, and it sucked as much as this cup of coffee.

How many grams of coffee grounds did Sean use? He was right. This coffee tasted like shit.

I set it back down, drumming my fingers instead against the countertops, needing something to do as I tried to process what to ask her next.

"What do you want to do, Pen?" If anything had been solidified for me yesterday, it was that I didn't want a fucking divorce. I didn't want to give up on us or our life together, but... if she needed that, it would kill me, but I'd give her what she wanted.

She rubbed tension out of her left shoulder, her eyes momentarily falling shut. "Before you left, I really thought I wanted to fix this." Oh, fuck. "But now, I'm honestly not sure."

"Are you saying that because you want to punish me, or because—"

"Because I'm honestly not sure, Dougie." She stared at her feet. "I don't know what it says about me that I," she winced, "that I kept a pregnancy *and* a miscarriage from you."

I rushed to assuage her. "That you didn't want to hurt me."

"I think it's more complicated than that." Pen tucked her hair behind her ear, glancing around the kitchen. "I worked so hard to not become the things I hated, to not be a replica of my parents, but I..." my muscles tightened as I braced myself for the axe to drop. "But I lost sight of what mattered to me while trying to protect myself."

"Pen—"

"Let me finish, please," she whispered, holding up a hand. "I need to get this off my chest or I may never."

My jaw flexed, but I kept a lid on it.

"I feel like I've spent more time trying to convince you that you were good enough than I spent on trying to actually be good enough for myself." Penelope exhaled, her arms wrapping around herself like that was all she could do to keep herself upright. "I lost myself, Dougie. I lost myself in trying to help you realize you deserved this life with me. And when my parents got involved in our wedding planning, I couldn't even remember that there was a time that I wanted to marry you with my ass exposed in a floral print hospital gown."

I sandwiched my tongue between my teeth, swallowing every calming word I wanted to spew.

I should have married her when we left the hospital. Things wouldn't have happened the way they did.

"I lost you in the process, and Christopher lost his parents. We were here physically, but we weren't emotionally. Not where it really counted." She shook her head, her bottom lip trembling. "I don't want to be my parents, and you're right, I am angry with you. But I don't want this loss or our struggles to define us. I don't want to be a scorned woman who spends the rest of her life hating her husband because he *almost* made a mistake that was brought on by his wife's decision to keep him out because she was ashamed of herself." She dropped her arms to rub her perspiring palms against the front of her sleep shorts. "I've been punishing you, because I've been punishing myself, too."

She held up a hand, instinctually realizing that I was going to remind her that my fuck up wasn't on her. "You wouldn't have gone to her if I hadn't," her leaden eyes squeezed tightly before she found the will to look at me, "*frozen you out,*" she quoted. That had been what I'd said to her. She had frozen me out with the strength of the arctic tundra and not even a flamethrower, nor even global warming, would thaw her.

"You wouldn't have thought about," she lifted her head, plucking her strength from somewhere, finally saying the name that had haunted her nightmares for months, "*Maria* at all if it weren't for me. We both know that."

I was transfixed, my mouth opening and closing. I didn't want to say that wasn't true, but it was. In the past, I'd seen Maria before in passing since I met Pen, but anything I'd felt toward her had been pity and animosity. It was only when I saw her experiencing what Pen and I had had with someone else that something snapped in my brain like a synapse misfire that made me think...

Think in a way I never should have. It had never been about wanting Maria, about regretting my decision to be with Pen. It had always been about Maria being happy in the way Penelope and I were supposed to be.

If we weren't happy on our wedding of all days, what the fuck did that say about our marriage? Nothing good.

"You were right when you said we need to take this slow, that we can't rush the process," Penelope said, summoning my eyes. "My instincts with you have always been to rush through things as a means of keeping you, because in some ways, I've always felt a little inse-cure." I wanted to tell her she never had any reason to feel that way, but I couldn't. I'd given her a reason to feel that way. "But we need to take our time and rediscover who we are as individuals before we can be a couple."

Hope. That was hope.

My emotional receptors went nuclear as she approached me nervously. Her trembling hands found my face, glossy Atlantic-blue eyes fixating on mine. "I love you, but I love you enough to know that our story as we once knew it is now over and we need to let those versions of ourselves… die." She swiped the single tear that left my eye. "But we get to write a new one, Dougie. If we want to, on our terms."

So why the fuck did I feel like I was losing her completely? "Where do we go from here?"

"I don't know," she confessed. "But I'd like the chance to fall back in love with myself," she wet her bottom lip, "and to rebuild some-thing new with you, too."

My face crumbled, my head weaving into a series of curt nods. "Yeah," I sniffled, offering her a small smile, "I'd like that." I dropped my head to her chest, wrapping my arms around her waist while hers twined around my neck. She pressed her cheek against the top of my head, running her fingers along the shorn parts of my neck.

We couldn't change what had happened, 'cause love was like a mirror. If you dropped it, the illusion of what you once were shattered. You could glue the mirror back together, but it would never be the same. It would no longer be used as a source of reflection, but as a place where something new could form.

A new piece.

A new story.

A new love.

Chapter Twenty-Seven

Dougie

Present

"I'm not getting in the car with you," I growled, glaring at Sean, who held the passenger door open expectantly.

Frankly, he looked like he'd rather be sitting on the Mass Pike during a six p.m. traffic jam on a Wednesday with his cock sandwiched in a steel bear trap than in a car with me, but he still stood there, his hand outstretched to the door.

His patience slipped. "Get in the car, or I'll knock you the fuck out." Ah, there he was.

I tugged down hard on my ball cap, glaring at him under the bill. "You wanna do this with me again, asshole?"

We were being sent out of the house to 'resolve our issues'. Although resolving things with Sean was the least of my priorities, Pen had insisted after Raquel had suggested it—and frankly, I was just about ready to do anything to get back in my wife's good graces again.

Going to breakfast with this blundering idiot included. But did he have to drive? Couldn't I just drive myself... and if my foot found the accelerator when he got out of the car and I got my revenge for Final Fantasy IV, my mug, and my sliders... alright, I was thinking in extremes again.

I still considered him my best friend, even if we were at each other's throats.

"The cock size comparison is getting old, real fast," Raquel snapped, marching across the lawn, the laces of her shit kickers undone, her sleeves swimming in Sean's hoodie. "Get in the car. Both of you. *Now*."

"Now you've done it," Sean muttered, storming by me, passing Raquel a pleading glance. She pointed at the car, the space between her brows wrinkling.

"And don't come back until you've said everything that needs to be said."

"So never?" I proposed, rounding the front of the Jeep as Sean opened the driver's side door, huffing out a breath. I heard him jerk the seat back, adjusting Raquel's preferred settings, his eyes hot as freshly melded steel on me as I opened the passenger side door.

"Dougie—" I slammed the car door shut, cutting her off. Her mouth moved, her ire exploding off her, but it was muted behind the safe confines of the Jeep's cabin.

She'd thrown her hands up in the air with exasperation, and if it wasn't for the small, controlled snort leaving Sean in the driver's seat, I would have thought he was gonna lay into me again for pissing her off.

He blew her a kiss. She retaliated by throwing him the finger.

"God, I love her," he said on a sigh, turning the Jeep on, tilting his head back to watch her stalk across my front lawn, storm up the steps and slam the door behind her. "But I hate her fucking ideas about as much as I hate Penelope's."

I pitched my elbow on the edge of the window, cradling my chin with my open palm. "I'm not interested in making eyes at you over a breakfast menu either. Let's get one thing straight."

Pulling the shift into reverse, Sean cranked his neck over his shoulder. "Feeling's mutual, sweetheart."

"You're a prick."

"And you're a coward," he seethed, rolling his eyes. "Together, we're a couple of whiny assholes. Now do you wanna shut up and stop spoiling my appetite, or do you want to build a bridge and get the fuck over it?"

"I don't want to get the fuck over it."

Then Sean said the one thing that could have changed everything if I'd said them sooner. "You fucked my sister," he uttered, my stomach hitting the floor. "If anyone needs to get the fuck over it, it's *me*."

I lost control of my expression, the comment a vacuum that sucked all the oxygen out of the cabin in the car.

How long had he known for? Fuck.

I ground my teeth, keeping my eyes fixed on the street as he pulled the car into drive and the tires gritted against the cold, wet ground.

I stole a glance at him, noting the tension in his profile, his knuckles whitening. "I always thought it was weird," he began, trying to modulate his tone, "how Maria could hate you more as adults when she saw you less. It never occurred to me you guys..." His jaw was as sharp as granite while his mouth rocked, like he was trying to control what he said next. "You should have told me."

Yeah, I guessed I should have. But his sister had literally made me sign a fucking NDA to ensure nothing compromised her integrity or her fucking career as the only female lawyer at her firm while she was trying to make partner—and when I had wanted to tell Sean... Maria reminded me of what I was good for.

"When did you want me to tell you?" I asked, remaining nonchalant even though my heart was literally in my throat. "Over Super Bowl Sunday?"

Sean scoffed. "When you thought about breaking your vows, you moron." He glared at me. "You almost ruined my sister's relationship, Dougie. And *yours*."

My throat worked as I draped my hands against my thighs, my gaze tipping downward. "I know." I knew it had been a mistake to go to Maria's apartment that day.

I knew she finally had a boyfriend.

She finally had a chance at happiness, and in my moment of weakness, I'd nearly ruined it for the both of us.

Sean concentrated on the street. "Don't you want to know who told me?"

I dropped my arm, leaning back. "Not really."

He adjusted himself in his seat, tugging the seat belt away from his thick neck. "Katrina," he volunteered anyway.

"Katrina?" That had been an unexpected curve ball. But who the fuck had told her?

"My kid sister is perceptive. She speculated, and when she put Raquel on the spot about it," he probed the inside of his cheek, "she sang like a bird because if there's one thing my wife is notoriously bad at despite her repertoire of talents and career in storytelling, it's lying." He drummed his fingers along the leather of the steering wheel.

I held in the laugh. It was ridiculous. I had full confidence in Raquel's ability to hide a corpse without a trace, but to tell a convincing lie? No dice.

I rubbed the corners of my mouth, fitting the pieces of the puzzle together. "So, Trina spilled the beans to you?"

He chuckled in disbelief, but it lacked any mirth. "You know this family can't keep a secret for shit."

Wait a minute. "Was *that* why she fired me?"

Sean frowned, his eyes thinning. "She fired you as an incentive to grow a pair and come talk to me about it." He pulled onto Main Street, taking us toward Eaton's idyllic town square. The benches in the brick paved square were empty, scattered around an octagonal Victorian gazebo in the center with ornamental trim and cheery white columns. The thinning maples circled the square, their limbs forming a canopy.

"Fucking with my income was a shitty thing to do."

"My sisters' all play dirty, you know better than that." Fact. Maria, Olivia, and Katrina didn't spare anyone. "Maria told Raquel her side of the story because she knew it would come up eventually." He drummed his fingers against the steering wheel. "She had a lot of tact and compassion about it, despite the shit storm it caused in her personal life. You can thank her later."

Thank Maria? That was never going to happen, but... maybe Raquel had told Penelope Maria's side and that was what had taken the edge off her anger a couple of nights ago.

Sean pulled the Jeep close to the curb in front of the only diner in town—Four Corners—his foot found the brake as he tugged the shift gear into park. Killing the ignition, he took off his seatbelt, then leaned back in his seat with defeat. "I'm real pissed at you."

"Feeling's mutual."

"And yet the reasons are different." He inclined his head to the right, dark eyes studying me. "Give me one good reason you're pissed at me."

I gaped at him, my mind racing to come up with the words.

Why was I mad at him? I'd stopped talking to him because Penelope had demanded it, but I didn't...

Nothing. I had nothing, because I'd been projecting for months. I knew that.

"That's what I thought," he announced, sounding every bit as smug and victorious as he intended.

I glared at him. "So, what? You're mad at me because of Maria?"

Sean's left leg bounced, his mouth a thin line. "I'm mad at you because I'm your best fucking friend and I asked you on your wedding day if you were having second thoughts and you looked me in the eye and told me you were fine and you weren't."

Jesus Christ, half a year later and his interpretation of that day was still wrong. "Because I wasn't having second thoughts about marrying *Penelope*, I was having second thoughts about the *wedding*."

"Oh, my fucking bad," he scolded, clutching his chest while feigning regret for his misunderstanding. "Next time I'll ask better questions."

God, he was such a fucking patronizing and entitled prick. "I don't need this shit, Sean. Not from you."

He twisted in his seat, leaning in my direction with his teeth bared. "Too fucking bad, asshole. Two years ago, you nearly stopped me from going to California to get my wife back, and I didn't listen to you." He was still obsessing about that, but I didn't blame him. I *had* tried to stop him. I'd tried to tell him to leave Raquel alone and let her move on with her life.

But shit, what if he *had* listened to me?

I swallowed, my silence acting as his green light to continue. "You don't have to listen to me either, but guess what? You're going to hear every goddamn word that comes out of my mouth. So, get out of the car and let's get something to eat." He glanced at the diner, the neon flashing 'OPEN' sign burning my retinas. "And maybe if Rhonda is lucky," he said, referring to the waitress who worshipped the ground he walked on and was old enough to be his mother, "we won't throw any more fists."

Chapter Twenty-Eight

Dougie

Seven months ago...

I WAS FREAKING THE FUCK OUT.

My clumsy hands fumbled with the bow tie—why fucking bow ties —trying desperately to get the clip in place. I hated how tight this thing was against my throat, the buttons on the dress shirt choking me. I felt like a sardine crammed into a too tight can. The sleeves were snug around my biceps and forearms, hardly affording me the room to lift my arms, which maybe was a good thing because I was sweating like crazy. The seams strained to contain my broad shoulders, and the neck-line felt closer to a noose.

Goddamn it.

The door opened behind me in the dressing room, revealing Sean's tall frame in the doorway. If there was one of us who looked tickled fucking pink to be here, it was him. The suit hugged his frame like a glove. No wool blazers in sight here. His dark hair, styled in a way I'd never seen before, slightly brushed back away from his eyes, while his unflappable shit-eating grin nearly hit his russet-brown eyes, practically consuming all the real estate of his face.

"I hate that wedding planner," he announced with a chuckle, toeing the door shut behind him.

The wedding planner I hadn't wanted. The one shoved on us by Penelope's parents that we agreed to because hey, that's all we'd done since we allowed them to get involved in our wedding.

Yeah, feeling was very fucking mutual. I had Moira the wedding planner at the low price of ten G's of Cullimore money to thank for this dress shirt that was a size too small because she didn't like the way the appropriate size was too loose around my chest.

So, I agreed, because this entire wedding had been one submission after the other.

What had started off as a peace offering to make up for, y'know, impregnating my betrothed out of wedlock, and simultaneously shattering every hope, dream, and illusion her parents had for her, had turned into an organza and three-hundred-and-fifty-two dollars per plate nightmare.

This wedding wasn't us—it was them.

When we had talked about our wedding, we envisioned eating roast beef sandwiches from that shithole on Charles Street in Boston that were tightly wrapped in aluminum foil wrappers. Pen had wanted to forgo the expensive dress with the train for a pantsuit with her favorite Iron Maiden tee under her blazer. An outdoor ceremony at the Boston Common near the Brewer Fountain. Go for beers after at O'Malley's and promptly get on a plane after to finally eat pasta in Italy.

None of that had happened.

I mean, beyond the compromise her parents had been willing to make by spending someone's life savings on an outdoor tent just so Penelope could say at least the reception had been outdoors.

In fucking *March.*

We'd discussed a summer wedding, but summer had turned into spring, and spring had turned into that awkward in between of winter and spring that was reminiscent of a prepubescent teenage boy's voice —totally fucking inconsistent and unreliable.

But by the grace of whoever was looking down on us, the weather was perfect today. It was just too bad my mood wasn't. All I could think about was how the stress of planning this event had wedged an iceberg between us that turned us into two strangers going through the motions.

Sean stared at me expectedly, waiting for me to say something.

"Same," I replied without looking at him.

Pen and I had nothing in common anymore. Nothing but Christopher.

He huffed. "She's blowing a gasket about Raquel's shoes."

"What about them?" I glared at the bow tie, trying once again to get my thick fingers to cooperate. That wedding planner had no actual problems. Her sole purpose was to drive me into a nervous fucking breakdown.

I should have put my foot down. I should have never allowed this wedding to get this out of control. Fuck her parents. Fuck their society and their guilt.

But maybe I was being ridiculous.

"Her feet and ankles are real swollen," he continued, stepping toward me. "She can't get them into her heels." Sean swatted my fingers away, tugging on the bow tie, momentarily choking me—my eyes bugged, I couldn't breathe—the clip snapping easily in place. He patted me on the back, pausing as the damp heat of my perspiration registered on his palm. "Dougie, Jesus Christ."

Last night, the night before our wedding, I called my soon-to-be wife, seeking reassurance that after the revelry of this over-the-top and gaudy affair for the wedding of the century—the wedding neither of us had truly wanted but were coerced into—that we'd go back to just being her and me.

That couple who joked about getting married in a hospital.

The couple who had feverish sex against their front door.

The couple who had sex at all.

She'd chastised me instead. *Don't be ridiculous, Dougie.*

Ridiculous. I was being ridiculous.

Sean took a step back. "You're sweating through your clothes."

The observation made my sweat glands flex their muscles, another flush of heat sweeping over me. "Thanks, Tips," I muttered, stepping out of his line of vision.

But the fucker's eyes followed me to the bar cart in the room's corner.

Whiskey. Whiskey would get me through this.

He stepped back, appraising me suspiciously. His mouth turned into a tight line. "Do you have…" Sean grimaced, like he didn't want to say it. "Cold feet?"

"Of course not." So why did I want to throw up?

My heavy arm lifted the crystal decanter, pouring four fingers' worth of the expensive, amber liquid fire into the match crystal glass. Who gave a shit if it was a ten o'clock in the morning?

I downed it, hardly feeling the burn.

It had been a long time since I'd felt something.

"Have you seen Christopher anywhere?" I asked, focusing on the door. If I went to Pen right now and asked her to get in the car with me and Chris—to say fuck this—would she do it?

Would she go back to being the girl in the truck who laughed with me, who let me make love to her, and be with her? I stared at the empty glass, staring at a single droplet running down the wall of the glass.

Could we go back to what we were?

Sean cleared his throat, arousing my attention. Regret swept through me as his mouth flipped down turned as though he'd tasted something bitter. "He's with your frigid in-laws."

I laughed to myself. My frigid in-laws, that was putting it fucking politely.

The crux of all our newfound problems. When we'd said we wanted a modest wedding, they came in swinging with the guilt. And who was I to stick my neck out and argue with them? I'd done enough damage, hadn't I?

I'd soiled their precious little girl just like she'd asked me to in my truck three years ago. Filled her up nice and good, put a baby in her.

Made a life with her.

Had a life with her.

And poof. It really was like a lightbulb went out, and no matter how many lightbulbs I screwed back in to brighten her up, nothing worked.

A stranger laid opposite of me in our bed. She looked like Pen, her waist dipped in the same space, the bed sheets settling there. She smelled like her, and in the instances I heard that posh lilt, she sounded like her, too.

It was almost convincing enough for me to believe it was my Pen, but it wasn't. The woman in our bed ripped away from me like my touch alone would turn her into ash.

I let it slide. I knew I shouldn't have, but I had.

When she circumvented my kiss, I let it slide.

When she avoided discussing anything short of Christopher, I let it slide.

When the prenuptial agreement ended up in my lap and no lawyer in New England would review it? I let her suggest Maria.

Maria.

Fucking Maria Tavares. An epic mind-fuck whose heated dark eyes were the kind that haunted you forever because Maria wasn't someone you could purge from your memory.

The last place in the world I'd wanted to be, and my wife-to-be, willingly thrust me back in her path because I needed to be someone else's problem while she focused on all of this. This opulence, this pretentious fucking affair of the century that was supposed to be for *us*.

Of course, she hadn't seen it that way. No, Penelope really thought she was looking out for me, for us. Who would be better suited to ensure your wealthy future in-laws weren't about to fuck you in the ass without lube while you bit the pillow but your ex-girlfriend?

Correction: Maria had never been my girlfriend, had she? I'd been her fuck buddy. A reliable cock for her to ride when she felt like it, because that was who I was. Reliable and steady Dougie.

I shouldn't have let that slide, either, but I had this uncanny habit of allowing people to walk all over me.

Now I was here. On mine and Pen's wedding day, thinking of pulling a runaway groom, only I wasn't fucking Julia Roberts, and I didn't want to leave Penelope at the altar. I wanted to bring her with me, and shit, maybe I wasn't as good looking as Richard Gere, but—

"Did you hear me?" Sean interrupted.

My head snapped back, my vision blurring as I tried to make out his figure. "Huh?"

"I said, is everything okay with you and Pen?"

No. No, it wasn't. And it hadn't been in months, and I didn't know why. It seemed like only yesterday we were mocking this whole fucking affair we'd been guilt-tripped into having at all. She even had made a point of building vision boards she knew her parents would outright reject, laughing through the whole thing.

Something had happened, though, 'cause almost overnight, she was as invested in this wedding as she'd once been in our relationship. Once been the operative phrases in that sentence.

It had been a long time since I'd felt relevant to Penelope. Important.

My chest clenched. How could I miss someone so much when she was always close by? I could just leave this room right now, storm into her dressing room. Risk her admonishment that I wasn't supposed to see her in the dress but fuck the dress. Fuck the wedding, fuck all of this.

I just wanted her. I'd always just wanted her.

"Dry spell." I cleared my throat, trying for casual, even though my heart was going to rip out of my fucking chest any moment now. "Just a dry spell."

Sean laughed, shaking his head. "What's it been?" he teased, scratching the back of his neck. "Forty-eight whole hours?" He turned to the rack, plucking another white dress shirt—someone had had the foresight to ensure there were multiple white shirts—just in case. He took it off the hanger, tossing it in my direction.

God, I wished it had been forty-eight hours. It had been well over forty-eight days, even.

I caught the shirt, but as my fingers curled around the soft woven cloth, and my eyes spotted the Armani logo on the tag, a burst of rage erupted inside of me. I didn't belong in fucking Armani or in a dress shirt.

I didn't belong here.

I didn't want to put it on.

"No," I croaked out, my throat growing impossibly dry. "Longer."

"I don't believe it." He waved me off.

Could I blame him? I didn't believe it either, but it was true. My future wife wanted nothing to do with me—physically, mentally.

Emotionally.

"Sean," I exhaled, kneading my chest. Fuck, when had my lungs shrunken? It hurt to breathe. "Seriously."

I was forgetting what her hair felt like. Sometimes, I experienced phantom sensations in bed where I thought I felt the instep of her foot brush against my ankle the way it always had when she wanted something from me.

It never was there.

It was just the empty, cold burden of the sheets and the hollowed ache in my chest reminding me of what we'd once been. Night after night, I lay wide awake next to her, listening to the evenness of her breathing, fighting with the desperation to just crawl into her mind—to nudge her awake and beg her to tell me what I'd done.

I was marrying her, signifying the start of our new life together, but somehow, it felt like the end. Dread pooled in my veins while I fought the bow tie, my chest caving in as I struggled to breathe.

Why the fuck couldn't I get this thing off?

Sean's expression collapsed, his golden complexion growing ashen. "Dougie, look at me."

But I couldn't. The room was fucking spinning, and my heart was hammering hard enough that I thought any second now, I'd drop dead. I tugged harder at the bow tie, the clip straining as my mouth grew parched and heat licked up my spine, my insides turning cold.

I couldn't do this. I couldn't fucking do this.

Sean's hands grasped my shoulders, shaking me hard. "Dougie!"

His baritone froze me in place, slowing my thoughts and my racing pulse.

I *had* to do this.

If we got this day over with, then we'd get back on track.

"You're right," I blurted, nodding my head just to get him off my ass. "Cold feet."

"You can tell me you know." His eyes softened. It was hard to discern which part of this was wigging him out. My newfound fear of getting married to the girl I'd dreamed about marrying from the beginning, or my general state of mind. He seemed as in disbelief over the situation as I was, but he soldiered on. "If you're having second thoughts, I mean."

Second thoughts. Was that what this was?

"I'm not." I tried for calm, pinching the buttons on my shirt open. "Not about Pen," I clarified, swallowing hard. I gestured to the door, knowing full well what existed beyond its barrier. "Just about... all those people." I shrugged my shoulders. "Nerves, I guess."

Sean's expression etched with manufactured understanding, his head weaving in a nod. He wasn't buying my bullshit, but he wouldn't force me to talk, either.

"I get it. I'd be overwhelmed if my guest list pushed four hundred people, too." He unclipped the bow tie when I undid the last button. "Just get out there and pretend like it's just you and Pen. Everyone else doesn't exist," he suggested.

Easier said than done, but I could do this.

"Things will get better when this is over," he added.

Would they? Would we get a clean slate once we exchanged vows and pledged forever to one another?

Would she fall in love with me again then?

I nodded my head, offering him a bullshit smile as I met his eyes. "Yeah. I'll be fine." I took the shirt off, the air cooling my perspiration as I tossed the shirt to a velvet lounge chaise in the corner. Feeding my arms through the clean shirt, I got my head back in the game as I pinched the buttons closed. I didn't fidget this time as Sean clipped the bowtie back in place. Accepting the blazer he held out to me, he clapped me on the shoulder, offering me a solidarity head nod.

"You're getting everything you wanted."

Yeah, it was everything I wanted, but when I envisioned it?

It hadn't ended like this.

Heading for the door on my legs that felt boneless, my hand extended for the knob as I prepared to seal my fate. "Sean?"

He looked at me, wide-eyed, as we both acknowledge the stalemate we'd encountered despite his best efforts because I couldn't be honest with him. "Don't mention this to Raquel."

Chapter Twenty-Nine

Dougie

Present

RHONDA STUNK LIKE A STALE PACK OF PALL MALLS AS SHE SHOVED A hand into my hair, ruffling my messed strands. "I thought you skipped town," she complained in a wheeze, pulling me against her in a bull-shit hug. "You and Penelope haven't been here in months."

Fact. Saturday mornings at Four Corners had been Pen and I's thing since we moved to Eaton, but we hadn't been here since... hell if I knew.

"Been busy," I replied, staring at the tired and scratched up table-top. I traced my fingers on the chipped edges, hoping Rhonda would get a clue to take her foot off the gas.

"Where's your lady?" she mused, burrowing into the pocket of her stained sugarplum pink carhop uniform in search of her notepad.

I heaved a sigh, leaning back in the banquette, catching her eyes flickering to the stretch of windows in search of Pen outside. "Home."

"And yours?" she glanced at Sean.

He kicked his bearded chin at me, answering begrudgingly. "At his place."

"Boys' morning." Rhonda nodded, propping the tip of her scuffed-up once-white sneaker onto the linoleum floor, flipping the lid of her notepad open as she untucked the pen from behind her ear. "What can I get you started with?"

"Egg white omelet, please," Sean said, settling the menu back down. His elbows found the edge of the table. "And another coffee refill."

"You got it," she glanced at me expectedly, tapping her pen against the notepad.

The faux leather of the banquette crinkled as I shifted in my spot, resting my chin on my fist. "I'm not hungry."

"Eat. You look like shit," Sean snarled.

"So do you," I observed. When was the last time he'd shaved? Gotten a haircut? Had over four hours of consistent sleep?

His broad chest rose and fell as he fought to regulate his ire, his punishing glare thinning. "I've got two kids under the age of six months." Sean leaned forward in the banquette, flicking his eyes up and down. "What's your fucking excuse?"

Well, first, my wife and I got suckered into a wedding we hadn't wanted.

Then she quit me cold turkey like cigarettes without warning.

Oh, and then I thought I wanted to have sex with your sister.

And if that wasn't enough—my wife was pregnant, lost it and never told me.

Was that enough of a justification, or was I the perfect example of what the formation of a nervous breakdown looked like?

I kept a lid on it, giving him my profile as I dipped my attention toward the window, the gray clouds churning outside. Droplets hit the glass of the window, blurring the street. When the fuck was it going to stop raining?

In my peripheral vision, I caught Rhonda stepping back, clutching the notepad to her chest as she worried her bottom lip with her teeth. "I'll get you the usual, Dougie."

"I'm *not* hungry," I told her reflection in the window.

"He'll take it. Thanks, Rhonda." Sean made a thumbs-up gesture, dismissing her. Quiet enveloped us despite the clinking of cutlery at nearby tables. The diner was surprisingly busy for the middle of the week, swimming with locals as waitresses hustled from one table to the next, rushing to get orders out. The bell on the door chimed as someone left and another person entered. Bacon grease and coffee touched my nose, stirring something in my gut.

My stomach growled involuntarily.

Sean tapped the handle on the mug, scrutinizing a chip on the rim. "Told you that you're hungry."

"I'm not hungry."

"So, what are you?" Sean asked, leaning forward. "Other than knee-deep in this 'woe is Dougie' bullshit."

I left him waiting in suspended silence. Prick.

Rhonda returned with a coffee carafe, tail practically tucked between her legs, as she filled both our mugs and then inched back the way she'd come from.

"You owe her an apology."

"Why?" I asked, observing him. "You all stick your noses where it doesn't belong, and then I'm the one who owes you an apology?"

Sean sniffed, his jaw setting stiffly. "Because we *care*."

Care? They cared? "Well, don't. I don't need you to care."

"Then next time, move states," he suggested. "That'll fix all your problems, right?"

My jaw ticked. "Dunno," I said, picking up my mug with a casualness that put me off. "Seemed to work okay for your wife."

Sean stiffened, the color draining from his face.

Fuck. I'd gone too far.

That had been the third worst moment in his life, and I'd stuck my dirty fingers into a wound I wasn't confident would ever fully heal. That wasn't me. We both knew it. I'd genuinely been the nice guy once, and sure, Sean and I always said it like it was...

But we never intentionally said things to one another for the shock value or intending to hurt the other.

I sobered, my small fleeting moment of victory souring my insides. It was a sore spot for him, years later, and I knew better. I wasn't mad at him. At least, I didn't think I was. I was just... "I'm sorry."

I took off my ball cap, tossing it to the space beside me, before I leaned forward and buried my face in my palms, driving the heels into my eyes. How the fuck had I ended up here?

After what felt like forever, he spoke, "I took Raquel here on our first date." I spread my fingers, watching him through the fence of my digits as a faraway look touched his eyes. "She sat right where you were, looking like she couldn't decide if she wanted to throttle me or fall for me."

"She chose wrong either way," I joked, lifting my head. My fingers bridged, creating a perch for me to place my chin.

Sean chuckled, his mouth curving into an asymmetrical smile. "She's always been this flight risk, but I think I always knew I'd chase after her no matter where she went," he hesitated, adding in, "fleeing the state, included."

I broke the link of my hands, reaching for a packet of creamer on a dish. Ripping the tab open, I added it to my coffee mug. I stirred, before adding sugar and finally finding the will to drink it. I kept the small groan in check, the bitter and fragrant notes hitting my palate. Now that, that was a decent cup of coffee.

"I know that right now, it seems like we're..." he searched for a word, touching his cutlery, laying neatly on a napkin to his right.

"Perfect?" I suggested.

"Sure." He shrugged, leaning back in the banquette with his arms folded across his chest. "I know it seems like we're perfect, but we're not, Dougie. We struggle. The last couple of months have been the hardest of our lives, but we choose each other. We embrace our flaws, we accept that we're gonna fuck up, that not every day is going to be easy." He squinted like he was trying to keep himself in check.

"Some days are harder than others. Sometimes I worry I'm going to wake up one day and she's not gonna be there. That she's going to leave me and our kids and I'm going to lose my mind all over again.

But… I trust her." He inhaled, then sucked his bottom lip between his teeth, getting a grip. "I trust her enough to know that she chooses me too, that she chooses this life with me. We work at it, and it's hard, and those are the days I know I have to love her a little harder because that woman is re-parenting the hell out of herself while trying to adjust to her new role, too."

He blinked, rubbing his eyes with his thumb and forefinger. "Sorry, I'm tired." Bullshit. He was blubbering, but I'd allow it because I got it.

"That was probably the best night of sleep you've had in months, though, huh?"

He threw his head back with a laugh, nodding. "I almost feel bad offloading the kids to my ma. Holly's in this terrible sleep regression and…" Sean's eyes flared, his brows hitting his hairline, "she better grow up to be a fucking singer because the pipes on that kid." He glanced heavenward, pressing his palms together in prayer. "It's brutal."

"Two must be hard."

He stroked his scruffy chin. "It's not easy, but I wouldn't want it any other way." He smiled. "We get little glimpses of their personalities here and there. They're both kinda goofy." Sean got that look, the kind dads got over their kids. His chest practically puffed out with pride as his whole demeanor changed. "They look so much like me it's scary. I mean, they got a bit of their ma in there, but damn," his eyes widened. "Those paternal genes."

"Just what the world needs. More Tavareses."

He nudged my foot under the table. "Asshole."

I rolled my eyes, sending him a shit-eating grin. "I didn't say it was a bad thing."

"Yeah, yeah."

I blew out my cheeks, marinating on everything he'd shared with me. It was hard not to compare our situations with one another, but he was right. What I saw between him and Raquel was surface level. It wasn't the harmonization of screaming six-month-olds, the frustration of not getting the garbage to the curb on time on collection day, the desperation for an hour of peace.

"I miss her," I said lowly. "Penelope, I mean. I've missed her." I lifted my eyes to his, no longer feeling uncomfortable under his observation. "It's the most isolating experience. Missing someone who you can hear moving in the house, who you can faintly smell, whose voice you can hear. It's like loving a ghost. You can sense that they're there, but there's this void that sucks everything you have and gives you nothing in return." I let out a harsh breath, scratching my cheek.

"Can I ask you something?"

He was going to anyway. I nodded.

"Do you want out?"

"I never have." I bent my neck, staring down at my wedding band.

"Why did you," he exhaled, trying to find his nerve, "go to my sister's that night?"

I lifted my eyes, shame burning a path up my spine. It was a question I'd asked myself repeatedly. I thought back to the night that solidified my decision.

Things hadn't gotten better after the wedding, like Sean had said—if anything, they'd seemed to get worse. Half the time Pen and I were arguing, the other half, we were ignoring each other.

Today was the prior. Today we were at each other's fucking throats, and I hated it.

"You are an asshole," she hissed at me.

Always with the name calling now. "For not wanting to drive two hours to see your parents?" *I demanded incredulously.*

"It's not about us." But it was, it always had been. *"They want to see Christopher."* Like hell they did. They wanted to make me feel like shit about myself, complain about my job, remind me where I was failing as a husband and father, and talk about how successful the prick they'd want Penelope to marry was.

"I was hoping that after we got married, we'd see less of them," I said, watching the muscles in Pen's back compress under her baggy, spaghetti-strap nightgown.

She scoffed. "Why would you think that?"

"Because you can't stand your parents."

Penelope's jaw tensed. She looked away, grabbed her hanging clothes on the closet rod, and tore them to the right. The grating sound ringing in my ears. She plucked a dress from its hanger, pinching it in her fist. "That's not true."

"Are you kidding me?" I demanded.

But she wouldn't look at me. "Penelope, they make me feel like shit."

She scowled. "You're being ridiculous."

"I'm getting pretty goddamn sick and tired of you minimizing how I feel." It hurt. Why couldn't she see that? She'd always been so aware, and now...

Pen dropped the dress at her feet, her hands balling at her sides. The silence was crippling as her shoulders rose and fell as she breathed, her stare still fixed on the closet.

I had nothing to lose now. "Why aren't we having sex?"

"Why is it always about sex with you?" she hissed. "Ever since I met you, it was always about sex."

She may as well have slapped me. I staggered back. There was a throbbing in my throat as my blood pressure heightened, tension settling between my shoulder blades. "It's never..." how could she say that?

Did she remember how this all happened?

"I just mean," she held up a hand, as though recognizing her error. "It's not really that big of a deal, is it?" Pen asked, sounding as sarcastic as her mother was on a good day.

I rocked my jaw, pitching my hands on my waist. "It's been months, Penelope. Kind of."

She swiped her palms against the front of her nightgown, her attention returning to the closet. "I see."

That was it? I see? "Penelope."

She waved me off dismissively, as though she was shooing off a fly, and I was this inconsequential problem. "If you don't want to come to Connecticut, you don't have to."

It wasn't about fucking Connecticut—it was about everything. I felt like I was playing house with my wife, who was as ambivalent about my presence as the temperament of Mother Nature, and it was destroying me. I felt like I was getting flayed alive every single day, with no end to the torture in sight.

She was keeping something from me. What, I didn't know, but it was the biggest head fuck and installing all kinds of thoughts and deep-seated doubts in my mind that I didn't want to have.

It left me thinking about things I shouldn't, with the romanticized version of a person who had no business being on my mind at all.

But the longer she said nothing, the faster those thoughts germinated. Her silence was like fertilizer, and the seeds spawned into trees that no axe, no matter how sharp, would take down.

My stomach dropped to my feet, my thoughts a mess of anger and frustration as I tried to see past her bullshit and the walls she'd erected around herself without warning. Somewhere in there lived the woman I'd fallen in love with.

Or at least, I hoped she was still in there—but I wasn't sure of what remained of my fight to keep her anymore.

"You don't care how they make me feel, do you?" *She didn't care that I could hear her parents every time we were there, rhyming off my faults the same way one might list their grocery shopping list.* "That's why you don't say anything to them anymore."

Pen blew out a breath. "They're always going to have something to say, just tune it out."

Just tune it out?

Just pretend like they didn't take issue with my entire fucking existence? My career? My family? I mean, for fuck's sake, these people had wanted me to change my last name and had nearly told four hundred guests at our wedding that I was.

I was never *changing my last name, and I didn't expect Pen to change hers either.*

But she expected me to change. She expected me to mold myself into whatever she wanted me to be, whatever they expected us to be.

And I was over it. "A year ago, you would have never let them say any of that shit to me." *I threw my hands up in the air.* "Never mind fucking pander to their emotional needs."

"I am not pandering!" *she shrieked, whipping around on the ball of her foot. Her frame rattled with her rage, her eyes hot on me. It seemed like she was always snapping now, these irrational emotional outbursts that seemed to get worse as the days waned into weeks. Ever since the day we were supposed to leave for our honeymoon, and I'd found her sobbing on the toilet with period blood everywhere.*

"You are conflating your sex addiction with your personal issues with my parents." *My mouth popped open, the tightness in my muscles burning as I stared at her, transfixed in horror.*

But she wasn't finished dressing me down. No, Penelope was only getting started. "Get over it, Dougie. We'll have sex when I feel like it, but I don't feel like having sex with you," *she seethed, practically decapitating me with her eyes. "You're working all day, and I'm a housewife. I'm tired at the end of the day. Your wants are the furthest thing from my mind when the day is over."*

The furthest thing from her mind.

My molars found each other, my jaw tensing as I clenched. For some reason, I thought about her rushing across the yard and leaping into my arms, peppering my face with her kisses over the jests of the crew when we worked together. Of her clinging to my side even when it was too hot to fuck, and she was just this affectionate little thing who didn't care about the unsavory circumstances. She just wanted her hands on me, and mine on her. I thought about the woman who had wanted to marry me in a hospital gown.

But here we were.

And I didn't think I had the strength to do this. I inched away from her, from this argument, from our marriage, heading toward the bedroom door.

"Now you're walking away?" she hollered.

"What do you want me to say to you?" I asked her soberly. "After every-thing you just said to me, what do you want me to say?"

I wanted to be wanted again. I needed to be wanted.

I…

I wanted to be held and loved and assured that I wasn't the biggest sack of shit. And I wasn't going to find that here, in this house, with my wife.

But I knew where to find it.

"She'd already lost the baby by then," I finished. It had been her anger talking, the grief… not her.

"That's messed up," Sean murmured, his expression rankled. "That she kept that from you, that you…"

"Yeah," I agreed, rubbing the corners of my mouth, staring down at my untouched scrambled eggs and bacon. "I shouldn't have gone, though." I was making a conscious effort to avoid saying his sister's name. "I was frustrated that you were hanging out with what's-his-face, maybe even a bit jealous." He'd asked Maria's boyfriend to go to a baseball game with him in Maryland, and I'd felt like I was being replaced there, too. Everywhere I'd looked, I wasn't enough.

"No." He picked at his omelet that had arrived as I'd filled in the blanks for him. "You shouldn't have gone there."

The fact that Sean had driven me to Four Corners and not to the edge of town to beat me to death and then ensure no one ever found me again like his wife had promised was a goddamn miracle.

I would have killed me.

Guilt swam in my insides, my mouth going dry as the lump formed in my throat. "I wasn't trying to mess things up for... Maria and..." Whatever the hell his name had been.

"Jordan." Sean filled in the blank. "His name is Jordan, and he's a pretty standup guy, believe it or not... even if he is from Baltimore."

At least he didn't cheer for the Yankees.

Sean put his fork down, his mouth pulling to the right with thought. His brown eyes landed on me, filled with neither judgment nor absolution. "You royally fucked up," he said matter-of-factly, earning my flinch.

No shit.

"You made a giant fucking mess, but that doesn't mean you can't fix it, Dougie. You just need to get comfortable being uncomfortable and remembering why you chose her."

"What if I can figure that out, and she can't, Sean?" I clenched my jaw, my insides shrinking as the gravity of our situation marinated over my mind. "What if we're too far gone? I mean, you don't keep a pregnancy from your husband, whether you wanted it or not, you just don't. And then to not tell me when she," I paused, finding my nerve, "when she lost it."

"People do fucked-up shit when they're scared. It doesn't always make sense, but it's their brain's way of trying to protect them from the things they're struggling to understand." He shook his head. "I went from feeling perfectly okay with never speaking to you and Pen again to feeling so fucking sorry for you both that I regretted hitting you."

"I hit you," I corrected.

"Whatever," he said, shrugging. "I felt bad, and I understood. Keeping a secret from your best friends is one thing, but from each other? That destroys marriages, Dougie. Lies ruin people beyond repair."

"I should have…" I trailed off. "Fought harder. Maybe if I'd just been transparent about where my headspace was, it would have made something register for her, too."

"I think she was worried about coming across as faulty."

I lifted my head, watching him sadly through my eyebrows. "She's not faulty."

"I know," he assured, his tone steady and even. "But the way Raquel explained it to me, if your body failed you in this way, the self-hatred…?"

I swallowed the lump of emotion in my throat. "I would be angry, too."

Sean pushed his plate back, linked his hands together, and pressed them to his mouth. "Go home and choose her, Dougie."

"I do—"

"No," Sean interrupted emphatically. "*Consciously* choose her. Choose her when she yells, when she acts in a way you don't under-stand. Choose her when she's crumbling and needs you to hold her up. Choose her when she can't choose herself."

An hour and three cups of coffee later, we strode out of the diner. Our relationship was far from mended, but I held onto the hope that we were on the path for recovery. I'd missed a lot in the few months since I'd seen them last.

I had a lot to make amends for.

Sean searched the pocket of his sweatpants for his keys, fishing them out. As I was inching toward the passenger door, I lifted my eyes, pausing when I caught sight of the antique shop across the street.

Hundreds of times I'd driven down Main Street right past this shop. But the shop had never had *that*.

"You in a hurry?" I asked.

"I got about an hour before we gotta pick the twins up from my ma's," he glanced behind him, trying to find the source of my wide-eyed curiosity. "What's up?"

"Penelope's birthday present." I kicked my chin at the antique shop.

Not that I had a goddamn clue how to pack it… or get it home.

But it was a start. It was something she could begin to reclaim as her own. Something I could offer her to choose herself, too.

Sean glanced back at me, grinning. "C'mon, any luck and it's still the old woman who sold me Raquel's typewriter."

Chapter Thirty

Penelope

Five months ago…

"COME ON, SEAN," I GROWLED, LISTENING AS THE PHONE RANG AND rang. "Pick up the fucking phone."

I'd called Dougie half a dozen times when he'd stormed out of the house after our argument, but he hadn't answered. Out of desperation to fix it, I'd pivoted and started chain-calling Sean.

If anyone knew where Dougie was, it would be Sean.

But he didn't answer, either. I slammed the phone down on the receiver in frustration, gritting my teeth till my TMJ screamed.

Charging toward the dryer, I clipped the dryer door shut with my hip forcefully, tossing the rogue sock into the pile of unfolded clothes I'd had clutched in my hand.

Pushing out a tight exhale, I stared at Dougie's plaid button up as I pitched one hand on my hip, the other on the dryer. The loud rush of water filling the washer basin drowned my thoughts out. My gaze trailed from his shirt tentatively to my polished short, fingernails, settling on the stack of rings that were supposed to represent our love and our union.

People in love didn't do that to one another. People in love didn't say what I said.

I'd been horrible to him.

My eyes stung, tears pricking the back of my lids while I fought to keep them contained. The urge to call him again made my fingers vibrate.

Lowering my head, I took a shuddering breath that didn't meet my lungs, my vitriol pin balling through my mind.

Your wants are the furthest thing from my mind when the day is over.

That wasn't true though, was it? I cared, I...

I still wanted him, too. I just... I just *what?* Lifting my hand to my eyes, my vision blurred as the tawny, warm laundry room lighting caught on the opal of my engagement ring. My fingers curled inward as I fastened my other palm around my wrist, clutching my rings close to my chest.

I just didn't know how to tell him that none of what was happening between us was because of him, it was because of me.

I would have torn out of the house too if someone had accused me of something so horrendous and out of left field. Dougie was right to question me; he was right to challenge my thinking. I'd turned into a WASP-y aristocratic version of Dr. Jekyll and Mr. Hyde—only there was nothing strange about my case. I was just struggling under the burden of my massive fucking lie that I kept hidden.

I was lying to my husband. I'd been lying to my husband every single day for almost four months. Another hurl of guilt taunted me, making my teeth gnash together.

I had to tell him. I couldn't do this anymore.

The shrill ring of the phone to my right interrupted my thoughts. Jolting, I stared wide-eyed at the phone, but when I told my legs to run for it, I couldn't move.

Strident, inward thoughts spun in my mind, screaming at me that something was wrong.

The fine hairs on the back of my neck rose to half-mast, practically confirmed the fear. Prickling crawled down my spine, goosebumps breaking out across my skin.

Now, who was the one being ridiculous? Me.

So why couldn't I move?

Just answer the phone, Penelope.

Apologize to your husband.

Beg for his forgiveness.

But something told me that wasn't my husband returning my calls.

My heart skipped a nervous beat as I took one hesitant step after the other to the phone, my hand nearly shirking back when another urgent ring came through.

I winced as my ribs turned into a vise around my lungs and I lifted the phone to my ear, my fingers finding the cord. "Hello?"

That sound. I knew with full certainty I'd never forget that harrowing, broken cry, nor that sensation of dread polluting my veins. "P-P-Pen," Sean stammered. "I-I-I,"

Terror struck me, my legs as heavy as anvils. My palm crashed hard against the laundry room wall, bracing myself as terror seized me. "What's wrong?"

God, please don't tell me that my husband was dead. I'd never forgive myself.

But what Sean told me threatened to ensure I entrapped myself in a purgatory unlike any other forever.

"It's Raquel," he gasped out. "She had an accident."

I flew out of the house at the sight of Eileen's headlights slashing across our living room window as she pulled her car into the driveway. My hands were rattling as I tore off toward my SUV as fast as my

Birkenstocks would allow me, while I kept my phone sandwiched against my ear, and my heart hammered like a war drum in my chest.

Why wasn't he answering his phone hours later?

"Penelope," Eileen called.

Any other day, the way her motherly Irish lilt enveloped my name would make warmth enter my veins. Now, the interruption just irritated me because it was delaying me from getting where I needed to be.

The hospital.

"Are you okay to drive?" My teeth chattered despite the unusually balmy late spring temperatures.

I turned my head away, covering my mouth with the back of my hand. I didn't have a choice, because I had no idea where *her* son was, and I...

The tingling in my chest said I had to go, every alarm and panic receptor in my mind melting down. Without answering her, I unlocked my car doors, my headlights flashing. I was so fucking lightheaded right now, but I didn't have time to wallow, second-guess myself, or question my stability.

I was a mother. That's what I was biologically designed to do—be okay in a crisis. Know what to do when the day came when Christopher tried to shove a bead up his nose or found himself inspired to recreate the scene from *Home Alone* where Kevin McCallister used a sled down the stairs, and we inevitably wound up in the ER with a broken or sprained limb. I knew I would pass the time educating him they used stunt doubles in movies. And I'd keep talking to him while ignoring the din of the hospital because it would keep my worry in check and give me something to do.

But no amount of talking would help me right now.

The engine roared to life, my hand searching the air to my left for the seatbelt that I eventually snagged and clicked into place. Eileen approached the front door, her arms folded across her chest and worry darkening her expression as she glanced at me over her shoulder.

The unanswered question still lived on her face.

Was I okay?

No. But I had to be.

As soon as my Bluetooth engaged in my car, I tried Dougie's number again as I shifted the SUV into reverse. Plumes of dust kicked up when I hit the accelerator too hard, my wheels grunting in protest.

"C'mon, Dougie," I pleaded, slamming on the brakes when my tires touched the street. "Answer the phone."

His voicemail kicked in once more.

I ended the call, redialing again.

Choking the steering wheel, a million things entered my mind. What if he'd been in an accident, too? What if the last thing I'd ever said to him had been a lie? I hadn't meant he wasn't important; I was just—I was projecting.

It seemed like I was always projecting.

By the time I saw St. Anne's hospital twenty-five minutes later, I'd called him twenty-two times. He hadn't answered once. As I punched the parking meter's button to gain entry into the visitor parking lot, I'd decided on two things.

One, I was going to tell my husband the truth. I was going to tell him I'd been pregnant, that I'd been angry about it, and then I'd wanted it—and that it was my fault I lost it.

As I reverse parked my SUV, my body trembled. I had struggled to handle it myself, but I had no idea how he'd take it.

There was a risk that he'd hate me.

But if he didn't… then number two was, I'd beg him to forgive me, because I didn't want a life or a world without my husband in it.

I needed him.

I needed him to look at me like he once had when I was the new girl, and he was the guy who stared at me like I was the best thing that had happened since the Pats drafted Tom Brady. I missed Dougie, desperately.

I missed him so much that sometimes, even when he was right beside me, his choppy breathing signifying he was wide awake, I fantasized about blanketing my body on top of his and just basking in his warmth and presence.

I wanted our lives back. I wanted him back.

So the horrifying, increasingly realistic visual that his truck might have flipped upside down in a ditch somewhere, long since erupted in flames and his body incinerated, had my hands sinking in my hair, tugging at the roots while my stomach churned.

He didn't even know I loved him.

But then another thought leeched into my mind, scarier than the first. God, what if he had been in the wrong place at the wrong time? I had read a story a few weeks ago about a man who'd been stabbed to death while pumping gas. Something so normal shouldn't have resulted in the loss of a husband and father of three from Revere, but all the BPD had confirmed was that it was a case of mistaken identity.

I was a classic example of mistaken identity, too, wasn't I? I'd sold Dougie on the illusion that I was someone else and he'd bought into it, and now, now he might be dead. Or I was just losing my fucking mind who knew.

Either way, my body and amygdala were reacting to it as if it were a sure thing. I didn't even know what kind of memorial service he wanted. I couldn't be a widow, no. Christopher needed his dad. I needed his dad.

We were supposed to be a family, the three of us. We'd promised each other in the hospital that our forever was all that had mattered.

My breathing quickened as my adrenaline charged through my system. I dropped my grasp on my hair to wrap my arms around my body in a consoling hug.

Please, don't be dead. I'm sorry, just don't be dead.

My blurring vision searched the sea of cars, the overhead street-lights illuminating the parking lot as I fought to find a focal point to help me calm down. A bright pink car, or a motorcycle, something unlike the nondescript sedans, SUVs and minivans.

What if that really was the last thing I said to him?

What if I'd never gotten to tell him the truth?

What if he—my heart stuttered in my chest, my expression slackening and a hollowed-out sensation swept through me.

What if he was just a few car lengths away?

I leaned forward, ignoring the way my head spun, my gaze fixating on the Ford F-150 and the silhouettes of two bodies. One I could readily pick out as my husband's body, but the other...

Was I seeing things? Was this the straw that broke the camel's back and had me emitted into the hospital for a temporary, involuntary psych evaluation?

I stiffened, a tingling sensation bursting in my chest as the sobs ceased and the heels of my palms dug into my eyes.

My gaze dropped to the license plate. The red serial number was bright and proud against the stark white metal illuminated by the streetlights.

2KT N20

I wasn't going crazy, that was his license plate. My heart sank, a shudder ripping through me while sweat licked up my spine. The tingling set off in my limbs as I studied the silhouettes.

Feminine. The one in the passenger seat was feminine, and she jerked the passenger's side sun visor down, her slender shadowed limbs swiping at her face.

Who was that? Who was in his truck?

I held my breath, spots entering my vision when the truck door ripped open, the red-bottomed soles entered my line of vision first, pulling me into an alternate universe where my worst nightmare came to fruition before she revealed the rest of herself to me.

Shiny, lush dark hair that spilled over her shoulders. That curvy, enviable figure. Her normally perfect makeup smeared around her eyes as though she'd been sobbing hysterically.

But she still looked elegant, even distraught, as she slammed the truck door like she wanted to take her anger out on the driver of the truck. The one I'd spent years loving, the one whose son I brought into this world, the one I'd married.

The one who was running around with *her* while I'd been at home, tearing myself apart for *him*.

I couldn't believe this. My skin burned hot, my hands rattling as I fought to get the car door open. The seatbelt jerked me back, my molars clenching together as I punched the button free, the polyester giving me a fabric burn as I ripped it away from my body.

No, no. This was wrong. I was seeing things, right? I had to be.

Dougie was the nice guy. The kind guy. He wasn't a cheat.

He wasn't.

And Maria Tavares had a boyfriend named Jordan. I'd been so

relieved when I'd met him during our wedding weekend. He was charming, dapper, and a little older than her. But he was hers.

Finally, I'd have nothing to worry about again because Dougie's 'one who got away' was off the market, and he was completely mine because the vows had to mean something.

They had to. He wouldn't have... he wouldn't have done that to me.

Not after what his father had done to his mother.

But the more I tried to reason with myself, the worse my rage grew. What was he doing with her then? There was no other explanation. My muscles twitched under my skin, and my pulse roared wildly in my ears as my Birkenstocks ate at the pavement. I had tunnel vision now as I put the pieces of the puzzle together.

I hadn't been crazy when I'd caught the way he'd looked at her on our wedding day. I'd ignored it from my spot at our table when I'd gone to get a seltzer tablet from my clutch to add to my water because I'd felt nauseous and when I'd lifted my head after finding the tablet buried at the bottom of my bag, my stare zeroed in on him with her with a sniper-like focus—his hand closed around her bicep, while Maria tilted her head down to meet his intense stare dead-on.

And the only thought I had in my mind at that moment as I clawed through the waves of nausea and discomfort was that they looked good together. They could have been together had she wanted him. Despite my best efforts to make myself feel better with the mantra to myself that what I'd witnessed was platonic, it didn't change that when she fled from his path, he looked at her like he should have looked at me.

He wanted to chase after her, to hold on to her, maybe even to love her again.

Now I knew I hadn't been imagining what I'd seen that day. No, that had been real. Their spark, their connection, their... their budding affair.

When had it started? Before our wedding, or after?

God, did I even want to know? There I'd been, trying to be the model wife, the perfect daughter, a halfway decent mother, harboring a secret pregnancy, and he had been off prancing around with her?

It must have started after the wedding. When he'd got argumentative with me, when he started demanding we talk and discuss things. And when I didn't want to, because I was struggling with the guilt, he sought solace in her.

My husband was cheating on me. I placed a hand on my stomach, my insides heaving as the visual of their naked bodies moving in tandem contaminated my mind.

Did they fuck in his truck like we used to?

He didn't notice my short figure as I rounded the hood of his truck. Dougie had his head down on his steering wheel, his shoulders slumped and his profile tense.

I'd loved him. I'd fallen for him despite my desire not to, for reasons just like this.

How could he do this to me?

Biting on the inside of my cheek, I pounded the driver's side window, the blunt ping of my rings against the glass cutting through the silence of the parking lot. My blood ran cold as he lifted his head slowly, his tired, green eyes widening with surprise and dread.

My eyes stung with a fresh batch of tears, my bottom trembling as I glared at him. I ripped my eyes momentarily from his, finding Maria's silhouette in the distance, charging toward the hospital entrance.

I hadn't made that up. That had been her with him.

They'd been together. He'd left our house to go to her.

He'd betrayed me.

I swallowed the lump of emotion in my throat, but ingesting gravel would have been easier. My head moved with bewilderment as he reached for the handle of the door. All I could do was stare at him with the competing thoughts of how much I loved him, and how much this moment had destroyed what remained of us.

Dougie opened the car door with control, an unspoken plea entering his expression.

My tears dribbled down my chin, cruising down the column of my throat, past my collarbone and disappearing between the tunnel of my breasts under the white-solid notched-collar three-quarter-length shirt.

I shook my hands out, the anxiety threatening to pull me over the precipice. "I've been calling you," I whispered.

He winced, his head turning toward the open truck door.

"I've been calling you and you didn't answer." I glanced back at the hospital doors, where Maria was nowhere to be seen. "You were with her?"

I wanted him to lie to me. I wanted him to gaslight me into believing that I hadn't witnessed what I did. But Dougie was still the nice guy, even when he wasn't.

Or at least I thought he had been. "Not the way you think I was, Penny."

I fought the urge to throw my head back with a laugh. That was the best he could come up with? Was that the byproduct of a public-school education? You didn't learn the art of telling a convincing lie? God, the blood crusted around his nose alone was a tell.

"What happened to your face then?" I demanded, my stare tapering.

This time, I couldn't control the laugh. It came out in a dry huff as I pieced the final missing puzzle piece together. "Did you two get caught by Jordan?"

Dougie held up both hands, attempting to pacify me. "No one got caught doing anything."

Liar. What a fucking liar, and a terrible one at that. He was the poster boy of an adulterous husband right now.

Folding my arms over my chest, I propped the tip of my sandal onto the paved ground. "I don't believe you," I confessed, my voice laden with guilt. This was my fault. I was responsible for this, wasn't I? If I'd just told him, then he might not have gone to her.

I couldn't expect that depriving my husband of affection for months on end would have kept him faithful to me. He was still a person.

Even the sanest one would have reacted the same way.

My next statement leaving my mouth was a sucker punch to my gut. "I've seen the way you look at her." I tried to swallow the bile tearing up my throat.

Dougie looked like he stopped breathing.

"At the wedding, *our* wedding... there was this moment where you looked at her like you should have looked at me."

"Penny—" *God, don't say my name like that.*

I shook my head, staring at a piece of chewing gum fossilized on the ground. "No, I really… I don't want to hear it." And I didn't. I wet my lips, and my nostrils flared as I willed myself not to cry anymore.

"What do you mean you don't want to hear it, Penelope?"

I refrained from rolling my eyes. "Exactly what I said," I replied, inching away from him, needing as much space as humanly possible. "I can't make you want to be in this marriage with me when you so clearly want to be with her."

Why else wouldn't he tell me he was at his breaking point if it weren't because he wanted out, too?

"Penelope, I gave her a ride to the hospital." Another lie. I created more distance between us as he leaned in, his hands flexing, as though he wanted nothing more than to pull me into him and keep me there. I couldn't recall the last time I'd felt the strength of his arms around me.

That was my fault.

"I want to be with you." The lies were becoming so fluid, so convincing now, that for a split second, the naïve part of me almost believed him.

Almost.

My jaw hardened, my teeth chattering inside of my mouth practically vibrating as the anxiety worsened. "How did you end up in the city, then?" I craned my head. "That's a long way from home."

All I received was his silence. And his silence? It was telling. It said all the things he wouldn't admit.

The WASP in me wouldn't allow me to scream in public. I couldn't hurl insults and accusations at him. I couldn't slap him. I couldn't crumble to the ground.

So, I did what I knew how to do, what Evelyn would have done.

I walked away.

I hardly felt my body as the soft shuffle of my Birkenstocks and quiet cries filled the stillness of the parking lot as I made my way to the entrance. I needed to get in there. I needed to make sure Raquel was going to be okay after everything.

His panicked voice called out as he pursued me, "I'll tell you the truth, just let me—"

I spun around, losing my hold on myself. I shoved my hands against his solid chest, a feral cry so unlike me slipping free. "Save it for someone who believes you, Dougie, because that person isn't me." I pulled my hands back, swiping the tears from my cheeks with the back of my knuckles. "Not anymore."

The hospital had been the last place I thought I'd end up tonight after my husband fled our house in a cloud of kicked-up gravel, devastation and rage. Over the sterile scent of bleach and polite platitudes was the unmissable scent of death permeating from below.

My stomach rolled. Could I blame him for having an affair? Could I truly justify my anger?

I'd accused him of having a sex addiction, but that wasn't true, was it? I'd been depriving him, slowly plunging him into madness because I couldn't make peace or find acceptance of what I'd done.

What I'd lost.

Dougie hadn't deserved any of it. He deserved nothing I did to him. I wondered if he had known when he'd broken my fall the day we met what life had in store for us, if he still would have wanted all this?

I'd made his life hell for the past few months. No, that felt like I was trying to minimize how awful I'd been toward him. I hadn't just made his life hell, I'd turned his life into one vicious nightmare after another with no peace in sight. I'd bounded him to a lifetime of commitment when I'd accepted his ring, but that hadn't meant he knew what he'd signed up for because I'd changed.

Ever since that fateful January day this year when I watched that faint positive blue line appear on a pregnancy test, everything seemed like someone had thrown life off course because the truth was, I hadn't wanted to be pregnant again.

Not yet.

The timing was just bad. Mother was harping on me to get serious about the wedding, reminding me of the mounting costs for an event we'd neither wanted nor asked for. I was convinced that I'd missed a lesson at Hotchkiss on how to effectively shame your adult children into anything and everything, but she had excelled and passed the class with flying fucking colors, and I became the "yes woman" I would have confidently sworn on a Metallica Limited-Edition Vinyl Box Set that I'd never become ten years ago.

But I had become a yes woman.

Giving my parents this wedding to plan, something to make them happy after I'd always caused them grief and anguish, had seemed like such an inconsequential thing. The joke was on me, though, and that wedding? It had cost me everything.

My pride.

My health.

My marriage.

It wasn't like I had intended to pretend the pregnancy wasn't happening long term. I was just stressed about the whole thing. But that hadn't meant I didn't want it. Some naïve part of me had just wanted to hit pause on it until I was ready to hit play again. But life didn't work that way, did it?

I had held onto hope that once Dougie and I landed in Italy for our honeymoon, with the gorgeous port city setting of Genoa behind us and the sun hitting the Liguria region just right, that I could apologize to my husband properly.

That I could serve him this surprise to get us back on track. That this pregnancy, however wrong the timing had been, could be exactly what bridged us back together.

I loved Dougie.

I needed Dougie.

And without me realizing it, I'd needed that pregnancy.

But the thing they didn't warn you about needs was that most of them were just wants disguised. Much like Christopher's conception, this one was unplanned. And just as I adjusted to our newfound situation, where toothless grins masked the discomfort of dress fittings and forays with the dressmaker's needles, and my overwhelmed mind's attempt at trying to conjure what another version of Dougie and I looked like, or the inward sound of laughter and joy drowned out Mother's snide remarks about my weight as I emotionally and mentally fell in love with the concept of our family of three making room for one more...

I lost it.

Just like that.

One minute, I was packing my positive pregnancy test alongside the first ultrasound wrapped in a box in my luggage, with my heart beating wildly in my chest and the surety that this would fix us.

The next, I was the victim of a horror movie.

Strangely enough, I hadn't expected there to be that much blood. The desire to die had blindsided me, too. I'd always been the happy girl, the funny girl, but with my soiled underwear and the cramps that made me want to vomit? I welcomed death.

We hadn't made it to Italy.

Instead, I found myself in this very ER, hours later, alone and shivering—Dougie at home and fucking clueless—listening to a doctor telling me that after running a series of tests, my hCG levels had fallen and they'd been unsuccessful in procuring a heartbeat.

Such a clinical and callous explanation.

"The pregnancy wasn't viable, Ms. Cullimore. Can we call someone for you?"

The pregnancy wasn't viable, and there was no one to call because I was going to take this loss to my fucking grave. Because what did that make me now? I was a shit wife, a mediocre mother, and now...?

After everything I'd done to my husband leading to this moment, everything we'd endured, I couldn't even make it up to him by giving him this.

I'd turned into a monster, someone I didn't recognize, someone I couldn't even look in the eyes.

I struggled to even tell Raquel about the pregnancy, because on top of keeping it from my husband, I'd kept it from my best friend, too. I'd never held a secret like this. I'd told her almost every inconsequential detail about myself, short of how many times I used the bathroom in a day since the moment I'd met her in college.

Part of me hadn't wanted to detract from her pregnancy—she was going to experience motherhood for the first time—and the other part of me hadn't been prepared to deal with it yet.

The joke was on me. My lack of gratitude? It had come back to bite me in the ass. And if Dougie and I had been in a shitty place before? It paled compared to what awaited us after I'd come home with the doctor's orders that while I wouldn't need any procedure; I needed to take it easy for a few days and to wear a pad to help collect the blood and clots.

It would pass after a week or two. I had to endure this for two entire weeks, and the rage brewing inside of me boiled out of control. My anger misdirected, I punished my husband. I turned him into a villain. I projected my weaknesses and insecurities, and he absorbed it until he couldn't.

That was why he'd gone to her tonight, hadn't it?

He'd left our home to go to her, to someone who once made him feel good, who loved him in her own fucked-up way.

I'd once been the source of his yearning. I'd been the beat in his heart, the thrumming in his soul. Now I was just the faulty wife who'd miscarried their child and made his life insufferable.

I didn't deserve him. I'd never deserved him. He'd always worried he wouldn't be enough, but it was me. It had always been me.

I was the poison. I'd destroyed us.

Me.

Not Mother and Daddy.

Not Dougie.

Me.

That was why I was holed up in this recently cleaned hospital bathroom, the sting of bleach in the air burning my sinuses. The walls felt like they were closing in on me, and some small part of me just wished they would.

I slid down the tiled, one-person hospital bathroom wall, my ass hitting the floor as the agonized sob ripped from my throat. I drew my knees to my chest, the vision of my husband in the car with Maria shredding what remained of my sanity and dignity.

What did I care anymore?

Trying so hard to be fucking perfect hadn't mattered in the long run, had it?

I'd ruined everything, all by myself. Pushed away my husband, talked shit about my best friend who had nothing while I'd always had everything.

Spoiled, stupid, rich girl.

Ungrateful.

I hated myself. I'd done this to my marriage. My thoughts put my best friend in the hospital.

Maybe I hadn't caused Raquel's accident, but I couldn't help but feel some small, twisted part of me was responsible for it. She'd been so nervous when she'd told me in my kitchen last summer that she thought she might be pregnant. I'd fished her positive pregnancy test out of the garbage, for Christ's sake. No one had been happier for her than me.

No one.

I'd daydreamed about Christopher having a playmate—but when I'd learned that she was having twins? I'd grabbed her hands in the coffee shop, and screamed excitedly, bouncing on my toes while she stared at me like she might have a complete and total breakdown and everyone else watched us. They'd never understand. They'd never recognize the full significance because this was Raquel's moment. Her life was hers and hers alone. She was going to create for her children a life she'd always dreamed of for her and her late sister.

I believed in her, implicitly. I knew she'd never be like the people who'd brought her into this world because she had so much to give. I slept a little easier knowing that she finally had everything she'd ever deserved.

A real family.

So why the fuck had I envied her?

I was being punished now. My green-eyed monster would endure endless suffering as my best friend laid in an operating room while her husband collapsed to his knees with the most distraught, agonizing sobs I'd ever heard in my life while I hid in the bathroom.

On the floor.

What right did I have to sob? None.

I'd wished ill on her. Unintentionally, but I had. I'd coveted her happiness, the beauty of her well-deserved happily ever after.

I'd made snide remarks to Dougie about why she got to be pregnant when she had never wanted to be.

Me.

All me.

I'd ruined a family. And if she didn't make it?

If she didn't survive? I would be responsible for killing her, too.

God, I couldn't stomach that. My hands fisted my hair, my mouth popping open as another flurry of cries ripped free.

"Please, please," I begged to no one. "Just let her live. Don't let her die, I'll give anything…"

The urgent knock wrapped against the bathroom door.

"You almost done in there?" A disembodied male voice called.

I couldn't hide in here forever. "J-j-just a minute," I stammered weakly, pushing myself up from the floor. My lungs squeezed as I fought to control my breathing, stumbling toward the pedestal sink. I punched the soap dispenser, lathering my hands, suds not forming because of the lack of water. I scrubbed until my hands were raw, despite the increasingly urgent pounding against the door.

I fixated on washing my hands, scrubbing them into oblivion like the act of attempting to cleanse myself would wash away my sins.

It would never be enough. I'd never be able to scrub the stains a way.

The door jumped as though someone had kicked it, but I didn't even have it in me to react. I turned the faucet on, rinsing my hands off, my skin stinging as the water spilled from the faucet, rushing over my tender, red skin.

I reached for a sheet of paper towel from the dispenser, tearing a sheet free and drying my hands off with it. Turning the faucet off, I stared at my blotchy complexion in the mirror.

"You have no right to cry." I met my glossy, red-rimmed eyes dead-on—hating the woman they belonged to. "You did this, Penelope." I swiped the remaining tears with the back of my wrist, then tossed it to the trash.

Gritting my teeth, I unlocked the bathroom door. The man on the other side sucked back a breath, stepping out of my way as I stumbled back into the hallway deliriously.

If I looked close to how I felt? I'd get the hell out of my way, too.

The fluorescent lights were so harsh out here, bouncing off the white walls and the cream floors. I squinted, the headache setting in as I stood in the hallway. The intercom paging a doctor sounded muffled, a ringing setting off in my ears as I tried to figure out what to do next.

Was I allowed to wait? Was I allowed to hope and pray that she was okay?

Was I going to lose my best friend?

I thought this was what it felt like to go crazy. The sensation of treading water despite your exhausted limbs, the deep inhalations only for your lungs to struggle to deflate, burning instead like they were waterlogged. Clutching at my chest to fight with the feeling that I was drowning, some small voice whirred in my head that I didn't deserve to lift my head from the disturbed surface of the water.

No, I needed to keep it there and serve my penance.

Just sink, Penelope. Sink.

"Don't you cry, goddamn it," I demanded in a whisper, shaking my head. But it was no use. I was going to cry, the ache ripping through me as I succumbed to my guilt and shame.

"Pen?"

I quickly swiped under my eyes as I turned to face the source.

Trina's features were soft and round, her face etched with compassion, the smoothed strands of her pastel pink hair tucked behind her ears. "Hey," she whispered, opening her arms to me with invitation. "She's gonna be okay."

She had no idea how much I needed that assurance right now, even if all it did was make me feel worse. I should have been with Raquel. I should have been present. She had called me earlier that day and I'd screened the call.

I screened most of her calls and texts these days.

I sagged into Trina's embrace, clinging tightly to her like she was my life raft, the only thing keeping me from sinking to the bottom of the ocean where I rightfully belonged. She was smaller than I was, but she held me with a herculean strength, her hands stroking my back. "Raquel's tough," she reminded me. It had always been obvious she adored her sister-in-law. "So fucking tough."

I knew that. I knew my best friend wasn't weak.

She hadn't escaped her demons just to die like this.

But I was scared. I was scared that I'd said so many horrible things about her, things I could never take back. And on top of that...

My husband was having an affair with my best friend's sister-in-law. With Katrina's older sister.

I choked on another sob, the suffocating hollowness in my chest so unbelievably fucking bleak that I wished that time would just stop for a minute so I could catch my breath.

No one stared at us as I rested my forehead on Trina's shoulder while she held me in silence in the middle of the hallway. When the shaking finally subsided, and my breathing evened out, her voice filtered through once more. "Do you want me to go get Dougie?"

"No," I hissed. He was the last person I wanted, the last person I needed.

Katrina recoiled in my arms, breaking our hold.

"No," I repeated this time, keeping my pitch soft and controlled, emulative to how I'd been raised. My shoulders slumped as I wrapped my arms around myself, stepping out of her embrace entirely, offering her my tight profile.

From the corner of my eye, Trina worried her bottom lip, her tone straining as she asked, "Did something else happen, Pen?"

What a loaded question.

Everything had happened. Everything.

I ran my fingers through my hair, forcing my posture to straighten and squaring my chin. "I just need to go sit down."

Illusions were all I had left anymore, like a party magician. I'd been brought into this world to bedazzle and fulfill someone else's life expectation. I hadn't been bred on love or on desire. I'd been the logical next step in my parents' life. My sole purpose had been to actualize their life plan for me, but I hadn't even done that right.

I hadn't done anything right in a long time, but this? This I would.

Taking one tenuous step after the other, I refused to falter as Trina called my name.

I didn't dare turn back and face her as I made my way back to the waiting room with the promise on my mind that as soon as I knew Raquel was okay?

I'd never speak to her again.

She deserved better.

And I didn't deserve her at all.

I wasn't sure how I'd driven home, but with exhaustion in my limbs and my mind numb, I turned the ignition off. Dougie's headlights sliced across the yard behind me as he sped up the drive, slamming his brakes.

He'd tried to sit with me when I went to the waiting room, but I got up and moved. I didn't want to pretend.

Maria had watched. She was supposed to be with Raquel tonight, maybe if she had been where she was supposed to be instead of with my husband…

"Penelope," Dougie called my name as soon as I got out of the truck, but I didn't meet his eyes. I just wanted it to stop.

His footfalls came down hard on the gravel of the driveway, but I whipped around, stilling him with a jut of my open palm. "Do not follow me, I can barely even look at you."

"Nothing happened."

"You're a fucking liar, Dougie. And you know it."

I slapped his hand away with everything I had in me when he reached for me. I'd never wanted to be that suburban housewife. The one trying to not yell at her husband on their front lawn in the middle of the night. I'd left as soon as Raquel was in recovery and the babies were stable, and Dougie was hot on my heels.

They had a son and a daughter. Children that would have grown up with my own.

But I was too ashamed of the things I'd thought and said. I couldn't imagine ever looking into their eyes, staring down at their small features. I'd always recall the time that my thoughts caused ill-will on their mother.

I'd nearly deprived them of her, so I didn't deserve her or them. I just wanted the noise in my head to stop. Staring up at the house, my bottom lip trembled.

"You weren't supposed to turn out like them," I said. This gorgeous edifice was the setting of our love story, the place where our son slept soundly, and Eileen laid oblivious in the guest room. "You were supposed to be different. The nice guy."

"I am the nice guy."

"No," I shook my head. "You're another lie, just like I am." I let the tears fall, squeezing my lids together. "We're strangers."

He stacked his hands on top of his head, exhaling a tight breath. Shifting his weight from foot to foot, he kicked at a piece of gravel, sending it across the yard. "Pen, just tell me how to fix this."

I forced my legs to move. I was going to sleep in Christopher's room tonight, on the floor with his little hand cradled in mine. My heart would only calm when I watched his tiny, even inhalations and saw the life in him. I had something; I had our son.

Our son was the only thing that would keep me here in this house of horrors.

"You wanna fix it?" I asked.

Dougie stared at me, wide-eyed and desperate.

"Stay the hell away from Raquel and Sean."

He paled, his arms collapsing to his sides. He opened his mouth to argue or reason with me, but I turned away, rushing to the front door.

Staying away would be our penance.

I wouldn't hear otherwise.

No matter how much it broke my heart.

Chapter Thirty-One

Penelope

Present

I CUT THE STREAM OF WATER FROM THE SHOWER HEAD, THE IMMEDIACY OF the cold draft settling across my skin as I watched an errant drop compete with another against the tiled walls while my wet hair dripped down my shoulders.

When I had turned thirty, I'd felt different. I'd been happier, too.

At twenty-nine, the prospect of my thirties had filled my head with notions of poise, self-acceptance, and an unflappable confidence.

But thirty hadn't brought me any of those things. It had given me pain, a chasm in my heart, and uncertainty.

Things were still unclear at thirty-one.

The seal on the glass door squeaked as I pulled it open, extending a hand for the white terrycloth robe hanging on the hook. Feeding my arms through the sleeves, I knotted the sash in the middle, then stepped out onto the bathmat. Slouching into the neckline of the robe to warm up, I pressed my thighs together to keep the shiver at bay as my eyes swept over the bathroom.

I'd loved this color palate when I'd initially picked it. But now, now I kind of hated it.

White tiles showed everything, no matter how much you scrubbed at them.

Flexing my fingers at my side, I took a fortifying breath and approached the bathroom mirror. Extending a hand, I swiped my hand against the condensation, creating a clearing. The bags under my eyes greeted me and it was hard to remember a time where they hadn't existed.

Things had been... weird, to put it simply.

After Dougie had returned home and Sean and Raquel had left, we sat together in the kitchen. Neither of us saying anything as we processed the turn of events. He knew everything now, and I couldn't help but recall how avoidable it had all felt in the grand scheme of things if I'd just communicated.

Like I'd needed to do at that moment.

"I don't know how to navigate this," I told him. *Dougie lifted his eyes to mine, his mouth a thin line as he shifted his gaze heavenward, nodding his head.* *"But all I know is that running away, avoiding each other, pretending like it's not happening... it won't work."*

He dragged his teeth over his lip, then scratched at the stubble on his cheek. "I agree."

"We skipped steps the other night. You were right," I continued, *drawing in a deep breath through my nose. I still felt him moving inside of me, and his hands on my skin despite being on the other side of the room. "We need to go back to the basics. Figure out what worked about us and what didn't."*

He nodded. "No more secrets, Penelope," he murmured. "From either of us. No more."

"And no more lies, either," I followed up.

The release of tension surprised me in my muscles as he met my stare once more and nodded his head again.

He repeated the statement back to me. "No more lies." Dougie stood up, plucking his ball cap from the counter, fitting it on his head. "I think we should," he bowed his head for a moment, trying to find his nerve, "go talk to someone. Together."

"Why does it sound like there's an 'and' there?" I asked, the heaviness in my stomach returning.

"And I think we should go see someone individually, too." He lifted the bill of his cap, glancing around the room, discomfort touching the corners of his eyes. "All my life, I dreamed of this. Of someone like you, of our son, of our life together. But when it got hard, I started wanting something easier."

"I did that—"

"I did that, Penelope. Not you. We all get choices to make." Dougie's jaw hardened, his arms crossing over his chest. "I'm trying to understand yours as much as I am trying to understand mine, but I need to figure out this part of me that wanted to default to something that I knew ended badly for my ma."

"Hurt people, hurt people..." I trailed off, reciting what he'd once said to me about Raquel as I wrung my hands together on my lap. "I'll, I'll find someone for us."

"And for yourself, Pen." He wasn't letting it go. "Someone who isn't that dorky asshole from Back Bay who blows smoke up your ass."

I blew out my cheeks. "He's not dorky." But he had enabled me. I knew that. Henry had never challenged my thinking, wasn't that why I stopped going? I was too ashamed to share my burdens and guilt with my therapist because I'd perpetuated this illusion of perfection and I hadn't wanted anything to compromise it.

"Start thinking about what you want out of life, and... when we're ready, we'll see where we're both at."

"I want this life, Dougie."

He seemed distracted for a moment, his eyes surveying the kitchen, until they landed on a photo on the fridge, partially buried under bill payment *reminders. It was a photo of the three of us at the beach two summers ago. He tilted his head in my direction, sadness entering his tone. "Me, too, Pen."*

"But?"

"But we need to want something more for ourselves, too."

What did I want for myself? That question had been heavy on my mind since then. It was the same question my new therapist had handed back to me as homework for the week when I'd gone to see her yesterday. She wasn't like Henry. She possessed an analytical and calm demeanor that had me unabashedly spilling my guts out, recreating the timeline of the last three years.

And at the parts I expected a big reaction. She kept her features neutral, the scratching of her pen eating up the air. Then she asked me that question just as our time ran out.

What did I want for myself?

Sure, I wanted to be a wife and a mother—but it was those identities that had challenged the parts of myself that I felt I needed to repress, too. In my pursuit of perfection, I'd forgotten what I loved, what I missed. I hadn't gone back to work after giving birth because I thought the next logical step in my life was to be a stay-at-home mother like mine had been.

But I'd never asked myself if I found that fulfilling or if it was something I felt I was supposed to do. Don't get me wrong, I loved our son. I loved spending my time with him and being able to witness as he discovered the world for the first time—I'd just never asked myself if I was done discovering the world, too.

I thought that might have been what Dougie meant. It wasn't about him trying to challenge the depths of my love for Christopher, him, or our life, it was him trying to question what I'd said in the kitchen about needing to fall back in love with myself again.

Who was Penelope Louise Cullimore?

What does she do? What does she love?

And would thirty-one be the year that she discovered it?

Picking up the hairbrush, I worked the fine bristles through my hair, allowing my leaden eyes to drop shut momentarily as I lost myself to the sweeping motions, one stroke after another, only stopping when an uncoordinated knock sounded from my bedroom door.

Opening the bathroom door, the steam escaped the hot confines as I stood in the bathroom doorway.

"Mama," Christopher called as the bedroom doorknob turned. He jutted his head inside, grinning at me. "Happy birthday!"

"Get in there, little man," Dougie said with a quiet laugh. "I'm gonna lose this whole tray."

What tray?

The door widened as Christopher sauntered in, his weight shifting from foot to foot in a bounce-like dance. His clothes matched green corduroy pants with a gray long-sleeved shirt. For some reason, it made me sad.

My eyes lifted from his only for a split second as Dougie's stocky frame filled the doorway, his eyes uneasy as they landed on me while his fingers tightened around the serving tray in his grasp.

"Happy birthday," he said breathlessly, his gaze sweeping over me, momentarily addling my brain. What was birthday etiquette? Did I get to kiss my husband if I wanted to? Or did I have to wish for it on a birthday cake?

I wiped my sweating palms against the side of the robe, nodding my head. "Thanks."

A week ago, my clothes had been scattered on the floor and he had buried his head between my legs. Yet somehow today, I felt more naked in front of him than I ever had before.

He glanced down at the tray. "Where do you want this?"

"You made me breakfast?" I studied the tray, the smile lifting the corner of my mouth.

"Uhm." He let out a throaty chuckle as he tilted his chin downward. "Full disclosure, I called Frieda yesterday for a recipe, but my hollandaise did not come together the way hers does."

"Eggs Benedict?"

"I tried." He lifted his shoulder in a half-shrug. "You don't have to eat it if you don't want to, though." My stomach fluttered as I took light footsteps toward him. His deep green eyes searched mine, a hyperawareness of my body percolating through me.

"Thank you," I murmured, not even looking at the plate. I leaned forward, pressing a chaste kiss at the corner of his mouth.

My pulse raced as I drew back, finding he'd shut his eyes for a moment.

Dougie's hard swallow was noticeable, his Adam's apple weaving. "Anything, Penelope. I," he faltered, glancing down at Christopher, who'd winded his body around my leg, staring up at me expectantly.

Dougie didn't say it, but I heard it all the same.

And I loved him, too.

"I don't know what they're doing out there," I whispered into the phone. "But he won't let me look." Actually, what he'd instructed as he weaved in and out of each room with a smirk playing with his lips, as he closed curtains and blinds was, 'stay away from the backyard facing windows.'

But same shit.

"Then don't look—*ow*, Jesus, Holly," Raquel hissed, her annoyance directed at her daughter. "This kid's a fucking piranha."

I snorted out a laugh.

"Don't bite the nipple that feeds you," she growled, shuffling on the phone, no doubt to adjust the baby who whined in protest.

"That bad, huh?" I asked, trying to steal a glance through the small sliver of a crack in the curtains, despite Dougie's orders to not look in the backyard for the next couple of hours.

That was pretty much an invitation to do the exact opposite, but he'd been out there with Sean for almost six hours and between the whir of the leaf blower, and the incessant thud of hard earth being dug into, the anticipation was killing me.

Raquel huffed. "My nipples could guide Santa's sleigh. That's how red they are. What the fuck do you think?"

I held a hand to my mouth, trying desperately to prevent myself from laughing as I flexed on my toes, trying to steal another peek outside.

I couldn't see shit. "What are you going to do if their first word is 'fuck'?"

"I dunno, beam with Southie pride—OW!" she yelped. She blew

out an exasperated breath, mumbling something to herself. "You're not trying to look, are you?"

Well... "Kind of."

"Pen, c'mon," she protested. "Step away from the window. Just let it happen."

"I can't help it. I'm so curious." I shifted my weight from foot to foot. "Do you know what they're doing?" It hadn't escaped my notice that they'd added in the element of a Bluetooth speaker that was pumping out an eighties and nineties playlist, intending to drown out as much noise as possible.

"May—" she made an indignant sound that earned my wince. Breastfeeding was hard enough as it was, never mind when they started teething and latching on awkwardly. "Pen, I gotta go."

"Okay," I said, stepping away from the window. "Try lanolin."

"That shit is greasy and stains all of my bras."

She was at her wit's end, her frustration and discomfort palpable even through the phone. "Hydrogel pads, then."

"What the hell is that?" she asked. "Almost six months into this and I feel like I'm still learning shit."

"It doesn't come with a manual, don't be too hard on yourself, Kell," I reasoned. "You can reuse them for twenty-four hours. It just helps keep your skin hydrated."

"Okay..." she trailed off, failing to hide the shame in her tone. "Can you ask Sean to stop and grab those when he leaves?"

"No problem."

"I'm not a terrible mom if I introduce them to solids now, right?"

I hated how crestfallen she sounded about it. "Of course not." I pulled myself away from the closed guest bedroom window. "The important part is ensuring they're fed. How you do it isn't relevant, and it isn't a measurement of your ability. And if you're worried, talk to your pediatrician."

"I don't mean to whine, and you never complained... sorry, is it... is it hard talking about this after...?"

I was quiet for a moment, staring at the bed. Dougie was still sleeping in here, little traces of him interspersed throughout the room.

His folded lounge pants, his pillow. An emptied glass with the dregs of water at the bottom that hadn't made it to the kitchen.

"No," I replied. "I'm a mom, regardless of what happened, and your experience is still valid."

She heaved out a sigh a relief, her mood seeming to brighten. "Okay, thanks, Pen."

"Anytime," I replied. "And thanks for the birthday gift." Sean had handed me a matte-black-and-gold polka-dotted gift bag when he'd gotten here, looking like a blast from the past. He was donning his beaten-up Tavares Construction T-shirt under his flannel camel brown jacket, jeans that had seen better days, and work boots.

"Open it," he'd insisted.

Inside was a jewelry box with a dainty and thin bracelet with music note charm on it next to a second charm with opal in the center, set around a gold plate.

Opal like my engagement ring. The one I'd spent an unreasonable amount of time wondering if I was ever getting back.

"You're welcome. See ya."

Hanging up the phone, I padded out of the room as quietly as possible. Christopher was still down for his afternoon nap, and I wasn't ready to disturb him.

Not yet, anyway. I was trying to ween myself from stealing glances at him during his nap at the behest of my therapist. Part of it had to do with my need to coddle him and keep him close after the miscarriage. The other part of me was just living in a permanent state of fear that something would happen to him if I didn't always have eyes on him.

But I knew it wasn't healthy, for him or for me.

I'd see him after he woke up. We were ordering in tonight. Dinner together had been a regular thing now. And while it was initially as weird as Dougie seeing me in a bathrobe this morning, I looked forward to those thirty-minute dinners together.

He made it a point to talk about something. Anything. Initially, it was hard for me because it felt contrived, but eventually, we found our footing and talked about things beyond the weather.

Goals, wants, dreams.

Although I still wasn't sure about the latter.

The back door opened below, two sets of heavy footsteps culling the quietude downstairs. "Beer?" Dougie asked, his voice distant.

"Nah," Sean said. "I gotta get outta here."

The seal on the fridge opened, followed by the rush of water from the kitchen sink. "You got dirt on your forehead."

Sean guffawed over the pop of a beer bottle being cracked open, followed by the tossing of a cap to the counter.

As I rounded the banister and padded toward the kitchen, my heart warmed at the sight of them in their element again. I didn't believe that things would immediately bounce back to the way things had always been between them, but there was an unshakable brotherhood between them I knew would endure anything.

I didn't probe Dougie on what was said between the two of them when they'd gone out, and he didn't share. Whatever it was, it changed Dougie's demeanor when he got home.

Their cheeks were ruddy from the cold, exhaustion lining their faces, despite the ease in their respective postures. Dougie straightened, his eyes lighting up at my presence, his expression etched with something I couldn't place. It sent a shiver down my spine all the same, my eager heart hammering in my chest.

I was desperate to know what the hell they'd been up to out there all day, but just seeing his face? It momentarily robbed me of all cognizant thought.

Whatever they'd been up to, it was important enough for Sean to leave the restaurants to his staff for the day and lend Dougie a hand.

Sean glanced behind him. "Hey, birthday girl." He shook his wet hands in the sink, reaching for the dishrag as he offered me a soft smile and interrupting mine and Dougie's moment. "How's thirty-one so far?"

I rested a hand on my hip, blowing out my lips. "Unremarkable." Confusing, really.

"Give it time. Your knees will start to crack." He wiggled his thick brows at me. "That's when things get interesting."

"That's thirty-two," Dougie corrected him, bringing the beer bottle to his lips, tipping it back. He smacked his lips, then smirked in a way that made my thighs clench together and that foreign, albeit familiar, burst of heat pulsed between my legs. "Thirty-one were the grays."

Dougie would look good completely gray, I knew he would. Even now, I could see little strands weaved through his dark hair. A headful of that stuff, though? Panty melting. The color would do something to the shade of his deep green eyes. I could practically envision the slivers of silver peppered around his mouth, too.

Sean's eyes rounded. "You got off easy, then. I started getting those at twenty-one."

Dougie frowned, squinting while he tried to find them. "I don't see grays."

Sean sniffled, his nose running from the cold. "I pluck 'em."

"Don't do that. You'll give yourself bald spots," I admonished, folding my arms over my chest.

"You sound like my ma," Sean replied, drying his hands off on the towel draped over the oven door handle. "But I think that's a myth."

Dougie probed the inside of his cheek, scratching at his head before sheepishly asking, "Isn't the whole salt and pepper thing in?"

"Hell if I know." Sean shrugged, glancing at me for confirmation. "Would you like to weigh in on this?"

I titled my nose skyward. "No comment, Princess." I slung his nickname for me back at him.

He chuckled, nodding his head. "I like the way you think." Well, that was a first. Sean clapped a palm against Dougie's. "Call me next week. We'll get the rest sorted."

"Rest of what sorted?"

Sean smiled, mischief glinting in his russet-brown eyes. He scrubbed his scruffy jaw, then shook his head. "Guess you'll see."

He hooked an arm around my shoulders, pulling me in for a hug. Despite the October cold still lingering in the fibers of his clothes, he was a warm mass of heat. He smelled like the autumn chill, spice, and leather all tangled in with the faint trace of sweat.

Sean kissed my forehead, his mouth dropping to the shell of my ear. "I'm not gonna ask you to forgive him until you're ready," he began in a whisper, "all I ask is for you to remember who he is beyond his fuck up." He broke away from me, squeezing my shoulder gently.

Then his voice projected, that loud and clear baritone filling the kitchen. "Happy birthday."

Snapping his fingers in Dougie's direction, he tossed him a pointed glance. "And don't forget to call my sister."

Dougie rolled his eyes. "I said I'll think about it." His mouth rocked from side to side, his brows raising a little. "Snow plowing is lucrative come November."

"Sure," Sean crooned. "If you want to live out your six-year-old Tonka truck fantasies."

Dougie threw back his head with a laugh. "Get outta here, asshole."

Sean grinned, flipping him off before turning away.

"Oh, Sean," I called as he cut through the family room, heading to the foyer. He stopped, craning his head a little over his shoulder to regard me. "Raquel asked for you to stop and grab hydrogel pads." He kneaded his neck, confusion touching the corners of his eyes. "They're nipple pads."

"Aw, jeez, is she bleeding again?" He grimaced, shaking his head. Obviously, she hadn't been exaggerating.

"No idea, but she's threatening to get Rudolph demoted, so I'm concerned."

Dougie snorted. "What a smart ass."

Sean didn't react. He was completely ambivalent to his wife's antics and word usage—it must have come with the territory of marrying an author. He simply nodded as though what I'd stated was completely typical, fishing his car keys out of his pocket. "Okay, on it."

"Just don't get confused with the nursing pads, okay?" It was an easy oversight, and I'd done it a few times myself when I'd relied on packaging.

"Thanks, Pen."

The front door opened and closed behind him as he left. Cold air circulating my way, making the hairs on my arms raise and my nipples harden under my shirt.

I shook off the shiver. "Why does he want you to call..." I began, turning around to face Dougie.

"Trina?" Dougie filled in the blank, staring at the beer bottle in his hand.

I controlled the urge to sigh with relief over which Tavares sister he'd been referring to. "Yeah."

He caught a droplet of condensation on the neck of the bottle. "She needs help with the windows on the Victorian." He didn't sound surprised at all. "Couple of casualties and the costs are mounting."

"So..."

"I'll do it as a favor for her, but I'm not going back."

"Dougie." He lifted his head, waiting for me to complete my sentence. "Maybe," I pressed a hand against my stomach. "Maybe we should stop punishing people."

He considered it for a moment, his jaw grounding. "Is that what I'm doing?"

"It's what we both do. Try to get the one up on people when they hurt us..." I stepped toward him. "If you don't enjoy working with Trina, then don't do it. But you always seemed to like what you did, and you're good at it." He'd always come home fulfilled. Exhausted and tired but sporting the biggest grin in the world. I had no recollection of Daddy ever coming home with that level of contentment, and he'd been a suit who'd never known a day of hard labor in his life.

Dougie studied his chokehold on the bottle, propping his foot against his ankle. "Will that make you happy?" he asked, his tone cautious. "Me going back?"

"What will make me happy is you making yourself happy." He evaded my gaze, and for a split second as he tipped the dreg of the bottle back, I thought he was going to fire a nasty remark at me, but he didn't.

Instead, came the nonchalant nod. "I'll think about it." His jaw flexed. "I've missed all of them. It's just... awkward to navigate."

My insides softened at his admission, the guilt tearing at me a little. "I know."

"Parts of me are scared to get too close to them again." He glanced up at me. "I'm afraid of there being any opportunity to—" he cut himself off, the slate of his face washing with shame.

I inhaled sharply, fidgeting with the sleeve of my sweater. "To run into Maria?"

His head snapped back, squeezing his eyes shut. "Yeah."

"We can't control who they have in their lives, and," I hesitated, "it's unrealistic. She's their sister." I flexed my hands at my sides. "And Raquel's my best friend… Maria's always going to be there."

"I don't want anything to compromise us." I understood that. Parts of me dreaded the moment I would see her again, if I'd freak out, if I'd fly off the handle… but this other part of me also recognized that Raquel was right. Maria wasn't at fault. Her initial choices had led him to me, and my choices had led him to her.

Dougie and I were both guilty, but Maria Tavares? She had nothing to do with us. "And if we're as strong as I know we are, then it won't make a difference." I fully meant that, too. "You should go back to work if that's important to you."

"Okay." It was hard to say if he was mollifying me, or if he genuinely believed that, but time would tell.

There was something else I wanted to discuss with him, though. It had been on the back of my mind since breakfast this morning while Dougie told me about a snow plowing gig he'd been offered that would start in a few weeks' time.

"I've been thinking that I," I didn't know why I was so nervous suddenly. It wasn't like this was the fifties or that I thought he'd have an adverse reaction. "I'd like to go back to work, too."

He lifted his eyes to me, rolling his lips together before he nodded. "I think that's a good idea."

I wasn't ready to restart my business again, but maybe work under someone. "I miss being creative, having something for myself besides…"

"Being a mom and a wife," he said, filling in the blank. "I understand."

We were silent again. He leaned against the kitchen island, holding the neck of the beer bottle while his eyes took in the kitchen. We'd made so many memories in here, mostly good ones, but…

"You ever think we'd end up here?" he asked, cringing a little.

I shook my head, my stomach dipping. "Never."

"I'm sorry I hurt you, Pen," he whispered. "I know it'll never change anything, because we can't undo the past, but," his eyes locked me in place, "I want us to have a better future."

"Me, too."

"I want to honor everything about us, the good, the bad," he sucked back a breath, "and the loss, because it's ours."

I flinched, my chest caving in, the tears coming hot and fast. I wondered if the sting of what could have been would ever cease.

Dougie set the bottle down, straightening his posture. He held out a hand to me, offering me a boyish smile as he drew me in. Wrapping his arms around me, he pressed a kiss against my temple, inhaling sharply. "I love you, Penny." I leaned into him, resting my head against his chest and allowing him to keep me grounded. We could never undo the things that we had done, erase the things that we'd said, but he was right.

We could honor everything about us, because every moment brought us here. Good or bad, and it was ours.

"I love you, too," I whispered back, bunching his coat in my hands. I inclined my head back, glancing up at him through a blurred vision.

I wanted him to kiss me, but instead, he brushed the tip of his nose against mine. His eyes falling shut for a moment as though he were committing this moment to memory. When he opened them again, they were glossy. He wrinkled his nose, his nostrils flaring as he took a step back. "Go get your jacket and boots."

Dougie broke away from me, clearing his throat with a quick sniffle that made my heart ache. I wanted to comfort him the way he had me. He gave me his back, pressing this forefinger and thumb into his eyes. Rolling his shoulders, he glanced at me with a gentle smile. "Go on."

I did as I was told, collecting my black knee-high Hunter rain boots from the front door and sliding on my car coat.

"If you hate it, I'll get rid of it," he said, uncertainty lacing every word. "Okay?"

My ribs squeezed, my heart thumping in my throat. Why would I hate it?

Dougie took my hand in his, then opened the door, the faint autumn muskiness perfumed the air, notes of decaying leaves, and the sweet earthiness tangled in the wind.

I swept my gaze over the yard, trying to find the source of his anxiety. The yard was tidy, the lawn cleared of leaves, a line of neat yard waste bags to the far left near the shed. They had wrapped the rest of the shrubs in burlap, the flower beds overturned. Everything seemed as it would have under ordinary circumstances. Confusion swirled through me. This couldn't possibly be what he had been nervous about. I lifted my gaze heavenward, staring at the proud maples in our yard, their remaining leaves somehow prettier in the setting sun.

The soft tinkling all the way at the property's edge had my attention shifting. I furrowed my brow, holding a hand over my eyes. "What is that?" I asked, squinting. I could make out a white bench that hadn't been there before and what looked like fresh mulch, but the source of the chiming was escaping me.

"Come on." He tugged my hand, leading me down the wooden porch steps. The flagstone transitioned to hard earth as he led me across the cleaned yard. The tinkling of what I now recognized were wind chimes grew more melancholic as we neared closer to the property line.

The woody scent of mulch touched my sinuses, the bright white bench welcoming me. A soft, weather-friendly striped, blue pillow propped up proudly on one corner, next to a table that appeared it might double as storage.

But as I worked my eyes over what I was uncovering for the first time, my heart stuttered in my chest as I narrowed in on a young bush.

"Dougie…" I released his hand, and he stood back, his eyes heavy on me as I stepped onto the padding of mulch, the twigs crunching under my feet.

They had planted a hydrangea bush in the corner, and while it was absent of its full, plush blooms, I knew with certainty that its planting symbolized our chance.

We could still grow here. We could still live and love.

"It'll bloom mid-spring, throughout early fall next year," he said softly behind me. "We can add more to the beds every year, but I know how much you like hydrangeas, and," I heard his hard and obvious swallow, "I want this to be a place where we can come and reflect… October is pregnancy and infant loss awareness month." My heart squeezed at his awareness. He'd been doing his own independent emotional work.

There were pretty, rust-colored solar lighted lanterns scattered throughout the garden, a small retaining wall erected around the base made of gray, old brick that ended abruptly. That must have been what Sean meant when he said they'd do the rest. "But if you don't like it, if it upsets you…" Dougie trailed off.

I shook my head. It didn't upset me, far from it.

I approached the bush, running my fingers along the green leaves. My gaze tipped downward, a glint of silver metal catching my eyes. Engrained in a metal garden plate at the base of the hydrangea was a tiny heartbeat, with the word "ours" beneath it.

I'd shown him the sonogram I hadn't been able to part with a few months ago, but I'd never asked for it back.

Then it hit me—that was why he'd been worried. He'd immortalized the loss alongside a four-lettered word that carried so much weight to it.

That had been our baby we'd lost, a chapter we'd written in our story, a heartbreak we'd had to honor and learn to live with. But it was ours.

Ours, and we'd never forget it. We could still bloom and flower into something beautiful.

Crouching to the ground, I ran my fingers along the etching. That tiny heartbeat, committed to stone forever, commemorating the moments we would never spend with them, the sounds we would never hear, the smiles we'd never see.

But they were here. In this stone, our baby lived forever. We wouldn't forget them. We'd honor what was ours—just like Dougie had said.

My body shook as I brought the back of my hand to my mouth, rising to my feet while trying to control the sob, but I couldn't. The mulch crunched behind me, his steps unhurried. I smelled him first before his arms winded around my waist and he pulled me back into him.

Dougie dropped his forehead against my head, taking a fortifying breath that shook his body. "I don't want to forget anything," he murmured against the shell of my ear. "Every part of us, good or bad."

"You did all of this for me?" I said, sniffling and turning around to face him. This time, he didn't mask the tears.

His head weaved with a nod as his throat bobbed with an obvious and tight swallow. "Do you—"

"I love it," I cut him off.

I flexed on my toes, not giving a shit about slow right now. I needed to demonstrate how much this meant to me. My mouth fitted against his, my arms looping around his neck. Dougie didn't fight me. He kissed me back, slow and tentative at first, until the urgency and passion entered the fold, and some dormant part of his brain came back online.

"I want to go wake up Chris from his nap," I said, scissoring my fingers with his. "I want him to see our special place."

The wind chimes extended on a hook against the fence rang out, sounding closer to rain drops as they swayed in the breeze, and it felt like a whispered promise from a higher power. Warmth expanded in my chest, and some part of me knew, without a doubt, that we were going to be okay.

'Cause our story was only just beginning, and the truth could set you free.

Chapter Thirty-Two

Dougie

A month and a half later…

MY BREATH LEFT MY MOUTH IN HOT VAPORS AS I NARROWED MY EYES AND reared the hammer back, hitting the nail pinched between my fingers.

The 'thwack' harmonized with the rest of the hubbub of the construction yard unfolding around me. I'd spent the last hour of my day installing siding fasteners to prepare for the replacement boards.

"What do you think?" Trina asked from below. "Done by next week?"

I glanced down at her from the top of the ladder, then looked around the stretch of fasteners. My lips vibrated with thought. Next week? If I came back tomorrow for a couple of hours… "Probably."

Trina blew out a breath. "I want to avoid the first snowfall, or we're fucked." She brought the side of her thumb to her mouth, sandwiching a hangnail and pulling on it. Her face crinkled with a wince, no doubt having injured herself, her mouth nursing the wound.

I snorted out a laugh, shoving the hammer back into my tool belt. "*You're* fucked," I corrected, the metal of the rungs on the ladder grunting as I climbed down, my grip tight on the cold ladder. "I don't work for you."

And I didn't. Erm, not really. I'd come back to help with the window installation, then I'd gotten pissed when I looked at the shit job they'd done with the electrical and plumbing rough in, because didn't these idiots remember anything about code?

"You *could* work for me," she said sweetly, batting her made-up eyelashes at me. She snagged my arm when I cleared the last rung, "C'mon, Big Head."

"You haven't called me that in forever." And I couldn't say I really missed it considering my ego hadn't felt huge in a while, but I was on the mend. Or at least I was beginning to feel better. Then again, that might have been a byproduct of the guy I was talking to on Saturday mornings. He was different, not like what I remembered Pen's therapist in Back Bay being like. He looked rough around the edges with his burly build, long beard and shrewd eyes, but was as wise and kind as could be. Most Saturdays, we didn't spend in his office, but strolling through Fall River, walking the streets of my old stomping grounds as a teenager. We talked, but it never felt clinical somehow. I didn't even really like calling him a therapist, but... he was giving me the tools to help me.

Trina leaned against me, attempting to either keep up with my long strides or slow me down. It was inconclusive. "Let's negotiate."

"You fired me, remember?" I reminded, shaking her off my arm. But like a soiled prom dress, Trina clung on. These fucking Tavareses... I couldn't help but smile.

I'd missed this shit.

"A means to an end," Trina replied. I tapered my eyes at her, but she just looked up at me all wide-eyed and innocent, reminiscent of when she was a kid

"You really think you're innocent in all this?"

"Nope." Her lips popped on the 'P' as she leaned her head against my shoulder once more. "I've got blood on my hands, but it should show you how far I'm willing to go for my family. Which includes you." She faltered for a moment, a shudder ripping through her as she pressed a closed fist to her mouth as though she were going to lose her lunch. "Even when certain family members decide to—"

"Don't finish that sentence," I warned. I didn't need the reminder about Maria and me. That was a lifetime ago, and I had no desire to reminisce about it.

She snorted, holding her hands up with a shrug. "She's pretty if you're into the whole ice queen thing, so like, I get the initial interest." She nudged me. "But I'm glad you married Pen. She's one of my favorite people. If it weren't for her," Trina glanced around the yard, smiling, "I might not have had the confidence to take this on without Sean."

I would agree with that sentiment. Penelope had been instrumental in rebuilding Katrina's confidence and showing her she could do anything.

Still, I didn't want to talk to Trina about her sister or about my wife. "I don't want to have this conversation with *you*."

"Aw, c'mon, I'm all grown up now!" she protested, shoving me back. "I know how this stuff works."

"You're still five in my mind, you'll never be a grownup." Even if she had gotten knocked up once. I preferred to pretend that had been immaculate conception. My knuckles still flexed at my side with the reminder of the asshole Sean and I had dealt with when he skipped town and she ended her pregnancy.

She might have gone through with it had he stayed.

Trina blew a lock of hair out of her face, her mouth rocking from side to side as her posture took on something tentative. "How's Pen, anyway?"

Warmth expanded in my chest. "I told you she got that gig." She'd met some woman at Old Maid's Café when we'd gone to lunch together a few weeks ago who ran a rehabilitation business for historical homes. She was older, and not quite as hands on as Trina was in her ventures, only working on houses when they were in their completed stages, adding final finishings while keeping in line with the houses era and fusing modern trends simultaneously—which was right up Pen's alley. She knew she could have just started her own thing again, but she wasn't ready for that level of involvement or responsibility. Not yet anyway.

"You did, but she could have come back and worked with me, too," Trina said, her brows folding inward. "No one wants to work with me."

"Weird, huh?" I tapped my bearded chin with feigned thought, only dropping my hand to snap my fingers as though a lightbulb had come on. "Oh, I know why, it's 'cause you're an ass."

"No, no," she held up a hand, "you've got me mistaken with Sean. I'm the fun, happy-go-lucky boss." She touched her messy hair. "My hair is blue, for fuck's sake. *Blue!*"

"Is that how you would describe your Satanic music preference? Fun?" 'Cause the only impression it gave me and everyone else on the site was that she was one bad day away from sacrificing one of us to her underworld lords.

She flipped me off, sneering. "Dick."

"Ah," I crooned. "There she is."

She held up both hands, face crinkling. "Okay, okay, I get it. Not everyone wants to work with Katrina." Something faraway and plaintive touched her eyes when she eased her features.

That reaction wasn't for me. "Did you call him?" I asked carefully, studying her reaction.

She flinched, her chest caving in on her. Trina shook her head. "No." She pressed her bottom lip into her upper one, rolling them together. "Not sure what I'd say. Too much time has passed."

"Most people start with 'hi'," I suggested. She was right that a lot of time had passed since her and Adam had been a her and Adam, but I wasn't suggesting she date the guy again or anything. Just, y'know, the kid was one newcomer who knew what the fuck he was doing—he was more efficient than six of the crew combined.

"And then you could apologize." For snooping through his past on the Internet.

"Dougie." She dropped her chin, staring at her work boots.

"Okay, I get it. Calling the ex-boyfriend is bad."

"He wasn't my boyfriend," she corrected me, shoving her hands into the pockets of her coat. She shrunk into the neckline, rocking on her heels to stave off the December cold. "Not... not really."

I tapered my eyes at her. I'd gotten my piece of universal karma a couple of years ago when I'd found the two of them in the basement of what was now Sean and Raquel's house before the fire. And if I could burn a layer of my retinas off to forget it... "What the hell's that supposed to mean?"

They bought me coffee for a solid week just to keep my mouth shut, but it wasn't necessary. No way in hell I was recounting to Sean what I'd seen. No one needed to relive that.

And I mean no one. But if he wasn't her boyfriend, then was he using her?

Or was she using him?

Trina straightened, pulling out one hand to wave me off. "Doesn't matter now." She forced herself to brighten, glancing at her watch. "You better go or you're gonna be late for your date."

Penelope and I had incorporated weekly Friday night dates into our lives. It was part of our homework from our marriage counselor to do something outside of the house with the sole focus on seeing each other in a different light—literally. While we were on our dates, we weren't allowed to talk about work, about the house, about Christopher, only about each other.

It was kind of like getting to know one another again and rebuilding the trust through a rediscovery stage.

"What time is it?" I asked, unhooking the belt around my waist, staring up at the dim sky. Daylight saving time messed with my perception of time every year. It got darker earlier.

"Quarter to four."

Cool, I'd be home in ten minutes. "I'm out of here." I handed her the tool belt she accepted with both arms, her body buckling a little under the weight. Trapping the laugh behind my teeth, I shook my head. She was on the smaller side, but she was determined, and that was what made her strong enough to be the boss. "See ya."

The gravel crunched under my boots as I approached my truck, fishing my car keys out of my back pocket. The headlights flashed across the darkening yard as the sun made its descent behind the dense conifers sewn in with barren deciduous trees that made up the woods the house abutted.

"Dougie."

I stopped, my ears craning to listen.

"I'll see you tomorrow?" she hollered out to me. She knew I'd be here, too. What? She wanted to be done the exterior next week. Who was I to not help her?

I stopped, cold air penetrating my lungs. I smirked, glanced over my shoulder, and nodded. "Sure, but I want an increase."

Katrina adjusted my tool belt over her shoulder, rolling her eyes. "Bring me a coffee tomorrow morning and you've got yourself a deal."

"Ten percent, Trina."

"Five," she volleyed back.

"You need me. *Ten.*"

I huffed out a laugh, a cloud of steam leaving her. "Fine. Ten. Don't forget the coffee." She waved me off, turning away as she stalked back to the cacophony of the busy yard. "Wrap it up, guys," she called. "I'm freezing my tits off out here."

No one dared to make a lewd joke. They all knew better. She was kind of scary when she was pissed off and equally merciless with firing people. Although Trina hadn't told them she'd fired me. She'd created an elaborate story about a vacation I hadn't been aware that I'd taken that she'd animatedly recounted to everyone on the yard the day I corrected the window installations at Sean's behest, because "he didn't have time to help right now."

Two restaurants, twin teething babies and shit. Y'know how it goes.

Personally, I thought it was a ploy to get me back here.

There had been a lot of relieved faces to see me, but I hadn't come back intending to return every single day. It had been a favor that went on for a month and a half.

But Penelope was right. I didn't hate my job. I never had. And being back on the yard, getting swept up in the revelry again, being needed and wanted, that made me feel good.

Just the continuation of my presence here required a ten percent increase. It was only fair after the chaos Trina had put me through, even if it had been for my own good.

Getting into my truck, the engine rumbled to life as I fumbled with the heat settings, rubbing my hands together as a chill charged through me.

God, I hoped it wasn't too cold to do what I had planned for Pen and me tonight.

My stomach fluttered as I glanced to the glove compartment. Extending an arm, I opened it and dug through the stack of napkins, the owner's manual, finally spotting the pretty red leather box with the gold curlicue on the edges. My heart raced in my chest as I found my nerve to open the lid, the latch clicking to a stop.

The ring was pretty. Dissimilar from her first one, but pretty.

The London blue topaz reminded me of her eyes, and even in the setting sun, its iridescent edges sparkled under my appraisal. There were two tiny diamonds nestled beside it, and thin prongs keeping the squared setting in place on a white gold band.

My stomach roiled as I considered the stark differences between this and her original engagement ring. For one, I knew she loved opal and preferred yellow gold, and two, she had loved that ring.

But that ring, that ring hadn't been given to her the way I'd wanted to. I had done it on someone else's timeline, and in some fucked-up way, it felt doomed from the start. I wanted things to be special between us, done our way, and give us the chance we both deserved. Closing the box, I tucked it back into the glove compartment, then headed home.

Our Christmas lights were on by the time I pulled into our driveway, thanks to the timer. The soft white lights twinkled along the roof of the house, bright and joyful against the inky night sky. We'd strung garland around the porch that also had a string of matching lights, with a gold bow spaced out every two feet. The porch light was on, and my stomach flipped at the gesture.

It always did. It had been weeks since I'd come home to a darkened house. We'd put the lights up outside shortly after Thanksgiving—a weekend we spent at home rather than in Connecticut—alongside the Christmas tree that stood proudly in the living room window right after Thanksgiving dinner. Pen's parents were surprisingly not bent out of shape on our decision. In fact, they almost seemed relieved when Pen explained we wanted to spend it privately. She'd murmured something to her mother out of earshot, but I didn't press her on it.

It was a miracle she was even divulging something I assumed was personal to her mother at all. All this was to say that the inside of our house looked like someone had detonated a Christmas bomb by the time I pulled all the Christmas decor out of the basement and Pen put me to work. There wasn't a single space that wasn't laden with Christmas decor, from the creepy ass Santa Claus figure Pen kept on the landing of the stairs that could have doubled as Hallmark's inter-pretation on a white-haired Chucky doll sans the scars, but with the same serial killer smile—weapon of choice would have been a sharp-ened candy cane—to the carved and painted wooden blocks counting down the days to Christmas on the fireplace mantel. She'd turned it into a space a Christmas fanatic would have lost their load to.

And I loved it, because seeing her happy, hearing her hum Christmas carols to herself, and split a piece of Christopher's advent calendar chocolate with him every day, gave me what the season repre-sented for everyone.

Hope.

Hope that our family could be something.

Hope that we still had something good here.

Turning off the truck, I inhaled a lung full of cold air and pulled my lunch cooler out with me. The muted, evocative music came from the house as I shut the truck door, making my mouth split into a grin.

I loved that exquisite sound.

The oaken, upright piano had been delivered shortly after Christo-pher had woken up from his nap on her birthday. Initially, with the way the gob smacked expression wouldn't leave her face, I thought I had pissed her off about it.

Sure, the piano wasn't the prettiest thing, but she liked antiques. And I thought even if, at a minimum, she never felt the urge to play, then at least it was a good conversational piece.

Right?

All I knew was that when I'd left the diner with Sean that day, I'd spotted the piano in the window and knew without any doubt that I had to bring it home for her. It was early twentieth century, had been desperately in need of a tuning, and had seen better days. But I had a plan. I'd get it tuned for her once it was delivered, and then I'd figure out how to properly restore the wood without ruining the dentil detailing around the small lip forming the music rack and polishing the pedals to its former glory.

It was a work in progress.

Her expression had pinched with something I hadn't been able to place as she took tentative steps toward it, and lifted the fall board up, revealing the ivory keys. She had sucked back a tight breath, then pressed down on the middle C, releasing the sharp, buzzed twang into the air that made her wince.

"*I know you and the piano have had a rocky relationship in the past, but I've been thinking about the moments where you seemed the freest to me, and the day you pissed your mother off with your rendition of Enter Sandman is in my top five,*" I told her. Even if she'd done it intending to get under her mother's skin, watching her surrender herself to the music and fall into it had been beautiful.

"*I love it,*" she murmured, swallowing the lump in her throat, a fresh batch of tears shining in her eyes. "*Thank you.*"

She'd played almost every day since—well, at least after we'd gotten it tuned.

The airy notes punctured the night air as I approached the house, keeping my footsteps light on the steps in fear she'd stop playing when I entered. Unlocking the front door, I opened it carefully, catching sight of her at the piano.

She was the prettiest thing I'd ever seen, my breaths slowing as I took her in. She wore a soft, cashmere white cowl neck sweater that, against the bright red of her lipstick and her fair complexion, made her look like a 1920s starlet. Her flaxen hair was pulled back in a smoothed, low ponytail at the base of her neck, her profile concentrated as her adept hands flowed across the keys, her body leaning into the piano.

Her jaw ticked, her mouth quirking in a smile as her evocative playing grew more urgent in the crescendo before halting. She turned her head, cocking a brow at me. "You just going to stand there, or are you going to come give me my kiss?"

I set the cooler down, then slipped out of my boots. "I smell like shit."

"Hmm," she hummed, appraising me through one eye. "So, sweaty and sawdust like?"

"No saw dust today, I'm afraid," I said, approaching her. Her head inclined so she could gaze up at me, the adoration in her Atlantic-blue eyes so brilliant it almost brought me to my fucking knees.

I'd never tire of her looking at me like that. I'd never take it for granted.

"Just sweat." I palmed her cheek, and she leaned into it despite the chill that rattled through her. Lowering my hand, I brushed my callused finger against her bottom lip, checking the lipstick for tackiness.

"It's matte," she informed me. "You can do your worst." Heat flashed in her eyes, and I knew she meant that comment to be sexual.

I wasn't ready to have sex with her, not yet. But that didn't stop her from trying to remind me the option was still there. I just needed to get over this hump—er—curve with the ring.

The new one.

And gauge how she felt about where we were headed. Sticking to the steps had been important to me. Acknowledging what happened, talking about it, grieving, reconnecting, rebuilding our trust, and eventually, intimacy. It wasn't just only on either of us anymore; it was collective. We'd both told lies, but we were committed to only ever telling the truth from here on out.

Leaning forward, I massaged my lips against hers. I felt the charge in her kiss, its magnetic pull sweeping through my insides when she tugged on the open folds of my button-down, pinning me to her. I hated my morals, my reservations and need to see this through.

I just didn't want another situation where we gave in, only to realize we weren't on the same page again. Sex made things complicated, even when you were married.

Penelope pulled back from the kiss, looking up at me hopefully, but I didn't make a move on her.

Shucking under her chin, I offered her a smile. "Let me go shower, and then we'll get out of here."

"Okay," she replied, releasing me. "I dropped Christopher off at your mom's an hour ago. I'll pick him up tomorrow and then take her to Costco."

I shrugged out of my coat, reaching for the coat hanger in the closet. "I'll come, too."

"Nope," she sang. "I'm planning on grabbing your Christmas present tomorrow."

Throwing my head back with a laugh, I glanced at her, loving the playful mischief glinting in her eyes and the quirk in her mouth with a smirk. Sounded like a new power drill to me... maybe a new hose storage unit. Shit, I could really use some new underwear, too, but truthfully? "You can't buy me a Christmas present."

"Why not?"

I paused mid-step on the stairwell, glancing at her. "'Cause I have everything I need."

Penelope

"Where are we going?" I asked, touching the blindfold. I couldn't see shit under the material and the complete and total darkness surrounding the truck as we drove didn't help, either. It had surprised me when he came down the stairs, dressed in clean blue jeans, a gray Henley with the makeshift blindfold in his hand—it was just a scarf—and asked if I trusted him enough to let him surprise me.

Of course I did... but that had been a decision I'd made twenty minutes ago, and now I was kind of regretting it because my curiosity was getting the best of me.

Dougie gave my knee a reassuring squeeze. "We're almost there."

The tires bounced along wooden planks, inciting my frown as I tried to recall Eaton's map to get a sense of which direction we were heading in at a minimum.

Driving on wood could only mean one thing, a curl of excitement sweeping through me. "Was that the kissing bridge?" I asked.

He laughed. "You can't relax for a minute?"

"You have me blindfolded and your hand on my thigh is doing something to my vagina," I informed him breathlessly, shifting in my seat to clench my thighs together. "No."

Really. I didn't know what it meant where such a subtle gesture from your husband literally created a pulse between your legs, but I imagined that had something to do with the fact that he kept his foot on the brake in the sex department and our marriage counselor said we'd know when we were both ready and to be patient when the other wasn't.

After what I'd done to him, it was only fair.

That didn't mean I wasn't always going to try with a heated glance here or there.

The odd remark.

The occasional half-naked stroll through the house long after Christopher had gone to bed for the night when I knew Dougie would be in the family room, watching a hockey game... and if the towel accidentally slipped from my frame when the Bruins scored, and I cheered.

I was trying to capitalize on his elation, and while he gave me the appreciative, hungered sweep of his eyes, he'd always bundle me back up.

The wooden planks transitioned into road once more, and my robbed vision somehow felt darker. A moment later, the truck slowed, then wobbled as the tires crunched along debris, leaves and... where the hell were we?

My ears perked up at the sound of Dougie pulling the truck into park, the engine humming under our feet. "Okay," he announced, his tone nervous. "You can take off the blindfold."

Finally. My eyes squinted as I tried to adjust to the bright headlights illuminating the thicket of trees.

Rolling the silk scarf of the blindfold in my hand, I chewed on my lip, surveying the space. From the corner of my eye, Dougie smiled to himself, leaning back in his seat. He touched the dial on the radio, the jingling of a Michael Bublé holiday number filtering through the truck's cabin.

He didn't look at me as he extended his hand to me over the middle console. I settled my palm in his, the warmth of his kiss on my knuckles inducing a flutter in my chest when he brought them to his mouth.

I let his hand go and ejected my seatbelt, zipped up my thigh-length coat, and opened the car door. The unpleasant December chill accosted me as I felt for the ground and shut the truck door. Rounding the hood of the truck, I stood at the illuminated clearing, circling in place, cocking my head back to stare at the pinprick of silvery stars above us.

The kissing bridge. The woods.

I knew where we were.

This was our spot.

My eyes found his in the truck. He raised his brows, his mouth tugging into a smile. Dougie opened the truck door, the cold claiming his exhale. "Know where we are yet?"

My insides squeezed, my eyes stinging. "Back where it all began," I murmured. At least part of where it all began.

He came to my side, brushing his knuckles against mine. "I knew the moment you showed up at the site in high heels that you were going to be trouble," he started, a smile touching his mouth, his eyes crinkling in the corners. "But it was when you opened your mouth that I knew I was going to fall in love with you."

"Oh, yeah?" I asked, leaning against him.

"Yeah, and when Sean told me not to fuck the new girl," he said, his laugh reverberating through his chest. "I knew I was going to marry the new girl."

My mouth popped open. "You did not!"

"I did," he assured me, nodding his head. "I didn't know how, I just knew that I would." He probed a dry crack on his bottom lip with his tongue. "And I would do it all over again in a heartbeat."

I swallowed the lump of emotions in my throat. "Even though everything happened the way it did?"

"Our lies almost cost us everything, Penny," he said, "But this story? This life?" He looked at me, and in his eyes, I found everything I'd ever needed. "It's ours." Just like the stone in the back garden said.

He dug into his pocket, drawing out my rings. My heart hammered with longing at the sight of them. Finally, this moment. I was getting them back, and it was taking everything in me not to bounce on my toes with excitement. He knew I'd always loved those rings, they were simple but pretty. I'd never wanted anything gaudy or cliché, no Tiffany diamonds. The iridescent opal stone caught on the stream of light from the truck.

Dougie held up the rings, sandwiched between his thumb and forefingers. "Give me your hand."

I extended my left hand for him, holding my breath as I prepared to watch him slide my rings back on my ring finger... but he flipped my hand over, placing the rings into the center of my palm, then folded my fingers closed around them, blanketing my hand with his.

He spoke before I could question him. "We're never going to go back to being those people we were, Pen. You were right." He held my eyes, the gorgeous shades of green no match for the forest enveloping us. They were the brightest, burning with a fire that could have leveled us both.

A fluttery sensation entered my chest, my lips pressing together as I stood in wait for him to continue. "But I don't want to be those people anymore, either."

Dougie closed the distance between us, his palm still curved around my fist, while his other hand cupped my face. My lids dropped, his shuddering chest shaking against mine as his lips found the pleat of my own and pressed down hard. "Throw them," he murmured against my mouth.

I leaned into the kiss, flexing a little on my toes. *Wait.* "Huh?" I ripped my head back, my eyes flaring.

"Your rings. Throw them."

"What?" I asked breathlessly, stepping away from him. I pulled my hand from his, bringing my clenched fist to my chest. "I'm not throwing them." Had he lost his fucking mind? We were getting back on track, not going backward.

I turned away from him, prepared to stomp back to the truck, but his voice stopped me.

"Throw them, Penelope, because those rings aren't us. They're who we were. We can't erase anything that's happened, but we can't hold on to who we once were, either."

I pursed my lips, the rings digging into my palm as the meaning of his words marinated in my mind. My jaw flexed under the tension. Wordlessly, I lowered my hand, opening my palm. The pulse thrummed in the center, but not from the pain of clenching too tight— but from realizing that he was right.

We'd still been holding onto the past.

The rings weren't us.

They weren't who we were anymore.

Turning around, I scrutinized him for a moment longer. Drawing in a deep breath, a trickle of anticipation flowed through me as I lifted my arm above my head and, with my eyes shut, sent the rings flying through the trees.

It was quiet enough that I heard them land.

I just didn't know *where*.

"Oh god," I whispered. I couldn't believe I'd done that. I shook my hands out, shaking my head. "Why—" I cut myself off, watching from the corner of my eye as he lowered himself to one knee. My eyes flared, a garbled sound leaving my slackened mouth.

Dougie held up a ring to me, the gorgeous topaz glittering in the bright LED headlights. "I choose you, Penelope. I choose you now, and tomorrow," he said, staring up at me with wide-eyed adoration that sluiced through me. "I choose you when we struggle, when life doesn't go the way we expected. I choose you when you're down, when you're happy, and," he paused, laughing through his nose, "When you steal my deodorant. You really gotta stop doing that by the way."

I snorted out a laugh, my shoulders quaking. "It works better."

"It's gross."

"Stop," I murmured, swatting him gently. "You can't say gross in a proposal." I paused. "Actually," I dug the tip of my boot into the hard ground. "Yeah, you can." It really was kinda gross, but it worked better, and then I smelled like him and...

"Good," he said, shaking his head up at me. "It is gross, but I let it slide because I love you and I'll share my deodorant with you in this life and in the next one." I snorted out a laugh, the emotions clogging my throat. "I choose you now and always." Dougie's throat shifted with his swallow, his focus unyielding as he held out the ring to me. "Will you choose me, too?"

I would choose him. Today, tomorrow. In this life and in the next.

I would choose him over and over and over again because we weren't broken.

Fractured and imperfect? Yes, but I'd never wanted perfect.

I wanted the nice guy, the good guy, the one who didn't always say the right things, who made sure I knew how much he loved me before he brought me into his world. Who loved me even when we'd made mistakes.

"Yes," I murmured, watching as he slid the ring on my finger. "I choose you."

Now, tomorrow, forever.

Always.

And as the first flakes of snow fell around us, blanketing the earth in white, I felt like the pieces of a snow globe, immortalizing our new story. One that was absent of the lies, the story that welcomed the truth and change as constant as the weather.

Some love stories lasted a season. But ours?

Ours would last a lifetime.

We'd barely made it in the front door before Dougie was fumbling with the folds of my jacket, drawing it from my shoulders. He was on me in seconds, my back finding the front door as he shoved me back gently, his icy, strong hands sliding up the hemline of my shirt and skimming my sides. I jolted, my breath snagging in my lungs as his mouth descended on me, his tongue gliding against the pleat of my mouth until my lips parted with invitation.

Hooking my fingers around my shirt, I tugged it upward, my vision momentarily blinded as he captured my lips once more before I'd cleared my head completely, earning my laughter. Lifting my arms, he helped me pull my shirt off the rest of the way. The snow had gotten heavier once we left our clearing in the woods and with his hand draped over my thigh, and my left hand folded over his, I'd watched each perfect flake as it twirled in the wind, my attention only leaving the snow when he summoned my attention with three words.

"I'm ready, Penny."

And now with his face buried between my breasts, his hot mouth worshipping each one while his palms clung to the pert swells pushed upward thanks to my bra and every nerve in my body charged to life, I knew this moment would mark a new start in our story. The chill in the air stung my skin when he pinched the clasp of my bra open. Dougie withdrew himself just a little to run his fingers over the straps and watch with the eyes of a possessed man as they slid over my shoulders and the cups fell from breasts, my nipples tightening.

He leaned into the crook of my neck, his teeth grazing against my hammering pulse, dragging downward languorously until he settled against my left breast, his teeth coming around my nipple. I released an eager cry as he alternated between nibbling and circling the sensitive bead with his tongue and then moved his attention to the other.

My hands clawed at his jacket, pulling it from him as much as I could until he helped me, and then before he could return his focus back to my breasts, I yanked at his Henley, peeling it over his head. My mouth salivated at the sight of him. Now that he was eating three meals a day again and back at work, he'd filled out again, his body hard, defined and familiar, just like it had been before. The skin in his face no longer hung, his skin healthy and not sallow. But it was his eyes, his gorgeous forest green eyes that were no longer tired and sad but filled to the brim with the promise of our future and his unending love for me and our life together that brought me a joy unlike any other.

"Like what you see?" he asked, his hand closing around my throat and pinning me to the door. I inclined my head back, my eyes closing halfway as I watched him close the distance between us and pressed himself against me.

Hard. So impossibly hard.

My thighs quivered, my panties sticking to my core. "Mhm," I murmured, my skin dimpled with excitement as he dragged his hand upward, grazing my jawline and pressing his thumb against my lips. I held his eyes as I accepted his thumb, sucking the digit and dragging my tongue along the pad of his finger.

Dougie hissed as he ground his erection against my belly, his forehead falling against my own, breath ghosting across my face. Releasing his finger, I slid away from him, forcing him against the door. Sinking to my knees, the front door mat rough against the tops of my bare feet after I'd ditched my socks when we got in, I undid his belt, the slink of metal dancing as I fed the leather out of the loop, the ends hanging open as I popped the button open and tugged his zipper down. Hooking my fingers at the waistband of his jeans and boxer briefs, I drew them downward, more need gushing in my core as his cock jutted in my direction, the pretty pearl of precum sitting proudly on the tip in offering.

He brushed his fingers along my cheekbones, his molten eyes emboldening me as I leaned forward and swept my tongue along the glistening bead.

"Penny, fuck," he groaned, his hand cradling the back of my neck.

I loved I did that to him. That I could still do that to him after all this time. Opening my lips around him, I moved forward, sliding him into the warmth of my mouth's cavern, accepting more of him as I hummed around his thick girth. His fist pounded against the front door, rattling behind him, his chest hollowing out as I glanced up at him through the veil of my lashes.

Dougie's face twisted with strangled control and pleasure, his mouth slightly parted as his breathing hitched with each bob of my mouth against him. Relaxing my gag reflex, I took him in as much as I physically could, the head of his cock massaging the back of my throat. His nostrils flared, and his eyes grew heavy as he watched me in a drunken daze.

Without warning, he wrapped his hand twice around my ponytail and jerked me back. I squeaked with surprise, another feverish pulse kicking off between my legs.

He'd never been rough with me like that before. Not sober, at least.

I liked it.

He'd always treated me like I was fragile, made of glass, something to worship. But I liked this side of him and feeling him without his inhibition and worry.

Dougie kicked his chin to the stairs. "All fours. Now."

I turned my neck as much as I could with his hand still bounded to my hair, staring at the stairs. When I didn't move, he guided me to my feet, staring at me hotly. I could barely catch my breath in the best possible way as I studied him. He was handsome, his beard freshly clipped and his eyes hungry. Dougie pulled me into him, kissing me with everything he had in him. I undid my pants, shimmying out of them alongside my underwear, never breaking our connection. He walked me backward, halting, when we got to the stairs.

I broke away from him, planting my knees on the second tread, leaning forward and resting my forearms against the fourth tread, my body arching in offering. His shadow danced against the wall as he fitted himself between my thighs, his hands planting on my sides. He pressed his lips against my spine, leaving a trail down each delicate bone, his strong fingers shifting from my side to grasp my ass cheeks, parting them.

"Dougie?" I asked, my breathing hitching as he shifted behind me, and I craned my neck to steal a glance at what he was doing.

His half-lidded eyes sent a curl of pleasure through me. "Look at you," he murmured, releasing one of my sides to brush an explorative finger across my slick seam. "Such a pretty pussy."

I yelped when his hand came down unexpectedly against the outside of my thigh, my blood coursing through me, making my core ache with need. I rocked forward, panting out a harsh breath.

"Sorry, too hard?" he asked nervously, breaking character, his hand settling against where he struck me to soothe the skin.

I let out a breathy laugh, shaking my head, wiggling against him. "More."

I'd always wanted this part of him. Less reserved, more... primal.

He grinned, then struck me again, this time, a little lighter than the first time, but the action made me tingle all the same. I could get used to this untethered part he let go of when he trusted himself to lose control.

And I wanted him to lose control in me, with me, on my ass, on my thigh.

Wherever.

Dougie lowered himself further, seating the tip of his nose against my entrance. His tongue swiped against me, my body rocking as he grazed my clit tentatively at first before he dove in, driving his nose against me, his tongue lashing at me with hunger as he feasted.

My body moved with him, an insatiable pleasure flooding me as he shifted his face to plunge his tongue inside of me, his mouth closing around me. His fingers dug into my ass cheeks and my body heated with the threat of his fingerprints marking my body. I wanted more of him, I needed all of him.

"Fuck me, Dougie," I goaded. "Give me your hard cock."

"Penelope." His voice came out like a feral growl against my pussy that made my stomach flip. I squirmed against him, my body aching for more of him.

"Give it to me hard and good."

"Is that what you want?" he asked on a growl, lifting his face. God, it sounded like a threat, and I loved it. "Do you deserve it?" He angled himself behind me, brushing his cock against my entrance painstakingly slow. I let out a whine.

I nodded. He clapped his palm against my ass cheek, and I cried out. "Tell me what you want."

"I want you to fuck me," I exhaled. "I want to feel you for days to come. I want your marks on me, and I want you to fill me up until you're spilling out of me."

"Jesus Christ." I gazed at him over my shoulder, loving the pinched concentration flushing in his face and the heat of his crazed eyes as he watched himself sweep the tip of his cock along my silky folds, coating himself in my arousal. Just when I thought he was going to prolong it again, he plunged forward, impaling me, and my hips bashed against the riser of the stairs, pleasure and pain exploding in my senses.

His firm fingers banded around my waist as he rutted forward, his hip bones eating into my skin. He sampled the skin on my shoulder, my body moving under his, absorbing his thrusts while he practically fucked me into the stairs. I could barely breathe, but I didn't care because I would give anything to relive this moment as we became one again—properly—for the first time in nearly a year.

Dougie slid his arm around me, nestling his hand between my legs, his adept fingers finding my clit as he massaged me in a dizzying combination of slow but firm. Pleasure bubbled in my gut as my mind fought to focus on which ecstasy to lose myself to first. My body grew feverish, my skin throbbing. The squelch of my pussy as he pounded into me filled the quietude of the house over our heavy breathing and murmurs.

"Come on my cock, Penny. C'mon," he murmured against the shell of my ear. "Lemme hear how much you like it."

Closing my eyes, my mouth popped open as his heated words filled my head and threw my body over the edge. Euphoria took over, an explosion of pleasure erupting between my legs, sending electric currents through my body and a kaleidoscope of butterflies freeing in my stomach. I cried out, and Dougie took that as an invitation to increase his tempo, my satiated body absorbing it all, thrust for thrust.

Seconds later, he let out a hot groan, his cock kicking as he spasmed atop of me and I clung around him as he spilled inside of me with his warm release. His sweaty chest stuck to my body, the trembles racking through him as he breathed against my skin.

Turning my head, I met his reverent eyes as he leaned forward, grazing my lips with his. He smirked, pressing his forehead to mine. "You were right."

"About what?"

"Your lipstick. It didn't move."

I smiled, brushing the tip of my nose against his. "Told ya."

My lipstick was infallible.

Just like we were, too.

Epilogue

Dougie

Eight months later...

SOMETHING SMELLED GOOD. I WRINKLED MY NOSE, GROANING AS I ROLLED onto my side. Burying my face in the pillow for a moment, I extended a hand, feeling her spot, her lingering body heat still trapped in the sheets.

Pen hadn't been up long, but she was up.

Sitting upright, I blinked back the sleep, taking in the landscape of our bedroom. She draped her housecoat over the arm of a gray Chesterfield chair in the bedroom's corner, next to her folded pajamas. My eyes found the alarm clock, shock sending my brows to my hairline.

Holy shit, it was after eight and I'd slept in.

Pushing the sheets back, I snagged my track pants from the floor, feeding my feet and legs through them, the waistband snapping against my waist. Approaching the window, I tore the blackout curtains open, the heat of the summer sunlight pelting me in the face.

It was gonna be another scorcher, and the lawn needed to be cut. The blades were an inch too long, but green and proud. Grabbing a shirt from the dresser, I pulled it on as I inched out of our bedroom, the meaty aroma growing more potent when I opened the door.

My stomach gurgled—bacon. Definitely bacon. Christopher's bedroom door was wide open. I heard him singing along to the opening theme song of *Sesame Street* downstairs. Taking the stairs, I found him sprawled out on the rug, in mismatched shorts and a T-shirt —we were teaching him how to dress himself, picking his outfits included—resting on his elbows, legs bent, feet suspended over his waist.

"Morning, Daddy," he said without looking at me.

"Mornin', little man," I replied, approaching him. Getting down on my haunches, I ruffled his shock of golden hair. He grinned at me, his dimples nearly hitting his eyes. We'd celebrated his third birthday a few weeks ago, but I couldn't believe how quickly he was growing up.

Some part of me wanted time to slow down. I wasn't ready to witness those soft swells melt into strong arches or for his voice to drop. And sure, that was still years away, but it felt like only yesterday, Pen and I were in my shithole apartment, and she was telling me she was pregnant.

"Did you eat yet?" I smirked. The sweetness of syrup on his breath had hit me as soon as I neared him.

"Yep," he replied, popping his 'P'. "Pancakes!"

Kid was a pancake monster.

I left him be, heading to the kitchen where Pen was already dressed. She had pulled her hair into a short ponytail, high on her crown, a pink tank top paired with her denim-covered hips gyrating to the beat of Dexys Midnight Runners "Come On Eileen" as she pushed bacon around. She raised her hands up, spatula in one hand, her engagement ring and new wedding band catching in a stream of sunlight from the garden doors.

We'd renewed our vows in the spring—our way. Boston Common Pond, roast beef sandwiches, an off-white cream suit with her favorite band tee, and me in jeans and a dress shirt.

We got matching Converses, and Chris got a pair, too. It was the wedding we'd wanted, the way we wanted it.

No lies, nothing artificial, just us.

Leaning against the kitchen archway, I watched her, utterly mesmerized by how effortless she was when she was happy—and she was.

Happy.

We'd both kept up with therapy and couples counseling, and she was glad to be out of the house every single day, working again.

She'd needed that just as much as I'd needed it, too. We were happier as a couple when our purpose as individuals was being fulfilled beyond our roles as parents.

Penelope had a job she enjoyed and was talking about the possibility of starting her own thing again in the future.

"Stop watching me," she called over the pop and sizzle of bacon, the song closing, transitioning into a slower tempo song—"Simple Man" by Shinedown.

I'd always loved this song, but I loved watching her more.

"You're hot," I commented, laughing, fighting the urge to dance with her. "I can't help it."

She glanced at me over her shoulder, her mouth pulling into a sly smile. Pen crooked a finger at me, summoning me to her. She lowered the heat on the burner, turning to wrap her arms around me. "You slept in."

"Yeah, funny story," I began, swaying with her before backing her against the counter. "This real hot blonde wouldn't let me sleep last night."

"Hmm," she murmured, feigning concern as her brows drew together. "Sounds dangerous."

"She is," I agreed, dropping my voice. "Had to throw a hand over her mouth while she fucked me, though…" the memory alone had my cock stirring, especially when heat hit her eyes and she pressed her body against mine. "Do you know who she is?"

Pen leaned forward, kissing the corner of my mouth. "Doesn't sound familiar. Want me to help you find your mystery woman?"

"Would you mind?" I asked, sliding my hands around to grip her ass. "I wanna take her to Italy."

I'd been waiting to tell her about my great idea for weeks, but rather than the excited jubilation I thought the statement would get out of her, Penelope tensed in my arms.

That was not the reaction I'd been expecting. At all.

She stared at my exposed chest, fitting her hands against my thick biceps, and squeezing me with... was that fucking sympathy I just detected?

"Wow." Pen let her breath leave her in a tight raspberry. "Italy?" she said, stepping out of my hold.

What happened here? "Yeah," I said, nodding my head. "I was thinking rather than us spending New Year's here, the three of us could go on a trip... Y'know," I trailed off, "Genoa? Pasta? Family vacation? Late Honeymoon plus your mini-me?"

"He's your mini-me now," she corrected with a blink, turning away to grab the spatula. True, Chris was looking a little more like me these days, but still. Pen flipped the bacon, her posture stiff enough that I could have balanced a scale on her shoulders alone.

"Penelope?"

"Could you go grab the eggs?" she said instead. "I fed them, but I forgot to grab the eggs."

Them being the chickens we'd got in the early spring.

Axel, Van Halen and Bruce.

Iconic names for chickens. Chickens she'd bought individual bow ties for and took a lot of pictures of. I'm not kidding. They had their own Facebook page.

And as cute as they were, they were the least of my priorities right now, especially when she was acting in a way I hadn't witnessed in forever. "Are you okay?"

"Yeah," she said, clearing her throat, taking a sharp inhale. "Eggs, though, please. Your bacon's going to get cold."

I stepped back, appraising her back. She wasn't dancing anymore, and it was hard to get a read on her. I'd get the eggs, we'd eat, and then I'd give her an opportunity to come talk to me. Part of our homework in marriage counseling beyond transparency was giving the other the chance to offer their thoughts when they were ready within a reasonable amount of time.

We never went to bed pissed off anymore.

Nodding my head, I gave her a reassuring smile even though my insides shredded, and I was nervous as hell. "Sure."

I thought she'd be excited about Italy, but maybe she had something else in mind. We hadn't thrown our New Year's Eve party last year, but I wanted to do... I dunno, something special for us this year.

Grabbing the wicker basket on the counter that we used to collect eggs, I opened the garden doors, and walked barefoot across the porch, down the steps. The flagstone was warm under my feet, the blades of grass lush under my footfalls, when the path transitioned. Sweat broke across my brow immediately as the blistering sun bore down on me, and the soft breeze made the wind chimes sing in greeting when I approached the small bright red chicken coop to the far right of our yard, framed by chicken wire fencing. The trio were pecking at the feed Pen had tossed there, clucking as they moved against the patch of worn-in dirt the coop lived on. I rounded the red building, opening the hutch door. Shoving my hand in the opening, I felt around for the eggs, frowning as I came up empty-handed.

That was weird. We'd had eggs consistently since the chicks turned eighteen weeks. It was unusual that there was nothing in there. Bending at the waist, I squinted to see if I could make out an egg in the distance. Maybe it had gotten shuffled out of place in the chaos of their feed being tossed—they turned into hound dogs when there was food.

There was nothing there.

Well, except something that seemed out of place. Swallowing tightly, I extended a hand once more, brushing against the thin piece of plastic. Pulling it out, my stomach dropped as I stared at the all too familiar test in my hand.

And that bright positive sign.

"I don't think Italy's gonna happen this year," Pen said behind me. "Next year's not looking great, either."

I turned, still holding the pregnancy test in my hand, my jaw slack.

"... surprise!" she added timidly, though she'd attempted for enthusiastic. Her thin laugh betraying her as she chewed the corner of her mouth.

"Are you serious?" I asked.

She nodded. "Confirmed it this week at the doctor's office."

I dropped the basket and the test, pulling her back into my arms. "You're pregnant?"

"Four weeks." She pressed her forehead against mine. "So not that far along." Fitting her hands against my cheeks, she tipped her gaze downward. "Are you..." she trailed off, but I caught the nervous bobbing her throat as the next word croaked out of her, "happy?"

Happy. A five-lettered word I'd never fully considered the weight of before. For some, happiness amounted to things they had in their possession, short-lived moments that eventually faded into memories. It came from life satisfaction, maybe being in the position to buy an Escalade, or winning the Powerball.

But for me, my happiness was right here, in my arms, and the byproduct of our happiness existed on our family room floor, singing to himself with maple syrup still glossing his mouth.

We'd casually discussed trying to expand our family in another year or two, but things changed—and I was perfectly okay with that. "Penny, of course I am," I breathed, cradling her face. "Are you?"

She nodded, but there was something in her eyes, a hint of worry she was afraid to voice, because I understood.

What if *it* happened again? What if, despite our gratitude and our renewed hope, we were plunged back into a dark place we'd fought so desperately to crawl out of?

Pen drew in a breath, lifting her eyes to me. "I'm scared," she confessed, a lock of her hair twirling in the warm breeze. "Of doing something wrong again, of..." the wind chimes swayed in the distance, the pretty tinkling carrying off in the breeze, "of it happening again."

I smoothed my thumbs over the arches of her pretty bone structure, my mouth pulling to the right. "I know."

"We weren't planning on this just yet, and I... I took on that new project at work, I finally have a groove of things and what if I get too stressed out and fuck up again?"

"Penny, you didn't cause what happened." After Pen had begun working with a new therapist, it became clear her grief over the last few months had edged into an undiagnosed depression... and my actions hadn't helped. It exacerbated her grieving process and intensified the weight of it all.

Not that learning that we'd lost a baby hadn't hurt—it killed.

But for Pen? Who'd carried our child and the secret of them inside of her, losing our baby and the vision for our family she'd woven into her head had been a devastation unlike any other. She'd lost sight of herself, of her perspective. That's what she was afraid of.

Regressing to a bleak place she'd worked so hard to get out of. I'd be lying if I said I wasn't afraid, too. But not scared enough that I'd let the fear taint our joy.

"When's your next appointment?" I asked.

"In a couple of weeks."

"I'll come with you."

Her eyes rounded. "You will?"

I touched her forehead with mine. "Of course. We're in this together."

She stared at the pretty blooms on the hydrangea bush in the distance. "This changes our plans for a bit."

I smiled at her observation. That was just us, though, wasn't it? We didn't plan the pregnancy, just like we hadn't planned the first two and it was abundantly apparent to me we shouldn't even share the same bar of soap at this point, but I didn't care about our plans because we hadn't met under ordinary circumstances.

Everything about our connection, our story, had been unplanned. It was fate. Nothing either of us could have foreseen because destiny didn't always make itself known to you. Penelope was a wish I'd made after I got my heart broken from someone else, and it was solidified when I'd watched her get back in her SUV three years ago, with the feeling of her in my arms still coursing through me like a life force.

If I'd been in cruise control before, Penelope had given me a destination, a place to be.

She'd given me a home in her heart.

I didn't care about the plan. I cared about her, about what was ours.

"Fuck our plans." I shrugged. So Italy was still on hold, and we'd have to clean out one of the spare room and turn it into a nursery. I'd love my wife a little harder and hold her hand every step of the way because nothing would taint this moment again—no matter what the what-ifs were. "I don't want our anxieties or our plans to overshadow this." Reaching for hands, I scissored our fingers together. "This is ours, Pen."

Her anxieties were valid, and normal—but the chances of it happening again were realistically about as comparable as someone who hadn't experienced a loss before. I wanted her to enjoy this pregnancy, to watch her with reverence in my gaze and warmth in my chest as she nested and sorted out the baby clothes she'd stored away in the attic. I wanted to catch sight of Christopher pressing his ear to her stomach, to feel the kick of his younger sibling. And I wanted her to cherish each day and each moment with our family of three as we made room for baby number three.

Because there would always be a baby number two that we would love, the baby that never was, the future that never took shape—but she wasn't alone. We'd loved, and we'd lost and through the chaos and the vines of pain, we'd found each other again under unlikely circumstances.

That was love.

A gust of wind kicked off around us, hard enough that it should have ripped the petals from the hydrangea, but it didn't. The wind chimes urgently sang, and it felt like a whisper of a promise that would be honored.

We'd be okay.

"Ours..." she echoed, a small smile touching the corners of her mouth. She shifted her stunning ocean blue gaze to me, the gloss of her tears fringing her lashes. Pen flexed on her toes, the pleat of her lips settling against mine and I held her there, absorbing the moment, love and reassurance filling us.

And with my arm slung over Pen's shoulders, and her side pressed against mine, I led her back to the house where our story started, ended, and began again.

'Cause stories like ours?

They lasted forever.

Content Warning

The themes found within this book focus heavily on the loss of a pregnancy and infidelity, and have the potential to be distressing to some readers.

Reader discretion is strongly advised.

Author's Note

I didn't think Penelope and Dougie were going to have their own book. When I met them while telling Sean and Raquel's story a few years ago, they were about as well-rounded and even keeled as could be. In fact, some readers preferred them over Sean and Raquel.

They were perfect—until Veritas.

I was taken aback when Dougie appeared on the scene. I hadn't accounted for him in Veritas' outline. I had no idea why I couldn't get his voice out of my head, or why he insisted he had to speak to me, but I listened.

And what he told me unnerved me. I questioned him several times. I tried to circumvent him, but he wouldn't let up.

So I pinned my outline and let him drive me to where he needed to lead me through Jordan and Maria's story. Did I like what I saw along the way? Fuck no—but I understood, too, because life isn't perfect. It's not always linear. And relationships, they're hard.

Especially when communication breaks down, when secrets mount, and shame unravels us at the seams.

Lies was one of the toughest books I've written to date. Dougie and

Pen are characters I truly adore and to see the "it" couple falling apart was hard, and for a while there, I was unsure if they were going to make it through the other side despite what my outline kept telling me —because while miscarriages are extremely common, so too is the percentage of relationships that fall apart in grieving.

Add in the element of Dougie's mistake with Maria? And we got a recipe for disaster here—and all of it paled in comparison to the inner turmoil Penelope was feeling, her conflicted feelings toward herself, Raquel and her marriage—and Dougie's regret for a near indiscretion that almost cost him everything; the life he'd dreamt of, his wife, and his friends.

This book was unbearably difficult at some points, but watching them rebuild and set off on their path to healing was rewarding (and made the gray hairs worth it). Lies reads differently from my other books. It was more challenging to write, more emotional, but also, in my opinion, the most beautiful, too—because it depicted hope in a time when the world needs it most.

So much of our lives are subject to change without notice. Plans go to shit, dreams change, life happens, and in those moments, we take these broken parts of ourselves, honor them, and reconstruct something new.

Whether Lies broke you and pieced you back together again, I hope you found love and forgiveness within these pages.

Thank you so much for reading!

Acknowledgments

I cannot believe I've had the pleasure of writing acknowledgements six times now in two years. Publishing Mirrors in 2020 was a dream come true, but to be here in 2022, sharing Dougie and Pen's story with you, it really just takes my breath away.

I have to thank the readers for that. I write because I love it, and my hope when publishing is that the stories and the characters that live in my head rent-free might be stories you'd love to read, too. The feedback over the last couple of years has truly rendered me speechless more times than not. I've had the pleasure of connecting with so many of you and I cannot thank you enough for your time and love. Your reviews, your edits, your conversations, they all mean so much to me.

I am immensely grateful to live in a time where, despite a global pandemic *(when's this shit gonna end?)*, I can still explore, experience and fall in love with Massachusetts all over again through the help of the Internet. I am indebted to sources like *Encyclopedia.com*, *Boston.com*, *Boston Globe*, *Wikitionary* (for slang usage) and various Wikipedia pages which have imparted so much insight into a city and local culture that I adore during a time in which travel and exploration isn't quite safe. (*Yet.* I'll be there before I know it.)

I'm also grateful to resources such as *Parents.com*, *Medical News Today*, *Very Well Family*, *RWJF.org* and *Mother.ly*—miscarriage, infant loss, and postpartum depression is one of the most traumatic experiences a person could go through, and these resources were vital in both educating me and helping me navigate telling Pen and Dougie's story.

The loss and the grief of a wanted pregnancy or infant is unparalleled, and I am indebted to these resources for their in-depth accounts.

This book was made possible because of some incredible people in my life—old and new—who have continuously had my back during the writing process of this book.

MAR — You read this book. I desperately *needed* you to read this book because I was genuinely scared. Penelope and Dougie were the 'it' couple, and to be writing their story, trying to pilot parallel time-lines, and constantly worrying about whether this was good enough—you kept me sane—and you surprised me when you told me you loved it. I am beyond blessed to have you as my partner and to have your unwavering support and belief in me. I love you!

ABC — That's number six in the books. (Yes, that was an attempt at a pun.) I can't believe that this whole thing started because you asked casually about my cover plans with Mirrors in early 2020—how far we both have come in such a short time. I am beyond grateful to have you as my best friend and creative director extraordinaire. Life has the funniest way of surprising us when we least expect it, and meeting you was one of the best gifts. Never forget how much you're capable of when you believe in yourself. You've come so far, and I'm immensely proud.

JP — Thank you for always scrolling by my TikTok's, LOL. I'm so proud of everything you've accomplished, baby brother!

MK — You are an absolute gem, never change. No, seriously. You're amazing to work with and I am so happy that our paths have crossed. Thank you for always being so thorough and for believing in my stories as much as I do! Three books down together, hundreds more to go.

NL — I feel like I've known you and S my entire life. Anytime I try to think of life pre-Soul Sisters, I draw a blank—and that's okay, because I'd rather not remember life before you two. You are such a source of inspiration, a magnificent bright light, and I am so honored to call you my friend. 2021 was the year you chose yourself, and in doing so, you inspired me to think beyond my self-limiting beliefs, too. You have a heart unlike anyone I've ever met, and I truly believe that you've found your calling. I can't wait to witness all the incredible and transformational things that 2022 brings you. Love you! *(If you are looking for marketing, proofing or promotional services, message nishasbooksandcoffeepr on Instagram!)* #SS2022

SA — My spicy little pimenta! How the hell do you do it all? Mama, author, wife and saving lives on the front lines during this shit show of a panorma—you inspire the hell out of me every single day. Seriously. What's your secret? N knew what was up when she told me to check out Power—all that witchy energy. Whether we're exchanging recipes, sharing 'oh shit' moments, or just going through the day-to-day motions, knowing I get to experience these moments with you and N means so much to me. Having you both in my life has been one of the most rewarding blessings of my author career—because I found my sisters. *(Go check out Victoria Woods Power Series. You can thank me later. Trust.)* #SS2022

GP —The entire Grey's Promo team: thank you so much for being so incredibly patient with me, answering my deluge of emails, and reassuring me I'm not a mess. You're all amazing and I'm so grateful!

Friends and family — Thank you for your immeasurable support. For always being the first ones to order, share my work, and root me on.

To the aspiring authors, the writers who want to hit publish, and the dreamers who need a little more encouragement — There is no better moment than this one to chase your dreams and make them a reality. I know it's scary, but what's scarier is looking back on your life and wondering, 'what if?'

About the Author

A.L. Woods is a bestselling author of roller coaster romances, caffeine aficionado, and collector of Sailor Moon paraphernalia.

She lives 40 minutes west of Toronto, Ontario with her partner, Michael, and their 8lb larger-than-life miniature dachshund, Maia.

She believes that burritos should be in their own food group, loves the fall, winged liner, and listening to metalcore at an offensive level.

For photographic evidence of her shenanigans, or cute photos of Maia, follow her on social media.

Website: https://amandawrites.ca/

Be sure to subscribe to her newsletter on her website so you don't miss out on exclusive content!

twitter.com/AmandaWrites_
instagram.com/amandalwrites
pinterest.com/ALWoodsBooks
facebook.com/AmandaLWrites
tiktok.com/@amandalwrites

BESTSELLING AUTHOR
A.L. WOODS

Want to read all about Maria and Jordan?

Turn the page to read the first chapter of Veritas!

Prologue

Maria

Four years ago...

No one fucked like Douglas Patterson. No one.

With my legs thrown over his shoulders, his thrusts quickened—the kind you felt under your bellybutton like a relentless, toe-curling euphoria you didn't want to end. He sent me a shit-eating grin, cocky as always, the rutting of his hips slowing to grind against me.

"Are you gonna come for me, Maria?"

I bit down on my lip, savoring each roll of his strong hips, my head weaving with a nod. His hand slipped between us, his index finger working against the sensitive bundle of nerves that made up my clit. My pussy contracted around his cock, a moan slipping out past my lips as white spots erupted on the back of my eyelids and my body convulsed in bliss under his.

Dougie dropped my legs, his hard body blanketing over mine while his mouth fastened on my lips, swallowing my moan. His tongue swept against mine in a hypnotic dance that I memorized over the past six months. It was a kiss I'd become comfortable with, but with feelings I'd never reciprocate. Dougie was living a teenage fantasy, and I was just enjoying a steady lay.

He shifted against me, my grip on his cock coaxing his orgasm out of him as I clenched. He shuddered above me, warmth registering between my legs as he lost his load in a condom. After another moment, Dougie retracted his hips slowly, his reverent forest-green gaze looking down at me.

"Hi," he whispered, his voice coating my insides with a tepid warmth.

"Hey yourself." I offered him a satiated smile, squirming under his weight.

Dougie rolled off me, drawing me closer to him as we both came down from our post-orgasm high. I was still feeling it through my toes, my legs boneless. He dropped a firm kiss on my exposed shoulder, his fingers splaying against my taut stomach.

"I've been thinking," he started, that deep, brassy baritone in my ear, the edges dampened by his exhaustion.

"About what to eat?" I asked in response, my eyes closing only for a minute. I was always hungry after sex, especially this close to dinnertime. The sun had only set a few minutes before we ended up in my bedroom, peeling each other's clothes off in a passionate frenzy. I had a shit day at work, and he was exhausted from roasting under the sun all day on a construction site. "I really want Indian." A spicy biryani sounded amazing right now. My stomach released a small gurgle at the thought. I waited for the reverberation of his chuckle against my back, but it never came. That was the first thing that tipped me off. "Dougie?" Rolling over, alarm resounded like a sharp, tinny sound in my ears, nearly deafening me when I met his intense expression.

Fuck, anything but that look.

Levity. We needed levity. "Did you want to order something else?" Pizza might not be so bad, either. I'd have to work out twice as hard this week to burn it off, but nothing a Pilates or spin class wouldn't fix.

"Not about what to eat," he intoned. "About us, Maria."

Us? Okay, Tavares, don't panic. There had to be a logical explanation for why he'd bring that ugly, two-lettered word up now after six months. An abject taste filled my mouth, a burst of soured notes on my tongue that turned my stomach.

I was careful not to react, despite the punitive deluge flooding my insides, screaming to abort mission because somewhere along the way, it appeared the lines of our intentions had gotten crossed.

Sitting up, I pulled the white silk bed sheet around my chest, pinning it in place with my arm. Dougie propped himself on a perched elbow. He studied me in a way I didn't want him to—with hope and devotion. "We've been doing this for six months," he started, scratching at the five-o'clock shadow peppering his cheeks. "I don't want to sneak around anymore. I know it'll be awkward if it comes from you, so I'll tell Sean."

My brother Sean, who was only a year younger than me, was Dougie's best friend—and *boss*. No, no, no, absolutely not. There was *nothing* to tell because we were just *fucking*.

"I figure worst case, he'll get pissed, maybe try to punch me, but we'll hug it out after," Dougie said casually. Confidence and humor existed in his tone, but his eyes were dead-fucking serious.

I blinked at him, my mouth involuntarily popping open. "What." The question came out as a statement.

What do you think is going to happen when you tell my brother?

What kind of reaction did you think you were going to get from me?

What did you think we were doing here?

My throat weaved, feeling as though I'd swallowed a fistful of sand, my stare flitting to look up at the smooth ceiling of my bedroom. Sean and Dougie had scraped all the friable popcorn material off it when I first took possession of the condo last October. I didn't like jagged edges. I preferred smooth, clean lines, no surprises. White paint. Dark floors. Simplicity. Those things made sense to me. I liked nothing that was sinuous, vibrant, or complicated—and no, we're no longer just talking about my design preference.

Dougie and I had a deal. An understanding. An arrangement. Those were things I could comprehend, things I liked... not *this*.

"Are you going to say anything?" The muscle in his jaw tightened, his green gaze glinting with worry—a disparity shining there that contrasted what I was feeling—annoyed.

"Why?" My mouth twisted grimly, an unnatural stiffness settling in my spine, each strand of hair on my head tingling with alarm.

"What do you mean 'why'?" he deadpanned.

It was quiet enough that I could have sworn I heard the fish swimming in the Boston Harbor my condo overlooked.

"Maria?"

"I felt I was clear on our arrangement," I finally replied, lifting a well-groomed eyebrow at him. "We agreed to these terms."

I'd constructed them with meticulous care, ensured that they were mutually beneficial. He had laughed at me when I presented them to him in my home office, but he had signed them.

Then he spurted an ink of another kind inside of me.

So why was he looking at me like I'd infringed on our terms? Dougie had mastered the art of looking like a kid who'd just witnessed the crushing loss of his favorite toy at the hands of a schoolyard bully.

He cleared his throat, sitting upright. "Yeah, but... I just thought..." he trailed off, my bedsheets bunching at his waist when he sat up, giving me a glimpse at the impress of his abs formed by hard labor. "We've been doing this a long time, Maria."

Six months, one week, and four days, to be exact. I always stayed current on the terms of the contracts that were stowed away in my filing cabinet. The intent wasn't to be a bitch. Any good lawyer would tell you it's just judicious.

"Exactly," I agreed, watching the muscles work in his back as he rolled the tension out of his shoulders. "Why ruin a good thing?"

It was a good thing. What Dougie lacked in terms of accolades and a résumé, he made up for in his ability to handle my needs with a reverence better suited for a long-term lover.

And we weren't that. We were fucking. I had told him time and time again that's what we were doing. Friends with benefits. Frenemies with benefits on a particularly bad day at work. He'd gotten me through an emotional time a few months ago when he'd found me yelling at my father's headstone. João Tavares was the only man I'd ever allow to hurt me, and I'd sworn the day he died that I'd give no one else the opportunity to do so, either.

Dougie was no exception—not then, and not now.

He was silent for a moment, then cleared the grit noisily from his throat. His forest-green eyes found mine over his shoulder, the moonlight playing on the curve of his nose that I'd broken when he had insulted me by suggesting he take me on a date to a McDonald's when he was fifteen to my sixteen.

As if.

Still, the way he asked his next question rehashed the feeling that sat like a brick in my gut. "Are you embarrassed by me?"

Was I embarrassed by him? Well, no. Not really.

Alright, no need to put me on trial about it—maybe I was a *little*. He wasn't exactly my type. We stood shoulder to shoulder when I wasn't wearing heels. I made more money in a week than he did in a month. He hadn't gone to college. He didn't own real estate, and after his credit card had been declined when we'd ordered sushi a few weeks ago, I was positive he had a concerning amount of debt.

We'd grown up together. He'd always lounge around my childhood home, eating at our dinner table, horsing around with my brother. He helped my parents with remedial chores and took my kid sisters to school when one of us couldn't.

He was a good guy, but I wouldn't date him.

We were too different. There was no scenario in which we ended up together.

"Maria?" He had the audacity to sound scorned.

"I'm not embarrassed by you, but I told you that wasn't what I wanted." I held my chin up. "You got the wrong idea."

"I got the wrong idea?" he parroted, before extending his fingers to rhyme off the facts. "I'm here three nights a week. I call you every day. We have a good time. What's the problem?"

My hand flitted the evidence away. "The problem is, we are incompatible."

And we were, weren't we? We came from completely different socioeconomic backgrounds, and sure, I wasn't born into money, but goddamn did I love having it. Money and power made this world go round, and I loved having both. Relationships were like deadweight; they'd drown you if you allowed them to.

Dougie's face crumpled, a whistle escaping his lips as my words clipped him in a barrage. Shit, that came out so much worse than I meant. "I don't mean it like that, I just—"

"That sounds an awful lot like embarrassment to me."

I supposed it did. Twisting my bedsheets in my fist, I resisted the urge to touch him. "Dougie, c'mon. We agreed to these terms. We both acknowledged what this was. Let's keep it easy. No one needs to be privy to what happens between you and me."

He jerked his head away from me, shielding his eyes. "Who talks like that?" he questioned, his tone growing reedy. "I know you think I'm a bit of a blockhead, but I hate to break it to you, Maria, I'm a person. I've got feelings."

Exactly. That was exactly the fucking problem. "We said no feelings," I reminded him, ignoring the prior half of his sentence. I didn't think he was stupid even without a degree, and I was more than aware of the inconvenience of the organ he romanticized beating behind the solid confines of his muscular chest.

"I know what we said. I signed your stupid contract," he spat.

I flinched. "I'm not trying to be cruel, Dougie."

"You're not trying to be a nice about it either, Maria."

Assuage and defuse, Maria. "You're a great guy, but—"

Dougie cut me off with a laugh that lacked any warmth. "Spare me, please. I don't need your pity." He shoved the bedsheets away from him, sliding over to the edge of the bed, searching the floor for his clothes. "I'm not that desperate."

"Where are you going?"

"Home." He pulled his T-shirt over his head.

"Why? You always sleep here. Your apartment doesn't have A/C, and it's the middle of a heat wave." He didn't need to suffer needlessly or make this a whole ordeal just to prove something to me.

"I'll survive." He huffed, shooting me a glance that struck me in the chest. I massaged it absently, wincing as I studied him. The wounded look had molted, agony alive in his eyes. "I've survived worse."

Pivot. I needed to pivot and engage in damage control. "I think you're overreacting to something that isn't that bad."

Honestly, it wasn't like I was saying we couldn't have sex anymore. I just didn't want to go out with him. Not that big of a deal.

But apparently, this was akin to mowing his heart over with a ten-ton truck. His anger exploded off him, slamming into me at full force. "Fifteen years, Maria," he seethed. "Fifteen fucking years. That's how long I've been in love with you."

My skin broke out into goosebumps, my heart kicking in my chest. I'd known. Of course, I knew how he felt when I had proposed our arrangement. At a minimum, it seemed like a win-win situation for us. Dougie got to feel like he had gotten the girl in the end, and I got a reliable bed partner I didn't feel I was going to have to threaten with a lawsuit to keep him quiet if he breached the non-disclosure agreement.

I was trying to make partner at the firm, and I couldn't afford anything getting out to anyone about my personal life—like I said, smooth, clean lines, and no surprises. Finding a bed partner was trickier than you would think.

"I know," I replied, trying to keep the edge out of my voice while holding up a mollifying hand. "But we said no feelings."

"Fuck what I said, or whatever I signed!" he shouted, earning my wince. My neighbors definitely heard him. "I don't care what I said. I care about *you*."

I swallowed, averting my gaze. "Maybe you should go." He needed to cool off, even if his apartment was sweltering, and I needed to think without him pouting in my bed. He moved too much when he was frustrated, constantly huffing, shifting from one side to the other, or fluffing his pillow.

"If I go, I'm not coming back, Maria." His declaration came out like a veiled threat.

God, he was as dramatic as my middle sister, Olivia.

Rolling my eyes, I inclined my head in his direction. I didn't react well to idle threats. I'd call his bluff if I had to. "Don't be ridiculous."

"What's ridiculous is that I thought you were capable of..." the words died in his mouth.

"Capable of what?" I sniffed indignantly. "*Love?*"

Love was stupid. Love *made* people stupid. Pathetic, really. Love invited hurt—no thank you.

He moved for the door, jerking it open. "Forget it, you're right. We said no feelings. I changed the terms. I breached on our stupid contract, so it's done."

Wait a minute, was he seriously about to walk out on *me*, of all people? I attempted to waylay him. "You can't just—"

Dougie spun around on the ball of his heel, baring his teeth at me. "Break a non-binding contract that wouldn't hold up in an actual court of law?" He took in a sharp, shuddering breath that I felt rattle through my bones. "Yeah, I can. And don't worry, our secret is safe with me."

Nothing. For the first time in my life, I was rendered speechless. Dougie found my silence amusing. "What's wrong? Shocked I'm not an idiot after all?"

My blood pressure soared. He was putting words in my mouth—that wasn't it. "I *never* thought you were an idiot."

"But you've never thought I was good enough for you either, Maria. Not in the way that mattered. I'm good enough to fuck you because I'm reliable, and when you've told me to jump, all I've ever done is ask you how high." He scrubbed a hand over his face, his calluses catching on his beard. "Well, I'm done jumping."

"All this because I won't..." I rolled my hand out in front of me, struggling to use the term. "*Date* you?"

"This isn't just about fucking dating me. It's everything." He hastened toward me, his hands balling into tight fists at his sides. "I am in love with you, and I think beyond your entitlement, need to remain indifferent and closed off, you love me, too."

I scoffed, throwing my head back. I was not entitled. Vain, yes. Entitled? No. I'd worked my fingers to the bone to get what I wanted. Entitled people were born into wealth and power. Not me. He wasn't going to fling me into some check-marked box to make himself feel better. "You're projecting."

"Then tell me you don't love me."

Aphasia greeted me, robbing the words from my tongue momentarily. I didn't love this man who thought he could woo me with a stupid McDonalds' coupon when we were teenagers. Who still wore denim on denim despite my protests and only took off his worn-out Boston Bruins' baseball cap to put on a hard hat. Who was terrible with money, but good with me. He was good to me. I knew he was, but we were wrong for each other. We desired different things. Dougie wanted a house back home in Fall River and a tiny facsimile of himself running around a dooryard with gap-toothed smiles and shrieks that made you dig out the aspirin for the onset of a headache. He vied for Sunday lunches with his ma, Super Bowl parties, PTA meetings, and coaching the Little League for his spawn.

And I wanted this—my life exactly as it was, as I understood it, because I'd climbed every rung on a ladder to get it—the waterfront condo that came with a hefty price tag, the closet full of designer shoes and pretty handbags I'd once dreamed about as a child to drown out the jests of my peers in elementary school for being the dumb Portuguese girl. I wasn't dumb then, and I was certainly not dumb now. Breaching the terms of our agreement, voiding our contract, would change everything. And I wasn't ready for that. Not with Dougie, not with anyone.

So it made saying the words easy—even if it was momentarily uncomfortable. My brittle voice came through, dissembling everything else I was feeling. "I don't love you."

Nausea imbued me, my heart pounding hard enough I heard the useless thing in my ears. There was no flare to the four words, just a finality. I wanted to follow up with an apology, but "I'm sorry" was acid up my tract, and the haunted look in his eyes indicated I'd done enough damage. I may as well have dug the heel of my favorite pair of Jimmy Choo's through his heart with the way the light diminished from his expression as the statement seeped in.

I'd lived my life on the motto, "veritas"—truth. It was the seal of approval on my Harvard degree—I'd sworn to tell the truth, the whole truth, and nothing but the truth, so here it was.

I didn't love Douglas Patterson. Douglas Patterson was an easy, reliable, good fuck who was my height, in desperate need of a shave, borderline insolvent, and my brother's best friend. He was kind, kinder than me. He adored my fucked-up family, was an expert with a hammer, and had always been there when I'd needed him—but I was *not* in love with him.

He knew it as well as I did. Perhaps he always had. Dougie blew out his cheeks, expelling every ugly thing he should have said to me that I rightfully deserved. Then with two languid nods of his head, as though fortifying himself, he squared his shoulders and left with the slam of my front door that I knew tilted the framed degrees in my office abutting the entrance.

I'd agonized over ensuring they were evenly hung. Flinging myself back on my mattress, the foam absorbed my petulance as I stared up at that smooth ceiling once more. I postulated that smooth, clean lines were easy for me to understand, because it was the foundation of who I was. No nebulous curves or forks in the road to catch me off guard, nothing but cold, hard facts and reality.

I didn't love Douglas Patterson.

I'd told the truth.

So why did it all feel like a lie?

Printed in Great Britain
by Amazon

25441586R00303